Sal Thomas likes to string wo[...]
amusing order. BBC Comedy onc[...]
who keeps on sending us scripts'.[...]
up, starred in an Edinburgh sketch show, tried her hand at film
writing and sitcoms (all to zero financial acclaim) and finally
settled on romcom novels as her genre of choice after realising the
world can never have enough of the mirth-filled mushy stuff.

Sal lives in Manchester, England, with her husband and son – the
two loves of her life. Her side hustle is managing her rampant
anxiety. She also works in marketing.

instagram.com/salthomasauthor

Also by Sal Thomas

The Accidental Housemate

COMMUNITY SERVICE

SAL THOMAS

One More Chapter
a division of HarperCollins*Publishers*
1 London Bridge Street
London SE1 9GF
www.harpercollins.co.uk
HarperCollins*Publishers*
Macken House, 39/40 Mayor Street Upper,
Dublin 1, D01 C9W8, Ireland

This paperback edition 2024
First published in Great Britain in ebook format
by HarperCollins*Publishers* 2024
1

A catalogue record of this book is available from the British Library

ISBN: 978-0-00-860941-2

Printed and bound in the UK using 100% Renewable Electricity
by CPI Group (UK) Ltd

Content notice: Please be advised that this book contains references to suicide.

To my family, without whom I wouldn't have learned to laugh so much.
Or have needed to.

Chapter One

Simone was more drunk than she'd intended to get. She knew this for three reasons. The first was that on the walk from the car to the flat, she'd gone over twice on her heel – her ankles and hips were loose and her stride was less forced than usual. The second was that she'd stopped tensing her stomach muscles about an hour ago, which was normally unthinkable given the tightness of the cashmere shift dress into which she'd poured herself that morning. And the third was that she couldn't make sense of how an important potential client of the reputation management & PR agency she worked for was jerking himself off, right there on her doorstep.

'Oh, that's right,' Finchley moaned.

How did she get here? She'd had no intention of making the acquaintance of his trouser contents when she'd agreed to drinks earlier. In fact, she'd had no intention of agreeing to drinks earlier – he was as wrinkled as a drowned corpse and only half as attractive – but Tony, her boss, had made it clear that refusal wasn't an option when he was capable of gifting them a half-a-million-pound contract. So she'd spent the evening drinking more champagne than she'd wanted, pretending to be more interested in his business than she was, and making all the right noises as he explained how much of a swinging big dick he was in the world of finance. Only now the swinging big dick's actual dick was out. On her doorstep.

She'd tried to keep things professional. She'd laughed off the compliments and the double entendres, made it clear she had a boyfriend, and had consistently steered the conversation away from anything too personal. But on the shared chauffeur-driven lift home that he'd been adamant she accept, he'd made the kind of overtures that only a man with too much money and too little charm would attempt. He'd then insisted on walking her to her door, having deliberately asked the driver to stop far enough away to do so.

'Aren't you going to ask me to … come inside?' he'd asked, pressing himself against her, hard on his own wordplay.

She'd been here before, of course. Different bloke, same lame game. It was a lose-lose situation. If she tried to extricate herself with a polite excuse, her vagina would be unfinished business to him, the threat of his penis hanging over her like a fleshy Damoclean sword. If she kneed him in the bollocks and went inside to eat half a block of cheese, she'd get into all types of shit at work.

It was a pussy-based puzzler alright. A veritable Snatch-22. But as she'd been weighing up her options, wondering how to play this grim hand for the best, he'd taken matters into his own hands. Literally.

She'd no idea when he'd undone his trousers, but there it was. He was wearing loose cotton boxers, doubtless chosen in the belief his testicles should be as free from restraint as he was, and his cock should enjoy the privilege of absolute freedom to go wheresoever it chose. She glanced at said cock now. It was small, with an excess of foreskin despite its hardness, like a child swamped by an adult's polo neck sweater. In the streetlamp's yellow sodium glow, it looked like it had been smothered in iodine in preparation for an operation. She swallowed the acrid bile that rose in her throat.

'Are you sure you don't want this in you?' he said.

Quite sure. What she wanted to do was tear it off and throw it in a storm drain, but even as the thought crossed her mind, she knew she wouldn't. She was at a critical point in her career. As far as Tony was concerned, watching some guy pound his prick in order to secure a big account could be considered a business transaction of sorts. A case of *Jizz Pro Quo. Quid Pro Cum.* He wouldn't give a shit. How the hell had it come to this? Some people drew the line at overtime, for fuck's sake! Thank heavens she'd had a few though. It would hopefully mean that, come the morning, the specifics of what was happening now would be harder to recall – the edges blunted, the detail in soft focus.

'I'm going to come,' Finchley mumbled.

It was the most considerate he'd been all evening because it gave her time to step out of the way of the globules of semen erupting like white hot lava from the skin folds around his bellend. She watched it spatter onto the black lettering of the doormat beneath her feet. WELCOME. Less of a greeting, more a commentary on his performance.

'Do you have a tissue?' he managed, all breathy swagger gone now, his face slick with the effort of ejaculating.

She wordlessly reached inside her bag and pulled out the monogrammed napkins she'd taken from the elite new bar they'd ended up in. There hadn't been a chance to get a word in edgeways earlier, let alone a selfie, so she'd intended to take some arty shot of them for her Insta to serve as proof she'd been there. She handed them over. Probably better not to have a memento of the evening after all. He dabbed at his rapidly diminishing cock, a deflating balloon in its final death throes, and tucked himself back into his trousers. By the time he made his excuses to leave, he was almost contrite, poor lamb. Perhaps he was fleetingly seeing himself for what he was: just a little man with a small dick and a narrow view of the world, spilling his seed onto a virtual stranger's coir matting. Still, the introspection wouldn't last.

She went inside and washed her hands, removed her make-up, gulped down two glasses of water, and looked at herself squarely in the mirror above the sink. The shit she'd put up with for this job. She'd better bloody well get this promotion.

Chapter Two

By the time Simone got off the tube, it was as though she hadn't showered at all. Her skin was clammy, her painstakingly straightened hair frizzed at the edges, and her face itched beneath her carefully applied make-up. The street offered little relief; it was unseasonably warm for mid-March, but at least the metallic screech of the train grinding against its tracks was gone, replaced by a cacophony of beeping and shouting from drivers who deemed their journeys to be more urgent than anyone else's. Caffeine was most definitely required.

'Spare some change, love?'

The homeless man was outside her favourite coffee shop, sat on a makeshift cardboard bed. He was holding up a plastic pint pot, as if waiting for a *cheers* that never came.

Oh crap. She'd never been very good with homeless people. She always became hugely awkward around them, a sensation she detested and therefore tried to tie up in self-righteousness, thus preventing her from having to feel bad about their plight. When she was a child, back in the nineties, vagrants had been a rare phenomenon. There'd be the occasional grizzle-haired, trolley-

5

wielding ancient who would scour bins and wear newspaper socks and make the whole thing look like an eccentric lifestyle choice. But nowadays, they were unavoidable. That wasn't going to stop her trying, however. She kept her eyes above pavement level. Do. Not. Engage.

'Can you spare any change, love?' he said again, but this time with such confidence, her gaze was drawn towards him.

He was definitely rough around the edges, his wan face was creased with dirt and sparse cartoonish whiskers pointed directly out from his chin, but his eyes were keen and alert. Damn! She'd made eye contact. He raised the cup again.

She'd received a government leaflet once advising that giving money directly to homeless people exacerbated the vicious cycle of substance misuse, and meant they continued to avoid the help they needed. She'd gratefully swallowed it without question. Not giving wasn't *mean*; it was *mandated*. By people who knew better than she did. Time to switch tactics. A gentle *sorry*, followed by a melancholy head shake and beatific smile, a facial contortion she hoped would convey *I sympathise with your plight, and if I could, I would almost certainly give you some money, but it's in your best interest that I don't.* This was usually met with a returned smile from the recipient, a tacit acknowledgment that, at its most basic, they were just two people trying to navigate life as best they could. Only today it wasn't. Today the man gave her a look that seemed to convey, *Nice try, sister, but I can't survive on your carefully contrived thoughts and facial expressions, I actually need to eat, so I'll ask you again.*

'Just a couple of quid's change to get some breakfast.'

She didn't have a couple of quid in change. True, she had a twenty in her purse, but if she could stop feeling like Hagrid had taken a shit in her brain at some point today, she was going to get her French bangs trimmed at the cash-only place near work. But the tractor beam of his gaze had her in its pull, and she didn't have the mental strength to resist it.

'Can I buy you breakfast instead?'

'Where from?'

She motioned to the coffee shop. 'In there?'

'What's on the menu?

'Pastries.'

'Empty calories.'

A nutritional expert. Brilliant.

'Anything with protein in?' he asked.

'They have protein shakes but…' But they cost eight quid, and cash flow wasn't the best right now.

'I'd prefer a butty.'

Opposite them was a greasy spoon with a flashing sign that made her eyes ache. She nodded to it.

'Nah, that gets terrible reviews,' he said.

'How do you know?'

'I read them.'

'How?'

'On my phone.'

He produced a smartphone from his pocket. So many questions. How had he got it? How could he afford it? She didn't need to know.

'I know what you're thinking,' he said.

'I doubt it.'

'How can I afford to have a phone?'

She wasn't going to get through the next three minutes, let alone the day.

'We're given 'em by the authorities. Easier to stay in touch and get you off the street.'

'How long have you been on the street?' Oh god, now she was having a conversation.

'Four years.'

'How long have you had your phone?'

'Four years. I've got good at Wordle though.' He grinned.

She took a deep breath. Terrible mistake. A nearby drain reeked of wet dog crossed with an unemptied food bin. Being sick in the street would not be a good look. She was also disconcerted to note that someone was taking an interest in their exchange, just there on the margins of her vision. Tall. Broad. Wearing a hoodie.

The homeless guy waved at him. 'Be with you in a minute, J.'

A mate of his? It didn't matter. Best to ignore him. She wished she'd done the same with old Whiskers here.

'How about a tea?' she suggested.

'Nah, you're alright.'

Great. Time to leave. But he wasn't letting her go that easily.

'Are you on Instagram?'

Of course she was on Instagram. She had over two thousand followers, and if she didn't get a coffee soon, she'd have to think of something else to post for their viewing pleasure.

'No.'

The hoodie watching them gently scoffed. She refused to turn around.

'I'm not gonna stalk you,' said the homeless guy. He grabbed a large piece of cardboard with the Instagram logo and @StreetPete scrawled on it. 'Can you post a picture of me? I'm raising awareness of homelessness.'

'I think people already know it exists,' she said.

The hoodie behind her chuckled throatily. A woman with a small wheely bag and an air of high-mindedness approached, pointedly put some change in Pete's cup, and cast her a barbed look. How was she at fault here?

'Money won't make the guilt go away,' Simone told her.

'If you cared, you'd post a picture of me on Instagram.' Pete winked at the hoodie.

Was he a stooge? Was she on some hidden camera show? She

really wasn't in the mood to be dicked around. Not on a Wednesday. And not after last night's doorstep shenanigans with Finchley.

'I think it's great what you're doing...'

Did she? She'd never really considered that anyone making a bed from boxes would be motivated to do anything beyond begging.

'...but people don't go on Instagram to be reminded of how shitty the world is. That's what the platform formerly known as Twitter is for.'

Another deep laugh behind her.

'It *is* only a picture,' the hoodie said. 'I'll happily take one of you together.'

She was too tired and hungover for some random stranger to be acting intellectually superior to her, even if at that moment an *amoeba* was intellectually superior to her.

'Tell you what,' she said, 'why don't you have your picture taken if you're so...' she spun around, curious as to which do-gooder's judgment she was being subjected.

'I've already posted. See?' He was holding up his mobile phone.

But it wasn't the post that caused her words to grind to a standstill; it was the guy himself. He was hot, like, unusual-looking ex-Prada model hot. Perhaps a bit too old for catwalks, but still way too fine for catalogues. He was all angles and strong lines, but his tawny skin was peppered with freckles, softening the architecture of his face and lending him a playful vibe.

'Bully for you,' she managed.

His lips were naturally pursed, like words were constantly perched on the end of his tongue ready to tumble out, and his bright blue eyes had a slight downward turn at the edges, as if the effort of being so gaze-into-able had tired them out. Soft twisted meringue-like peaks of afro hair poked out the front of his hood.

And he was tall, much taller than her in her heels, and she was five-eight without them. She scanned the screen for his handle; made a mental note: @Jasp-err.

He shrugged. 'I guess it is.'

Simone didn't like very attractive men; they were too self-aware and not to be trusted. As last night had demonstrated, men were troublesome enough creatures even without the constant temptation of eager women wanting to land themselves a superior specimen. No matter how attractive you yourself might be – and empirically she was doing okay for herself (not that it was something for which she could take much credit) – it was only ever a matter of time before they did something unutterably dickish. You know, like getting their twenty-three-year-old assistant pregnant when they were meant to be in a committed relationship with you. But unusually for her, she felt ambushed by this guy's handsomeness, as if by not expecting it she'd been caught on the back foot. Best not to show weakness, though.

'I don't recall asking for your opinion, Jasp-err.'

'I'm just saying it's not that big a deal.'

'Maybe not for your feed, but for mine it's the equivalent of a turd in a box of turmeric buns.'

He smiled. She didn't.

'You seem angry about something,' he said. 'Are you okay?'

'Who are you? *The woman whisperer*?'

'Whoa!' He raised his forearms in surrender.

The hoodie was tight. No label, but his muscles had been designed by Michelangelo.

'Didn't realise it was Snark Week on the Discovery Channel,' he said. 'I was just asking.'

Snark Week. She'd have to remember that.

'It's nothing that a coffee and a handgun wouldn't resolve.' She checked her phone. It was getting late. 'Seems I won't get my hands on either this morning.'

'Cheer up,' said Pete. 'Could be worse. You could be me.'

'Very reassuring.'

'True though,' said Jasper.

Normally, whenever she encountered someone on an equal-ish attractiveness footing as herself, they would square off, almost daring one another to disappoint on other levels. It was a stupid game, probably some evolutionary bullshit at play. But this one wasn't engaging in the usual way. The body language was all wrong. It was as if how she looked, or indeed how he did, were of no bearing on this situation. She was confused and, she hated to admit, slightly peeved.

'Is it? Sure, I have a roof over my head, but I pretty much *only* own the roof. The bank owns the rest and charges me a fuck ton percent for the privilege. The walls are so thin I can hear the mice screwing next door – at least I can when my neighbour isn't playing his frigging tom-toms. On top of this, I have a shitty boss whose idea of staff motivation is to use the carrot as a makeshift ball gag so he doesn't have to listen to your cries whilst he beats you with the stick. I'm so hungover the Red Cross has opened an emergency care base in my brain, and all I really want to do is curl up on that cardboard and go the hell to sleep, which, if you look at the state of it, gives you some indication of just how bad I'm feeling. So I am sorry that I'm not capable of bringing you the happy-clappy *are you alright, mate* version of myself this morning. Or indeed any morning.'

Jasper was doing his best to appear contrite.

'And out of interest,' she said, 'did you just come over to lord your virtuous superiority over me?'

'I came to have a chat with Pete.'

These two went together like strawberries and bream. Curiosity got the better of her.

'Are you some kind of double act? Sherlock Homeless & Doctor Hotson.'

Jasper and Pete exchanged a half-smile and an admiring nod. This was also unusual. Most men she met resolutely ignored the fact that she could be witty. Women like her were there to appreciate men's jokes, not make any for themselves.

'Not bad,' said Jasper. 'You could also have had Django & Cashless.'

'Who's the double act?' she asked.

'Tango & Cash.'

'Never heard of them.'

'Really? Sylvester Stallone and Kurt Russell. Two cops with very different approaches who have to team up to clear their name.'

'When was it out?' she said.

'Late eighties.'

'How old are you?'

'Thirty-five.'

He was a year older than her.

'Best era for buddy cop movies,' Jasper said.

'Yeah,' said Pete, all misty-eyed. *'48 Hours.'*

'Another 48 Hours,' said Jasper.

'Lethal Weapon.'

'Lethal Weapon 2.'

'Bad Boys.'

'Bad Boys 2.'

'Not seen it,' said Pete.

'You've not seen the latest one?' said Jasper.

Pete gestured to his surroundings. For a fraction of a second, she wondered what his life was like before he became Street Pete.

'Ah man. We'll have to watch it one day,' said Jasper.

She was also no clearer on what the relationship between these two was.

'Well, I'd love to stay listening to you two list films all day, but I need to go to work.' She pulled the twenty out of her purse, bent over and shoved it into Pete's cup. 'Here. Have it. I was going to get my hair cut, but the way this day has started, I'll probably tear it out instead.'

'You said you didn't have any money,' said Pete.

'I said I didn't have any *change*.'

'Semantics,' said Pete.

How did this guy know about semantics? Nope. No further engagement.

'Spend it on Spice. Crack. Popcorn. Whatever gets you off, mate.'

She sensed Jasper wanted to say something to her, as if her impending departure had nudged the natural order of things back into alignment. Perhaps his disinterested vibe was a ruse – something advised by that pick-up artist book *The Game* which had done the rounds a decade ago. Still, the sooner she got to work, the sooner she could sit and stare at her screen and not do any work. She turned and strode off, not even bothering to acknowledge Jasper as she went. Two could play that game. She was about twenty strides away when she heard urgent footsteps behind her. That was more like it.

'Hey!' He was next to her. 'This is a bit awkward but—'

'The answer's no,' she said.

'Eh?'

'You're going to ask for my number.'

'Am I?'

'I know how this works.'

'Do you?'

'Yeah. First you play it cool, get me all intrigued. Then you ask for my number. Then you leave me waiting days to text. Then we go out, possibly a few times. Then we bone. Then, having got exactly what you wanted, you get bored and move on.'

The only guy she'd ever been certain didn't have an ulterior motive, or wouldn't mess her around in some way, was her dad, but even he'd betrayed her by dying.

'I'm flattered,' she said, 'but I already have a boyfriend.'

Jasper's whole face was an apology. She'd been right.

'Erm … actually I was going to point out that you have bird excrement on your back.'

'What?'

'One crapped on you when you put money in Pete's cup.'

This wasn't in *The Game*. Was he kidding? It was an interesting gambit if so. She took her jacket off. Sure enough, there was a streak of bird crap down it.

'Goddammit! I knew I should have given up fucks for Lent. Tell Pete I want my twenty back.'

Jasper reached in his pocket and pulled out a handkerchief. An actual cotton handkerchief.

'What's this?' she said. 'A Regency drama?'

He smiled and passed it to her. A lesser mortal might have been disarmed. She laid the jacket over a bollard and dabbed at the splotch. It was like smearing wet chalk and coal together.

'Why the hell would bird crap be black and white anyway?' she said. 'Worms aren't black and white. Bread's not black and white.'

His eyes twinkled. 'You could argue that nothing in life is black and white.'

She cast him a withering look.

'Not into philosophical jokes,' he said. 'Noted. You know it's meant to be lucky.'

'That's bullshit.

'No, that's bird shit.'

He was quick. And enjoying himself. There was no sorting the jacket now, so she turned it inside out and lay it across her bag. The hangover sweats were kicking in anyway.

'Do you want this back?' She held the soiled handkerchief out to him.

'You're alright.'

'Great. Well, if I need to unconditionally surrender from anything today, like my life, at least I can wave this. Have a good one.'

She walked off, trying not to think about how much of an egotistical idiot she must have seemed. She could deal with the egotistical bit. She'd spent her whole life having people assume she was *up herself* just because of an aesthetic configuration of her DNA and a desire to cloak her emotions, but she didn't like being proved wrong about men. It was disconcerting. It went against her confirmation bias. Still, there was an eight-million-to-one-shot of bumping into this one again, and despite the stain on the back of her jacket, or her genetic good fortune, the rest of her life thus far had proven that she wasn't actually that lucky.

Chapter Three

Dixon & Astley (aka Dickwad & Ghastly) had offices on the upper floor of one of London's most sought-after buildings. When first constructed, it had garnered headlines for its unusual shape, and the fact that the light reflecting off it had burned the paintwork on someone's Bentley. It was her boss's car (Simone worked for the Dickwad half), and he'd created the headlines in the first place, seeding the entirely fabricated story to a press eager to pour scorn on the edifice and its occupants. Instead, they had inadvertently created more publicity for the business than several thousand pounds of advertising could have achieved. The company could well afford the premises and the car, operating as it did at the most lucrative end of the Public Relations spectrum. Dickwad was responsible for pure-play PR on behalf of uber-wealthy organisations and individuals, raising their carefully crafted profile through events, stunts and grand gestures. The other side of the business, presided over by Ghastly, existed to wipe away any trace of negative stories that might already have surfaced on clients. They erased information where possible, and where not, flooded the internet with benign propaganda about them, undertaking such algorithmic alchemy that only the positive stories would rise to the top of the search engines. There's a joke in SEO that if you want to hide a dead body, you do it on page two of Google. This was the purpose of Dickwad & Ghastly. So broken were the Directors' moral compasses that they offered to neutralise the negative publicity the Bentley story had garnered, but only in return for a five-year-long rent reduction from the building owners. But that was not before every possible acquaintance of Dickwad could have read the original story, and therefore known that he now had a Bentley and a plush office in the city's hottest (pun intended) new postcode.

Simone stepped out of the lift and into a human fish tank, with floor to ceiling views of architecture far more elegant than the space-age dustbin she'd just shot up. No sign of the directors yet, so there was still time to slum it with a coffee pod before she got started.

'Look at what the cat dragged in.'

Just what she needed. Oliver Young-Ward was already in the kitchen, gazing at his reflection in the glass-fronted fridge. His name couldn't have been more appropriate: he was thirty-three, but looked more like a brattish ten-year-old caught in the crossfire of a grow-ray gun. He had permanently narrowed eyes, like he was constantly weighing up what use you might be to him, and a cowlick fringe that pointed in the wrong direction, because the rest of him had never done as it was told, so why should his hair bother? His pasty white ankles were bookended by deck shoes and cream chinos, in the back pocket of which was a rolled-up copy of *The Spectator*.

'Do you ever actually read that, or is it to warn passers-by that you're a right-wing, pro-hunting, polo-playing aristocrat who's secretly insecure about his moral legitimacy?'

She'd seldom hated anyone in her life, but Oliver Young-

Ward was a genuine nemesis. He was Hannibal Lecter to her Clarice; kryptonite to her Superman; dogshit to her Kurt Geigers.

'You look like you've just come off the set of *Ten Years Older*,' he said.

'Put a cork in it, Ollie. Or would a silver spoon be more appropriate?'

He was a perfect specimen of the upper classes, the kind to whom life had come as easy as his pecker doubtless did, hunched over a soggy biscuit at the boarding school where he'd failed to learn anything – except how to be a grade-A asshole.

'Heard you were out with Finchley last night,' he said. 'Do you reckon you'll get it?' His voice was steady, but his eyes betrayed his concern that she might.

Her stomach turned at the thought of what had gone down on her doorstep, but it would be worth it – just – to get one up on Oliver. He had arrived at the company eighteen months previously, utterly lacking in experience, but with a familial connection that secured him a position she'd slaved to attain. He'd failed to make any kind of impression, except one of a man trying to talk with a tongue three sizes too big for his mouth, until his father-in-law, high up in a chemical company, had needed to bury a story about a cancer-causing pesticide capable of drifting thousands of feet from where it was applied. Since then, the father-in-law had channelled a steady stream of business their way, just as his chemical company had channelled a steady stream of deadly compounds the way of an unsuspecting public. Nepotism was alive and well and shitting all over her potential promotion parade.

'It doesn't matter,' said Ollie. 'I've got Papa coming in shortly. Got a contact in government to float my way. And you know how lucrative those contracts can be.'

Not what she needed to hear this morning.

'Doesn't it ever bother you that you rely on your family for your career?' she asked.

'Come on, Little Bo Peep,' he sneered. 'You're not so pure. I use my connections; you use these.' He gestured to her boobs. 'We're not so different, you and I.'

'We're nothing alike.'

'I know you. A working-class kid trying to break the confines of her social stratum. Wanting to mix with the big boys, but crying foul when they do grown-up things.'

He leered at her. Did he know what Finchley had done? But no, that was impossible.

'The only thing you crave more than money is status,' he said, 'whereas I have both and a desire to keep hold of them. Same same.'

He was wrong. She just wanted the money. She'd had to make her own way in life, and having come from nothing, she knew all too well how easily you could return there.

'Anyway,' said Ollie, suddenly bored of her presence, 'Papa is going to be here in ten minutes, just time for Nora to grab me some proper coffees.'

'Nora has work to do for me this morning.'

'Is it to book you a facial? You really do need one.'

'Perhaps she can get you a new aftershave whilst she's at it. That Dior *Halitosis for Men* just isn't working for you.'

It was a lame comeback and Oliver knew it. He slithered away, whistling.

Her period was due any day, which meant she was even more sensitive to his barbs than usual, but was she guilty of using her sexuality to get ahead? Was there something she'd done last night to warrant Finchley's actions? Could she have gotten away with walking away sooner? Her experience suggested not. But what about the clothes she wore that accentuated her body rather than shrouded it? And the make-up she applied because it made her feel more confident. Was that being deliberately provocative? Or was it just using to her advantage what little advantage she did have? And wasn't the point that, even if the entire male population had a boner for you, you still had agency over which boners you chose to engage with? Wasn't it the guy's responsibility to keep it in his pants until such a point at which you made your wishes clear? Surely anything else was a symptom of their weakness, not confirmation of her abusing her so-called 'power'.

Come to think of it, though, she'd definitely not exhibited any such power over that Jasper guy this morning. He had been entirely resistant to any such charms that Ollie claimed she was exploiting. Fuck it! She was too hungover to be contemplating feminist code. She was good at her job – better than good. She'd worked harder than anyone there to earn her place on the next rung of the ladder, and if she so happened to have an appearance that people noticed as much as her professional capabilities, so be it. Even so, Ollie casting shade meant he was clearly rattled that the dangled carrot of a promotion was swinging in her direction. Because, make no mistake, if the deal with Finchley did come in, she was a shoo-in for director. The only thing to do was to not let him get to her.

Chapter Four

'Don't let him bother you, eh?'

'But I am looking old!'

'That's your concern? He's a bad man.'

She'd come to see her beautician, Wei, for her fortnightly fix. Wei was an open-hearted peach of a man, with a soft face that belied a hard childhood, growing up as openly gay in Jiangsu province. She'd stumbled across him at a nail bar years ago, where he'd regaled her with tales of his second job working in an S&M dungeon on the Old Kent Road. He'd joked about how handcuffs should have been a playing piece in Monopoly, although everyone would have to beg him to pass go, and he'd be the one collecting the £200. He'd given it up when he met his now-husband David, a financial advisor with a penchant for stocks (not of the restraining kind). Instead he'd set up a mini salon in the spare bedroom of their Crystal Palace flat, where he now offered Gua Sha facials and other delicious treatments. Her nostrils tingled as Wei smoothed lemongrass-fragranced massage oil onto her face.

'What if he's right about the other stuff?' she said.

It still rankled.

'He's a woman hater. Men like that, they only like their nannies, the ones who mollycoddle and tit feed. He's just jealous.'

'Hmm.'

'You need a different place to work.'

There were precisely three reputation management companies of such scale in the city: Dickwad & Ghastly; a second place run by a pit bull of a bloke famous for worse behaviour than the clients he represented; and the third owned by her walking perineum of a cheating ex-boyfriend. And whilst a lot of water had passed under the bridge since he'd done the dirty on her, given what she'd been told about her own reproductive chances, coming into contact with the child he'd fathered as a result of his affair might prove a little too much.

She tried to relax under Wei's constantly moving fingertips, the rhythmic stroking acting as a balm to her apprehension. After several delicious minutes, he spoke again.

'You know it's Mother's Day?'

All too well.

'I called again. No joy for me.'

'I don't know why you bother,' she said.

'She'll come round eventually.'

She doubted Wei's mum would. Homosexuality had been legal in China for over two decades, but Mrs Yang hadn't got the memo; she continued to consider it the mental disorder it had been classified as up until 2001. She'd even spent a huge proportion of her modest income to pay for aversion therapy, where Wei was instructed to have sexual thoughts about men whilst receiving electric shocks. It didn't work. He stubbornly continued to fancy men, but now joked that he could only come with his balls in the toaster.

'Things are changing,' said Wei.

'Not that quickly. I saw they opened Bohemian Rhapsody in China without the gay bits. Must have been a short show.'

He wiped away the oil with soft cotton pads. 'You never talk about your mum. You miss her, eh?'

Wei knew that her mum had died suddenly nearly two years ago, but he had no idea of the circumstances. She hadn't told anybody the truth of her death; it would invite too much cross-examination and counter-questions, and their terminal earnestness would be entirely at odds with the anger and confusion with which she regarded her mother's actions. She still hadn't felt the weight of any grief settle on her – not in the way she'd been consumed by it when her dad was snatched away nearly twenty years ago. It was more surprise at the absence of her mum's murmurings of disappointment, like finding yourself free of tinnitus after years of affliction. She made non-committal noises.

'It's hard for everyone without a mum today,' he said. 'It's in all the shops and everything.'

The fact was, she had always hated Mother's Day. It was a nonsense, fake-ass, celebration of someone selfishly propagating their genes without consideration for the future feelings of the person to be foisted upon a broken, dysfunctional world. She hated the compulsion to play along with the commercial shitshow, performing a dutiful daughter tap dance with the gifting of overpriced flowers and saccharine cards written by someone with candyfloss for brains. And maybe the tiniest bit of her hated the fact that she'd probably never get the chance to be a crap mother herself.

'It's not all bad though', said Wei. 'David's mum is so lovely.'

Lucky David. Whereas there were no Mother's Day cards that could truly sum up the relationship she'd had with her mother.

Roses are red. Violets are blue. You pushed me out of your vagina. And then expected me to thank you.

You propagated your genes and then blamed me when you could no longer fit into your jeans. #blessed.

Thanks for trying to live your life vicariously through me after you made terrible choices with your own.

She'd have been better off searching in the 'with sympathy' area. She made more non-committal noises for Wei and was relieved when he popped her under his photon therapy LED light and told her he'd be back in twenty minutes.

'So what are you doing for the rest of the weekend?' he asked when her time was up. 'Meeting the girls?'

'They're away.' She gathered her belongings.

He tutted. 'You need a boyfriend. You're a beautiful lady.'

This was his customary response whenever she didn't have plans, but then again, he also had no idea about Marcus.

'I'll probably do some work.'

He tutted some more. 'You work too hard. Didn't Dolly Parton say it's as important to make a life as it is to make a living? She's a wise lady.'

'Who do you think is wiser, Dolly or Confucius?'

He looked at her like she'd grown a second head.

'How the hell should I know? I reckon Confucius had bigger tits though. That's why he had long eyebrows and a beard – to try and take attention away from them.'

She laughed.

'Don't laugh too much, I only just got rid of those lines.'

There wasn't much danger of that.

'I'll see you in a couple of weeks, Wei.'

'You take care.'

She ignored the concern in his voice. Everything was absolutely fine.

Chapter Five

Simone gazed at optic upon optic of cordial bottles, hoping one might magically transform into gin. The various sodas and seltzers in the fridges below did nothing to improve her mood.

'It's a Temperance bar,' the barman said.

'It's an abomination,' she said.

When the girls had invited her to tag along to the opening of Canary Wharf's latest shit-hot night spot, she'd been anticipating getting a little merry. Fat chance of that. Surely there should be some rule that any establishment catering to adult humans, in a part of the city frequented by hard-working hard-partying finance folk, was one in which you should be able to mainline hard liquor.

'Millennials and Gen Z'ers don't need alcohol to have a good time,' said the barman.

'Yes, they do,' she said. 'They've just forgotten how to have a good time.'

'Do you know how to have a good time?' He flashed her a grin.

She coolly appraised him. Quite fit from the neck down in his denim tabard and tight-fitting white T-shirt, but far too young and far too barman-y.

'Not here I don't.'

She turned her back on him and watched as Nancy tried to take countless arty shots in various corners of the premises. Perhaps Ziggy, who was late as usual, might have had the foresight to get a small bottle of something potent from the supermarket down the road.

It made no sense for young people not to drink. Faced with the cataclysmic list of fuck-ups bequeathed to them by the Boomers, how else would they deal with their gnawing anxiety and escalating sense of helplessness?

'Isn't this place amazing?! So cute!' said Nancy.

Simone had never considered a venue of any description to be *cute*. This one, with its pastel velvet seating, pale green pearlescent tiling, and soft lighting, was at the prettier end of the spectrum, but the distinct lack of ethanol on offer meant it scored nil points in her book.

'You can do without a drink for one night, grumpy pants!'

Nancy, by contrast, was looking extremely cute. She was wearing an embroidered white button-through dress, tan suede slouchy boots, and her naturally straw-blonde hair was wrapped in braids around her head. She wasn't exactly pretty – her eyes were a little too wide-set and her nose just a little too snubby – but she was the epitome of wholesomeness, and completely non-threatening to the horde of followers she'd amassed for her lifestyle schtick on social. She slung an arm around Simone's neck and took a picture of them both. Simone grabbed the phone to ensure the image met her exacting standards prior to its publication.

'Can you order me a hibiscus and rose petal agua fresca?' said Nancy. 'I'm going to get a shot of the toilets.'

She got the attention of a different server and ordered herself a kombucha – not for the health benefits, but as a fermented drink it was the closest thing to wine she was going to get.

Someone tapped her on the shoulder. It was Ziggy, pneumatic in a cropped vest and spray-on leather leggings. She wasn't wearing a bra, and her perky nipples were clearly visible through the tight white fabric of her top.

'I see you've gone for the subtle look this evening.'

'You never know who you're going to bump into,' said Ziggy.

'Your nipples are sticking out so far, I'd be surprised if you *didn't* bump into everyone.'

Ziggy gave Simone her best crazy emoji face. She looked like a cross between Aladdin's Princess Jasmine and Lilo's Stitch. 'Are the drinks free?'

'From alcohol, unfortunately.'

'You know when I went to Dubai…'

Simone switched off. She'd heard the story, or ones like it, a hundred times before. Ziggy (not her real name) was a well-known travel vlogger, although Simone often thought her success had little to do with the quality of her content, and more to do with how much her arse (not her real arse) was on show in her pictures. It wouldn't matter where she went, her pert, rounded, Kardashian-like bottom was always front and centre. Still, it contained so much silicone it probably classed as a beach, so technically every day was a holiday.

'…you really get a sense of the authentic Bedouin culture…'

Authentic experiences: the ultimate battleground of the travel influencer. It wasn't enough to see a place anymore, you had to ride the national animal up its most treacherous mountain pass, and then convert to the local religion at the top. Ziggy would probably do a stint at Guantanamo if it meant a few more eyeballs.

'Order me a lychee and yuzu martini mocktail. I'm getting a shot of the toilets.'

Ziggy waltzed away, the twin bowling balls of her bottom jostling for position within her skin-tight pants.

Simone wasn't entirely sure how the three of them had become friends. She'd met them at a media conference a few years ago, and professional interests had provided enough glue for the connection to stick socially. With work being so crazy for so long, her social circle wasn't exactly extensive, and there was only so much drinking a girl could do on her own.

Eventually both girls returned, and after a who's-who breakdown of the other personalities at the party, talk turned to the holiday they were planning together.

'I've been offered a suite gratis at The Bellagio for three nights, so that should cover the Vegas leg for us,' said Ziggy, who had her good points, aside from the obvious two that were still standing to full attention despite the heat in the room.

'We have to go swimming in Slide Rock State Park,' said Nancy.

Ziggy searched for it on her phone. 'Good 'grammage. Approved. How does everyone feel about doing the Grand Canyon by mule? Helicopters have been done to death. There's some Apache stables you can stay at overnight. We can do the whole campfire thing.'

Nancy shrugged. 'We can do s'mores, moonlight yoga. I don't see why not.'

They continued to talk about potential itineraries, experiences, and whether San Fran or LA would be the best ultimate destination.

'Sure you can afford all this, Sim?' asked Nancy.

It was true the trip was going to cost more for her than for them, what with their sponsored posts and freebies. And yes, she was pretty much up to her eyeballs in debt having stretched herself paper-thin on her mortgage. But she was credit-carding it and would pay it off when she got her promotion. Besides, it would be worth it. Her dad had always dreamed of travelling across America after he retired, but he'd never got the chance to do either. She'd do it for him.

'So long as we get to drive a convertible down Route 66,' she said smiling, 'it's all good.'

'I don't think I've ever seen you so excited about anything before,' said Nancy.

'I get excited about stuff.'

Ziggy snorted. 'Come on, Sim. If we were the Scooby Doo team, I'd be Daphne, Nancy would be Scrappy Do, and you'd … well you'd be the guy in the mask bemoaning the pesky kids.'

'What?!'

Nancy fiddled with her straw. 'You are pretty cynical.'

'I'm just a realist.'

'It's okay. I'm just saying, you know, it's nice to see you looking forward to something.' Nancy picked up her phone. 'Shall we explore car options? Soft top, yeah?'

They stayed at the bar for another hour or so, but she couldn't quite shake Nancy's words. That was the problem with being sober: you remembered what people said. She'd always thought of herself as being the one that tolerated their idiosyncrasies. It had never occurred to her that the door swung both ways, and that they had to put up with her too. Not that she agreed with Nancy, but she'd been in the city a long time; a holiday was just what she needed.

Chapter Six

'Simone. Come in. Shut the door.'

Tony Dixon was reclining in his leather office chair, his lower shirt buttons straining under the pressure of his gelatinous belly. The morning sun streaming in made his gossamer thin hair look like a dirty brown aura. He had a face that even the most committed pacifist would gladly punch.

'Good golfing trip?' she asked.

'Good enough to secure the Coral project. The full brief will be in next week.'

His ruddy complexion was even redder than usual. No surprises that he hadn't used sun cream: he was the type of man who thought his wealth afforded him immunity from everything, even a burning hot ball of gas a million times the size of the planet they were on.

'So, when are you going to make me a director?'

She had worked for Tony for six years. In that time, she'd earned the company more money annually than any other account handler in its history, as well as won countless awards for creativity and effectiveness.

'No one deserves to be promoted more than you, Simone.'

'Great.'

His calf-leather chair groaned as he leaned forward. 'But I'm afraid there's a complication.'

'Which is?'

'There's been a report of bullying.'

That was hardly surprising. The place was essentially a high-functioning bear pit, with regular bollockings from the bosses being the norm.

'Which one of you is it against?' she asked, not entirely sure what it had to do with her promotion.

'You.' He pointed his pen at her.

'Very funny.' She was firm with her team, but also fair.

'Not that funny. It's Oliver.'

What the fuck? What was the little toerag playing at now?

'You're kidding me.'

'He said you've refused to assist him when requested, and deliberately excluded him from after-work socials.'

'That's because he's a lazy, boring asshole!'

Tony half-smiled. 'And what about verbal abuse?'

'He does exactly the same to me. Yesterday I politely asked him why he hadn't sent me the action notes from the Glennich meeting, despite my asking three times. He came right up into my face and shouted that I was "making a fucking mountain out of a molehill, was it my time of the month?" This was in front of my team.'

'He said you'd mention that. He told me it was a joke.'

'And what if I said what he's accusing me of was a joke?'

'You can't expect me to dismiss a colleague's claims out of hand. Imagine if it happened to you.'

'It does!'

There was a steadily building pressure at the back of her skull, like someone was grabbing her hair from behind and slowly and deliberately wrapping it around their fist.

'If you get so upset by these jokes—'

'He isn't joking.'

'Then why didn't you report it?'

She gave him an exasperated look. Like Tony gave the slightest shit about bullying in the workplace. He'd be the one on the sidelines, cheering it on.

'Just cut to the chase. Are you saying I'm not getting promoted because Oliver's pretending to be a snowflake?'

Tony came round to sit on the corner of the desk in front of her. His crotch was at eye level and his flies weren't done up properly. She edged her chair back.

'I'm saying it's no longer a one-horse race. He's shown that he's prepared to play dirty. He's trying to mess with your head.'

'You make it sound like a good thing,' she said.

'Isn't it? He's hungry. He's ruthless. This industry isn't for the faint-hearted.'

'But you promised me—'

'Shush now. Don't be such a baby. You know very well he brought in a huge account this quarter.'

'You mean his father-in-law? It's not like he had to go out of his way.'

How did she end up here? These were people who would sell their granny to their other granny and make the first granny pay a commission on the sale of herself.

'But on paper it stacks up. His billings aren't much shy of yours and he gets glowing testimonials from his client.'

'Again, his father-in-law.'

'And he has a lot of connections.'

'Hah!' she barked.

This is what it always came back to: sodding connections. She could grind for the rest of her life, but without an old boys' network to tap into, she'd always be left having to put up with pudding-pulling wankers to try and even out the score.

Tony picked up a ruler from his desk and absent-mindedly tapped it against his palm. 'I like you, Simone. You're like the daughter I never had.'

'You have a daughter.'

'But she's not smart like you are. Listen. You know what Oliver does. He makes stories about people go away. But he's shown he can also make them appear. Be careful, that's all I'm saying.'

This was too much. She got out of her seat and scanned the office.

'Where is the floppy-haired fucktard?'

'He's at a meeting.'

Oliver was nowhere to be seen, but at that moment Clarence 'Ghastly' Astley passed by. She shivered. He was the physical opposite of Tony, all pinched and skeletal, like Death in an expensive suit. No ageing portrait in the attic for him, but probably a rotten soul that not even the Devil had wanted. His only redeeming feature was that he'd never hit on her, but that was out of sexual preference rather than gentlemanly honour, so it wasn't much of a recommendation.

'And Clarence likes him,' Tony was saying. 'He's got the creepy old bastard on side.'

There was no love lost between the two partners, but as long as they were making oodles of money, they were happy to put aside their personal differences.

'So, what happens now? Am I being disciplined?'

He slapped the ruler against his palm. 'Would you like me to discipline you?'

She shook her head. If the irony in this office got any thicker, she'd choke on it.

'You're really going there, huh?'

'I'm kidding! Honestly, who made you the head of the fun police? Besides, there's no procedure in place for bullying.'

'That's reassuring.'

'If we had to investigate every time someone got shouted at, the whole operation would grind to a standstill. Just watch your back.'

'I can handle Oliver.'

'We'll review in a month. Right, get out, I have a conference call.'

She picked up her notebook.

'And Simone. Finchley got in touch. The account is yours. Said he's really looking forward to seeing more of you.' He winked.

She headed to the toilets, sat in a cubicle, and put her now throbbing head in her hands. That douchebag Oliver. He'd done nothing but make life difficult since his arrival, but this was an escalation. Should she leave as Wei had suggested? Do her own thing? She'd considered it, but there were contractual covenants in place that meant she'd be stuck working for tiny clients and tiny budgets, and there were loads of people already doing that with whom she'd need to compete. Nope, better the devil you know. Oliver's little prank hadn't actually got her into trouble, and the promotion could still be won on merit. It was just going to be harder than she'd envisaged. She needed to keep her head down, her nose clean, and her eyes open.

Chapter Seven

Simone had never got her head around threesomes. Sure, she'd seen porn in which bad actors demonstrated the pure physics of the proceedings, various permutations of penises and vulvas adding up to a triumvirate of titillation, but what about the etiquette in real life? Especially in England, with its social mores and politeness. If there was going down to be done, did everyone wait to eat together? If you were about to be screwed by two men, would most of the time be spent in a sequence of *no please, after yous*, or *you were here firsts*? Yet here she was with the averagely pretty face of Marcus's wife Bryony bearing down on her with all the beatification of Mary Magdalene. It was disconcerting enough to take her mind off the expert tit sucking to which she was being subjected.

'Can you take that picture down?' she asked.

'Which one?' Marcus wasn't really paying attention. He buried his face in her cleavage. 'God, I love your tits.'

Now she examined the wall above the bed properly, there were three pictures. The biggest one was of Bryony, in full Princess Diana pose, head slightly cocked to one side, like she was open and ready to listen to someone's problems. A second was of Marcus with Bryony and their two boys in what looked like Richmond Park, but which, given Bryony's connections to royalty, could equally be the Balmoral Estate. And there was one of Marcus and the two kids, taken before Marcus's hair turned salt and pepper, and his eyes became sexily creased by nearly fifty years of disarming smiles.

'The one of your wife,' she said. 'It's like being judged by Darcy Bussell on *Strictly Come Fucking*.'

'Darcy hasn't been on Strictly for years.'

He flipped her over, pulled her bum up into the air and slipped his cock back inside her. She grabbed a pillow to rest her upper body on, her nipples already missing the stimulation of his mouth. The feeling of being watched was worse now she was upright.

'She doesn't look as awful as you make her out to be,' she said.

'Darcy?' His breathing was getting heavier now.

'Your wife.'

'Just ignore her. I do.'

She almost felt sorry for Bryony; she had her own parents to thank for that. They hadn't had a good marriage, but they loved each other in the way that only people who liked to make one another truly miserable could. Indifference, on the other hand, was too terrible a concept to contemplate.

'Yeah baby.' He grabbed her buttocks and grunted.

He was fucking her quickly now, like he was on a deadline, which she supposed he was. As editor-in-chief of London's biggest newspaper, there was always a scoop to be unveiled, an edition to get printed, advertisers' needs to be met. She wished he'd do more to meet her needs at that moment. With zero clitoral stimulation in this position, there was as much chance of her coming as there was of him introducing her to his kids.

'God, I love your arse.' He gave it a light slap.

Not that she'd ever want to meet his kids. But sometimes she wished she could introduce Marcus to the people she knew, or tell someone that she was sleeping with one of the most well-connected and understatedly powerful men in London. But their eighteen-month relationship was strictly off the record. It wasn't like Bryony didn't know he was having an affair; she was having one of her own. Although, strictly speaking, could you call either arrangement 'an affair' if the marriage was long since dead? The appearance was only being kept alive for a deeply religious and extraordinarily wealthy set of Catholic parents (Bryony's) who had hinted at disinheritance should they ever divorce.

'Spread your legs wider.'

He slammed into her cervix. She groaned.

'That's good, huh?'

Normally it was tolerable, but not today. This was the first time she'd come to his marital home. What was wrong with the five-star hotel room he usually expensed for their trysts? The weekends away? Was she no longer worth the investment? Was he making cutbacks?

'Ooh, yeah. Please, sir, can I have some more.' No sense in telling him she wasn't feeling it. She too needed to get back to work.

They'd met at a film premiere after-party, and even though he was ten years older, his middle-aged good looks had a touch of the very bad about them which she'd found hard to resist. He also had the type of eyes that wouldn't just undress you, they'd undress you, put you in expensive lingerie of their own choosing, and then undress you all over again. When they'd first started seeing each other, he'd treated her like a precious object to be marvelled at, but recently she felt more like a fidget toy, there to be routinely fingered.

'Ahhughugh.' He arched his back and stiffened against her.

The tightness and expectation in her pelvis ebbed away. She'd have to masturbate later. Bryony looked almost apologetic.

Marcus flopped back onto the bed, leaving her to clear up after him. Perhaps she needed to play harder to get, or to play the field again. Trouble was, guys her own age and social standing just couldn't measure up in the status department and, as Kissinger said, power is the ultimate aphrodisiac.

'God, I love fucking you.'

She noted the order of the words. He'd never said he loved her in her entirety, just parts of her, and what he loved doing to them. That was okay, though; at least she knew where she stood. The one power he didn't have was to disappoint her; not emotionally at least.

'I might be able to wangle us a weekend away next month,' he said. 'Got a contact with a place in Southwold who owes me one.'

She lay down next to him, put her head on his chest, and let him kiss her forehead. In these more tender moments, she imagined that he recognised something of himself in her: the desire to be someone more than their respective backgrounds might ordinarily allow. But mostly he just liked to see himself in her, legs spread, brow moist, begging him to screw her.

Still, a weekend near the beach would be nice, wouldn't it?

Chapter Eight

Simone returned to her desk to find Oliver leching over Nora, their office assistant. Nora was a terrible office assistant, but one with creamy legs up to her armpits, blonde hair down to her bottom, and a pout like a bouncy castle. He stopped chatting when she approached and made his excuses. He was still pretending to be uncomfortable around her, which suited her down to the ground. She was feeling quite chipper. Another tough week at work finished, and a night out to look forward to.

'What are you wearing?' Nora asked.

She was heading to Secret Cinema, a slightly wanky affair in which you got to watch a classic film you'd probably already seen, only in a secret location, in fancy dress, with purpose-built sets and interactive performances justifying the exorbitant ticket price. The girls had organised it for her birthday.

'It's a hazmat suit.'

The movie was *Hot Fuzz*, and with a dearth of sexy females to emulate, she'd opted for the next best alternative: wacky. She was dressed as Janine, a blink-and-you-miss it cameo by Cate Blanchett, unrecognisable as a forensic scientist at a crime scene.

'Oh.' Nora's mouth took on the form of a rubber ring. 'But you're quite attractive for a thirty-four-year-old.'

Thirty-five now.

'Thanks Nora. I'll see you on Monday.'

———

Ninety minutes later, she was in a posh disabled Portaloo watching Ziggy and Nancy hoover up coke from a compact mirror balanced on the top of the cistern.

'Sure you don't want some?' said Ziggy.

'It is your birthday,' said Nancy.

Simone didn't do coke. She'd tried it, but it wasn't for her. For a start, it was too expensive. For another, people talked enough shit without spending top whack in order to augment that bad character trait. She had to hand it to Ziggy, though, watching her bend over. She'd wondered how she'd find a relevant fancy-dress option that allowed her to get her arse out, but here she was in the tiniest bodysuit and painted top to toe in gold paint, in homage to the 'living statue' street artist that briefly featured in the movie. Nancy was Eve Draper, the terrible am-dram actress who met a grisly end for her annoying laugh. Simone had nailed it with her own outfit; it had already drawn lots of admiring comments from purist fans, and the post she'd put up earlier had racked up a lot of likes.

'I really loved what you did with that bircher last week, Nance.' Ziggy rubbed her gums.

'I know, right?'

Nancy licked the twenty-pound note she'd had jammed up her nose moments earlier. Some committed vegetarian she was – didn't she know they contained animal fat?

'People said it couldn't be done,' she continued, 'but as I say, nothing is impossible. The word itself says "I'm possible", doesn't it?'

They were already as high as vacuous kites.

'Did I tell you I heard back from the detox retreat in Sedona?' she went on. 'Three days in return for three posts. It looks amazing. They tap into your emotions to release past trauma stored in the body and clear the mind of any old beliefs that might be blocking breakthroughs in your life. We're talking total holistic cellular renewal.'

'How do they do that?' asked Ziggy.

'Juices, mainly.'

Simone told them she was going to get a large drink.

The bar was noisy and rammed, but she weaved her way to the front and ordered a glass of red wine. She was stood next to some tall guy who'd come as the Lurch character. Like her, he'd opted for amusing rather than attractive, with his bloody blue plaster-dotted face, and fake goofy teeth. He won, though, because despite having dark skin, he was wearing a bald cap made for a white guy. She couldn't help but laugh.

'Nice cossie,' she said.

The guy turned to her. 'Thanks,' he managed in spite of the teeth. 'You too.'

She was still wearing the full regalia of hazmat suit, face mask and protective eyewear.

But now she came to regard him properly, he *was* attractive. There was also something familiar about him. 'Don't I know you?' she asked.

'I don't know. Do you?' His voice was baritone deep, the kind that reverbs in your chest.

'Maybe. Did you go to Lea Manor school?'

'No.'

'Do you live in Brixton?'

'I wish,' he said.

'Hmm. Must be mistaken.'

But she was seldom mistaken. She had a very good memory for faces, and her brain was busy racking itself to try and place this one in the correct context. The man took a sip of the very frothy beer he'd been served, giving himself a foam moustache. He licked his full lips, smearing some beyond their boundary. The teeth weren't helping.

'Er, you still have a little something on your lip.' She was acting a lot like she was coming on to him, but if she kept him talking, she might put her memory out of its misery.

'Who's to say I'm not saving it for later?' His eyes were smiling.

'Fine. Leave it. You can spend the rest of the evening looking like a negative of Rhett Butler.' She'd also seen *Gone with the Wind* at Secret Cinema once.

'There are worse people to look like,' he said.

'And it'll start to itch.'

'Then I'll scratch it.'

'And it might attract wasps.'

'Fine,' he said, 'you win.'

But rather than wiping it with the back of his hand, he removed the teeth, reached inside his Somerfield overall pocket, and pulled out a handkerchief. She'd only ever seen one person below the age of seventy-five carry a handkerchief before.

'Holy shit! You're the dude with the homeless guy!'

'Eh?'

'The one near the coffee shop.'

'That's not narrowing it down.'

How many homeless people did he know?

'He was giving me grief about social media. Come on, don't act like you don't remember.'

'I'm really sorry.' He grimaced. 'Any other clues?'

What was the handle of the guy again? The one he'd tried to foist on her.

'Street Pete! That was it.'

'I know Pete. But I'm not sure…'

She removed her hood, mask and glasses, and flicked her hair out of the suit's collar. In her head it was like a movie scene, in which the leading man suddenly realises the weird-looking chrysalis with whom he's been fraternising is, in fact, a really fit butterfly. His face made all the right moves: initial surprise, a flicker of recognition, building into fully formed delight that this was the creature in front of whom he now found himself.

'You're the woman who got shat on!'

Great. That was how she'd been lodged in his neural pathways.

The barman put a wine down in front of her. She took a large swig.

'I remember now,' he said. 'You thought I wanted your number!'

Another thing she'd tried very hard to put into the recycling bin of her mind.

He chuckled.

'I should have left you to the wasps,' she said.

'I'm sorry!' He tried to arrange his face into something more sorry seeming.

'It's Jasper, isn't it?' she said.

'Yeah. You?'

'Simone.'

She expected him to put out a hand to shake hers, but he took another sip on his pint. The natural order of things was officially broken.

'What's your story anyway?' she asked. 'Are you some kind of Good Samaritan God-botherer?'

It would explain his apparent lack of interest in her more visual virtues.

'How inclusive and sensitive of you to ask in such an accepting and tolerant way.'

'It'd just be a waste, that's all.'

'Of what?'

'Of'—she held her palm out and gestured to him—'this.'

She immediately wished she hadn't. She didn't want him thinking she was into … she gestured to him again … that.

His mouth curved regardless of what she didn't want him thinking.

'I'm just saying it'd be like opening a Tiffany box and finding an Argos charm bracelet inside.'

'I'm not sure I follow the analogy,' he said, 'but luckily for you, I'm not religious.'

'It's not luckily for me. I'm not into…' She did the bloody gesture again. What was it about this guy?

'And you already have a boyfriend,' he said.

For a guy who didn't remember her face, he'd recalled what she'd said well enough.

'I merely meant you hadn't offended me with your clear disdain for religion,' he clarified. 'I'm sure Jesus was a lovely guy, but not for me.'

'Yeah,' she said. 'I've often thought the second coming wouldn't work in the modern age. No one could tolerate that level of self-confidence. *You think you're the son of God, do you? Think you're a bit special. We need to take you down a peg or two, mate.* He'd be trolled to shit. *Blessed are the women*, he'd tweet. *But what about the transgender people? Are you saying they're not blessed?* I'd give him about six days before he was cancelled.'

Jasper was regarding her in a peculiar way. Like he was both amused and perplexed. She was used to being looked at, but there was something in the way he was peering at her that was different. More like a scientist examining a lab rat that was behaving unusually.

'Anyway, this was horrible,' she said. 'I'd better get back to my pals.' She didn't need to embarrass herself in front of him any more than she had.

By the time she got to the bar's exit, however, Jasper was alongside her once more. Twenty years of conditioning made her wonder if perhaps…

'No, I am not following you,' he said.

A mind reader too. How transparent was she?

'Technically you *are* following me,' she said.

'We were both walking in the same direction.'

She waited by the door, for some stupid reason expecting him to open it for her. He was very deliberately waiting for her to do the same.

'Wow,' she said. 'Who said chivalry was dead?'

'Is this a quiz? Was it Ralph Waldo Emerson?'

She smiled sarcastically.

'Is there something that prevents you from getting the door?' he asked. 'You seem like the type who can handle a door handle.'

'Oh, I can handle a door handle.' Ugh. She sounded like an idiot, even to her own ears.

'So why would I disempower you from opening a door?'

'It's called gallantry.'

'It's called benevolent sexism.'

'What?!'

'It is! I read an article about it.' Earnestness only magnified his handsomeness.

'But what if I like doors being opened for me? Am I in breach of some feminist manifesto?'

'Sexism isn't just catcalling and crap wages. And I happen to believe that opening doors, like lots of other things in life, should be consensual.'

No one really considered things in this way, did they?

'Does this help you get laid more?' she asked. 'Playing the sensitive nice guy routine?'

'No!' He seemed genuinely appalled at the notion. 'Let's just say I know a thing or two about unconscious bias.' He pointed two fingers towards himself.

His freckles popped like confetti on his skin. She wondered if the dapples covered the entire taut body hiding under that Somerfield overall. Not that she was interested in finding out. And she probably shouldn't be having lewd thoughts whilst talking about sexual equality. But her libido had never been liberal. It was Neanderthal.

'Fair enough.' She made a grand gesture of opening the door for him and ushering him through.

'How did that feel?' he asked.

'Really empowering,' she deadpanned.

'I'm glad to have been of service. Enjoy your evening, Simone.'

'You too, Jasper.'

For the next two hours, unable to fully concentrate on the film, she scanned the huge screening hall for him. No sign. At one point, she surreptitiously pulled out the phone she should have surrendered at the start of the event and looked him up on Instagram. His account was set to private, just as it had been when she'd searched his handle after their last encounter, and his bio was giving nothing away. Still, what did it matter? She didn't like nice guys, even vaguely intriguing ones like Jasper. What she liked was Marcus, who, as she now saw, had very thoughtfully sent her a dick pic, along with the message, *Here's your birthday present. You can blow it and make a wish when I see you next.*

It was on the dance floor, once her and the girls had taken their fill of the shooting range and village fete stalls, that she saw him again. Adam Ant's *Goody Two Shoes* was playing. How apposite. From what was visible through the swamp of bodies that separated them, he was doing a good job of dancing to it. And then she saw the girl he was dancing with. Fair hair. Petite. Pretty. But in a not-trying-too-hard way. That figured. Hmm ... she was vaguely disappointed. Perhaps it was because she was a sore loser, although she wasn't certain what she was losing. Perhaps it was the four large glasses of red wine, which had notched her beyond tipsy and into vaguely melancholy. Perhaps it was because it was her birthday and she could feel life getting ever shorter. Whatever it was, it meant that when she became aware of the blonde guy watching her, she was ready to engage. Not pull, but what harm was a bit of flirtation? And if Jasper happened to glance across and see, well ... so be it.

Blondie had really gone to town with his get-up. Not some cheap and nasty nylon simulacrum of a police uniform for him, this one was accurate right down to the accessory belt. His short shirt sleeves were tight against well-defined biceps. He wasn't her type, but he was definitely an archetype that lots of girls would be into: the boy you'd have circled in a yearbook as *most likely to be a personal trainer*. He was staring straight at her. He grabbed his toy walkie talkie and spoke into it, raised an eyebrow, and started walking directly towards her. She smiled. Role play, huh? She continued dancing until he was in front of her. Ziggy and Nancy spotted him and grinned. She winked at them as she leaned forward and purred in the guy's ear, making herself heard above the music.

'Is there a problem, officer?'

'There might be,' he said. 'We have reports of drug use in the area.'

The lights were playing across his face. He was somewhat more attractive up close, the eyes a little more interesting.

She tapped the side of her nose. 'I wouldn't know anything about that.'

He didn't smile. 'Are you sure?'

Perhaps he didn't like drugs. Although steroids were clearly on the acceptable list.

She squeezed his tanned bicep. 'Are you sure *you're* not hiding anything illegal in there? They seem unnaturally large.'

Another man joined them, dark-haired and stocky, dressed in the same way.

'I'll have to ask you to get your hands off him, miss.'

'Oh look, there's two of them. So cute. Just like Simon Pegg and Nick Frost. Should I call you Sergeant Angel and PC Butterman?'

'We're both PCs,' the newcomer said.

'Yep, I got that from the uniforms.' She wondered if Jasper had clocked any of this. 'You haven't got another friend, have you? Only there are three of us.' She motioned to Nancy and Ziggy.

'I'm going to have to search your bag,' the goodish-looking one said.

Odd. Surely this was the bit where he asked to frisk her, or something equally cheesy. 'And if I refuse to let you?'

'Then you'll be obstructing an officer in the execution of his duty.'

He was really getting into this. Maybe it was another interactive element.

'Would I now?' she said.

'I'll ask you again. May I search your bag?'

'It's okay. You can drop the routine now. Let your hair down a bit.'

'It's not a routine,' said the dark-haired one. He was almost certainly into cosplay.

'Your bag,' said the blonde one.

Perhaps she was in trouble for still having her phone on her.

But they could chill out; she hadn't taken any pictures to spoil their secret. Still, she didn't want to be kicked out before the end, so best to play dumb.

'I think you're doing a great job,' she said. 'You sound just like real officers.'

'That's because we are real officers,' said the blonde.

'Aren't there rules against impersonating a police officer?'

'Not if you're a police officer,' he said.

Okay, this was getting boring, and Jasper wasn't even on the dance floor anymore.

'Well, this has been great, but if you'll excuse me, I need the toilet.'

She turned to the girls to let them know, but the brown-haired guy grabbed her by the arm and pivoted her back around. She pulled her arm free.

'Seriously, guys. You need to give it a rest.'

This time the brown-haired one grabbed her more roughly. She wasn't in the mood to be manhandled, and whether they were actors, oversensitive security guards, or horny dickheads, this was overkill.

'For fuck's sake.' She pulled her arm free again.

'Ma'am,' said the blonde. 'You're leaving me no option here.'

Somehow Ziggy hadn't noticed the souring of relations and she sashayed into the mix. 'Are you trying to arrest her, officer? She's been a very naughty girl, haven't you, Sim?' She winked. 'She's always leading us astray.'

Blondie shoved Ziggy back in a way that clearly demonstrated these pair weren't a couple of second-rate actors getting all Stanislavski on her ass. A million thoughts scrambled for purchase on the slippery surface of her consciousness. Not quick enough, though, because when the brown-haired guy grabbed her again, this time pulling both arms behind her back, two years of self-defence training kicked in, and she instinctively booted her leg back, straight into his bollocks. She swallowed hard, her reward circuits and dopamine structures suddenly channelling energy the way of rational cognition. Everything came into stark focus – the illusion of what she'd been seeing from one perspective, now seen from a truer angle. They were actual on-duty police officers. But why the fuck were they singling her out? And for drugs? She was probably one of the few people in here who wasn't taking them! Her hands were yanked behind her back again and a hundred eyes fell on her.

'I don't have any drugs.' Something tightened around her wrists.

'That doesn't matter anymore.' Blondie motioned to the stocky one, who was now doubled over and clutching his crotch as if it was a beloved turtle she'd just crushed to death.

'I am arresting you for assaulting an officer in the course of his duty.'

Nancy and Ziggy looked on helplessly, finally waking up to how close they'd been to getting busted.

'You do not have to say anything, but it may harm your defence if you do not mention when questioned something which you later rely on in court.'

'Happy fucking birthday to me,' she said.

'It's your birthday?'

'Yeah. Maybe you could put the siren on for me. Make it a real treat.'

As she was led through the crowd, at least she could content herself that Jasper and his girlfriend hadn't seen how things had ended. This was far, far worse than pigeon crap.

Chapter Nine

The bed in the cell felt like it was made from bricks and the toilet flush wasn't working, so for the last two hours she'd been in the uncomfortable company of someone else's turd – and they did not have a healthy diet. If she hadn't been considering self-harm when asked by the duty sergeant before, she was now. Were it not for the seriousness of the situation, she might have enjoyed its novelty. She'd never been in trouble with the law before; never had her fingerprints taken. Charing Cross Police Station was quite the venue on a Saturday night, far more interesting and immersive than Secret Cinema. The prostitute in the cell next door shouted, *if you let me out, I'll give you a blow job and I won't even charge you*. Such generosity, although somewhat self-damning. The worst thing was not having her phone to distract her. She hated having time on her hands. At school she'd once had to imagine being a middle-class Victorian woman for a day. She'd said the first thing she'd do was contract typhoid, preferring to shit herself to death than spend a single second with only flower pressing or embroidery to amuse her. She'd forgotten the restlessness of not having anywhere to channel her energies, and her eyes and fingers subconsciously sought the device out every few minutes. The only alternative was to think, and she did not like thinking. It was therefore a huge relief when she was told the duty solicitor had arrived, a relief that lasted right up until she met him.

John Foxsmith had bags under his eyes that were so big, it was like his eyelids had been put on upside down. He had the oddest streak of ginger hair across his upper lip, as though seconds before he'd drunk a glass of orange juice and had forgotten to wipe his mouth. And when he walked her to their private interview room, he did so in a lolloping zigzag, like he was trying to avoid flak from his past mistakes, of which he seemed the type to make many. Still, you could look like crap and not necessarily be crap at your job, right? He ushered her inside, closed the door and scanned the room.

'Don't say anything,' he whispered, 'but I've been drinking.'

'You're drunk?!'

'Shh! Keep your voice down. If they find out, I could get rebuked.'

She slumped into a hard plastic chair and gave him some sharp rebuking of her own.

'I just need to get my head straight,' he said. 'Have you got any water?'

'No.'

'I took a gamble on not being called out.'

'On a Saturday night?!'

You didn't need to have watched many police dramas to know that Saturday was the busiest night of the week at a station. He started explaining himself.

'I'm not interested in your life story,' she said.

'Don't panic. No one has to know.'

He paced up and down in the tiny room, focussing on his feet in an effort to maintain a straight line.

'Er, any chance we can talk about me for a second?' she said.

'Sure, sure.' He seemed unsure.

'What did the police say when you got here?' she prompted.

'Erm…'

He'd forgotten.

'I've been arrested for kicking a police officer in the balls.'

'That's it!' He clapped his hands. 'Did you do it?'

'Not deliberately.'

'Oh well, that makes all the difference.'

'Does it?'

He sniggered. 'No.'

The guy was sozzled.

'Are you a real solicitor? Is this some kind of extended joke?'

This whole thing could still be an extravagant ruse.

'I'm a real solicitor.' He said it as an apology.

'Jesus Christ.'

He laughed. She looked at him blankly.

'Did you just say Cheesus Crust?' he said.

'No.'

'Because that would be pretty funny because, you know, Cheesus Crust. Like Jesus Christ, only cheesier.'

'I didn't say it. I said Jesus Christ.'

'Are you religious?' he asked.

'Yeah, I'm Church of Royally Fucked, mate.'

He laughed again. She gripped the edge of the table in front of her, fingers making contact with spongy chewing gum on its underside. She'd have to bathe for a month after this.

'I didn't know he was a police officer,' she said.

'Was he in plain clothes?'

'No.'

He regarded her like she was the drunk one, but the effects of the alcohol had long since dissipated. Being in a cell could be a real buzzkill.

'It seems unlikely you wouldn't know then,' he said.

'It was a party. There were lots of police officers around.'

'And yet you still assaulted one. Seems a bit stupid.'

'Pot. Kettle.'

He laughed again, an idiotic barking laugh, like a seal on helium.

'Do you have any current convictions?' he asked.

'Just the one that you're an imbecile.'

'Easy!'

She slammed the table with her fist. 'This is so unfair!'

'Just admit you made a mistake.' He hiccupped. 'It's your first offense. A lapse in concentration. Tell them you're sorry and they'll probably let you off with a caution.'

'What does that mean?'

'It means you'll be let off with a caution. And you think *I'm* the slow one?'

'I know what it is. But what does it mean legally? Do I have a criminal record?'

'No. We just established that. This *is* a first offence, isn't it?'

She dug her nails into her palms and asked again. He explained that a caution was something that stayed on your record for six years, and would only really be a problem if she was arrested again.

'Be compliant in the interview, act apologetic, and with any luck we'll both be out of here before the bars shut.'

An hour later, having done as she was told, John returned to the cell where she was waiting for news.

'I'm afraid they're going to charge you.'

Her skin suddenly felt very hot. 'But you said… I did…'

'I think someone up there's got it in for you. Well, out there actually. They do have the option of letting you off, but it all depends on the officer. Afraid you got a particularly sensitive one. Although all men are particularly sensitive down there.'

Shit.

'You'll be charged and asked to attend magistrate's court at a future date.'

She slumped onto the unyielding bed, bones jarring. 'Should I plead guilty?'

'That's your choice. I can only advise.'

'And what would you advise?'

'It's up to you.'

'Great.'

'Oi. May I remind you that you're getting this advice for free.'

'You're not giving me any advice.'

'Is it any wonder? You're not paying me! Anyway, I can't hang around here all evening. I've got a case—'

'Ooh. Someone else gets to have the five-star counsel, do they?'

'If you let me finish, I was going to say *of lager*. To be drinking. At home. It was nice to meet you…'

He'd forgotten her name.

'Simone,' she prompted.

He rapped on the door to be let out. Should she dob him in about drinking? She wanted to be as cruel to someone as fate was being to her. But what would that achieve? She just needed to get home and crawl into a bed that wasn't crawling with god knows what. She'd figure it all out once she got out of here.

Chapter Ten

'My little bunny. I can't believe you were arrested.'

Marcus was lying on the hotel bed, hands intertwined behind his head, looking dashing in a linen shirt, striped braces and tweed trousers. He hadn't bothered to remove his brogues.

'Were you scared?'

She nodded. She hadn't been, but having not seen him for over three weeks, she was ready for some sympathy. The girls had tried to offer some, but she couldn't shake the annoying fact that she'd copped the rap for something they'd been doing.

He leaned across, nuzzled her neck and nibbled her ear. She'd been there barely a few minutes, and, as hot as he looked, she wanted a glass of wine before they got down to it.

'I have to go to court.'

'You'll be fine.' He began to undo her trousers.

'I'll be fined. It could be up to two grand!'

After the shock and frustration of the charges had worn off, she had gone to work on the problem. She'd done her research, reading widely on the subject, and wangling informal chats with criminal lawyers. She'd applied to the Crown Prosecution Service to refer the case back to the police for a caution, which would be a more proportional response to a first offense. She hadn't yet heard back, which meant she needed to prepare in case it ended up in front of a magistrate. From what she'd gathered, representing herself, albeit following some judicious advice when doing so, would be the most cost-effective way of dealing with the situation. There was no defence to be mounted, no extenuating circumstances to be brought to the court's attention. If it got that far, she would likely get a rap on the knuckles, a conditional discharge (so definitely no getting in trouble for eighteen months) and be liable for a fine that she'd get to pay off over a period of time.

'Just ask for a pay rise,' said Marcus.

His hand was in her knickers, a five-fingered octopus searching for a hidey-hole. She hadn't told work. It wasn't that it would have repercussions for her job, but Ollie would only lord it over her. She'd keep it on the QT and pretend like it never happened. Her promotion would cover the fine. She removed his hand, got off the bed and poured herself a glass of wine.

'You don't want to be a character witness for me, do you?'

It was worth an ask.

'You know I can't do that.'

'But you're the most impressive person I know.'

'I assume you mean in the trouser department.'

She shook her head. For an intelligent man running a grown-up newspaper, there was plenty of tabloid hack lurking in there.

'Sorry,' he said. 'Come back here. I've missed you.'

She returned to the bed.

'So where did Bryony go at such short notice this evening?'

His call to meet up had been an unexpected surprise.

'The opera. Be there for hours.'

She'd been to the opera once. It was like watching a musical being played at the wrong speed, in the wrong language. When her date had suggested it, he'd insisted she'd be in paroxysms of emotion by the end. He was wrong. The closest she'd come to tears was when she'd dropped her grab bag of chocolate on the floor during the first act, and therefore had nothing to enjoy for the remaining three hours.

Marcus resumed his digital overtures. 'Pity about America, though, baby.'

'What about it?'

'You can't get a visa if you have a record, can you?'

'What the fuck?'

She jumped back up, grabbed her phone, and googled frantically, her mood darkening as every avenue of hope turned into a cul-de-sac. After several minutes she conceded defeat. Unless she got let off, it would be at least five years before she could apply for a visa.

'It might still get dropped,' he said.

She flopped onto the bed and took another gulp of wine.

'Why do I feel that this isn't entirely coincidental? Of all the people, why did they make a beeline for me?'

'It's probably because you were the hottest person there. I wanted to frisk you when I first laid eyes on you.' His fingers played eency-weency spider up towards her chest.

'I was really excited about it.' Her voice almost cracked. She coughed and focussed on the bad art on the opposite wall.

'Don't sweat it too much. Most of the places on your list are shitholes anyway.'

Her jaw tensed. She slammed the wine down, flinching at the squeal as it hit the mirrored bedside table. Her dad had wanted to see those places, and that was good enough for her. She yanked his hand away and turned from him.

'Go fuck yourself, Marcus.'

A sudden tiredness took hold of her. It had been another long week, it was only Thursday, and the very thing that had been keeping her going now hung in the balance. She hugged the corner of the duvet to her chest.

Marcus shifted his weight on the bed. Was he going to put a loving arm around her?

'Jesus, you're being a real bitch, do you know that?'

Clearly not.

'I'm upset, you dick!'

'I was trying to make you feel better.'

'Well, you suck at it.'

She tried to focus on the steady hum of the air conditioning. A door closed further down the hall, a muted thump followed by someone talking as they passed the door.

'I've had a shitty week too,' he said. 'That's why I wanted to see you.'

'Oh, is this suddenly about you?'

'I just meant—'

'You know what? I'm going.'

She was off the bed again. Her bag was by the door, but where had she put her bloody shoes? Without them, this wasn't going to be the dramatic point-making exit she'd envisaged. She glanced sideways at him. It was his move.

He lifted himself up on his elbows. 'Hey baby. I'm sorry. I didn't know this trip meant so much to you.'

Why should he? She'd never mentioned her parents and he'd never asked about them. He pouted. The lies those lips must have told.

'Why don't we have a bath? Help you unwind,' he said.

'Is that your subtle way of getting the rest of my clothes off?'

He shook his head. 'I don't even have to get in if you don't want.'

He held her gaze. He had a knack of gazing into her eyes like someone who had seen a lot of eyes in his lifetime, but found hers particularly appealing.

'I'll make it extra bubbly. I'll even throw in a back rub.' He unbuttoned his cuffs and began to roll them back in readiness. 'Please don't go.'

He held his arms out in supplication, palms up, like a magician trying to prove he had nothing to hide; but Marcus always had something up his sleeve.

'Besides, I haven't told you all my news yet. I have some gossip for you.' He slipped his braces off, undid his trousers. 'Come and have a bath and I can tell you all about it.'

She was still narked off with him, but the dickhead next door would only be cranking out some bongo bullshit back at her flat, and the wine here was infinitely better. Plus a bit of salacious news might be fun to hear.

'Fine. But order us another bottle first.'

She was officially drowning her sorrows.

Chapter Eleven

The room wasn't as grand as those in courtroom dramas. It was about the size of her gym's spin studio, but an excess of wood panelling the colour of wet sand made it seem smaller. It smelt like her gym's spin studio too: the pungent reverb of all the nervous bodies that had passed through hung in the limp air. Hers was the second hearing of the day, and with any luck she'd be back in the office just after lunchtime. She'd had to lie to Tony to get the morning off; said she needed to go for a smear. In fairness, she'd prefer to be legs up in stirrups having cells scraped off her cervix right now. She knew she was guilty, but as she listened to the monotonous-voiced prosecution sum up the evidence against her, she felt like a proper criminal. Aggravated assault. The copper who'd copped one practically wept during his witness statement. Where did they recruit them from nowadays? RADA? So much for a proportional response.

'Do you have anything to say in your defence before sentence is passed?' asked the middle one of the three magistrates on the bench. Her greasy hair was the colour of dishwater, in a style that was part bob, part combover.

'Yes, your honour.'

'Then proceed.'

She stood up. She'd worn ballet pumps along with a simple plain trouser suit. Used to heels, her calves felt taut, and she rocked slightly on her feet. The page on which she'd printed her statement quivered disconcertingly in her hand. She needed to get a grip. Fifteen years of creating compelling pitch presentations had primed her for this. She'd written the modern-day equivalent of the Gettysburg Address. She took a levelling breath, faced the magistrates, and began.

'Your honours. I want to assure you, in the strongest terms possible, that this misdemeanour was a momentary lapse in judgment. I'd had a particularly stressful few weeks at work, had consumed too much alcohol, and wasn't in complete control of my faculties. Let me explain...'

She told them that the kick had been instinctual, much regretted immediately afterwards; she believed every officer should be free to execute his duties without the risk of personal harm, and she'd pleaded guilty at the earliest opportunity to demonstrate her contrition. She would, of course, demur to their better judgment, but felt it wasn't in the public interest to punish her beyond the punishment she'd metred upon herself every day since the incident.

'This is my first offense,' she said, eyes wide and blinking, 'but I promise it will be my last.'

She went on, telling them it had been easy to imagine they weren't real officers, given the circumstances, and as a young woman, hadn't she been warned to be vigilant about potential impersonators? But she greatly admired the force, and found it reassuring to know that they were mobile and active in the places where she and her single female friends spent their time.

She stole another glance at the bench. The woman on the left had a close-cropped bleached afro, and wore tortoiseshell glasses through which she was regarding Simone with benign interest. The balding forty-something guy on the right, who looked like he did this in lieu of a social life, was leaning forward and practically nodding along.

'I wish to reassure you that I am a productive, hard-working individual. By pleading guilty as I did, and standing here to accept my punishment without any legal counsel, I hope to save the State any further burden on its limited resources.'

The outer magistrates seemed to appreciate that bit, half-smiling like she was telling them exactly what they wanted to hear. But the middle woman didn't seem to be buying it. Her arms were folded across a bosom that spread and lolled, and she almost lost her place when she thought of their lumpen mass beneath that turquoise jumper and mismatched tweed jacket. The woman should have been at a spinster conference, not sat there pouring expressive scorn on Simone's carefully crafted lines. She pressed on.

'And regardless of what happens here today, I think it's only appropriate that I make a donation to Police Care UK, who work to help officers injured in the course of duty.'

She glanced back up to the bench. Mrs Blond and Mr Boring were barely supressing a round of applause, but the puritanical dowager was staring at her with all the expressiveness of a crash test dummy. Simone had once been on a naked bike ride through London, but felt far more exposed under this dame's gaze.

'Thank you, Miss Stephens. Very … impassioned. Would you excuse us whilst we deliberate on an appropriate sentence.'

Sentence? Just the single word *bravo* should do it. But the glint in the old bird's eye was troubling. Why the deliberation? Her concern grew with every minute they were cloistered away in their side room. What was happening in there? Surely the two human-seeming ones would go minimum fine and be done with it. Even if the old maid was going hardball, they'd outnumber her.

Two against one was enough. Still, she'd watched *Twelve Angry Men* with her dad enough times to know that anything could happen behind closed doors. The wicked witch of the Westminster courts was clearly the type who got joy from other people's pain.

'Please stand, Miss Stephens.'

They'd returned, looking significantly more punitive than when they'd left. The witch's mouth twitched at the corners; there was the tiniest hint of a smile.

'Thank you for your patience. We have considered your statement along with the events of that night and taken into account that this is a first offence to which you have indeed pleaded guilty.'

She sensed a but – a big cellulite-ridden one coming her way.

'But an officer was compromised. And every time an officer gets hit, or spat at, or talked down to in the line of duty, a small chink in the armour of our civic safeguarding appears. When you struck that constable's testicles, you struck at the very fabric of the respect and deference necessary to maintain order in society. There were witnesses. People who may be more inclined to wrongdoing in the future as a consequence of seeing your actions. You failed to take seriously the nature of the enquiry being made of you. You directly ignored an officer's instructions. And, frankly, your statement suggests you imagine this to be a matter more for posturing than penance.'

Maybe she'd trowelled it on a bit thick, but she hadn't realised she'd be coming up against Ms Dowdy Dementor here.

'Contrary to the contrite figure you have attempted to paint with your pretty words, I see a young woman who holds authority in contempt. Whose instinct is to lash out. I believe you to be cynical and self-interested, Miss Stephens, and my colleagues and I are duty bound to try and provide a steer – a gentle redirection of your energies, if you will – away from such conceits.'

The outer two magistrates were staring at their pads.

'Which is why we have decided to impose a community order.'

Shit. Shit, shit, shit.

'You will undertake one hundred and twenty hours of unpaid work. Your probation officer will instruct you as to where these duties will be executed. You will also pay reparations to the court in the sum of twelve-hundred pounds, in accordance with your means, and a sum of eight hundred pounds for court costs. Failure to comply with any of these covenants will result in a custodial sentence. But given your desire to, as you so eloquently put it, not place any further burden on the State's limited resources, I am hoping they will suffice to help ameliorate your attitude.'

A hundred questions formed a disorderly queue in her head. But before she could get any of them out, the old hag stood up and left the courtroom, followed by the other two weak and malleable shit-munchers. She quickly texted the girls. America was off; she was beyond poor, and now she was going to have to do some minimum-wage style work god knows where.

'Cheers,' she muttered as the door closed behind them. 'This has ameliorated my attitude no shitting end.'

Chapter Twelve

'Why didn't you tell me?'
    'Because I thought you'd be mad.'
'I am mad.'
'Which is why I didn't tell you.'

Tony was pacing his office, rosacea-tinted face further flushed with the effort of actually being on his feet. She'd had to come clean. She'd met her probation officer. She was going to work in a homeless shelter. Her skin itched just thinking about it. There was no way she'd fit the hours in around her existing workload without anyone noticing something was off. Still, he should be thanking her; this was the most exercise he'd done in years.

'How long?'
'Three weeks.'
'Fuck's sake Simone.'
'I know it's not ideal.'
'It's pretty fucking far from ideal.'
'Calm down. I was due to be off for two weeks anyway. I can tag it on to the end. Unpaid.'

'This is a setback.' He stopped pacing and nodded to the glass behind her. 'Astley is going to take a dim view of this.'

There he was, grey as a storm cloud and looking half as cheerful, talking to Ollie, who was looking like a twat.

'Does he need to know? It's only five extra days. I could call in sick.'

The most important thing was that Ollie didn't find out.

'You know the man doesn't tolerate sickness.'

'That's because he's already dead.'

'This is a crucial time in the business.'

'I know. I'm the one doing most of the work around here.'

'Now, Simone. You know you're the sister I never had.'

'You have a sister.'

'Yeah, but she's a miserable cow. You're going off the boil. Jeffers called me this morning and says you're neglecting him.'

Jeffers was another man-child client who seemed to think that, because she worked on his account, he owned her. He'd invited her to a three-day corporate event that she'd politely declined – ironically because she had to work on his account – but he'd been pissy ever since.

'He's being unreasonable. I'm doing everything he needs me to,' she said.

'Everything?'

'Are you suggesting I actually go away with him for the weekend? You know that doesn't end in twin rooms, don't you?'

'What harm can it do?'

'Why don't *you* sleep with him if it's so important to you?'

'Because I'm not a ponce.'

'Jesus. 1980 called. They want their homophobia back.'

'It's not homophobic to not be a ponce, Little Miss Wokeness.'

'Everything's ready for my handover,' she said. 'If anything, this is better for you because I can check in every evening, so you won't have to. I wouldn't do that on holiday.'

He tore a piece of paper off the pad on his desk and used it to pick between his teeth. There must have been some remnants of his long lunch trapped in there.

'Fine. But you better come back fighting fit or else you are going to get knocked out by twinkletoes out there. He's hungry for it. He's already got you on the ropes; now he wants you on the canvas.'

'I'm the heavyweight, Tony.'

'Perhaps you can try and get some time off for *good behaviour*.' He tried to raise an eyebrow but struggled to overcome the downward pressure of his jowls.

'I'm not getting off with anyone at a homeless shelter.'

'Suit yourself, Florence Nightingale.'

'Just don't say anything to anyone, okay? I'll deal with it.'

She'd already posted some nonsense about a digital detox on social media, so she wasn't left having to try and fake a whole trip to the States. Although faking your life was par for the course on Insta.

Tony made some vague gesture in the region of his chest. 'Cross my heart. We'll see you in three weeks.'

Chapter Thirteen

Simone was sat in her lounge, aimlessly scrolling through make-up tutorials on TikTok, when a video call request popped up on screen. It was Nancy. They'd be at the airport now, filling up on the Duty Free. She wasn't in the mood to talk, but with Marcus away and Wei at a wedding, this would be her only company all weekend. She swiped to accept the call.

Nancy's face filled the screen. She was wearing a two-tone gold hippie hairband, her hair sea-salted into carefully orchestrated beach curls that fell from a centre parting.

'Hey Sim. How are you doing?'

'Oh, you know.'

'I so wish you were coming with us.'

'Me too.'

'Aww.' Nancy turned away from the camera. 'Hey Zig, come and say something encouraging to Sim. She's all down in the dumps.'

Nancy's head gave way to an image of Ziggy about five metres away, standing at a long sleek bar bathed in red and lilac lights. It was the Virgin Clubhouse.

'Have you been upgraded?'

Nancy ignored her, probably not wishing to pour salt into the wormhole-sized wound she was already nursing. Instead she approached Ziggy, who was wearing a pair of denim short shorts, tan leather chaps, a fringed racer-front vest, and a cowgirl hat. Just the outfit for an eleven-hour flight.

'Did you both ram-raid Coachella before you set off for the airport?'

'Gotta look the part, babe.' Ziggy raised a glass of champagne to the camera.

She ignored the urge to reach through the screen and knock it out of her grip.

'Don't be jealous. We'll be lying around in boring old spas or luxury hotel rooms, whilst you get to have a proper real genuine authentic experience.'

She missed 'bona fide' in her list of synonyms.

'What could be more fun than getting up close and personal with some of London's most put-upon people?' Ziggy said.

'Erm. Norovirus? A root canal? Brain surgery in the late nineteenth century?'

Nancy was back in frame. 'Zig's right, Sim. I've always wondered what it's like to be homeless.'

Always? This is a girl who refused to stay at a three-star hotel once as it would have been *slumming it*.

'And will you actually be able to mix with them?' asked Zig.

'It's not a zoo. They're not behind bars. I guess they'll be coming and going.'

'That's so nice,' said Nancy. 'Like free-range chickens.'

It didn't get more free-range than not having anywhere to live.

'You know, not many people get to do what you're doing,' said Nancy.

She'd read a stat that there were nearly three hundred thousand people classed as homeless in the UK. Even at a conservative ratio of one person working in homelessness for every five people in the system, that didn't really class as *not many*.

Ziggy butted in. 'Yeah, it'll be like the week I spent at that South American ape sanctuary. It was sooo rewarding. Remember?'

She remembered it perfectly. Ziggy had been terrified she was going to get her face ripped off by a gibbon, so she'd taken all the pictures she needed to in a single day, even changing hair and clothes to complete the illusion of a week's volunteer work. She'd confessed when drunk and had clearly forgotten having done so.

'Yep, you guys are still comparing homeless people to animals.'

'No. These were apes. That's different.'

'Yeah, they're really intelligent,' said Nancy.

Were they saying that homeless people were stupid?

'They can't be that smart to have ended up on the street, can they?' said Zig.

The truth was, she had no idea why or how someone could end up homeless, but she supposed in three weeks she'd know all she needed to.

'Are you going to keep us updated on Insta?' Ziggy was now scrolling on her phone. 'People will go batshit crazy for that stuff. Hot babe helps homeless.' She glanced up. 'Actually, that's a catchy hashtag.'

It was, but there'd be no posts. There was a loud announcement over the tannoy.

'That's us, sweetie!' Nancy tried hard to hide the excitement in her voice.

'Make sure you send me some pics.'

'Just follow along on Insta,' said Zig. She grabbed Nancy's hand and dragged her off. 'We've gotta go!'

She half-hoped they had an incredible time, and half-hoped

the plane crashed into a tall, impassable mountain and they'd be forced to drink their own urine to survive.

'I need to go too,' she said. She had a date with a pillow into which she was going to scream very, very loudly. These next three weeks were going to be the worst of her life.

Chapter Fourteen

The shelter to which she was going to have to make her daily pilgrimage was called Cedar Lodge, although some wag had replaced the E with an I, so now the sign read Cider Lodge. It was in Whitechapel, only one extra stop on the District Line from where she worked. She'd expected some towering monument to charity and good deeds, but this was an ugly prefab box tacked onto the side of an ornate Edwardian terracotta building. Apparently, it was a former psychiatric unit added on to the Barnabus Mission Hospital in the 1960s, during an era in which the recently discovered antipsychotic drugs were seen as the great white hope for curing all mental illness. By the 1980s, these small cottage hospitals had been deemed uneconomic, and the original building had been turned into offices. Its ugly appendage had limped on as a halfway house for people who had recently become homeless, and it offered additional day services to those who had lived on the streets for some time. It was completely unfitting of its modern-day neighbourhood. Whereas the rest of the street had been pimped, preened and pruned into a sweetmeat of middle-class gentrification, this had stayed resolutely untouched. It stuck out less like a sore thumb, and more like a wart-encrusted one on an otherwise perfectly proportioned and beautifully manicured hand. How it hadn't been pulled down and replaced with trendy apartments was remarkable.

She approached the double doors, their paint flaking to reveal decades of layers beneath, and steadied herself. What the hell lay on the other side? Whatever it was, she'd handle it. Suck it up, get it done, get back to normal. The door swung open without her touching it, and a man emerged. He had prematurely aged skin that reminded her of the paper she used to crumple and stain with tea to look like parchment.

'Don't mind me, love.'

The grey blanket around his shoulders might just as well have been made of lead for all he looked crushed by the weight of it.

'Do you know where the office is, mate?'

Mate? She never called anyone mate.

'It's through there, sweetheart.'

She made her way down the corridor and stopped at a door on which a manager placard hung vertically from a single screw. It wobbled when she knocked.

'Come in,' a cockney accent replied.

She pushed open the door and could immediately see why the sign had tried to make a run for it. It was less 'office' and more 'tip'. It was crammed with desks on which it looked like someone had played Jenga with box files, but then abandoned the game once the towers had fallen. Half of the floor was hidden under small chipboard filing cabinets, presumably unused, and there were piles of archaic computer equipment whose once white plastic casings had turned cream. Light streamed in through a Venetian blind that looked more like shredded paper.

'I said come in!'

She gingerly stepped into the room.

'Come where I can see you.'

She inched towards the voice, carefully stepping round the flotsam and jetsam, until she found its source, a muscular spiky-haired woman doing press-ups on the floor.

'Take the weight off. I'm nearly done.'

She nestled on the edge of a chair, avoiding a pile of newspapers. Her gaze alighted on a half full cup of coffee which had tiny white flotillas of mould on the liquid's surface.

'Ninety-eight … ninety-nine … a hundred.' The woman sprang to her feet.

She wore blue jeans, an open short-sleeved check shirt over a grey vest, and a large man's watch. Her face was surprisingly feminine, with cupid's bow lips and soft brown eyes, although the shaved eyebrow slits were doing a good job of drawing attention away from the latter.

'Feel that!' She leaned down, flexed her arm, and offered up a sinewy tennis ball of muscle and bulging veins.

'That's okay, thanks.'

'Don't be shy. Feel it!'

'Do I have to?'

'Course not.'

'Great.'

'Go on, though.'

Simone reached out and tentatively poked the bicep with a freshly manicured nail.

'It's very muscly,' she said.

'I know, right?'

The woman thrust out a hand. This was a far better part of the body to be offered. Simone took it.

'I'm Gay, by the way.'

As if that wasn't obvious.

'That's cool.'

The woman regarded her expectantly. Was she meant to say something else?

'I don't have a problem with homosexuality, if that's what you want to know.'

Still the hand persisted. In fact, there was a fair bit more pressure on it.

'As in short for Gayle,' said the woman.

'Oh, right.'

'Did you think I was a lesbian?'

The grip tightened.

'Erm … no?'

Gayle stared at her. 'So, are you one of these do-gooding, little pony princesses with lovely hair, good intentions, and a pocket full of giving a shit, here to ask about volunteering? Because I can categorically tell you that you won't last three days.'

Simone stared back and reminded herself that if she could handle Tony, she could handle someone like Gayle. The trick was to show no fear.

'No. I'm here on community service for kicking a police officer. I'm as close to Mother Theresa as Rasputin is, and I just want this over so I can return to a life of wilful ignorance, hedonistic abandon, and corporate whoredom.'

Gayle released her grip and slapped her hard against the side of the arm. 'You might just last the week.' She leaned against the desk. 'Three rules. No violence. No drinking. No drugs.'

'Shit,' said Simone. 'I might not last the day.'

Gayle raised an appreciative eyebrow. 'What's your name?'

'Simone.'

'Ah, yeah, Paul said to expect you.'

Paul was her probation officer.

'Do you have any experience of the homeless?' Gayle asked.

'I've seen them around.'

'Is that your attempt at a joke?'

It had been.

'Interesting. Well, you're going to need a sense of humour. Do you have any relevant skills?'

'I work in PR and events.'

'We've got as much use for that as a cock ring at a eunuch convention. Fill out this form then I'll find you something to do.'

She cast around for a pen and some clear desk space. Neither were forthcoming.

The door opened and a man backed through it, mug in each hand. 'Hey, Gay. Just got to grab some files.'

'Simone, this is Jasper.'

Jasper. The only person she'd ever met by that name was...

He swung around. 'Simone?'

WTAF. It was the guy. That guy. The *that guy* guy.

'You know one another?' asked Gayle.

'Jasper once instructed me on the merits of opening my own doors.'

What were the chances of bumping into him again? He looked even hotter than he had three months ago, tight white T-shirt tucked into dark blue jeans, and cute green Nike Blazers adding a pop of colour. His hair was longer than it had been, and a little curl hung down across his forehead.

'What are you doing here?' He sauntered over to pass one of the mugs to Gayle. He smelt of cedar wood and citrus. Probably Chanel Bleu.

'I'm volunteering.'

'Really? You don't seem the type.'

'Why don't I?'

'No disrespect, but I suspect there are human traffickers with more empathy.'

Gayle snorted. It was a pretty solid burn.

'She's not voluntarily volunteering. She got into some argy-bargy with a police officer.'

'That sounds more like it. What did he do? Enquire after your health?'

'No. He was trying to open the door for me.' She smiled sweetly. So he and his girlfriend (if there was still a girlfriend) definitely hadn't seen her being led away.

'Who sent her?' asked Jasper.

'Paul,' said Gayle. 'I think he's punishing us.'

'Hello. I'm right here.'

'I'm sure we can make some use of her,' he said.

'Still here.'

'The men's khazis look like a cow with cholera has taken a shit in them,' said Gayle.

'I'll have you know I once worked with disadvantaged teenagers.'

'Was it offering to buy them booze from the off-licence?' said Jasper.

'No.'

It had been. Still, it was worth a try to prove him wrong about her.

'And what makes you so uniquely qualified to read people?' she asked him.

'I'm a psychotherapist.' The wink he gave her was entirely lacking in flirtation. 'It's kind of my job.'

Psychotherapist. That explained a lot.

'Come on, admit it,' she said. 'You're pleased to see me.'

'No, it's true, I am.'

She allowed herself a smug smile.

'Those toilets really do need a clean. It's like there's been an explosion in a Marmite factory.' He scooped up some files with his free hand and headed for the door. 'I'd better get on.'

She watched him leave the room. Damn, his arse looked really good in those jeans.

When she dragged her gaze away, Gayle was watching her.

'You don't stand a chance, sweetheart.'

'Who said I'd be interested?'

'Who are you kidding? There are Orthodox monks that are interested.'

But it wasn't what Gayle was thinking; not precisely anyway. Sometimes the only thing more annoying than people finding you sexually attractive was people *not* finding you sexually attractive.

'Are you listening?'

Gayle had said something.

'Sorry, what?'

'I said I'm as busy as a cat trying to bury a turd in a concrete floor, so don't you be adding to my woes. No messing around with the staff. That's rule number four. Understood?'

Was it too cliched to suggest that he might be gay? Perhaps the woman he'd been with hadn't been a girlfriend after all. But even a gay man could appreciate the artistry of a beautiful picture, even if he had no interest in nailing it up against a wall.

'Hello! Is there anybody there?' Gayle knocked on the desk. 'I said understood?'

'Uh-huh.'

'Are you ready for a little tour?'

'Sure.'

She followed Gayle to the door.

'For clarity, though, why do you think he wouldn't be interested?'

'Darling. You spend money on getting your nails painted to look how nails look when they *haven't* been painted.'

She took in her French manicure; she'd never thought about it like that. Still, if it was because he was gay, she'd have said so.

'This isn't the la-di-da world of PR. The people you're going to meet are fighting for their dignity, respect, and basic human needs to be met. The fact that you happened to get lucky with your skin suit counts for nothing around here. And it definitely won't count for anything with Jasper.'

'Okay, cool. Good pep talk.'

Gayle led her down a dingy corridor. 'We're a small operation, but vital nonetheless. There are sixteen bedrooms, with folks staying with us anywhere between one to six months.'

They entered a sparse magnolia room. On the dark linoleum was a metal bed draped in a blanket the colour of despair. Next to it was a cheap teak-veneered MDF cabinet, its drawer front missing. Some large plastic boxes filled with clothes were piled up against the wall.

'This is cosy.'

'Throw cushions aren't high on the priority list.'

They continued on their tour.

'There's a range of reasons why people come to us, the most common being a breakdown in relationships with family. But we do have some here because of substance misuse, gambling, mental health issues and spousal abuse. The four horsemen of the modern apocalypse.'

'Sounds like a riot.'

'Everyone's required to keep their room tidy, but we also clean them once a week. You'll be helping with that.'

Gayle told her how the building was council-owned, but the shelter was run by a charity, one operating in difficult circumstances as income sources became increasingly hard to come by. 'Which is why we'll take whatever help we can get. Even princesses like you.'

'Gee, thanks.'

'Just use your loaf, pull all eight stone of your weight, and I won't get you sent to prison.'

They entered the kitchen where a young woman was removing pans from an industrial dishwasher, clattering them loudly onto the hob of a double-fronted oven.

'Tasha. This is Simone.'

Tasha stopped for a moment and glanced at her. 'Another one?'

'Yep.'

'They do like to send them.'

She watched as Tasha went back to her pans, her long pink and black braids swinging like ropes. She was wearing a loose black band tee over a short tight jersey skirt. Around her neck was a spiked dog collar, along with multiple silver chains. She had a bullring piercing through her nose, a small hoop through her bottom lip, and two vertical black lines running across the centre of her large dark eyes, like she'd been twice slashed with a Sharpie. She was, presumably, some form of goth or emo, not that she understood the difference. To her they were all just girls being less hot than they could be.

'Gary's texted to say he won't be in,' Tasha said with an eye roll. 'Again.'

'Fuck's sake!' said Gayle. 'Lazy bastard.'

'Yeah. And Fairshare have been delayed. Food won't be here until this afternoon.'

'Fuck's sake! Is there anything in?'

'Not much.'

Gayle reached into her back pocket and pulled out a wallet. She counted out six pound coins and five twenty pences, and handed them to Simone. 'I need you to go to the market and pick up enough stuff to feed twenty people.'

'Do you need me to do a sermon on the mount too?'

She held out her hand for more money, but Gayle's demeanour made it plain there wasn't any.

'Seriously?'

Gayle nodded. 'Welcome to the real world, darling.'

'What am I meant to do with this?'

The girl sighed. 'You should be able to get two big bags of

pasta, some garlic, half a dozen onions and five tins of chopped tomatoes. We've got dried herbs and spices. I'll make an arrabbiata.'

She pocketed the cash. She'd barely made it to the end of the corridor, though, when Tasha shouted her back.

'You'll need these.' She held out a couple of bags that looked like they'd been recovered from a litter pick in the grounds of Chernobyl.

'Err, it's okay, I'll pick up some fresh ones.'

Tasha's eyes narrowed. 'Err. That's twenty pence wasted. You'll use these.'

She was pretty bossy.

'Err, how about I buy the bags out of my own money?'

She was now having an err-off. Nice vibes. Very mature.

'Err,' said the girl. 'If you want to waste your cash and destroy the environment, be my guest. But you could get a grapefruit for that.'

'Do you need a grapefruit?'

Tasha defiantly swept her braids behind her shoulder. 'No, I'm just saying you could.'

She ran her fingers through her own hair. 'Because if you need a grapefruit, I can get you one.' She sounded like she was offering the girl outside for a fight.

'I don't need one. And besides, we all eat the same thing here.'

'We?'

Surely the staff were allowed to head out and get their own lunches. She'd been banking on it. There was a little sushi place she'd picked out for lunch that got rave reviews.

'The residents,' said Tasha.

This was confusing.

'You're not a resident, are you?'

'What did you think I was?'

'I assumed you were the cook.'

Tasha tutted. 'That's Gary. I help out because he's got issues. And it keeps me busy. There's not exactly much else to do around here.'

'How old are you?'

Tasha lifted her chin. 'Eighteen. Why?'

She was almost twice the girl's age, but looking into eyes whose dark rings probably hadn't solely come from a make-up palette, she sensed there wasn't such a gulf between them life-experience-wise. A litany of questions welled up in her, but she didn't dare ask any of them.

'I should get going,' she said.

Tasha thrust the bags at her and held her gaze until she took them. She then marched back down the corridor, stopping suddenly at the kitchen door.

'Go to the second fruit and veg stall on the left. He likes the pretty ladies, that one. You might get a discount.'

She disappeared and Simone deposited the money in her pocket. He'd have to give it away for it to be much cheaper. Still, after Jasper's point-blank refusal to seem in any way gratified that, of all the homeless joints, in all the boroughs, in all of London, she happened to have moseyed into his, charming a street trader might just help get this day back on track.

Chapter Fifteen

I t was a glorious afternoon, weather-wise at least. Simone leaned against the shelter's wall and turned her face to the sun, squinting into its heat, pinpricks of sweat forming on her upper lip. She'd spent the last three hours scrubbing at grout with a toothbrush, so when home time swung around, she'd found herself doing something she hadn't done for a very long time whilst sober: having a cigarette.

She inhaled deeply, welcomed the mild nausea and taste of burnt popcorn as the smoke hit her throat and lungs, then exhaled a spectral ribbon into the still air. She knew she shouldn't indulge, but she welcomed the light-headedness and taut sensation of need, one drag propelling her to the next, nothing to do except relinquish herself to the inevitability of the cigarette's conclusion, and the feeling of regret that would doubtless follow. She looked around, the world temporarily more vibrant than it had been a minute ago. Her gaze alighted on an old Škoda in the car park. It had flat tyres, and its windows were practically obscured with dirt and algae, as if nature was trying to reclaim the parking space. It was weird; this was valuable London real estate, where renting your driveway could bring in thousands, and it couldn't have been hard to get it towed away. Still, that wasn't for her to worry about. She took another drag and let the sun bleach her retinas once more.

'So, you smoke, huh?'

She almost choked with surprise. Blinded as she'd been, she'd not seen Jasper approach.

'Are you going to tell me that this makes me an addict, and therefore no different from any of the other addicts you work with?'

He regarded her blithely. 'No, I was going to ask you for a light.'

'Oh. Right. Yep, here you go.'

She reached inside her skirt pocket and held out the lighter she'd borrowed from the kitchen. He took hold of it, fingers tantalisingly close to hers, his nails like tiny ghosts. His hand lingered longer than expected.

'And a cigarette?'

'Wow.' She let go of the lighter.

'I've given up,' he said.

'Solid move. I don't smoke either.'

She tossed the pack to him and angled her head so that a sliver of shadow fell across her face, enabling her to see the whole of him better. The sun was behind him, giving the effect of some heavenly interloper.

'It's interesting you should say the other stuff though,' he said. 'It's amazing what you can reveal about yourself in the most innocuous moments.'

'Are you psychoanalysing me?'

'I'd need something stronger than a cigarette to attempt that.'

He lit the fag, holding it like a joint. He moved to the wall alongside her, put one foot up against it, and rested his free hand on his thigh. They watched in silence as sparrows flitted fitfully between the small, spindly trees that lined the building's rear driveway. Jasper seemed entirely comfortable to stand there enjoying his cigarette, but she considered all silences around men to be awkward ones.

'So are you a psychologist or a psychiatrist?' she asked.

'You know the difference?' There was a note of surprise in his voice.

'Isn't it that psychiatrists can prescribe drugs to change the brain, whereas psychologists can only study it?'

'That's about it.' He took a large drag and sent smoke rings into the ether. He turned towards her, a wisp of smoke still trailing from those full lips like it was clinging on for as long as possible; a straggler at a party. 'I'm a psychologist.'

'Which means you get to observe the action, but you don't get to influence the outcome. Isn't that like being an extra in a porno?'

He half-smiled, tiny dimples appearing at the corner of his mouth. 'Also interesting you should mention sex so early on in the conversation.'

'Is it? I don't hold much store by all that Freudian stuff.'

'He's only the godfather of psychoanalysis,' he said.

'Yeah, but didn't he claim all men want to bang their mothers, whilst banging a ton of patients who bore no resemblance to his mother, thus disproving his own theory?' She'd come to the point in her cigarette where she should stub it out, but she continued to let it smoulder. 'It's a classic bit of misdirection. *Hey, check out zis guy, he vants to bang his mutter*! Then when everyone's checking out that guy, Freud sneaks off and bangs a paying customer.'

'I notice you're also consistently referring to sex as *banging*. Is that indicative of something?'

'Perhaps it's indicative of the fact that sex with me is always banging?'

She shuddered inwardly. That's right. Always best to double-down on sounding like a dick when you're talking to someone who already thinks you're a dick. Jasper stubbed out his cigarette and flicked it into a bin about eight feet away.

'Am I meant to be impressed?' she asked.

'Funny. I was just thinking the same thing. Tell me, do you think everyone's actions are done with the intention of eliciting a reaction from you?'

'I asked first.'

'No. I am definitely not trying to impress you. What I'm actually doing is trying to take my mind off the fact that one of my patients died this weekend.'

'I'm sorry.'

'Are you? People die all the time.'

'Okay, I'm not sorry. What happened? Did you psychoanalyse them to death?'

He smiled, as she'd hoped he might.

'Heart attack. But also booze which probably led to the heart attack.'

'And you're worried that you're bad at your job?'

'No!' he said.

'Other people are worried that you're bad at your job?'

'You can only try to help. It doesn't always work.'

'Would a psychiatrist have done a better job do you think?'

'Jesus!'

'I'm only asking what any self-respecting person would.'

'And are you a self-respecting person, Simone?'

'That's a big question.'

He looked directly at her. 'Only if the answer isn't yes.' He passed the lighter back to her and effortlessly pushed himself off the wall.

Her own cigarette was almost up to the filter, but she took a final drag anyway, noting the burn against her flesh. He was so infuriatingly *on it*. It was like her brain slowed down around him, and there was something in his bearing that made her doubt …

well, everything. If this were a sparring match, the judges would almost certainly have awarded the advantage to Jasper for that one. She'd have to try harder next time.

'There you are.' Gayle had rounded the corner. 'Any chance you can go and help Tasha serve dinner?'

She waited for Jasper to answer, but he was looking at her.

'I think she means you.'

She checked her Fitbit. It was bang on six. 'I was about to head off.'

'I'm sorry, Cinderella, do you turn back into a pumpkin at one minute past?' said Gayle.

'My probation officer said I'm entitled to work set hours.'

'Oh, I forgot about your entitlement. Perhaps you'd like to take it up with HR, get them to email a timesheet you can complete. You can pop your eight hours in, print it off for me, and then I suggest you jam it straight up your back pipe. Not all the way though; I want you to leave a little bit poking out. Then I want you to set fire to it. When, and only when, your ringpiece looks like a little asterisk drawn in charcoal, then you can still come and help Tasha with serving up. Does that sound agreeable to you?'

Jasper suppressed a smirk.

'What finishing school did you say you went to again?' said Simone.

'Follow me.'

———

That evening, with a large glass of Pinot Grigio in hand, she reflected on the day. As she'd passed out plates in the dining area, she'd been surprised by the mix of residents. Some were exactly as she'd imagined, like the hunched-over man she'd bumped into that morning, while others could have been out for a casual bite to eat. There were also a few other regular volunteers. No one particularly interesting, but it was still surprising that people gave up their own time to volunteer. Where was the sense in inducing your own misery to observe the misery of others? Wasn't the net effect simply more misery? She'd spoken to one woman, clearly religious, for whom the whole thing was probably some kind of afterlife insurance policy. But Simone didn't believe in heaven. She didn't even believe in hell, and she'd once spent a Sunday afternoon in Ikea.

The Tasha girl was a harder one to work out. She'd barely spoken when they were serving up, but after everyone had been given a plate of pasta, smothered in a rich deep red sauce whose sweet and smoky aroma filled the dining room, Simone had asked her how she'd learned to cook. *By not having a choice in the matter*, the girl had said. Eight words that spoke volumes.

Gayle had finally let her leave at 7:15, but not before she'd had to rinse off all the plates and stack them in the dishwasher. It was funny, she didn't mind that Gayle was some OTT hard nut type – Tony had asked her to do far worse than touch a bicep – but it was her dismissiveness that rankled. She didn't need to be liked, but she liked the *level* of liking to be on her own terms. She wanted to feel in control of the variables. It was the same with Jasper. There was no benefit in him fancying her – the guy worked in a homeless shelter after all – but it was a matter of principle that he should. She took a sip of wine and stretched her long legs out on her velvet couch. Still, she hoped he was working tomorrow. If nothing else, she now had a little side hustle to make the next three weeks more interesting.

Chapter Sixteen

The next morning, she was in the kitchen working at its large stainless steel-topped island. Gary was still not in, but the food delivery had arrived, so she'd been promoted to peeling potatoes. They were green on the outside, and Tasha had told her she'd need to remove several layers to get to something edible. Given that the peeler she'd found was about as sharp as a marshmallow, and made for someone right-handed, this was easier said than done. She had just frustratedly launched a particularly shitty specimen of a tuber across the room when Jasper came in. It skidded to a stop at his feet, which, she was horrified to note, were clad in the type of zigzag-patterned Velcro-fastening walking sandals that crusty environmental warriors wore. Despite this crime de fashion, the rest of him was still, undeniably, extremely easy on the eye.

'What's with the spud missile?'

She shot him a warning look. 'Don't.'

He eyed the mound of skin next to the paltry pile of potatoes that she'd managed to prepare. 'Have you peeled a potato before? Do you need me to show you how it's done?'

'I'm fine, thanks.'

He picked up the jettisoned potato from the floor, rinsed it under the tap, and returned it to the worktop. 'So you enjoy cooking then?' His voiced dripped with sarcasm.

'I find cooking for yourself is a bit like wearing your best underwear to clean the bathroom; unless there's someone around to appreciate it, what's the point?'

He cocked his head on one side, puppyish. 'So you're saying you only ever make an effort if there's someone to witness it?'

'Is this about to turn into one of those *if a bear shits in the woods, does it still stink of shit* debates?'

'I don't think I've heard it phrased quite like that before.'

'Isn't everyone driven by external validation?' she said.

'Partly, I guess. It's a natural human instinct. But I'd say it's not healthy for it to be a primary source of motivation.'

'Thanks for the life hack. I'll try to be more intrinsically motivated by removing skin from this potato. Maybe I could start a new religion. Call it Zen Spuddism.'

He stifled a smile.

She motioned to his footwear. 'Although I'm not sure I should be taking advice from a man in those sandals.'

He looked down at his feet. 'What's wrong with my sandals?'

'Let's start with what's right with them. They're not espadrilles. The end.'

'It's going to be thirty degrees today.'

'I don't think there's a heatwave strong enough to justify the visibility of men's feet in an urban setting.'

Although, in fairness, his weren't the calloused hooves that many men sported. They were, like the rest of him, extremely tidy.

'Are you foot-shaming me?' he asked.

She groaned. He was so right-on. She re-examined the potato he'd retrieved. It was covered in tiny sprouts, dead eyes that needed to be gouged from its surface. She pushed the pointy end

SAL THOMAS

of the peeler into its squeaky flesh, but fumbled it and sent the blade into the base of her thumb instead.

'Christ,' said Jasper, as blood oozed out onto her starch-dried skin.

'Don't worry, it's nothing.'

She rubbed at the nick by way of illustration, deep red mingling with chalkiness, making it look like she'd tested a pink lipstick there.

Jasper winced.

'It's fine,' she reiterated. 'You don't need to look so concerned.'

'It's just…' He hesitated. 'I'm not very good with blood.'

She laughed, genuinely surprised.

'Thanks for the sympathy,' he said.

'You know you *are* ten percent blood, right?'

'I know. But I don't like it when any of that ten percent makes a break for it.'

It was too good an opportunity. She smeared some of the blood around the gap in her fist, making a large-lipped hand puppet. 'Jasper doesn't like the sight of blood,' she said in a Mickey Mouse voice, her hand miming along.

He averted his gaze. 'For your information, haemophobia is actually one of the most dangerous phobias you can have.'

'Is that because you get torn to shreds for being a big girl's blouse?'

'It's because you can sometimes faint and hit your head. I'm not that bad though. Still, if you could just…' He made a shooing motion at her.

She went and rinsed her hand off at the sink, then held it up for his inspection. 'Better?'

'Thanks.' He poured himself some weak squash from one of the large jugs Tasha had prepared. 'Are you not afraid of anything?' he asked after gulping it down.

Of course she was. Living alone in London meant there were

92

plenty of things to fear, but she'd be blowed if she was speaking to some hot head doctor about them.

'This pile of potatoes never being finished,' she said.

'That is a legitimate concern.'

He continued to eye her curiously. Was this what psychotherapists did? Just stared at you long enough until you felt you had to fill the silence?

'Isn't there a tree somewhere you should be chaining yourself to?' she snapped.

He smiled. 'Don't worry, I'm off. I only came in for a quick drink.' He put the empty cup in the dishwasher. 'I might catch you later.'

'Sure. Say hello to your friends at Extinction Rebellion for me.'

———

He'd been gone barely a minute when a man she'd seen at dinner the previous night appeared at the door. His face was the colour of overdone toast, and as creased as the pin-striped suit he was wearing. His greasy hair was scraped back from his face and hung like oil-slicked seagrass across his shoulders. A pair of pale amber eyes looked out from under black eyebrows that were strikingly bushy, but still paltry in comparison to his beard, which didn't so much require the attention of a barber as a landscape gardener. He was holding a small old-school camcorder, its red light winking at her.

'I know what you're doing,' he said.

'Preparing lunch?'

'You're watching me.'

'I'm not watching you.'

'You're watching me now.'

He spoke with a thick accent, like his tongue was too heavy for his mouth.

'Now I am, yes, but that's because you're in my eyeline. And you appear to be filming me so, you know, people in glass houses…'

'What about them?' he said.

'Who?'

'The people in glass houses.'

'It's a saying. People in glass houses shouldn't throw stones.'

Although *shouldn't wank during daylight hours* would be similarly good advice.

'Why would they be throwing stones?' the man asked.

'I don't know.'

'Nobody should be throwing stones.'

He grabbed his throat through his beard and rubbed it anxiously. She returned to the potatoes, but his presence was hard to ignore.

'You know Rumi?' he said.

I no roomie? Was he asking her if she lived alone?

'*A stone I died and rose again a plant,*' he said. '*A plant I died and rose an animal; I died an animal and was born a man. Why should I fear? What have I lost by death?*'

His tone was odd. Not robotic as such, but notably detached. The usual inflections and rhythm of speech stripped away. It was a bit like speaking to Siri.

'Was there something you wanted?' she asked.

'I know where you're from.'

'Brixton?'

'The government sent you.'

Strictly speaking, she supposed they had, but she was getting the impression that wasn't what this guy meant.

'You took my hat.'

Judging by the state of his hair, there was every chance it had crawled off his head of its own accord.

'You want what I've got,' he said.

'Nits?'

'You'll never get it.'

'I'm sure we can work this out, whatever this is.'

'You don't belong here.'

'You're not wrong there, dude.'

'How old are you?'

'Don't you know you should never ask a woman her age. Or film them without their consent.'

He flicked the viewfinder closed. She was surprised how relieved she felt. For someone used to sharing her life with strangers on social media, the individual attention of one person felt oddly exposing.

'I'm thirty-five,' she told him.

'When were you born?'

She was reminded of when she'd use a fake ID to get into nightclubs, although this guy was a bit more troubling than your average bouncer. She told him the date.

'And what day was that?'

She had no idea.

His eyes narrowed, great fuzzy black caterpillars crawling closer to the bridge of his broad nose. 'It was a Sunday.'

Oh yeah. Her dad used to tell her that *Monday's Child* poem. She was destined to be bonny and blithe and good and gay. One out of four wasn't bad. But how did he know that?

He tapped his temple with a coarse finger. Okay. She was officially creeped out.

'Why did you take my hat if you have nothing to hide?' he said.

'I didn't take your hat. I've been in here for the last hour.'

'And yet you've only prepared seven potatoes?'

The unpeeled pile taunted her.

'April eighth, 1990,' he said. 'Jose De Vega, American actor, dies of AIDS. Ryan White, youngest American haemophiliac to contract HIV, dies of AIDS. Some people think that AIDS was created by the CIA to punish homosexuals. What do you think?'

'I'm sure that's not the case,' she said.

'Also the day Twin Peaks was first broadcast.' He cast her a slightly unhinged Kubrick stare. 'Agent DB Cooper. Named after a man who hijacked a Boeing 727 mid-flight and, when he received his ransom, parachuted out over Washington, never to be seen again.'

He continued to regard her like she might have information about the guy's whereabouts. He was obviously some kind of wacko, but was he dangerous? He didn't seem dangerous, but then she didn't have much experience of foreign oddballs. He stepped towards her. She gripped the handle on the peeler more firmly. What was she going to do if he tried anything, pare him to death?

'What are you doing?' she asked.

'Getting the tin foil.'

'Are you going to make yourself a new hat?'

He peered at her like she'd lost her mind. 'I'm going to bake a potato. If I wait for you to be done with lunch, I'll wait forever.'

Gayle was scowling at her computer when Simone burst into the office.

'Is the guy in the suit dangerous?' she said.

Gayle didn't look up. 'Why?'

'He thinks I took his hat.'

'And did you?'

She told Gayle what had happened.

'You've only peeled seven potatoes? What the bleeding hell have you been doing in there?'

'I'm serious, Gayle. I'm not qualified to deal with mad people.'

Her heart was beating quickly, and it wasn't the dash to the office that had caused it.

Gayle tutted. 'We don't say mad. We say reality challenged.'

'Okay, reality-challenged people.'

Gayle sniggered. 'We don't really say reality challenged. That'd be ridiculous. No, he can be a bit mad.'

'Well, the mad one is—'

'No, *I* can say mad, because I'm a certified mental health professional. You can't.'

'For fuck's sake. I can't call him mad, and I can't call him reality challenged, what can I call him?'

'How about Hozan?' Gayle's lip twitched.

'Well, *Hozan* really doesn't like me.'

'Then he's a very good judge of character. And it'll be that he doesn't trust you yet.'

'And how can I make him trust me?'

'Make him like you.' There was another twitch of the mouth. It was like there was a verbal tripwire attached to Gayle's lip, which she kept blundering into.

'Brilliant.'

Gayle tapped on her keyboard. 'What does it matter if he doesn't like you? You're only here for three weeks.'

'I don't need him to like me, but I do want him to *not* look like he wants to kill me.'

'Don't flatter yourself. He's more likely to think you want *him* dead.'

'What's wrong with him?'

'What's *different* about him, you mean?'

'Yeah. Whatever. That.'

'He has some interesting ideas. Conspiracy stuff. He thinks big corporations are out to ruin the little man.'

'That's not a conspiracy: that's capitalism.'

'He thinks we're under surveillance 24/7.'

'We are. It's called the internet.'

'And he thinks the government has planted a cognitive enhancement chip in his brain as part of a global experiment in human warfare.'

'What the fuck?!'

Gayle waved a dismissive hand. 'He's fine. He just gets antsy around new people. Speak to Jasper if you want the full diagnosis.'

'Yeah, I might do that.' She genuinely wanted greater reassurance.

Gayle finally looked up from her computer. 'On second thoughts, do not speak to Jasper about him.'

'But you just—'

'I do not want you and Jasper...' She swirled her hand around.

'Waving?' said Simone.

'You're about as funny as a clown. Now go and make yourself ... less here.'

She reluctantly returned to the kitchen, but there was no sign of Hozan. Even so, she finished off the pile of potatoes as quickly as possible and was happy to be asked to help out at an art therapy class in the main communal area. She wasn't sure how therapeutic art could be for a bunch of wildly untalented amateurs – Van Gogh cut off his own ear and shot himself in the chest, and that boy could actually draw – but it was better than being alone.

Chapter Seventeen

Simone had been consigned to the laundry for the afternoon. It was creepy as hell, tucked as it was in the bowels of the building, with the only functional strip light barely illuminating its bare brick walls. A huge metal washing machine loomed before her. She'd seen one like it once before. Her and the girls had been to a secret bar in Soho that had been done up like a launderette on the outside, but if you stepped through the washing machine, you were transported to an exclusive cocktail bar beyond. No Narnia on offer here, though – just a pile of towels that looked like they'd been used as tissues by a fluey Demogorgon in the Upside Down. She gingerly picked up a hand towel with two fingers and swung it into the drum.

She wondered what the girls were up to. Not that she needed to wonder too much; they'd documented every inch of the trip so far, or at least Ziggy had documented every inch of her arse on the trip so far. It had been photographed in the Phoenix Desert Botanical Gardens, the Phoenix Art Museum, the Phoenix Zoo, and two Phoenix nightclubs, where it had been barely covered by a pair of 'shorts' made entirely from rhinestone chains. Jasper, by contrast, was proving far harder to keep track of. She'd caught a brief glimpse of him in the main common room on her way back from lunch, but they hadn't spoken. Pity. A bit of bants would have helped the day pass a little more enjoyably.

The pile beckoned. The bath towels were trickier, but by hanging them across the open door, she could kick them inside in increments. Where the soap went was anyone's guess though. After a couple of minutes of trying to remove a welded-on panel at the front, she conceded defeat. She pulled her phone from her pocket and was searching how a Mag Primer RS works when Gayle came in. She was followed by a tall man on whose stringy frame hung a nylon shell suit that he appeared to be wearing in a non-ironic way. His thinning blond mullet had clearly wanted in on the eighties action, the hairline of which was beating a retreat towards the midline of his head in a pronounced M shape. His sparse facial hair was only moderately more committed to the skin-coverage cause.

'Slacking so soon?' said Gayle.

'Do you know how to get powder into this machine?'

'Is it to add an extra day onto your community service for every second I find you on your phone? Maybe that'd do it?'

'I was searching for an instructional video.'

Gayle turned to the man. 'Reckon she's telling porkies, Steve?'

Steve's eyebrows met beneath a line in his forehead so deep, it was like he'd spent a long time trying to work out where his fashion sense had gone wrong, but he was still no closer to a solution.

'It's not for me to say.' He had a thick Mancunian accent.

'Get down off the fence, man; it can't be comfortable having one bollock hanging either side of it.'

'Who am I to judge? I tell you…'

Gayle held up a finger. 'Not an invitation to chat.'

The man opened his mouth.

'Shhh!'

'Bu—'

Gayle pressed a finger to his mouth.

'Hnnn.'

'Nope.' She turned to Simone. 'Simone, this is Steve. He rabbits on more than a whistleblower on sodium pentothal.'

'Truth serum,' said Steve with a shrug. 'I looked it up after the third time she said it.'

His voice had a soporific quality to it; a melodic lilt that sounded like he was either stoned or in a constant state of conflict resolution.

'I thought he'd make excellent company for you,' said Gayle. 'And it gets him out of my hair.'

'She loves me really,' said Steve.

'No, I don't.'

'You do.'

'I don't. But I'm sure Simone here would love to hear your life story.'

'I'm fine for life stories,' said Simone. 'I once read the first three pages of *Becoming* by Michelle Obama.'

'And if I find you on your phone again, when you should be working,' said Gayle, 'I'll be testing its torch function where the sun don't shine.'

Interestingly, Dickwad and Ghastly had once hidden a story about a politician who had been caught doing precisely that. Right now, she missed the place.

Gayle left. She would have to throw some powder in the drum and hope for the best.

'Don't mind her,' said Steve. 'She's a bit stressed.'

'Don't worry. My real boss makes her look like a pussycat.'

Steve whistled. 'So, did I hear right that your name's Simone?'

'Hmm.'

'After Nina Simone?'

'No.'

'Because I really like her music. My dad didn't. He was a bit of a racist. I'm not. Live and let live, that's my motto.'

She'd met guys like Steve before, the kind her dad had worked with. They always had a motto.

'It takes all sorts to make the world go round, doesn't it? That's what I say, anyway.'

It seemed that Steve had a few mottos.

'Some of my best mates are—'

'Probably best to stop you there, Steve.' She held up her finger like Gayle had done. 'I'm not really one for small talk.'

'Right, okay then, yeah, no problem. I'll make myself useful, shall I?'

'Could you?'

There was a tumble drier equal in size to the washing machine on the opposite wall, and Steve opened the door and pulled out the tangle of bedding within. For several minutes, the crackle of static electricity was all that could be heard as pillowcases were separated from duvets. It reminded her of the ASMR meditation videos she'd been into for a brief period. Perhaps she should listen to one now. Enjoy a few tingles to help see her through the last hour of the day. In fact, she was annoyed she hadn't thought of listening to something before now. She'd just retrieved her earbuds when Steve spoke.

'I bet you're wondering how I came to be here, aren't you?'

'No.'

'It's 'cos I'm a gambling addict.' He wrestled a resistant ironing board until it yielded with a metallic squeak. It rocked unevenly on its open legs. 'That's the first step. Admitting you have a problem.'

'Admitting I have a problem with you talking doesn't seem to be helping me, Steve.'

'I was a chippie, doing alright for myself. By the end I'd sold everything, all my tools, the lot. It was the horses that did it.'

'Right.'

'It wasn't all bad. I once put a hundred on a nag that came in twenty-five to one.' He gazed at her expectantly.

'And?'

'Pity the rest of them came in at twelve-thirty!'

The guy was a doofus.

'So, like I said, I'm just going to…' She made a show of putting her earphones in. If only she'd brought her noise-cancelling ones.

'Do you believe in God?' he asked, apropos of nothing.

'I did before you started talking to me.'

She opened the YouTube app.

'The Twelve Steps is the best thing that's ever happened to me,' said Steve, seemingly not registering her excellent comebacks.

She calculated the distance to the door. She really wanted him to take twelve steps in that direction.

'You have to give yourself over to a power greater than yourself,' he said.

She suspected he could give himself over to a scarecrow, and it would have greater power than him. And it would dress better. She found a video she liked the sound of, but the damned thing wouldn't load.

'I said most people are a bit more surprised. About the gambling thing.'

So he was listening enough to realise she hadn't responded to whatever it was he'd said.

'I don't mean to be funny, Steve, but that hairstyle was a bit of a gamble, and let's face it, that hasn't paid off for you, has it?'

She went back to her phone and was relieved to hear the breathy hiss of the iron. He didn't stay quiet long, however.

'It's odd isn't it, people saying *I don't mean to be funny*. If they knew they were being funny, which they clearly do because they're using the phrase *I don't mean to be funny,* and if they genuinely *didn't* mean to be funny, they could just stop after the phrase *I don't mean to be funny* and not be funny, couldn't they?'

She refused to feel bad. This was probably the kind of voodoo he used to guilt people into lending him money, which he'd spunk up the wall on bad bets.

'But you carry on, love. Don't let me stop you. I deserve it. I really do. You know what they say: true humility and an open mind can lead you to a better way of life.'

Who said that? Probably nobody. Ever.

'What are you trying to listen to anyway?' he asked.

'A meditation.'

He nodded his approval. 'Nice one. Prayer and meditation are in Step Eleven.'

Was he trying to suggest some kinship with her?

'I'm not interested in your approval, Steve. I just want to try and get through the day without losing my shit.'

Steve smiled. It was an odd enigmatic little turn of the mouth, like he knew something she didn't. 'Sounds a lot like what I'm doing with The Twelve Steps, mate.' He whistled. 'Ironic really. My sponsor says meditation is all about learning to live in the present moment. Yet here you are trying to meditate to avoid it.' He shrugged, placed the iron back in its cradle, and slowly folded the duvet cover.

He was right, of course, but she'd rather wear that shell suit than admit it. Still, he was proving far more sage than a man who'd hit rock bottom had any right to be.

'Jesus. I'm trapped in a room with the poor man's Oprah Winfrey. Or should that be Oprah Losefrey?'

Steve smiled again, a proper heartfelt grin. 'You remind me of my mom.'

'Great!'

'Everyone called her Barb because of her sharp tongue.' He dropped the folded duvet into a tatty plastic basket. 'That, and her name was Barbara.'

She laughed despite herself. He was impossible to work out. Was he a manipulative genius, or some hapless halfwit with impulse control issues?

'What's your plan, Steve? What are you going to do?'

'I've made a list of everyone I've harmed. I'm going to make amends where I can. Just not yet.'

She tutted. Of course *not yet*.

'No, you're right to tut. It sounds like I'm making excuses. I'm gonna do it, but I need to get out of here first. The people I've hurt, they need more than words. They need proof. When I'm in my own place, then I can start to piece it all back together. But the problem is...'

Steve's mouth continued to move, but the washing machine decided it had heard enough, and went into a loud spin. It was hard not to be judgmental. If he wasn't gambling any more, just how difficult could it be to get back into work, earn some money and let everything flow from there?

When the noise subsided, he reached inside his jacket pocket and pulled out a wallet. He passed it to her. It was empty except for a picture of a teenager with a messy mop of brown hair falling over large soulful eyes.

'That's Declan. Not seen him for over twelve months. He'll be doing A-levels next year.'

She wondered if she was being hustled. Was it even his son? This could well be a routine he pulled with unsuspecting members of the public; he could ask her for money at any moment.

'If I could only get my Universal Credit sorted.' He gave a resigned shrug.

She wasn't buying the woe-is-me routine. 'So why don't you?'

'I need help with the forms, but my case worker's off on long-term sick, so she can't go to the benefits office with me.'

Perhaps it was better he wasn't given any money; he'd probably only bet it away. Steve reached for the picture. She looked at it once more. There was a resemblance: the same long thin nose, the downturn at the sides of the mouth. Perhaps he was telling the truth. Seventeen was a tough age not to have a dad around; she knew that better than anyone. Hang on, though, this was how people like Steve got you, with their plausible sob stories, back stories and tall stories. If he was so keen to sort himself out, he'd try harder.

'It can't be that difficult,' she said.

'You'd think so, wouldn't you? But honestly, you'd need a degree to work it all out.'

She didn't have a degree, and she'd always hated the assumption that you needed one to make anything of your life.

'Oh come on. I bet I could do it.'

'I'm not in a position to be taking bets, mate.'

She tossed the wallet back to him. At the end of the day this was his problem, and it was her home time.

That night, after she'd answered all of Tony's emails (who knows what he'd have done if she'd genuinely been incommunicado), she was in the bath, trying to slough off the day's grime. The cut on her hand stung every time she put it into the soapy water. She traced her finger over it, thinking about Jasper's reaction at the sight of blood and the way he'd readily admitted to his phobia. How did he get to be so at ease with his vulnerability? Many men would be embarrassed by such a weakness. She also couldn't help mulling over his question to her yesterday. Was she a self-respecting person? From someone who presumably should be impartial, the question had felt somewhat judgmental, like he'd made his appraisal and she'd been found wanting. At Dickwad & Ghastly, she was hyperfunctional; she was the person who got shit done, and she took pride in that. Just the volume of emails she'd had to field from Tony proved how capable she was. Usually, insecurities were like harem trousers to her; she'd tried a few on for size, but found them better suited to other people. She preferred to deal with difficult feelings by not having any. But the moment she went through the doors of that shelter, it was like she was stripped of her abilities. She was Thor without his hammer. Khloe K without her filters. Donald Trump without his gibbering white privilege.

She wondered where Marcus was right now. She was too tense, too thinky; she needed a diversion. He was probably still in his office. She leant over the side of the bath, retrieved her mobile, and took a selfie. Most of her body was submerged in the bubbles, but her glossy boobs were exposed. She fired it off to him with a couple of hashtags. #nofilter #needfucking.

A response came through within a minute.

You naughty girl. I'm at a dinner. Sat next to boring politician. Now can't move for stiffy.

She smiled, pleased with her capacity to turn him on.

Wish I was under the table right now. Would make amends.

Oh yeah. How?

She let her legs fall open.

I'd unzip your trousers and place my warm mouth around your dick.

Wouldn't people notice?

There's a long tablecloth. You'd just look like you were rocking on your chair.

Nice detail.

Not as nice as me fingering myself whilst your cock is sliding in and out of my lips.

Are you fingering yourself now?

Maybe.

She most definitely was.

Hang on. Making excuses. Luckily have jacket with me…

She continued to stroke herself. A minute later, a video call came through. Marcus was in a large cloakroom toilet.

'I only have a few minutes. Show me your pussy.'

She swept the bubbles to one side, lifted herself slightly and angled the phone there. She gently spread herself and continued to apply pressure to her clitoris.

'Yeah, baby. You are so fucking hot.'

'I just couldn't wait until the weekend,' she said.

'See what you did.'

Marcus's cock filled the screen. As much as she liked it, out of context of the rest of him, it was cartoonish. She'd never been a fan of dick pics; it was like trying to see the erotic potential in an uncooked sausage. But the thumbscrews of desire were already tightening, and in just a few more turns, she'd be begging for release.

'So, tell me again what you're going to do with this,' he said.

She closed her eyes, gently teased her index finger inside herself, and told him exactly what she'd do with it. It didn't take long before she heard the guttural moan he made when coming. She was close herself, she just needed a little extra encouragement.

'And then you reach down under the table and you—'

'I'd better get back,' he said.

'You can't go anywhere yet; your dick's still hard. Tell me what you'll do to my tits.'

'I've already been too long.'

'Just one more minute.'

'Babe, I need to get off.'

'Yeah, me too Marcus!'

She opened her eyes. The screen had gone dark. She heard a tap running, then a dryer start up. After a minute, he reappeared.

'I'll see you at the weekend. I'll tell you anything you need me to then, okay?'

'Marcus—'

'They're going to wonder where I am. This was great.'

He hung up. Fuck's sake. She tried to carry on without him, furiously grinding herself against her palm, but the water was cooling as quickly as her desire. She'd been cheated out of her moment of release. It was like being on a rollercoaster and the carriage getting stuck at the top of the big dip; no plummeting in a moment of complete abandon, just the ignominy of being left hanging. She gave up and pulled the plug on the bath.

Self-respect indeed. It would be a long time before she got to sleep that night.

Chapter Eighteen

'Does anyone know what the recovery position is?'

'Is it the one that comes after the doggy position?' said Steve, expectantly looking around the room for a laugh that didn't come. 'I'm only trying to lighten the mood. If you can't laugh, what can you do? That's what I say.'

Luckily no one seemed too keen on joining Steve in the bants, because the St John's Ambulance instructor could no more control a room than he could his own sweat glands. Dark patches bloomed on his shirt like ink on blotting paper. The cobwebs on the ceiling had more presence. But the mood today was sombre.

'So, we use this position if they're not responding, but are breathing normally.'

The instructor wasn't breathing normally. He'd fetched a couple of large bags in five minutes before and the effort was still evident in the whistle of laboured breath through his nostrils. She hoped he didn't keel over; you could no more put him in the recovery position than you could a lubed-up seal.

'Simone, perhaps you can help me demonstrate?'

'You want me to get on the floor?' she said.

'Is there a problem?'

The floor was grotty, and she was wearing a white broderie anglaise jumpsuit. Attaching the name sticker to it had been torture enough.

'I think the last time that carpet saw a vacuum cleaner, it was being operated by a dinosaur.'

Steve laughed, which made her wish she hadn't said it.

'Can't Steve do it? His tracksuit is wipe clean.'

He was wearing another shell suit combo. The St John's guy took as deep a breath as he could manage.

'It doesn't matter who goes first,' he said. 'You're going to be taking it in turns.'

Several pairs of eyes bore into her.

'Fine. I'll go first.'

By the time St John's got round to the tilting her head back part, all dirt was forgotten in favour of hoping the growing beads of effort on his forehead didn't break ranks onto her face. When Gayle told her she needed to attend that morning, she'd questioned her logic. She was only here for three weeks; she wasn't going to be saving anyone. She had gotten a lecture about death rates in homeless services being significantly higher than for the general population. When she'd continued to whinge, Gayle threatened her with the kiss of life. At least it was better than cleaning windows, which is what she'd been doing all morning.

Once everyone had mastered the art of folding someone into the correct shape, they moved onto resuscitation. The bags that St John's had brought in contained training mannequins.

'Hey, it's *First Aid for Dummies*,' said Steve, with whom she'd been reluctantly partnered. 'Get it? Like those books.'

Everyone roundly ignored him. They'd already learned not to engage for fear of inviting further conversational reprisals. She took in the pale face of the model, a male one, named Brayden. Its skin was the rubber of cheap dildos, and its pained face looked like one had been stuck up its arse. Not that it had an arse; it was entirely dismembered. Just a death mask and chest with LED lights embedded within, there to give real-time feedback on their resuscitation technique. St John's asked the group to watch him demonstrate first.

'Place the heel of one hand on the breastbone at the centre of the chest, your other on top, and then interlock your fingers.'

'I spoke to Gayle,' Steve whispered to her. 'About you coming to the benefits office.'

'Position your shoulders above your hands and, using your body weight, press straight down by five or six centimetres.'

'Huh?' she whispered back.

'You promised to help me sort out my benefits.'

St John's doll made a clicking sound. 'That means you're doing it correctly,' he said.

'No, I didn't,' said Simone.

'It's important you keep the compressions at 100 to 120 times per minute until an ambulance arrives.'

'Yeah, you did,' said Steve.

She hadn't said she would go, just that she'd be able to sort it if she did go. He was trying to get her on a technicality.

'Remember the Bee Gee's "Staying Alive",' said St John's. 'That's the rhythm you're aiming for.'

As his dummy's heart stuttered to life, the pink radiating around its chest, she had a sudden memory of watching ET with her dad. She hadn't wanted to – she'd have been about ten, and the film would have been almost twenty years old by then – but he'd insisted. When the alien died, calcium-white and zipped into a clear body bag, she'd surprised them both by climbing into his arms to sob, as grief-stricken as Elliot. But then there was the merest hint of a glow, meaning ET's family were coming and he was finally going home. She wondered if anyone had tried CPR on her dad when he'd collapsed.

'I wouldn't want "Staying Alive" to be the last thing I ever heard.' She tried to clear the mental image of his suffering.

'What would you go for?' asked Steve.

'If it was the choice between going to the benefits office with you, or a premature death, I'd opt for "Going Underground".'

'Hah! Top one.'

'If you do this properly,' said St John's, 'you can triple survival rates.'

The instructor went on to demonstrate mouth to mouth, or rescue breaths to give them their proper name, before inviting the group to practise for themselves. The whole thing was easier said than done. Steve attempted to get the circuit from heart to forehead to light for over five minutes, but even without any medical training, they knew it was time to call it a day. Near to collapse himself, given his boil-in-the-bag outfit of choice, Steve went to get some water. She was determined to do better, but Brayden's face stayed resolutely pallid. Even with her lips firmly clamped across the doll's, she just wasn't getting the clicks that would tell her the lungs had been inflated correctly.

A pair of plimsolls came into view.

'Ah, you make a lovely couple!'

She ran her gaze along the full length of the body attached to them. It was Jasper.

'But I think you're losing him,' he said.

'This one's faulty.'

'A bad workman always blames his resuscitation doll.'

'I'm doing everything I was meant to.'

'Have you thought about asking for help?'

'I don't know where the guy is. Probably on a scheduled shower break.'

She regretted the words as soon as she said them. She had no truck with St John's or his weird bodily issues; she was just in a permanent sulk at the moment.

'Be nice to Neil. He's a good guy.'

'Do those exist?'

She turned her full attention to Brayden's chest, increasing the pressure and trying very hard to look competent. No joy. She gave it another go, but try as she might, she just couldn't get the damned lights to create a complete circuit. She sensed Jasper above her, still there, still watching. His amusement at her fruitless struggle was practically audible. She glanced up and, sure enough, he was smirking. She got to her feet and despaired at the grey patches on her knees.

'Tell you what, why don't you have a go if you feel so confident?'

'Okay.' He knelt on the opposite side of the dummy. 'Did you check the airways?'

'Yes.'

He placed his index finger into the mannequin's mouth with the gentleness you might use to fish something out of a child's. 'All clear.'

'I know. I did it already.'

'Then you tilt the head back.' He gently cupped its chin and lifted it a little, as if it was made from porcelain, not plastic.

'Yep. That too.'

He then pinched Brayden's nose, taking great care that the heel of his hand didn't touch the mannequin's forehead. 'And then you need to create a complete seal, so the air from your lungs goes directly into theirs.'

'Oh really. You don't say.'

Jasper lowered his lips to Brayden's, his skin dark against the blanched nougat of the dummy's. His jeans had ridden down slightly, and his top had ridden up, revealing another patch of smooth flesh. He glanced up to check that she was watching what he was doing. She was watching alright.

'And then you blow.' He blew slowly and deliberately into

Brayden's mouth. The dummy's chest expanded steadily and made the requisite clicking sounds. Jasper repeated the breath. Brayden clicked his approval. He then interlocked his hands and started on Brayden's chest. The lights stayed illuminated for the full thirty compressions he counted, cancelling out any enjoyment she might have gotten from how Jasper's triceps popped with every downward push. Brayden looked mockingly up at her. Then Jasper did.

'I did all of that.'

'Are you sure?'

'Yes.'

He deftly jumped to his feet. Brayden seemed sad to see him go.

'Then I guess he just wasn't that into you.'

He did a little *what are you gonna do* shrug. If she'd had hackles, they would have been up. Steve reappeared.

'Hey, Steve. Did you tell Jasper that I've agreed to go to the benefits office with you?'

'Have you?'

'Yes. I have.'

'I'm pretty certain you refused to—'

'Let this crazy situation continue,' she said.

'But you said you'd rather die than—'

'See you go without the money that you're entitled to.'

Jasper cocked his head to one side. 'Really?'

'Yeah, really?' asked Steve.

'Yes, Steve.' She kept her eyes on Jasper. 'Because I am a smart woman.'

'That's great, though, because then I can—'

'Capable of handling whatever is thrown at me.'

'It's gonna be tricky but—'

'Perfectly adaptable to any situation.'

'I don't doubt it, mate, I reckon we should—'

'Regardless of what Jasper may think.'

'Eh?'

Steve looked from Simone looking at Jasper, to Jasper looking at Simone. 'Do you two need a minute?'

'No need,' said Jasper. 'I have a session I need to prepare for. If you'll excuse me.'

She watched him go. He hadn't pulled his jeans back up, and the tops of his supermarket boxers were still showing.

'I'm confused. Are we going to go?' Steve's daft eager eyes regarded her uncertainly.

She sighed. 'Yes, Steve. We're going to go.'

'How did you get on with Brayden?' Neil was at their side.

'I let him die,' she said. 'Look at him; he's got no quality of life.'

Neil chuckled nervously and said something about leaving it to the professionals to decide things like that, but she wasn't really listening. Just not that into you. From anyone else it would have been funny.

'I'll take him back to the front myself, shall I?' said Neil.

'I'll bring it up for you, mate,' said Steve.

She needed to stop letting her emotions get the better of her. If she didn't, who knows what she'd agree to next. She checked the time on her phone. It was ten to five. Screw it, she'd done everything that was asked of her today; she was going to find somewhere to hide and mindlessly scroll for a bit.

The bathrooms of Cedar Lodge were as depressing as the rest of the place. Knotted emergency cords hung like strings of clotted blood from the ceiling. Ribbed plastic handles spoke of age and infirmity. And the toilets, with their odd horseshoe seats, had been hung too high, meaning that as she'd caught up on the day's developments, her legs had gone numb. Her jumpsuit top was scrunched on her lap, stopping it from falling onto a floor that already glistened with errant urine dribbles, even though she'd only mopped it yesterday.

Tony was still taking full advantage of her not being on holiday. He wanted her to pull together an intel file on a potential client. Not a problem though; no one was any the wiser about her absence, and it would give her something to do in the evenings until the girls returned.

There was a knock on the door. She ignored it.

The prospect was some big investor who, from first glance at least, seemed to own large slabs of London. The grapevine had it he wasn't happy with his current agency, and Dickson & Astley would almost certainly be on the pitch list if it went to tender.

The knock came again. More insistent. Whoever it was could go find another bathroom.

The guy's name was Gerald Wolfe. Property tycoon. Multi-millionaire. Tax exile. It could be big. Really big. His profile pic on the corporate website gave him the appearance of a US gameshow host: tanned, coiffed and avuncular.

'Can you hear me?'

She didn't respond. She didn't recognise the voice, but if it was another volunteer, she didn't need them reporting to Gayle that she was hogging the bathroom when she should be helping with dinner.

Wolfe's biography on the FT painted a less friendly picture with tales of staff intimidation and bullying – the usual litany of asshattery from the mega-rich. Still, she was prepared to ride those coat-tails if it meant she got promoted. She tapped out a message to Tony.

No problem. All over it.

And if the opportunity came in, she wanted to lead the response. There was no way she'd let Ollie get his hands on this.

It was nearly home time. She'd squeeze out another pee then head back and continue her investigations; perhaps tap up her network to see who might be connected to Wolfe in some way. Pitches were won and lost before you even presented.

The handle on the inside of the door turned then fell back into position. Someone was trying to get in. She tried to grab some tissue, but it was one of those stupid single-piece dispensers that made getting some as easy as dragging a flannel through a nipple. She got a tiny square with which she dabbed herself. It instantly soaked through and stuck to her fingers.

'We're going to have to break it,' came a voice from the other side. Gayle's.

Shit! She stood up, turned on the tap and rinsed the tissue off. She yanked up her pants, wiping her wet fingers on them as she went.

'Ready?' said Gayle.

She set about the jumpsuit, but the damned thing was as about as easy to get into as a fastened straitjacket when you're already wearing a straitjacket.

'Stand back.'

She had one arm and one boob in, the neckline bisecting the flesh-coloured mesh bra that provided support but absolutely no coverage, when the door flew open and Gayle fell in after it. She rushed to get the other arm in only to hear the sickening sound of cotton-sewn seams being forced beyond their stretching point. She also saw the sickening sight of Jasper standing behind Gayle.

'For fucks sake!' shouted Gayle. 'I thought someone was dying in here!'

She was: inside. She continued to wrestle the jumpsuit until her second boob flopped into place like a defeated blancmange. Jasper backed away, eyes to the floor.

'What the fuck, Gayle! I was having a wee. This is harassment!'

'You weren't answering.'

'So? Is it so much to ask for a little privacy? What kind of lunatic would assume I was dying?'

The relief on Gayle's face had been replaced with fury. 'I didn't know it was you. Anything could have happened.'

'You can chill out. I'm fine.'

If you didn't count the light grazing of the left breast and a ripped jumpsuit.

'What were you doing?' asked Gayle.

'Urinating.'

'Were you on your phone?'

'No.'

'Tell the truth.'

'No!'

'Christ's sake, woman! Just a little bit of effort, that's all I ask. You think you're better than us because you've got a fancy job and fancy clothes? You think you're a poppy in a field of wheat? You're as exotic as a supermarket coffee!' A little bit of spittle formed at the edge of Gayle's mouth. 'What were you really doing in here?'

She felt like a naughty schoolgirl. 'Some research for my boss,' she muttered.

'Sorry, what?'

'Some research for my boss,' she said louder.

'Who's your boss?'

'His name's—'

'Nuh-uh-uh.' Gayle waved a finger at her. 'Who is your boss right now? Go on, say it.'

She wasn't going to say it.

'Say it,' said Gayle.

'I'm not saying it.'

'Say it!'

'Fine. You're my boss.'

'Louder.'

'Jesus, Gayle, this isn't *Jerry Maguire*.'

'Louder!'

'You are my boss for the next three weeks.'

'For you, it's just three weeks of your life. For these people, it *is* their life. Come with me.'

Gayle grabbed her by the hand and led her down the corridor.

'You like research, I'll give you some research to do.'

They reached the office.

'I'll drown you in so much paper, you're going to be shitting origami for a week.' Gayle opened one of the filing cabinets and pulled out several folders. She threw them onto a desk and rifled through. 'This is a good one. The NCH Report on Hate Crimes Against Homeless People.' She thrust it at her. 'How about this one? Homelessness as a Violation of Human Rights. Or this. Incidence of Sexual and Physical Abuse in Homeless Youth.'

Gayle continued to pass her reports with equally depressing names. They were getting heavy in her arms.

'Okay, I get the picture.'

'Do you? Because I don't think you have the faintest idea of what the picture is. You're so far from getting the picture, you're like a blind person asking their guide dog to work out a magic eye poster!' She rubbed her hands over her face. 'Go home, Simone. And be grateful you have one. I've got work to do.'

Gayle left the office, passing Jasper in the doorway. Great. She was going to get a side helping of awkwardness to go with her post-being-undressed dressing-down. He couldn't look her in the eye, even though moments before he'd been able to look her in the tit.

'Er…' he said to the space over her shoulder. 'I just wanted to say, I'm sorry I saw what I saw.'

'Was it that horrifying for you?'

'No, I meant—'

'I don't care what you meant. Do you know what? I don't care about any of this. I'm off.'

'For good?'

'Yeah, why not. I'd rather go to prison than hang out here another day.'

She sounded like a petulant child, but Gayle was the one being unreasonable. As she glared up at the ceiling, its suspended polystyrene tiles browning at the edges like parchment, one of the reports slipped from her grip and onto the floor.

'Fuck's sake!' She kicked the desk leg. Pain shot through her foot. Fucking sandals.

Jasper bent down and picked it up for her. He caught her gaze this time. 'Simone.' His voice was gentle.

'Yes?'

'I think you think that by not really trying, you somehow win.'

She tilted her head. 'Oh really?'

'But you don't. It's just that everyone else loses out.'

'Did you get that from Psychological Claptrap magazine?!'

He gave her a bent smile. 'I think it was Bullshit Therapy Today.' He slid the errant report into the stack she was holding. 'But that doesn't make it any less true.'

She wanted to throw the reports in his face. He was so bloody measured, a perfect counterpoint to her fury. Instead she pushed past him, only to find Tasha hovering in the corridor.

'Hey, look, it's Wednesday Adams lurking in the shadows. Got something you wanted to add?'

Tasha was holding a couple of loosely scrunched-up plastic bags. 'You might need these.'

She felt her nose prickle. Jesus, was she going to cry? Her eyes moistened. She took a deep breath and feigned a yawn that Tasha pretended not to notice for what it was. The girl held the bags open. She fed the papers in. By the time her arms were empty, she'd swallowed the worst of it.

'Listen, I'm sorry about the Wednesday Adams thing.'

The girl gazed at her with complete equanimity and shrugged. 'I've been called worse.'

'That doesn't make me feel better.'

The girl shrugged again.

She wondered how heavy the weight on Tasha's shoulders would need to get before it was no longer possible to shrug it off. Best not to think about that.

She took the bags. 'Sure you can spare them? That's twenty pence worth.'

'It's nothing.'

But it wasn't nothing. It was a kindness. And she had received so little in recent years, she'd forgotten what to do with them.

'You can bring them back tomorrow,' said Tasha.

She really didn't want to come back tomorrow. Perhaps she might call in sick and get a doctor's note. Or call her probation officer and ask to be transferred to a gig cleaning graffiti, or litter picking. Anything but having to walk back in here in the morning. She allowed herself a moment to consider the implications, but the one that overshadowed all others was the safe and certain knowledge that if she didn't turn up, it would confirm Jasper's suspicions about her. And the only thing more unbearable than sitting at home thinking about that smug look crossing his face was not being around to actually wipe it off.

Chapter Nineteen

Simone woke to the sound of the cooker beeping. It took her a while to orient herself. She reached out for her phone, then it all came back to her, the cogs turning. She'd lugged the bags of reports all the way to the underground, only to get there and realise Gayle still had her mobile. She'd endured a whole evening without it. It was like a piece of her had been removed, reminding her of when her mother threw away her favourite teddy, telling her it was childish to still want one past a certain age. It had been the first time she'd realised an absence of something could feel as solid and unyielding as its presence.

She wondered if Gayle had kept the phone deliberately. It meant that the bags of papers had been harder to avoid the previous evening, winking at her from the kitchen surface as she refilled her wine glass. On the third visit to the refrigerator, she'd relented, dragging them into the lounge and spreading the contents across her rug. She was still reading when the streetlight flicked on outside her window, illuminating the pages, but not dissipating the gloom that lay within them. Something unfamiliar had lodged in her chest, an unwelcome squatter that once let in couldn't be moved on. *Shame*. The concern on Gayle's face when she'd burst in that door had been genuine. Reading these reports, she could understand why. Suicide was the second most common cause of death in homeless people. Not sickness. Not drugs. Self-annihilation. And she knew all about that.

She traipsed to the kitchen to turn off the cooker timer and flicked the radio on. Two perky DJs were asking listeners to text in and tell them what their favourite colour was. She changed the channel.

She'd showered and dressed and was fixing herself a smoothie when the travel report came on. Her tube line was closed. Replacement buses. Expect delays. Blah blah blah. She was going to have to take the car. She instinctively looked around for her phone, then cursed herself for her conditioning. That meant no satnav, which would make things tricky. She fetched her laptop, powered it on, saw the blue screen of death as it told her it was undertaking a software update, and reached for her phone to see what time it was, only to again remember that she didn't have it. The cooker clock told her she had an hour. It would take at least half an hour, possibly three-quarters, given the extra traffic. She was cutting it fine before she'd need to leave. She checked the computer. Only twenty percent completed. What the hell was it updating into? Optimus Prime? She considered hitting it with a brick, but restrained herself long enough for it to complete its pointless machinations and enable her to print off the directions, like people used to in the Dark Ages.

Luckily the gods had decided she'd eaten enough shit for one morning, and she was relieved to see an available space in the car park, albeit by the filthy car that appeared to have been pulled from the seabed. It was one minute to nine. She opened the door a little too vigorously and it banged against the Mary Celeste next to her. The window inched down, dirt accumulating on the perished rubber seals, and Hozan's eyes peered out at her. Was he living in his car? She scanned what little was visible through the gap, and sure enough was met with a panorama that looked exactly like that. Despite the fact that he was wearing a hat, which surely meant she was off the hook for stealing it, he slowly reached across to the passenger seat where his camera was sitting. She didn't wait for him to turn it on.

'I'm sorry I'm late.'

It was two minutes past nine and Jasper and Gayle were in the office.

'It's learning,' said Gayle, like she was some kind of AI. 'It understands humility.'

'I made you a tea,' said Jasper, pointing to a cup on his desk.

'Oh. Thanks.'

For some reason she'd expected a run-in, but Gayle seemed too preoccupied by a spreadsheet on her screen.

'I wondered if I might take Steve to the benefits office this afternoon,' Simone said.

Jasper tried to suppress a smile.

'It doesn't mean I want to be here,' she said quickly.

'You think any of us do?' said Gayle. 'Here. You might need this.' She pulled open a desk drawer and passed her the phone. 'It's been pinging like Babs Windsor's bra in a *Carry On* movie.'

There were no messages of any importance; just a neighbourly WhatsApp group banging on about bins and a missing cat, and one for an exercise class she never made it to. She passed it back.

'Perhaps you could keep hold of it until later.'

'Bleeding hell.' Gayle's eyes widened. 'Now it's trying to problem solve!'

'I guess if you feed it with enough data,' said Jasper.

'Still in the room,' she said.

'You can take Steve,' said Gayle, 'but be warned, you'll have a nightmare.'

'It can't be that hard.'

Gayle laughed bitterly. 'Tell you what. If the money comes through before your time is up, I'll give you the rest of your stint off for good behaviour.'

'You can do that?'

'I can do whatever I like.' She went back to her screen. 'And besides, it's not like we can't do without you. You're about as much use as a garden gnome.'

If Gayle had been holding a mic, she'd have dropped it, but Simone didn't care. If there was the tiniest chance to make it out of here sooner than anticipated, she'd take any piss-taking Gayle could throw at her.

Chapter Twenty

She'd been sat on the cheap plastic sofa for so long, her buttocks had gone numb. At least she could no longer feel the sweat pooling beneath them. Her skin was ready to melt off her body like a satin kimono in an eighties' porno. Even Steve, who was fidgeting next to her, had made some small concession to the heat by unzipping his shell suit jacket to the navel and not wearing a vest underneath it.

A voice rang out. 'Number three hundred and seven!'

Everyone glanced down at the tickets they'd pulled from the dispenser on arrival. Clutching it reminded her of being a child, waiting at the supermarket deli counter whilst her mother flirted with the faux 'butcher' over slices of corned beef. Finally, it was their turn.

The person behind the counter – Denise according to her name badge – had the air of a woman for whom breathing was too much trouble.

'How can I help you today?' The words dawdled out of her mouth with little intonation.

'I'm here to help this man claim benefits,' said Simone.

'Has he created an online account?'

'Steve?'

Steve shook his head. 'I wasn't sure how to.'

The woman gave them the supercilious smile of the carnival tin can stall man, the kind who hands you the rifle knowing full well the sight is skew-whiff and the barrel is bent.

'I'm going to need you to do that first.' Denise made the slightest inclination of her head. 'You're welcome to use the PCs over there.'

There were three PCs, all looking like they belonged in a museum. Two were occupied by young people shouting at them. An old man sat at the third, looking confused.

'Or there's an internet café round the corner.'

'I've not got any money, love,' said Steve. 'I'm homeless.'

'I can't do anything without an online account.'

'I'll do it on my mobile right now,' said Simone. 'It shouldn't take long.'

'I will have to ask you to do it elsewhere and then re-join the queue,' said Denise.

'The queue that we've already been in for several hours?'

'That's the one.'

'If I go in that queue for any longer, someone's going to file a missing person's report on me.'

The woman's eyes lazily rolled in their sockets. 'It's not that bad.'

'Isn't it? We met a baby when we joined that queue, and she's just had her first period.'

The woman shrugged, glanced at the clock on the wall behind her, and sighed. 'I'm due on a break now anyway.'

'Then we'll stay here until you get back.'

'I can't let you do that. Security issues.'

'What do you imagine we might do? Steal this biro?' Simone

picked up the pen that was attached to the desk with a bit of string and some Sellotape.

'I'm going to have to ask you to put the writing implement down.'

'Why? Are you scared I might fill out some forms correctly?'

'Leave it,' said Steve. 'It's not worth it. We'll do it another time.'

But she wasn't going anywhere. Except back in the queue it seemed.

It was another forty minutes before they were recalled to the same counter. She'd attempted to persuade Steve to go and get some water, preferably from somewhere several miles away so she didn't have to listen to his inane jabbering for a bit, but he'd politely declined on the basis that he couldn't take a hint if one abducted him in broad daylight and told him to shut the fuck up or else it would remove his fingernails one by one.

'How can I help you today?'

Denise spoke the words as if she didn't remember them. What was this? *Eternal Sunshine of the Spotless Twat?*

'You have got to be kidding me,' said Simone.

'Oh, it's you,' said Denise. 'Do you have the account details?'

She gave her the account details.

'I'm going to need his home address.'

Steve shook his head in resignation. 'I haven't got one.'

'We told you, he's homeless.'

'Is he in a hostel?' asked Denise.

'Cedar Lodge in Whitechapel. Run by this amazing woman called Gayle. She once—'

'Not now, Steve,' said Simone.

He nodded.

'We can use that as a care of address in exceptional circumstances,' said Denise. 'What are his bank account details?'

'Steve?'

'I don't have one.'

'Hmm. That's a problem.' Denise looked like problems were among her favourite things, along with dog bites, bee stings, and people feeling bad.

'Why?'

'Because it is.'

'You're saying he can't get money unless he has a bank account, but presumably he won't get a bank account unless he has money going in.'

'I don't make the rules,' said Denise.

'Is there a workaround?'

'You could designate an account for the first payment, but he'll need his own for them to continue.'

'He can use my account.'

'Ahh, thanks Sim,' said Steve.

'Don't ever call me, Sim.'

'And then do I get my money?' asked Steve.

'We need to confirm your identity. Do you have a passport, driver's licence?'

Steve shook his head.

'What about a utility bill?' said Denise.

'Are you taking the piss?' said Simone. 'For where exactly? HE. IS. HOMELESS!'

'We'll have to ask that he confirms his identity in person,' said Denise.

Simone took a deep breath. She waited. Denise also waited. Simone broke first.

'Perhaps we could do that then.'

'Sorry, you can't,' said Denise.

'Why not?'

'You need to book an appointment with a Work Coach.'

'Who's that?'

'Me.'

'We're seeing you now,' said Simone. 'You're just there.'

It would have been less frustrating talking to a malfunctioning Alexa.

'I can't do it now.'

'Why not?'

'Separate thing. And I have other people to see. They've been waiting a long time.'

'I know. Several days ago, I was one of them.'

'I told you it was impossible,' said Steve. His chipper attitude had finally given way to that of Eeyore being told Christopher Robin had developed a taste for donkey flesh.

She tried to unclench her jaw. Her neck was cramping. 'Can you book an appointment with *Work Coach* you for us?'

'No. But you can do it at one of the PCs over there.'

The old man was now using the keyboard as a pillow. Or perhaps he'd died trying to work out how to make an appointment.

'You'll need his national insurance number.'

'Steve?'

Steve could barely muster the energy to shake his head.

'You can find it on a payslip,' said Denise.

'Are you fucking kidding me?!'

She had read once that the human body was capable of exploding with the ferocity of several Hiroshima bombs, if only scientists could harness its atomic energy. They'd clearly never met Denise.

'If you're going to get aggressive…' Denise pointed to a sign that stated physical or verbal abuse would not be tolerated. Someone had put their fist through it.

Simone took a deep breath and exhaled slowly. Her mouth was claggy and dry. 'Okay, so supposing we make our appointment and then we somehow magic up the documents, is that it? Job done? He gets his payment?'

'It'll be five weeks from completion of his application,' said Denise, 'but you should get confirmation sooner.'

Five weeks. There went her chances of clocking out of the shelter earlier.

'You can apply for an advance at the Work Coach session,' said Denise.

She allowed herself a brief moment of relief.

'But the Work Coach appointment needs to have been booked within one week of the application being made, or else you need to start the whole thing again.'

'We can do that,' said Simone.

'Yeah, only I'm on holiday next week.'

'Where to. Miseryland Paris? Universal Credit Studios in Florida?'

'Tenby,' said Denise.

'So we can't actually make that appointment now.'

'You could call and see if there are any cancellations.'

'Who do we call?'

'That would be me.'

'And do you have a number?'

Denise began to write the number down on a scrap of paper.

'It's okay, I'll put it straight into my phone.'

Denise dictated the number. Seconds later, her phone began to ring. She picked it up.

'Fuck you very much,' Simone shouted into the mobile she'd just called Denise on. 'Come on, Steve. We'll find another centre to go to.'

Emerging into the blinding sunshine, she took a moment to collect her thoughts. She totally accepted that there should be checks and measures ensuring only those in genuine need could avail themselves of government cash, but these had not been small hoops to be jumped through – they called for contortion-grade moves.

'Looking for a new job? It's probably for the best.'

It took a second to register that it was Ollie who had spoken. Brilliant. She'd managed to keep the truth of her situation secret for six full days. There had always been the chance she might see someone from the office – it was only a fifteen-minute walk away – but it was four in the afternoon, nowhere near home time, and of all the possibilities, it had to be Ollie she ran into.

'What are you doing here?' she asked.

'Taking a stroll to clear my head.'

'It's always seemed pretty empty to me.'

He stepped right in front of her. 'You should be nice to me. When I'm made partner, I'll have a lot more say in how things are run. Feel free to *suck up* whenever you like. That's how you operate, isn't it?'

'You could come at me wearing a suit made of dildos and you still wouldn't do it for me,' she said. 'Although you'd have a better chance of hitting the right spot.'

He grabbed her by the upper arm, his thumb digging into it. She had no idea where Steve had got to. Still, so long as he stayed out of the picture, she could pretend her flight had been delayed or something. Ollie didn't need to know she'd been *inside* the building they were now stood outside of.

'What are you staring at?' he said to someone over her shoulder.

She pulled herself out of his grip and swivelled round in time to see a flash of neon heading straight at them with some speed. Next thing, Steve was running off and blood was streaming from Ollie's nose. It took Ollie a few seconds to play catch up on the unfolding events, but when he did, he bent over and moaned like a ghost train.

'He fucking headbutted me!'

He really had.

'Who the fuck was that?'

'Beats me,' she said, acting ignorant. 'Well, beats you.'

Blood dripped with metronomic regularity from Ollie's nostrils.

'Ow! That fucking hurts!'

What with the trodden-in chewing gum and the crimson streaks, the pavement was starting to resemble a Jackson Pollock.

'Don't just stand there, do something,' he moaned.

She did nothing except enjoy the fact that no one else passing the scene seemed to want to do anything either. Ah, London.

'Maybe he sensed that you were a dickhead. Like a pheromone that you give off. A twat signal. You just sent it up into the sky and now here we are.'

'Have you got a tissue or something?'

'Just give it a pinch.'

'I think it's fucking broken!'

'Give it an extra hard pinch then,' she said.

'You are such a bitch.'

'I have to go.' She turned in the direction Steve had headed.

'I am getting that job, Simone!'

Good job Jasper wasn't there – there really was a lot of blood. But weren't nosebleeds notorious for appearing worse than they were?

'Sorry, I just heard *I bag ebbing stat jom sibome*.'

'You'll pay for this.'

'It'll make a change to Daddy paying for everything.' She walked away with her middle finger held up over her shoulder.

A few hundred metres down the road, Steve beckoned her from an alleyway. Ensuring Ollie hadn't followed her, she ducked into it. His forehead was miraculously injury-free.

'Jesus, Steve. What did you do that for?'

'You looked like you needed help. I tried to help you.'

'Why?'

This seemed to be the stupidest question in the world to him. 'Because you tried to help me.'

'But I didn't have a choice in the matter.'

'Neither did I. I guess the urge just comes from a different place.'

Huh. She didn't know what to say.

'Who was that chief anyway?' he asked.

'A work colleague.'

Steve whistled. 'If that's what it takes to get the big bucks, I'm better off out of it.'

'Shall we get some water?' she suggested.

'That'd be sound.'

'And then shall we try and get you a bank account? You're going to need one eventually.'

She checked to see if the coast was clear.

'You won't tell anyone to fuck off when we're in there, will you?' asked Steve.

'Not if you don't drop the nut on anyone.'

'Okay, our kid. It's a deal.'

Later on, she sat at her laptop, googling how to work the system. Steve had been right – it was a joke, engineered to obfuscate and befuddle. The whole thing was like that movie *Inception*: layers within layers of bullshit, masquerading as something good. But she was determined to nail it. This was precisely the kind of thorny problem she liked to resolve. Having done her research, she would be better prepared for next time.

It was only when she finally closed her computer and was vegging in front of the TV that it finally dawned on her that Oliver hadn't been at all surprised to see her still in London. Had Tony buckled so soon?

Chapter Twenty-One

The next day, the tube issues were still ongoing, so she'd driven in again. Gayle must have seen her park up, because as soon as she poked her head round the office door, Gayle asked her to take Tasha to see a flat she'd been offered. There had been no sign of Jasper.

Now the girl was sat next to her, a human-shaped black blot on the cream leather interior of her Mini. She would ordinarily put the roof down in this weather, but it seemed ostentatious; an affront to the girl's situation; a slap in her pale made-up face. Instead she put the air-con on, its gentle hum drawing attention to the wedge of silence between them. The girl didn't attempt to fill it; she just stared out at the city as it crawled by, clutching the piece of paper on which the address of her potential new home was written. It was going to be a long way to not talk. But what did you chat to an eighteen-year-old about? Simone was out of the loop on music. She was culturally inoperative. The only trend she kept up with nowadays was fashion. When she first came to London, she enjoyed what the city had to offer: afternoons at the Tate; the Barbican; Royal Festival Hall. Wandering down the

South Bank, she would imagine people watching her, a star in the movie of her own imagination. She was a modern-day Edie Sedgwick or Mary Quant, ready to be part of a scene in no time. As it transpired, she never was adopted by bohemians. Sure, she'd been an artist's muse for a brief time, but not in the way she'd hoped.

They were headed to Dagenham, an outpost of London recently named the capital's unhappiest place to live, eleven miles east from here; she'd have to find something to say.

'So, where are you from originally?' It was a shit opener, like a speed-dating question offered up by the terminally uninteresting.

'Luton,' said Tasha.

'Really?'

'Why would I lie about that?'

'It's just I'm from Biscot.' It was only a ten-minute drive away from Luton. 'What school did you go to?'

'Dutfield.'

'I was Lea Park.'

'The performing one?' said Tasha.

'Yep.'

'We thought the people from your school were dickheads.'

They'd stopped at a traffic light and Tasha glanced across to observe the effect of her words.

'I thought the people from my school were dickheads too,' said Simone.

The girl didn't react. She was ice.

'You're a long way from home.'

'Not far enough,' said Tasha.

The girl – was it even appropriate to call her a girl? – stared out the window once more. They were coming up to a carriageway, intersected by a roundabout, and there was a tent encampment under the overpass. Tasha rubbernecked as they passed, as if expecting to see something notable, but to Simone it looked like all the other shanty encampments that had sprung up around the city.

Ordinarily she found it easy to make small talk. It wasn't something she enjoyed necessarily, but it was a skill she'd perfected by being in PR, giving off the façade of an easy conversationalist, fluidly recalling clients' kids' names, suppliers' wearisome anecdotes, where people went on holiday, what kind of pets they had. The interest she took was invariably false – an actor reading lines without emotional investment – but with Tasha it wasn't so easy. She might not know much about her, but she still felt she had some understanding of her situation, and that she probably wouldn't enjoy hearing more.

A car stopped suddenly ahead of them, its red rear lights perforating her reverie. She pumped the brakes, the ABS kicking in, and the car juddered as it tried to slow without locking the wheels. She reflexively put her arm across the girl, like her father used to, somehow imagining that his fallible bone and sinew could be more effective than a specially engineered belt. When the car finally stopped, just inches from the other's bumper, they bounced back into their seats. The girl rubbed at her abdomen under the lap strap.

'Are you okay?' asked Simone.

'Uh-huh.'

The car up ahead moved off, taking a wide arc around a pigeon that was pecking at some chips on the road. She'd nearly totalled her car so some vermin could have a snack.

She opened the window, shouted 'Wanker!' at it.

The pigeon looked up, unperturbed, still not moving even when the car behind them beeped impatiently.

Tasha popped her head out of her window. 'Wanker!' she shouted at its driver.

As the car swerved round them, finally sending the pigeon fluttering off in alarm, they exchanged the briefest of smiles.

The landlady, one aptly named Mrs Grimshaw, had a head like a skinless watermelon, her bright red face peppered with dark pockmarks. Tiny teeth like a toddler's leered out from her bulbous skull. She was unsettling, but not as unsettling as the flat.

The portents hadn't been good from the outside. It was part of a large red brick tenement with the datestone so crumbled it was hard to tell when it had been erected, but judging by the decay, around the time of the Pyramids. Litter gathered like snowdrifts against its walls. The interior was an insult to habitation. There were two rooms, although that was far too generous a description for what was essentially a single space, dissected by a partition that didn't even extend the full height of the ceiling. The smell was like wet soil in her nostrils, and damp crept like chromatography across paper that clung desperately to the walls and ceiling. Tasha's shoulders drooped as she took it all in.

'And this has been approved by the council?' asked Simone.

Gayle had told her people needing social housing in London outstripped property availability by three hundred to one. This particular flat was a private rental to be paid for by the local authority.

Grimshaw didn't respond, and instead proceeded to show them round like she was a tour guide for the National Trust.

'This is the bedsitting room. As you can observe, it offers a generous living area, complete with solid pine wooden wardrobe and small oak drawer unit. There's an abundance of light that comes in through the original sash window, which offers a view of the shared courtyard.'

She went to take in the view. The 'courtyard' was a grey slabbed area that housed huge rotund skips for collective waste.

'There's a capacious, comfortable full-sized double bed.'

The bed was a cheap divan, bedecked in bright blue patterned fabric to hide the stains, and with a flimsy hollow base in which you could hide bodies. In the centre of the mattress was a patch that had defied the camouflage.

'There's blood on the mattress,' she pointed out.

'It's coffee,' said Grimshaw.

'That doesn't make it better.'

The woman shrugged.

'What's behind that?' asked Tasha. She pointed to a grubby curtain hanging on a piece of stretched washing line that further divided the truncated room.

Grimshaw pulled it aside with a flourish. She regarded them expectantly, as if anticipating a round of applause. Behind it was the tiniest of shower cubicles, no bigger than a public phone box – and in no better shape than one – its glass frosted with limescale, and its sealant peeling off like ribbons of dirt.

'Where's the toilet?' asked Simone. The shower looked like it might have been used as one.

'There's one along the corridor.'

'And how many have access to that?'

Grimshaw didn't answer. 'If you'd care to step through into the annex, there's a fully fitted kitchen.'

She went in. There was no window, only the light coming in from over the partition wall. A single bulb hung from a wire that had grown furry from accumulated dust.

'It has all the modern conveniences you might expect. Fridge with freezer compartment, electric four ring cooker and oven, hot running water between the hours of ten and three.'

She opened her mouth, but the landlady cut across her.

'It's a pressure thing. You'd need to take it up with the appropriate water authority.'

With her snivelling voice, peculiar parlance and artful manner, the woman might have been a Dickensian character. Simone went to look inside the cooker. Quick as a flash, Grimshaw inserted herself between her and the appliance.

'Granted, the stove requires a little spruce up. The previous tenants left in a rather, shall we say, precipitous fashion.'

'Did they die suddenly in that bed?'

The woman continued to lean against the hob, a human in Chupa Chups form. A patch of black mould bloomed like a Rorschach test on the wall behind her. She thought of Jasper. *What do you see?* Asthma. Fungal infections. Bronchitis. She pointed it out to Grimshaw.

'Just a soupçon of condensation. It's imperative that the air be allowed to circulate in these old buildings to prevent such predicaments.' She glanced over Simone's shoulder. 'Now where's your acquaintance got to?'

'Let's face it, she can't be that far away.'

The woman ignored the barb.

They stepped back around the divide into the bedroom. Tasha was gazing up at the ceiling with intense concentration. Both Simone and the landlady fell silent. Something was scurrying around in the cavity above them, making an urgent tapping and scratching sound.

'What is that?' asked Tasha.

'Let's hope it's rats, or the cockroaches are going to be frigging gargantuan.' Simone pretended to listen more intently. 'Hang on. I think they're communicating in morse code. *What's that you're saying? Run away. Run away.*'

But far from being disconcerted, Grimshaw redoubled her efforts. 'It's just these old houses. Pipes and things. Always lots of unusual noises. It's part of their charm.'

Simone peered squarely at her. Seeing how horribly she'd turned out as an adult, she was glad she'd had such bad acne as a teenager.

Tasha continued to examine the ceiling. 'There aren't any smoke alarms. What if there was a fire?'

'It might improve the place,' said Simone.

But the girl wasn't listening; she was calculating. Grimshaw sandwiched herself between the two of them; she sensed prey and was preparing to pounce.

'I suppose I could see my way clear to installing one, if that offered you the reassurances you required.'

She was like Fagin, snaffling an orphan and putting it on the pathway to bad deeds.

'You're not actually considering this place, are you? The council can't possibly know it's in this state.'

'It certainly represents excellent value for money,' said Grimshaw. 'It's half the price of most other flats in these environs.'

'Because it's literally half a flat!'

'The plain fact is, there are a multitude of individuals who've already expressed an interest.'

'Who? Fumigators? Vermin exterminators? Showrunners for *Britain's Next Top Hovel*?'

Grimshaw's perpetual red face darkened, and her tiny teeth set into a contemptuous grin. She quickly rallied. 'It seems to me that your acquaintance is, perchance, facing a shortage of alternatives. But'—she made a sweeping gesture and half-bow—'I'm not an ungenerous woman. I am cognisant of the difficulties of finding accommodation in this fair city, which is why, out of the goodness of my heart, I have agreed to consider renting this particular abode to someone of her unemployed persuasion.'

If she played join-the-dots on the woman's face, and created a picture of another face, it would still be ugly.

'How very generous of you. Come on, Tasha, let's go.'

But Tasha didn't move. In fact, she very much seemed to be actively weighing up the place's non-existent merits.

'You can't be serious. There's condensation. In Summer!'

'As I think I intimated before, it merely requires the frequent throughput of air.'

'Come on! There's so much damp in here, we could have ditched the satnav and used a divining rod to find the place!'

'Could you fit an extractor fan?' asked Tasha.

Grimshaw opened her arms. 'Why increase the burden on the electricity, and your coffers, when opening a window whilst preparing the evening's repast would suffice?'

'The window that's been taped up to hide the gaping holes in the frame?'

'A common problem with sash windows in these historical properties. It would be a crime to replace them.'

'This isn't a listed building; it's a grade-one shithole!'

Grimshaw's mask of affability slipped. 'Have you heard the expression beggars can't be choosers?'

She had. To her shame, she'd been close to using it during her run-in with Street Pete.

'Simone,' said Tasha. 'It's okay.'

'Tasha, you can't let this walking wankstain persuade you that this is anything other than a hovel.'

Grimshaw threw her hands up in the air. 'That's it. You can't have it!'

'But—' said Tasha.

'I've decided. Sorry, little lady. Your … whatever she is … has just fucked your chances of getting your own place.' All pretence of poncy language had gone now. 'Good luck finding anywhere better than this.'

'But I barely know her,' said Tasha.

'I don't give a shit.' She ushered them out the door. 'Go on. Get out, the pair of you. You try and do something nice, something charitable, and this is the thanks you get.'

She attempted to slam the door in their faces, but she'd left it on the latch and it banged against its wooden surround, instantly creating a crack in the plasterboard fascia within which it was housed. Simone was about to throw in a final rejoinder, but Tasha had stormed off down the corridor.

All the way back, Tasha gave her the silent treatment, staring straight ahead with her arms folded across her chest. It was perplexing; she'd imagined Tasha might be the type to appreciate her having put the landlady in her place, but perhaps the goth exterior hid a much more emo interior. It was only when they passed the tent encampment again that the girl's gaze shifted, once more lingering on the tents that sat incongruously in their urban surroundings.

When she finally pulled into the car park (thankfully not next to Hozan's car) and switched off the engine, Tasha aggressively yanked her seatbelt off, sent it flying behind her, and opened the door.

Simone stayed her with a hand on her arm. 'I'm sorry if I did something wrong back there.'

'Finally, you apologise!'

'I was doing you a favour. That place was terrible. You need to wait for something better.'

'Oh, yeah, because I am overflowing with options.'

'It wasn't fit to live in.'

'Neither is the doorway of a KFC.'

Ouch.

'I know you must be keen to get somewhere.'

Tasha turned in her seat. 'What? You work in a shelter for a few days and now you know everything? You know what's best for me?'

'I only meant—'

'What the hell do you know? Do you know I got kicked out of

home at the age of fifteen? Do you know I slept on friends' sofas for six months so that I could do my GCSEs? Six As and two Bs if you're interested, not that it'll do me any good. Do you know what it's like to walk the streets all night for fear of what might happen if you stop walking? To be called a lazy bitch every day? To be spat at? To have food thrown at you? To be picking rice out of your hair and not know where your next shower is coming from?'

Simone shrank back in her chair.

'What's that? You don't know?' Tasha shook her head in contempt. 'You don't know shit about what is, or isn't, good for me.'

'But you have the shelter for now, right? Until something else turns up?'

'I can't stay here.'

'I know it's not ideal, but at least it's not crawling with mould.'

'I can't stay here.'

'Gayle isn't going to throw you out.'

'Listen to the words I am saying. I. Can't. Stay. Here.'

'Is it because Steve might talk you to death?'

The joke didn't land.

'Because I'm pregnant, okay! I'm fucking pregnant. And when you're homeless and you have a baby, you go to a women and baby shelter. And I don't want to raise my kid in a fucking women and baby shelter.'

'Oh.'

'Oh.' Tasha rubbed her abdomen in the same spot where the belt had dug into her. 'Not so talkative now, are you?'

Whilst Simone was processing this latest development, Tasha swung her legs out of the car and stormed off.

'How's it going?'

Jasper had seen events unfold from the patch of grass next to the car park.

'Really badly, thanks for asking.'

He was wearing a pair of Wayfarer knockoffs and, despite the accompanying naff Gap top, looked exceedingly cool.

'Want to talk about it?'

'I don't believe that a problem shared is a problem halved. I'm more of a problem shared is still a problem, but now you have someone giving you unsolicited advice that you almost certainly don't intend to take – *and* a problem.'

'You're very passive aggressive.'

'That's hurtful. I was aiming for aggressive.'

He smiled, his cheekbones infuriatingly augmented by the sunglasses.

'Advice is like the clap,' she continued. 'No one wants it, but there's plenty of folk out there prepared to give it to you.'

'Advice is like a sexually transmitted disease.' He nodded. 'Got it.'

He was too calm for her liking. Too in control of his emotional thermostat. She took a tin of lip balm from her pocket, smeared some on, and offered it to him.

He shook his head. 'Not if you've got gonorrhoea.'

He was also too verbally deft.

'Not smoking today?' he asked.

Christ no. If she had a cigarette for every time she got stressed in this place, she'd end up with a mouth like a Shar Pei's butthole.

'Did you know?' she asked.

'About the pregnancy?'

'So you did.'

'We talk. She's a great kid, despite everything she's been through.'

'But she's just a kid.'

'She's got her head screwed on.'

'That's not the only thing that got screwed.' She gazed heavenward. 'It's the preventability of it. What is wrong with these people? Why can't they see what a mess they're making of everything and pedal back a bit on the catastrophic life decisions?'

'You think it's just a question of choice?'

'Yeah.'

'And you think you're in complete control of your actions?'

'Yeah.'

'So you never get angry?'

'Yeah, but—'

'Or excited?'

'Yeah, but—'

'Or frustrated?'

'I'm getting frustrated *now*.'

'Precisely,' he said, pleased to have illustrated his point. 'You don't have complete control over your emotions. And if you don't have control over your emotions, how do you imagine that you have control over your decisions, especially if they're emotionally motivated?'

'You're talking bollocks.'

'That's not a robust enough rebuttal. I expect better of you.'

It surprised her to imagine that he had any expectation of her at all.

'I'm just pointing out that changes in brain chemistry alter our behaviour,' he said. 'But how much control do you have over your brain chemistry?'

She had to admit probably very little.

'The brain is a physical system like any other,' he continued. 'You can no more will it to operate than you can will your heart to beat.'

'But your job is to try and change how it works, no? Are you saying you can't? Are we back to you being shit at your job again?'

'I'm not saying I can't have a marginal impact. Flick a small switch that leads to better decision-making, that might lead to further better decisions. But I am saying that some people are, through life, luck, whatever, predisposed to being bad decision-makers. Therefore, we need to cut them some slack for their bad choices.'

'But they still have choice, right? They could still decide to *not* make shitty decisions.'

'That depends on how you view it,' he said. 'I believe we have a lot less control than we imagine. If any.'

'Are you saying you don't believe in free will? David Hume would be most disappointed.'

'You know about free will? I'm impressed.'

'Yeah, it was a movie about some orphan befriending a killer whale, wasn't it?'

'Sorry. I didn't mean to patronise you.'

But she wasn't letting him off the hook that easily.

'Why be impressed in the first place? If you reject free will for determinism, there is no *being impressed*, right? I was always destined to know about David Hume because I was always destined to do philosophy GCSE.'

'Touché.'

'Besides, it's too convenient an excuse. Oh, I can't stop drinking, I have no free will. I was *bound* to end up on the streets. That's too depressing.'

'Really?' he said. 'Isn't there something quite freeing about the notion of the *unfolding of the inevitable*. You just have to wait and see what happens.'

'But I've worked hard to get to where I am. Are you saying it's all luck?'

People like Ollie were lucky. *She'd* pulled herself up by her bootstraps.

'It's funny,' he said. 'People who are doing badly will put it down to luck, but people who are doing well will always say it's their own doing.'

'But you make your own luck.'

'How can that be when you consider all the stimulus acting on you? You can never truly be independent of the influence of other people, no matter how much you tell yourself you are, or how much you might like to be.' He pulled his glasses down and peered over the top of them at her. 'Can I give you some advice?'

'Are you kidding me? After what I said before.'

He chuckled.

'What are you going to say? That we should be fine with her throwing her life away? That the whole thing should be allowed to play out because it's just some inevitable consequence of the Big Bang?'

'I was going to tell you that a wasp has landed on your hair. You might want to shake it off.'

'Shit!' She waved her head around in an ungainly fashion until it flew away.

'You're welcome.' He leaned back on his elbows, more relaxed than ever. 'For someone who claims not to care about anything, you're getting very worked up.'

'I don't want to get stung!'

He gave her a lazy *you know exactly what I mean* eyeroll and pushed his glasses back up his nose.

'Come on. How hard can it be to *not* get pregnant?' she said. 'How difficult is it to have a coil, or wear a condom, or get the morning after pill? It's her decision if she wants to screw her life up. I don't care.'

'You don't care. If you say so.'

He said it in a way that made her want to rip the glasses off his face and shove them up his arse.

'Try and cut them some slack, though. Choice isn't black or white. It happens in tiny increments, and under the influence of a gazillion things out of our control. And undoing that programming, that soup of interference, that myriad of mental molecular movements, is far from easy. Understanding that makes it easier to have empathy.'

'I have empathy.'

'I didn't say you didn't. But this isn't about you.'

'I just find it frustrating when people are idiots.'

He pushed himself back upright. 'I should be getting back to work. But out of interest, how much can you forgive *yourself* for your actions?'

'This isn't about me, remember.'

He smiled.

'How do you think it's going to turn out for her though?' she asked.

'I don't know. I'm a psychologist, not a psychic.'

'That flat we went to see, it was genuinely horrific. It's hard not to be concerned.'

'There are six billion people in the world, six million in this city. Perhaps something, or someone, comes along and changes things for the better?'

He rubbed some dirt from his palms. They had a crosshatch pattern on them from where he'd been leaning against the heat-scorched grass.

'I'm offsite this afternoon,' he said. 'You'll probably be gone before I get back, so have a good weekend.'

Disappointment nibbled at her as he walked away, his languid stride emphasising the topography of his bottom. She'd forgotten how much she enjoyed a philosophical chinwag, and it would have been fun to pick it up again later. She consoled herself with uncharitable thoughts of what charitable deeds he probably got up to at weekends. Litter picking in the grounds of a children's hospital. Volunteering at a shelter for depressed donkeys. Crocheting socks for Syrian refugees.

Nothing that she'd ever be into, that was for sure.

Chapter Twenty-Two

On the last stretch to Wei's from the tube, she found herself walking alongside a slow-moving funeral cortège. A string of cars glinting like black pearls crawled along the street. A Fulham crest made from flowers was leaned up against a coffin festooned in *Dad* and *Brother* floral tributes. At least his family had the small comfort of knowing there was one less Cottagers fan in the world. She subconsciously crossed herself, a liturgical hangover from a Catholic mum who loved the drama of ingratiating herself into other people's sorrow.

Inside Wei's flat, a portable air-con unit was cranked up to eleven, yet still her skin prickled with the echo of the heat outside. As Wei fussed around, his miniature dachshund Otto trotted in wearing a small straw hat on its head and a sorry look on its face.

'Just because you once worked in a dungeon,' she said, 'doesn't mean you can torture a little sausage in this way.'

'I need someone to take care of him for a few days when we go to Pride in Amsterdam. Want to volunteer?'

'No.'

'I told David you'd say that. He wondered if the hat might help swing the deal.'

'It did. In the wrong direction.'

Otto dropped his bottom the full two inches it needed to travel to reach floor level, then dropped his head onto his paws.

'It's okay, baby,' said Wei. 'We'll get you signed up to Borrow My Doggy.'

'Why would anyone want to actively care for a dog that isn't their own?'

'You don't need to possess something to get pleasure from it.'

Marcus scampered into her thoughts. She was seeing him tomorrow, although she still hadn't entirely forgiven him for leaving her high and wet the last time they'd chatted.

'It's called unconditional love,' said Wei. 'You should try it sometime.'

'Love is always conditional.'

He pulled over his nail cart. 'What is it today then?'

Her nails were an absolute mess from all the cleaning she'd done.

'Maybe back to natural for now.'

'If you wear gloves, the lacquer should be okay.'

She hadn't forgotten what Gayle had said. 'No. I'll get them redone in a few weeks.'

The bowl of water he soaked her fingers in was refreshingly cool and smelled of rosemary and peppermint. She lay back and breathed in its soothing aromas.

'How's things at the shelter?' he asked.

She told him a little about what she'd been up to. 'I'm not sure whether I'm out of my comfort zone or out of my depth. I don't know how to handle them.'

'They're not poisonous snakes. They're just people like us.'

She told him a little more about Hozan, Tasha and Steve. 'They're definitely not like us.'

He removed her hands from the water and towelled them off. 'What about the staff? Are they all hippies?'

An image of Gayle flashed through her head. 'Not really, no.'

Wei began snipping away at her cuticles. The peppermint stung the remaining skin, but not unpleasantly.

'There is this one guy…'

'Is there now?'

'No, I don't mean like that.' She described her early run-ins with Jasper, surprised by the amount of detail she recalled.

'OMG. You already have history!'

'Hmm. I can't work him out.'

'Like a puzzle you want to undress?'

'I don't fancy him.'

'He sounds fanciable.'

'He works in a homeless shelter, Wei. He's not exactly operating in my league.'

'And you don't do nice guys.'

'I wouldn't say he's nice, exactly.'

As Wei filed and buffed her nails, she recounted all of Jasper's digs, which she could also recall in full technicolour. He was definitely funny, but it was more than that.

'Most guys, they recount some crap they've read in a Substack newsletter and assume they're smart. But he really thinks about things and puts the time in to form his own opinions.'

'It sounds like you've been thinking about his thing quite a lot,' he cackled.

The dog pricked up its straw hat. Had she? It was probably because she had nothing more mentally strenuous to get her head into.

'I'm not interested in him. I just find him interesting.'

'Isn't that how it starts?'

Wei picked up a bright vermillion polish and waved it at her. 'Shall I at least do your toenails?'

She nodded her approval. He unscrewed the bottle and set to work.

'Are you not a little bit tempted?'

'He doesn't go for girls like me.'

'What, bitches?'

She prodded him with her free foot. 'Do you think I'm a bitch?'

'No.' He seemed uncertain.

She frowned.

'Stop that. You'll get wrinkles.'

'Do you think I need Botox?'

'The best time to plant a tree is twenty years ago. But the second-best time is now.'

'So that's a yes?'

'I'm kidding! You shouldn't have Botox.'

She smiled, satisfied.

'How would you be able to do those withering looks of yours if you did?'

She kicked him again, causing him to smudge her last toe. When he'd sorted it out, he spoke again.

'So, have you got a picture of him?'

'Who, Jasper? No!'

'I'll Google him,' he said. 'What's the name of the place?'

She doubted he'd turn anything up, but gave him the details. She lay back again and listened to the gentle snores of the dog whilst her toes dried. Wei sniffed loudly. She glanced across. He had tears in his eyes.

'What's wrong?'

He passed the phone to her. There was a picture of Hozan, wearing a cap and sunglasses, but unmistakably him, stood on one side of his far-less-filthy car. On the other side, looking apologetically awkward but unapologetically gorgeous, was none other than resident psychologist and Mr Do-Gooder himself, Jasper. She read the article. The gist of it was that Hozan was a vulnerable refugee for whom the shelter didn't have enough room, and so Jasper had put an appeal out on social media for a tent in which they could temporarily house him. Someone had come forward to ask if their about-to-fail-its-MOT car might offer a more secure solution, and so Hozan had moved into the car park, still able to avail himself of the shelter's day services.

'I'm in love,' said Wei.

'I can't believe you're taking the side of someone you've not even met!'

'Who said I'm taking sides? What a sweetheart though. And what about the guy who gave him a *car*...' He theatrically wiped away another tear.

'Ah well, if you were to speak to Jasper, he'd probably say something like *he had no choice but to become a good person because it was a natural consequence of everything that had gone before, and therefore doesn't deserve too much credit*. That's ridiculous, right?'

'Dolly says be whatever your dreams – and *luck* – lets you be.'

'You don't buy the *you can't help the way you turn out* bollocks too, do you?'

'I couldn't help being gay. And trust me, I tried.'

'But that's genetic.'

'Maybe it all is?'

'You sound just like him!'

'So he's deep, kind and good-looking. Tell me why you don't like him again?'

'Because ... oh, forget it. I can't describe it.'

'You sure you're not just upset because he's out of your league?'

'No. *I'm* out of *his* league.'

'Babe. You're hot, but...' He struggled for the right words. 'It'd be like Cruella De Vil trying to bang Gandhi.'

'I don't want to sleep with him. I just want him to want to sleep with me.'

'You see. That's a crazy thing to say. But don't worry, he'd probably say you can't help being a mad bitch.'

'You said I wasn't a bitch!'

Otto jumped up and whimpered.

'It's okay, baby.'

Wei picked him up, removed the hat, and planted a huge kiss on the dog's head. She leaned across and fussed him too. She knew Wei was exaggerating for comic effect, but the use of the word *bitch* niggled at her in a way it might not have done previously. So she wasn't the simpering, nurturing type. That didn't make her a bad person; it just made her a different person from the one society expected her to be.

'Supposing I wanted to do something thoughtful to prove him wrong about me,' she said.

'You can't do a nice thing just to prove someone wrong. It cancels it out.'

'He'd probably say that if the net effect was good, that's what counts.'

Wei looked into the dog's eyes. 'She's also spent a long time thinking about what he'd say, eh Otto?'

She frowned.

He motioned to her forehead. 'Maybe you do need Botox?'

The door buzzer sounded. Otto wriggled in Wei's hands. He put him down and the dog ran out of the room.

'That's my next appointment. Go on. Get out.'

She heard David answer the door and invite whoever it was into the lounge to wait. Wei picked up the bowl and ushered her out of the room ahead of him.

'They're just people who want to be treated as such. When I first came out, people treated me like I was an alien. Like they believed my feelings weren't the same as theirs, that I didn't care about being called names. The whole time I just wanted to be seen as me.'

Simone had experienced something similar when her dad died. Not able to understand, or not wanting to, her friends had given her a wide berth, her grief somewhat harshing the vibe of being sixteen and wanting to drink own-label vodka and get titted-up behind the bike sheds. She opened the front door and stepped onto the communal walkway between the flats. The heat enveloped her in its clammy clutches.

Wei was still holding the bowl. Faint rainbows danced on the water's surface. 'For them, it's the same,' he said. 'They'll just want to feel normal again. So help them feel normal.'

Chapter Twenty-Three

Marcus was sat naked on the hotel's desk chair, arms restrained behind his back. He had compared himself to James Bond in Casino Royal, a throwaway statement that he'd then escalated into a full-on role play situation. She wasn't really into pretending to be someone else during sex; she preferred to think that just being herself was enough to turn people on. Clearly Marcus was no longer feeling the same way.

'Okay then, Miss Drippy Pussy. Show me you have ways of making me talk.'

When she'd arrived at the hotel room, he'd seemed genuinely excited to see her. He told her he'd bought her a gift and was impatient to give it to her. He'd produced a black velvet-coated box, about the size of a paperback book, that had tinkled when she shook it. Jewellery. He'd bought her some jewellery. But when she prised open the case and felt the lid spring up in her hands, she hadn't found a beautiful necklace nestled in the silk interior, she'd found a cheap pair of handcuffs. She'd turned them over, pretending to admire them, but really searching for a maker's mark, some proof they weren't just a trashy novelty he'd snuck into superior packaging. There hadn't been one. Not Agent Provocateur. Not Coco De Mer. Not Saint Laurent. Just tat. Well, not just. More like tat serving as an irritating reminder of the circumstances leading to her having the very week she'd been hoping to forget all about. Of course, Marcus had insisted they put the cuffs to immediate use.

She leaned over him, breasts brushing across his flushed face, and kissed him roughly.

'Interesting torture technique,' he said.

She said nothing, but went again, this time gently biting his lip. He murmured his approval. She bore down harder, wondering what pressure would be required to draw blood. He pulled away before she got to find out.

'Careful! I'm seeing the in-laws later. You can't leave any trace.'

It was tempting to do the precise opposite. To press her nails into his flesh and leave deep, half-moon tracks that wouldn't fade before he returned to his family. Instead, she pulled his head back.

'Apologies,' she purred into his ear. 'It's just that I've had a very bad week and now I intend to take it out on you.'

'I do hope so.' He didn't seem to notice the genuine intention in her tone.

She traced her nails across his chest, wound one of the hairs around her finger. He tensed in anticipation.

'Are you not going to ask me what I've had to do?' she asked.

He *never* asked her what she'd been doing.

'Was it a threesome with some fit Russian agents?'

She pulled at the hair, felt the resistance of his skin. Then it gave way. She held it up and examined it closely. It was grey.

'I'm afraid not. Want to try again?'

He clearly did.

'Did you have to suck snake venom out of someone's cock to save them?'

She grabbed another hair, pulling it more slowly, letting the tension settle for longer. Then ping!

'Nope.'

'Was it diffusing some massive weapon with your bare hands? Because I think this heat-seeking missile is due to go off in a couple of minutes, so you might want to contain the situation.'

He was enjoying himself. She wasn't.

'What I did was try to help someone claim benefits they were entitled to.'

An uncertain look crossed his face. 'Not sure of the relevance to the present situation.'

'Think of it as important backstory to what I'm going to do to you. Like when the baddy tells them the plan.'

He wasn't convinced, but she gave his dick a stroke, which satisfied him things were still moving in the right direction.

'And it was very, very hard,' she said.

'Was it now?'

She spread her legs and stepped forward across his lap. His penis strained to reach her, but she kept herself just out of range.

'I wondered if it was just me; if I was missing something.' She cupped his balls in her palm.

He shifted his weight forward, pressing himself against her hand. 'The only thing you're missing is having this inside you.'

'And then I did some research.'

'Ooh, going for a politico vibe. Erin Brockovich style. Unusual for you. I like it.'

She palpated the hard jewels in their soft pouches. So delicate. So vulnerable. So utterly grim if you thought about them too much.

'And the whole thing is far more ludicrous than I could have imagined. Unlawful refusals of help by councils. Discrimination against disabled people. EU workers left in limbo. People

SAL THOMAS

financially penalised for trying to find work. Shouldn't you be drawing attention to this?'

'I am drawing your attention to it. See, it's waving.' He was tensing his muscles, getting his cock to bob up and down, beckoning her like a giant's finger.

She squeezed his balls harder, felt the pressure of them against each other. Instinctively he backed off, but his balls weren't going with him. A flicker of uncertainty crossed his face.

'Are you serious right now?' he said.

Was she?

'Just getting into the character, babe.'

He wasn't going to be convinced a second time. 'Well, can you get more into the character of someone in an X-rated movie? Turn around. Show me your asshole.'

She was normally happy to acquiesce to his demands during sex. It made her feel desirable, like he wanted to take in every inch of her. But today she didn't want to do as she was told.

'No,' she said.

'Eh?'

'I said no.'

She felt decidedly odd, like she didn't want to play act at hurting him, she really wanted to do it. With the girls away and nothing else to do this weekend, she'd been looking forward to seeing him, but now she was here, she wondered whether she'd rather be at home.

'And yes, I am serious,' she said. 'Why aren't you reporting on it?'

What was up with her?

'I'm sorry to break it to you, babe, but my readers aren't interested in the plight of poor people; they're interested in exploiting poor people.'

'But it's not fair.'

162

'Aww, sweetheart. Are you having a moment of awakening? Are you starting to think about people other than yourself?'

'I'm just saying that—'

'How charming. Not great timing, though. Perhaps we can dissect the relative merits and demerits of the welfare state after I've ejaculated over your bum? I find I'm more able to concentrate on political discourse when my balls are empty.'

His penis wilted. She was reminded of the dummy that she'd tried to massage to life. That place. Those people. Invisibly worming their way under her skin like fragments of fibreglass. She was uncertain what to do. It was a matter of pride that she could get him off in seconds if she so chose, but equally, she was starting to wonder if perhaps the real power lay in not giving him what he wanted. She was caught between a cock and a hard-on.

'I'm sorry,' he said, when it was clear she wasn't going to comply. 'I'm a bit stressed.'

She gazed at his reflection in the room's full-length mirror. The slightly sagging belly, the T-shirt tan he'd developed since she'd last seen him. He was more M than 007.

'You really are cute when you're thoughtful,' he said.

She wondered what Jasper might look like if he were sat here. Or what he'd think of this situation. He'd probably approve of the subjugation of Marcus, less of the spreading of her arse cheeks. But when had Marcus been anything less than an egotist who used her primarily for his sexual pleasure? And when did that start to become a problem?

'Hey ... baby.' His voice was like molasses, trying a different tack. 'I don't have to be away for another hour. Let's finish up here, we can order a drink on room service, and then you can ask me whatever you like. How does that sound?'

He did his best sad little downward smile which crinkled his eyes in all the right places. She didn't want to relent, but her resolve was crumbling. Her problem wasn't really with him, was it? And did she really want to be talking about the intricacies of government policy when she had her own special benefits to claim right here? It was just the frustrations of the week imposing on the moment. Nothing more than that. She straddled him, felt him fatten against her thigh as he nuzzled her neck. She closed her eyes, ground herself against him, and attempted to get back in the mood.

Then she smiled wryly to herself. Perhaps there was some fun to be had in pretending *he* was someone else for a change.

Chapter Twenty-Four

The heatwave in London was continuing into its third week. The air was as still and torpid as stagnant water, rendering sleep impossible. She wished she'd stayed at Marcus's hotel, with its cooling air-con and soothing white noise, rather than have to open her windows to the sound of urban foxes screeching, or the restless sense of countless other bodies tossing and turning in the night.

She'd had too much time to think about the previous evening, too much brain space given over to the way she'd felt. When her and Marcus had got together, the whole thing had felt exciting and illicit. The casual stolen moments and hot sex had been more than enough. But the shine was wearing off and an unattractive patina was developing from continued exposure.

It was six in the morning. She cast off the sticky sheet that had wound itself into a wick during her nocturnal thrashings and got up to make coffee. Whilst the rich aroma of Columbia's finest filled the air, she replied to her emails.

There weren't nearly enough for her liking. A sum total of seven cc's (completely ignorable), three requests from her team asking where to find files (quickly actioned), and one note from Tony promising that he hadn't told Ollie that she wasn't on holiday. Lying bastard. At least Ollie had two black eyes and an expensive corrective surgery bill to fix a nose that was definitely broken. But things were going more smoothly in her absence than she was comfortable with. Why else did you take holidays from work, if not to prove how indispensable you were at your job?

On the street below, some beefy guy was standing idly by the flats' garden wall, seemingly waiting for someone. He turned his head and spat, a lumpen oyster of gob landing on the path to the front door. She considered shouting at him, but she'd probably get a stone through the window. Such was the lot of women: putting up with men's unshakeable sense of entitlement, never fully expressing themselves for fear of the consequences.

She poured herself a coffee and pressed her fingers to the side of the mug until they stung. Okay, she wasn't so cliched as to think all men were wankers. Forgetting the gambling stuff, Steve had done her a solid by standing up for her. But Ghastly was a horrible specimen of humankind, and Tony also an absolute horror show. Wei was a darling, but he was a friend, so couldn't be bunched in with the other dick-toting detritus. And Jasper? So he wasn't the type to spit anywhere at any time, but his faults probably manifested in other ways.

She needed a shower. No, she needed to go for a swim, preferably before everybody else had the same idea.

Twenty minutes later, she plunged into the local lido and allowed herself to sink to the bottom, loose hair waving like anemones in the refreshing water. She held her breath, waiting until the dull ache in her lungs turned to a desperate burn, before breaking the surface of the water again. That was better. She started swimming, trying to put all thoughts of the shelter out of her head, letting the water cleanse her of the faint tug of anxiety the whole thing brought up. When she'd spoken to Marcus yesterday, he'd been typically dismissive. *What do you propose you do?* he'd said. *Start a petition? We both know that's not who you are.* And no, she wasn't about to become *that* person. But last week Jasper had made her question her assumptions and, rather annoyingly, herself. He'd made it clear from day one that he considered her to be superficial, which made her oddly determined to defy his expectations. She'd worked hard to educate herself beyond her schooling precisely so she could confound people's preconceptions about her. And what about Tasha? She was smart – she had something about her – yet she was screwed before she'd even got going. It just seemed so wasteful.

After several lengths, she got out, pulled on a pair of shorts, and meandered into the park to find a spot to dry off. The sun made light work of the job. The day stretched out before her. No work to do. No pressing engagements. No one to hang out with to pass the time. She could go shopping, but the idea didn't hold the appeal it might ordinarily. It was too hot to be wandering around, too syrupy to be trying on clothes, and besides, what did she really need?

A dog slowly hobbled over the brow of the hill towards her. It had a greying snout and sad rheumy eyes that met with her own. It seemed harmless enough, so she allowed it to lick her hand. Just as she imagined it might be a stray, another ponderous figure ambled into view: a homeless person, lugging a heavy rucksack on his back.

'Sorry if he's bothering you, love,' he said.

The dog continued to lick her with its rough tongue.

'Come away, Gyp.'

Gyp seemed torn. It was as if the dog sensed her need for company.

The man waited patiently. 'He likes people.'

She ran her other hand down the dog's back. It was almost

certainly rescued, and probably had better reasons than she did to feel aggrieved at the world, but here it was, offering affection regardless.

'Come on, mate.' The man began to walk away. 'Let's leave this lady be.'

She was tempted to call him back, perhaps have a conversation with him like Wei had suggested. She wondered what Jasper would do. Whatever it was, she was sure it would come completely naturally to him. But she wasn't Jasper. Nor was she Gayle. She was Simone Stephens, and in situations like this, she was as comfortable as a lap-dancer's shoe.

'I think you need to go.'

She removed her hands from the dog's fur and it trotted off on arthritic legs.

She lay back down on the grass, closed her eyes and thought about the week ahead. On Tuesday, it was the funeral of the man Jasper had mentioned. It was difficult to imagine what a crematorium full of homeless people might be like. How would a guy like the one she'd just seen go about getting ready for a funeral? Was it possible to properly pay your respects whilst wearing dirty tracksuit bottoms? And then an idea popped into her head. What was it that Wei had said? *Everyone just wants to feel normal.* Well, she might not be capable of being a different person, but perhaps she could make good use of the one she already was. It turned out she was going shopping after all.

Chapter Twenty-Five

S imone dropped by the office to let Gayle know she'd arrived.
'You came back then?'

'Yeah. I went to the alternative option store this weekend, but they were all out.'

'At least that gives you something in common with everyone else here.'

Tasha wandered in eating toast. She caught sight of Simone and walked straight back out again. Simone ran to catch up with her.

'Tasha!'

No response.

'Just give me a second, would you?'

Tasha stopped and pivoted. 'One,' she counted, then turned tail again.

She followed her. 'Okay, maybe sixty seconds.'

They reached Tasha's room.

'I'm sorry for what happened on Friday,' said Simone.

Tasha grabbed the door handle.

'Genuinely. I'm really sorry for upsetting that landlady.'

'Really?'

'Okay, I'm not sorry for what I said to her, but I am sorry that it upset you.'

Tasha turned the handle, strode inside, and sat down on the bed. Simone took the still-open door as enough of an encouragement to follow her in.

'But Jesus, Tasha. Pregnant? Holy fuck!'

'That's generally how these things start.'

She was determined to keep things light. Absolutely no lecturing.

'Is it definitely yours?' she said.

She was rewarded with a scowl. 'Very funny.'

'And you want to keep it?'

'Yes.'

'For fear of sounding like every grown-up I have ever despised, you're still practically a child yourself.'

Okay, she was lecturing.

'I don't feel like one,' said Tasha.

She scanned the room. There were no posters or personal touches of any kind.

'How far gone are you?'

Tasha smoothed her top over her belly. No bump yet. Not far then.

'You have options.'

'As I've said before, the one thing I don't have many of are options.'

What had she been up to at Tasha's age? She'd have been working for a few years by then, a little nest egg of savings sitting in the bank from the modelling jobs her mum had once forced her into.

'And I'm not having an abortion, if that's what you mean.'

'There are other ways.'

'I'm not giving it up either. I couldn't live with myself.'

It would be far harder to live with herself if she had a baby that she then screwed up.

'Didn't you have sex ed at school?'

'I learned on the job.'

'Do you know who the dad is?'

Tasha tossed her braids over her shoulder. 'What, do you think I'm some kind of slag? Yes, I know!'

'For the record, I don't believe in slags. I believe in women who haven't met the right penis yet.'

Tasha laughed, a lovely mellifluous chirruping sound, and her entire face transformed.

She chanced sitting on the edge of the bed. 'Okay. What you do is your choice, even if I think you're fucking mad.'

Tasha seemed to appreciate the sentiment.

'And I didn't come here to give you a talking to. I came to ask a favour.'

'What favour?'

'You know everyone around here. With the funeral tomorrow, I thought it might be helpful if I brought in some suits for people to wear.'

Tasha eyed her suspiciously. 'You brought in suits?'

'I also bought you an outfit – in case you fancied a change. Although I realise you dress like you're going to a funeral every day, so…'

Tasha scowled contemptuously.

'I'm going to set them up on a rail in the lounge. Could you tell people to come and see me if they need one?'

Tasha was examining her through her sceptical lens. 'What happened?'

'What do you mean?'

'Last week you're all *I'm too good for this shit*; this week you've bought in a haul of free clothes. Were you visited by three ghosts in the night?'

'It's just some suits. They were on the *everything's-a-pound* line at the Red Cross.'

This was a lie. She was surprised by how much the suits had cost. She'd assumed charity shops existed to enable poor people to buy things more cheaply, but a supermarket suit probably wouldn't have been much dearer. Still, at least the Red Cross would make better use of the funds.

'Chill. No ghosts. I get it.' Tasha got up from the bed.

Simone cleared her throat. 'I really am sorry if I was a bit of a dick the other day.'

She offered to contact Mrs Grimshaw to smooth things over. Tasha waved the idea away. 'You were right, it was a total dump.' She smiled hesitantly. 'To be honest, I really appreciate you standing up for me. I don't have many people who'll do that.'

An awkward silence descended like a piece of theatrical scenery. Simone jumped up off the bed, breaking it with some babble about needing to get on.

'Just let me know if you want to take a look at this dress I got you.'

Tasha had found something uncommonly interesting about her feet to focus on. 'Thanks, Simone. I will.'

Jasper came in as she was struggling with a guy called Mike's tie.

'Hey,' shouted another of the day visitors who'd availed himself of a pale grey cotton suit. 'Bet you never thought you'd see the day.'

'Where is Andrey,' said Jasper, 'and what have you done with him?'

'I feel like a new man!' Andrey gave him a twirl.

She'd been genuinely surprised at the reaction a few smart two-pieces could elicit. She'd been here for just over forty-five minutes, and the room had transformed into an impromptu catwalk, albeit a rowdy one with lots of heckling.

Jasper sidled up to her. The required fabric folds were even more tricky under his watchful gaze.

'Do you need a hand with that?' he asked.

'Yes. I have no idea what I'm doing.'

'So I see.'

'It's not like I've ever had to dress in a man's suit.'

'Really? Because I can definitely see you being someone who wears the trousers.'

He deftly created a perfect knot, allowing Mike to amble off and admire his reflection in a nearby window.

'So,' he said. 'This is all very … unexpected. This is the most animated I've ever seen them.'

'Is that because they're usually on spice?'

She cursed herself. It was a stupid reductionist comment, one for which Jasper would doubtless mark her down in his mental inventory.

'It's okay,' he said. 'Some of the people who come here do, in fact, do spice.'

His trying to make her feel better only made her feel worse.

'What the fuck is going on here?!' Gayle's voice careened towards them. 'Is it *Homeless Fashion Week*? Only I missed my front row invite.'

'Hey, check me out, Gayle!' said Mike. 'Bet yer fancy me now, dontcha?' He grabbed her by the arm and tried to twirl her round.

'Get off me, you bleeding imbecile. I wouldn't touch you with Terry's barge pole, and he's had gangrene in his.'

Another man, presumably Terry, saluted.

Simone glanced enquiringly at Jasper. 'Gangrene?' she whispered.

'From injecting heroin,' he whispered back.

'Jesus!'

'Oi! Jasper!' shouted Gayle. 'Are you planning on working today, or were you going to stand around pretending to be Karl Lagerfeld?'

'I was just helping Simone to—'

'Were you now? Well, Miss Anna Wintour, these aren't the offices of Vogue. I've got a list of errands that would make Martha Stewart shit a brick, so if you don't mind, perhaps you can wrap up Queer Eye for the Homeless Guy and get some fucking community service done?'

'Well, I think I was done here anyway.'

Jasper looked at her with something like … oh god, was it pity?

'This was a stupid idea,' she said. 'I just thought … you know … with the funeral.'

She saw how this might seem to him. She was some vacuous idiot, imagining that an outfit would change anything. It was like trying to cure skin cancer with concealer.

'It wasn't a stupid idea… I—'

Gayle shouted at him again. There wasn't anything going on between them, but the woman could still enjoy a second career as a professional cockblocker.

'I do need to go,' he said.

'That's fine.'

'I'll… I'll try and catch up with you later.'

'No need. I'll leave these here. People can help themselves.'

When he got to the door, he glanced back briefly and gave her a half-smile that said … what exactly? She awkwardly waved in response. She was still staring at the spot from which he'd disappeared when something moved in her peripheral vision. Steve, already dressed in a suit (and not of the shell variety), was taking another from the pile.

'Oi! It's one each,' Simone said.

'Sorry, I was just—'

'Are you nicking that? Are you planning on selling it?'

'No. I swear down, I wasn't.'

'Because that is pretty fucking despicable.'

Steve held up his hands like he was facing spooked US armed cops, not a marginally slighted woman who'd hoped for a better reaction from a woman whose approval she hadn't (until that moment) realised she was seeking.

'I was taking it for Hozan. I figured he could use a change.'

'Oh.'

Steve slowly lowered his arms. 'Is that okay?'

'I'm sorry. That was out of order.'

Two apologies in an hour. What next? Writing confessional poetry?

'It's okay, mate.' He looked like he was going to hug her, but then clocked her facial expression and thought better of it. 'Gayle doesn't mean it, you know. It's one of them – what do you call 'em – coping mechanisms.' He scooped the suit up.

'I'm fine,' she said. 'She doesn't bother me in the least.'

'Yeah.' He gave her one of his little sage nods. 'Denial's another one.'

Chapter Twenty-Six

With most of the residents due to be out at the funeral, Simone was anticipating a quiet morning. Along with some of the other volunteers, she was making a 'buffet' for everyone's return, a meagre affair consisting of some disturbingly cheap frozen sausage rolls, white bread sandwiches, and a box of broken biscuits from a discount food shop on the market. Not quite a wake, but something masquerading as one.

She was daydreaming about the ramen lunch to which she intended to treat herself when Steve appeared in the kitchen looking like he'd been dragged through a hedge backwards. And forwards. And sideways.

'What the heck?'

He paced up and down, his previous mullet now a confection of butchered locks sticking up in all directions, as if held aloft by an invisible halo of statically charged balloons. There were also several bloody nicks on his face.

'Let's start with your hair. What happened?'

'I tried to cut it.'

'What did you use? A jet propeller?'

'Don't. I'm stressing out, man.'

'And what about your face? Did you try to cut that too, because you've done a great job if so.'

'I wet shaved. Not done it for a while.' He pulled on a lock of his hair. 'Can you do something with it?'

'Put some crime scene tape around it, and cordon off the area?'

A little anguished cry escaped his lips. She'd not seen him stressed before.

'Please?' he said. 'I was really hoping to be smart today. I can't turn up like this.'

'Can't you wear a hat?'

'It's boiling out there.'

'Okay fine. I guess I can't do any worse.'

She grabbed some kitchen scissors and got to work. When Tasha found them, she'd made him look slightly less police mugshot, and slightly more crap passport photo.

'I didn't know you cut hair,' said Tasha.

'Neither did I.'

'Gayle is asking if you can drive us to the crematorium.'

'What happened to the minibus?' said Steve.

'It's too mini. We won't all fit.'

'Isn't there anyone else who can do it?' asked Simone.

'Probably. But she asked for you. Do you want to take it up with her?'

Trying to reason with Gayle was like trying to reason with a starved Rottweiler whilst wearing a coat made of pork scratchings. She sighed. Bang went her quiet morning.

'I'll get my keys.'

When she got to her car, she was disconcerted to see that Hozan, looking particularly murderous, would also be joining them. Brilliant. This day just got better and better. He climbed into the back seat, his gaze never leaving hers as he did so.

'Where are we headed?' She held her mobile, ready to input the coordinates.

'No phones,' said Hozan.

'Well, I never did get round to doing *the knowledge*, so unless you know where you're going, we—'

'Turn right out of the car park,' he said without hesitation.

She saw Tasha smiling in the rear-view mirror. 'He knows where he's going. He knows everything.'

Presumably objecting to mobiles was one of his quirks. What was it these 5G conspiracy theorists banged on about? The masts were all bird-killing, cancer-causing, brainwashing, virus-spreading, autism-triggering, spy-enabling tech?

'I'm guessing the radio isn't allowed either,' she said.

Hozan looked at her like she'd lost her mind. 'Put on Heart. It's the best music mix.'

They made their way through the streets, Hozan's occasional monotonous instructions punctuating the anodyne fare offered up by the mid-morning DJ. Everyone seemed in a relatively sombre mood, but when the presenter announced a general knowledge quiz, Hozan sat forward in his seat and demanded she turn the volume up.

'He loves quizzes,' said Steve.

She also loved quizzes, not that she'd admit that out loud. Always had. Probably because she was good at them. In a world that increasingly confused knowledge with intelligence, her ability to absorb and recall meaningless nuggets of information gave her an additional platform on which to compete. Up went the volume. She stayed quiet for the first round of questions, just listened as Hozan plucked the correct information from the ether. But come round two, she couldn't help herself, and as questions rained down, she beat him to the punch on six out of ten of them.

Steve whistled. 'How do you know all that stuff?'

'Yeah,' said Tasha. 'Those were tough.'

They were pulling into the crematorium. She'd drop them off, then go and find somewhere to park afterwards.

'I don't know. I just remember random stuff. Always have.'

She brought the car to a stop and Tasha and Steve climbed out.

Hozan lingered, his eyes darting as if he was searching his internal systems for something. He placed a hand on her shoulder. 'You're one of us,' he said, then he climbed out without another word.

Tasha leaned in through the window. 'I think he likes you now.'

'Hmm. Why am I not reassured by that?' she said.

Hozan continued to stare at her, but something had shifted in his demeanour. Distrust had been replaced with … was it sympathy? Understanding? Yep, she definitely preferred it the way it was before.

She parked up and strolled back. She'd only put an hour on the meter but didn't expect proceedings to take long. Twenty minutes to be shunted along the conveyor belt – literally – before the next one came in. It was like YO! Sushi, only for corpses. It wasn't so long ago she'd been through this for her mum. Hers had been a joyless affair; Simone couldn't furnish the celebrant with much to celebrate. She'd tried to make the best of it, like baking a cake with wartime rations, and the few guests had made all the right noises in a blitz spirit kind of way, but the whole thing had left a bad taste in the mouth. When you're talking about someone's legacy, successfully taking their own life tends to trump any of their more humdrum achievements.

She'd barely had time to find a memorial bench and check her emails when, sure enough, people began filtering back out of the crematorium. She recognised some of yesterday's ragtag bunch amongst them, from the midst of which emerged Jasper. He was wearing a light brown linen suit, white shirt and maroon tie, like he'd just stepped off the set of *The Great Gatsby*. Good job she was wearing sunglasses, because they enabled her to stare to her heart's content without him knowing. Good lord. In a T-shirt and jeans he was fairly damned fine, but in a suit he was positively Adonic. She was enjoying the view so much that when he caught sight of her and waved, she forgot she wasn't meant to be staring and waved straight back, thus revealing that she had in fact been staring at him the whole time.

He ventured over and sat down next to her, a little closer perhaps than the size of the bench necessitated. He stared ahead and massaged his palm with his thumb.

'Funerals, man,' he said. 'Always make you want to reach out to the people you're closest to, don't they?'

A huge bee passed, heavy and drunk on nectar, and landed on a nearby rose bush.

'I think his wife might object.'

'Oh,' he said.

'Yeah.'

The bee crawled its way to the centre of the flower, abdomen pulsing with pleasure.

'Funny.' He loosened his tie and undid his top button. 'I'd envisaged you as more of a full helping, not a bit on the side.'

A bit on the side. Not an expression she'd heard for a while. She wasn't sure if he was complimenting or insulting her, but it was interesting he'd envisaged her as anything at all.

She shrugged. 'It's complicated.'

'It sounds it.'

'They're separated, but still live together for the sake of the kids. And appearances.'

'Really?'

'It's a weird upper-class thing. Like tweed dishcloths or Jacob Rees-Mogg.'

He smiled. 'So how long do you have to wait?'

'For…?'

'Until you can be together properly.'

'I don't know if I'd want to settle down with him.'

Jasper's brows furrowed. 'This really is complicated.'

The bee was off again on a lazy arc across the aquamarine sky. She watched it until it was out of sight.

'Men are like buses. Okay for a quick ride, but never there when you really need them.'

He shook his head. 'Does a fairy die if you express optimism or something?'

She took off her shades and regarded him insouciantly. 'Love is just a rumour, designed to keep people from thinking about their inexorable crawl to the grave.'

'How poetic. *I'm with you because the alternative is staring into the void of my futile existence, and you distract me sufficiently from my own mortality.*'

'You got it.'

'Ever considered cheering up?'

She glowered at him. 'This is my happy face.'

He laughed, a throaty chortle that seemed to break ranks from his lungs, so unexpected that she couldn't help but laugh too.

'Simone. I have worked with people who have been sexually trafficked, beaten up, urinated on by members of the public or lost their worldly belongings in horrible scams. But you are by far the most cynical person I have ever encountered.'

'Why, thank you.' She took a bow in her seat. 'I've always tried to excel at everything I do.'

'How did you get to be this way?'

'With a lot of practice.'

He reached inside his pocket, pulled out a packet of mints, and offered her one.

'First handkerchiefs, now mints. Did you spend seventy years frozen in the Arctic tundra, like Captain America?'

'Okay, don't have one.'

He went to snatch them away, but she grabbed the pack before he could. It was better than craving a cigarette.

'How about you?' She tried to sound casual. 'Any girlfriend?'

'We split up about six months ago.'

So he really was single. That made about as much sense as Crocs.

'Ahh. Did she break your heart?'

'No. It just wasn't working.'

'She dumped you?'

'No.'

'Did you dump her?'

'It doesn't always have to be about who dumped who.'

'Relationships are always about power,' she said.

He stood up and shrugged off his jacket; the sun had burned off what little cloud cover there'd been that morning. Over by the entrance, everyone was still milling around like they had nowhere to go. Then she remembered many of them didn't. As Jasper was about to sit back down, she spotted a tiny money spider crawling up his trousers near the back of his knee.

'Hang on. You've got a…'

She lightly placed her hand a few centimetres ahead of it, trying to encourage it onto her palm, but it detoured around the obstacle. She placed her hand slightly further up, but the spider wasn't interested. After a couple more attempts trying to get the kamikaze little critter to safety, she realised her fingers were now on Jasper's buttocks. He was peering down at her with a mixture of surprise and amusement.

'…hand on my arse?' he finished for her.

She snatched the offending digits away. 'There's a spider.' She motioned for him to see for himself, but the bloody thing had disappeared. 'It was right there.'

'Really?'

She told him to turn around, to see if it had moved to his front. Great. Now she was looking at his crotch. Still no sign of the spider, but something akin to mortification was crawling across her face.

'I don't see it,' he said, examining his own junk.

The trousers were very slim-fitting and, as he bent over, they further accentuated the bulge.

'It was right there.'

'Most people offer to buy me a drink before going in for the grab.'

'I wasn't trying to grab your arse.'

'So you say.'

'Why would I? It doesn't add up.'

'And yet here we are.'

'I wasn't!'

'What would your married man think?'

She had taken the bait and he was toying with her.

'God, you are so annoying!' she said.

He laughed and sat back down. 'Sorry. Couldn't help myself. Didn't think of you as easily embarrassed.'

'I'm not.'

He regarded her thoughtfully. 'Or as a rescuer of spiders. Somewhere in that cavity of a chest lies the tiniest beating heart.'

She picked up the jacket sitting between them and threw it at him. 'I can assure you there isn't.'

'I'm not convinced. What about yesterday? The suits thing.'

'Just playing to my strengths. Vacuous fashionista.'

His countenance clouded. 'I think we both know your strengths extend beyond fashion, Simone.'

The way he said it made everything feel a little wobbly. It was as though he saw something in her that she herself only half-suspected existed. For all Tony was an asshole, there was something about him giving her a *well done*, or a patronising *good girl*, that validated her in a way she hated needing, but still required. Jasper seemed to recognise that.

'And they can wear them for all those job interviews they've got lined up,' he said.

Hmm. Perhaps he was mocking her after all.

'You're right,' she said. 'It was stupid. I just thought...'

She couldn't formulate the sentence. Couldn't say that what had started as a bit of a way to say *fuck you* to him had turned into a small matter of ... what ... pride? That she had, in some miniscule way, made the teeniest tiniest difference, and it had felt the teeniest tiniest bit unshit to do so. She let out a long sigh instead.

He reached out and gently squeezed her upper arm. 'It wasn't stupid, Simone. It was very considerate. I was being sarcastic. I thought that's how you communicated?'

She felt the weight of his hand on her, noted the contrast in the colours of their skin. 'Sarcasm is my first language,' she managed.

Another hearse was slowly making its way up the driveway to the crematorium.

'I think we should be heading back,' he said.

'Yeah.'

As they drifted towards the group, Tasha waved at her.

'You two made up then?' he said.

She nodded.

'Be careful with that one. She may act tough, but she has a

deep-seated need to attach. Best not to get too close, given you're not going to be around for much longer.'

She stopped walking, making sure they remained out of earshot.

'You might need to take that up with Gayle,' she said. 'Because she's already arranged for me to take her to her scan later.'

Chapter Twenty-Seven

The grainy black and white image was like a blizzard at night, snowflakes swirling, drifting and clustering in haphazard patterns against the blackness. And then it came into view, the tiny form of Tasha's baby, wriggling like a jumping bean.

'Oh,' said Tasha, as if she hadn't truly believed she was pregnant until that moment. She gaped at the screen, eyes almost as wide as her mouth.

'Are you okay?' Simone couldn't tell if it was in wonder or terror.

'Shit. She's really there.'

Noting the word *she*, the woman pressing the wand to Tasha's belly told her it wasn't possible to be certain of the sex until the next scan. But Tasha wasn't really listening.

'How big is she?' she asked.

The sonographer – one Donna Sanders according to her badge – wrinkled her nose. It wasn't the first dismissive action Simone had picked up on since they'd arrived. At first, she'd assumed the staff's perfunctory attitude was efficiency in disguise. Then she'd seen how the other expectant mums – the older ones there with their simpering partners – were treated far more warmly. Cooed over even. She felt strangely protective of Tasha in that moment, lying there as the weight of what she was getting herself into pressed down as heavily as the ultrasound wand. As if fate hadn't dealt her a shitty enough hand, she didn't need the silent judgment of this woman thrown into the mix too.

Donna huffed. 'I'll come to that.'

Simone searched for the answer on her phone, repeating the question out loud and side-eyeing Donna as she did so.

'About the size of a plum,' she said.

The girl's eyes were noticeably glassy, even in the darkness of the room. Jasper was right; she wasn't as tough as she'd originally assumed.

As Donna continued to prod, the machine clicking and beeping as she went, she recalled the time when she'd undergone an ultrasound examination. It was over ten years ago now, but she hadn't been in the antenatal ward; the thing growing inside her abdomen had been a very different beast.

'The foetus is measuring around twelve weeks old,' said Donna. 'Does that match with your dates?'

Tasha looked confused.

'Do you know when you conceived?' the woman asked impatiently.

Another dig. This clearly wasn't planned.

'No.'

'Well, you can stop taking folic acid tablets now.'

'Folic acid?'

Donna's mouth took on the pinched characteristics of a cat's bottom.

'I didn't know you needed to,' Tasha said quickly.

Donna's attention turned to Simone, as if perhaps she should have furnished the girl with this information.

'Haven't you seen a midwife yet?' Simone asked.

Tasha shook her head. 'Not yet. This appointment was made by a doctor.'

'Well, it can't be helped,' said Donna. 'The next scan will identify if there are any neural tube defects.'

Tasha really did look terrified now. Simone couldn't get over the woman's attitude. She had the bedside manner of a robot whose mode had been set to 'tosspot'.

'But that would be very rare, no?' she prompted.

The woman checked Tasha's notes. 'You're young,' she said.

They waited, expecting her to add something more. She didn't. Instead, she stridently pulled out a metre's worth of blue tissue from the dispenser and tore it off with a flourish. She handed the wad to Tasha, who wiped the jelly off pristine porcelain skin that would be stretched thin in several short months.

'When's the next scan?' asked Tasha.

'You'll get a letter in the post.'

'Can I just check the address you have, only—'

'You can do that with reception.'

Their time was clearly up, and the moment Tasha climbed off the bed, Donna opened the door for them to leave.

'Wait,' said Tasha. 'I forgot to get a photo.'

'You can ask for a print-out at reception.'

Tasha nodded.

'It's eight pounds a copy,' Donna added, a little too gleefully.

'That's fine,' said Simone. 'We'll get a whole set.'

A wry smile passed Tasha's lips.

As they made their way back to reception, Tasha thanked her for the offer, but told her she didn't need to buy the image. They both agreed it sucked that you had to pay.

'What next?' mused Simone. 'Get the contactless machine out halfway through the birth. *That'll be twenty pounds for gas and air, and fifty for the forceps.*'

But they both understood the subtext. If Tasha couldn't afford to pay eight pounds for a scan picture, how the hell was she going to afford to pay for all the other accoutrements that parenting required?

They requested the pictures and found a couple of seats in the busy reception to wait for them to be printed.

'So dare I ask where the dad is in all this?'

'Not really in a position to help.'

'What about moral support?'

'Especially not moral support.'

Regardless of how capable Tasha appeared to be, this whole thing was a disaster waiting to happen.

'Do you think I need to worry about the folic acid thing?' she asked.

Simone reassured her that young women got accidentally pregnant every day. If they weren't taking precautions, they almost certainly weren't taking prenatal vitamins, and the world was full of perfectly healthy unplanned children. That bit, at least, would be fine.

Tasha stroked her stomach. 'Do you want kids?'

She was ready to trot out the lines she used whenever anyone asked her that.

'There are only two things wrong with babies,' she said.

'Which are?'

'Everything that comes out of their mouth, and everything that comes out of their arse.'

She sensed the disapproval of the woman two seats down.

'It's not like I have anything against kids particularly,' she continued. 'Some of my favourite clothes labels are manufactured by children.'

Tasha cocked her head to one side and waited for her to quit dicking about.

'And they are brilliant at fitting up chimneys,' Simone added.

'I get it. You don't like kids.'

The truth was she didn't know if she liked them or not, at least not since becoming an adult. When she was much younger, her parents had taken in foster children to supplement her father's meagre income. It seemed farcical now, given her mother's indifference to motherhood, but a not uncommon way to earn extra money back then. Before she'd turned ten, she'd seen a succession of children come and go. Initially, she'd found the whole thing exciting. If they were old enough, they would attend her school, where she would offer them up as flesh-and-blood show-and-tells. But the novelty soon wore off and the reality set in. For every lost but loveable youngster she would come to adore like a sibling – like the gentle Taiwanese girl who had been forced to live in a shed for not being a boy – there were the feral ones, whose troubled backgrounds were never excuse enough for the breaking of her toys, the kicking of her shins, and the taking of her precious parental attention.

'Natasha Davis?'

They approached the desk where the receptionist held out the payment terminal. Simone tapped her card and the woman handed over two tiny pictures on thin, waxy paper. Surely for sixteen pounds you should get an arty canvas? Tasha traced her fingers over their silky surface, her face set in grim determination. There were obviously some great kids out there – she was standing in front of one – but ever since the doctors had told her what they'd told her about her own reproductive capabilities, she'd taken great pains to remind herself only of the shitty ones.

Chapter Twenty-Eight

The next day, the Tube was finally running again. She could have enjoyed a more leisurely morning, but she'd woken up far earlier than her alarm, and so arrived at the shelter before anyone else. She exchanged pleasantries with the night security man, a Nigerian whose broad smile and easy laughter she was sorry not to have experienced before. It was nearing eight, but barely anyone seemed to be up and about.

She'd intended to stop at a coffee shop on the way, but had wandered past all of them lost in thought. Instead, she made herself a cup of tea using the own-label offering in the shelter's kitchen. Despite dunking the bag several hundred times and using only the tiniest dab of milk, she couldn't get the drink to go darker than the kind of barely-there cream colour that Farrow and Ball would probably describe as Camel's Wheeze.

She trundled over to the kitchen window. Hozan was in the front seat of his car, door open, reading a book. He wasn't wearing a hat, and his hair looked like you could no more pass a comb through it than you could find a needle in it.

'Have you spoken to him yet?'

She started at Jasper's voice, spilling tea all over her hand.

'Fuck!'

The scald was instant, a split-second between the sensory stimulus and her brain screaming *get this boiling hot fucking lava off me, you slow-witted imbecile!*

'Shit, sorry,' he said. 'I didn't mean to make you jump.'

The liquid had pooled in the place where her fingers were gripping the handle. She tried to take the cup in her other hand, but the rim was too hot. Her skin throbbed in protest.

Jasper grabbed it from her and placed it on the windowsill. 'I really am sorry.'

She frantically shook the liquid off, trying to release its grip on her epidermis. 'Wow, that smarts.'

He gently took hold of her wrist and examined the patch. It was already deep red, like a raspberry birthmark.

'Come over here.' He calmly led her to the sink, turned on the tap, ensured the water was running cold, and then held her hand under its flow.

Her pain receptors progressively numbed until only the faint echo of the original sensation remained. It was then she became fully aware of how closely Jasper was standing, his soft palm bearing the weight of her forearm, the water snaking over their entwined limbs. Their gazes locked.

She cleared her throat. 'I think I can take it from here.'

'I'm sure you can,' he said, 'but as a qualified first aider, it's my duty to ensure you're properly seen to.'

Hah. *Properly seen to.* She couldn't stop the smirk that spread across her lips.

He tutted. 'Good gracious, woman! Get your mind out of the gutter.'

'My mind may be in the gutter,' she said theatrically, 'but at least it is looking at the stars.'

His eyebrows crept inwards. 'I wouldn't have you pegged as

an Oscar Wilde fan.'

'I believe it was *Lady Windermere's Fan*.'

She only knew this because of a production she'd been in at school.

He ignored the sass. 'Let me see if I can find something to rub on it.'

She smirked again.

'Jesus! Why does everything have to be about sex with you?'

'Shouldn't *you* be able to answer that?'

He strode over to the freezer and pulled out a bag of peas. 'I don't fancy my chances of getting to the bottom of it.'

She sniggered.

He realised what he'd said and threw his hands up in resignation. 'I give up!' He wrapped a tea towel round the peas and handed them to her. 'Here. Hold this on for another few minutes.'

He went to fetch the first aid box. As he stretched to grab it from the top of a cupboard, she tried hard not to notice the two little pits where his back met his glutes.

'So, just out of interest,' he said, 'what is it that you do when you're not doing community service?'

She had a feeling Jasper wouldn't approve of the whole reputation management gig, even the events part of it, so she told him how she was meant to be on her road trip.

'Where should you have been today?' He unscrewed the cap on a scraggy old tube of Savlon.

Hmm. Weird. For the first week that Ziggy and Nancy were away, she woke up every morning knowing exactly where she should have been. This week she wasn't so certain.

'Arizona, I think?'

'I'm sure you're not missing much. Isn't it mostly sand?'

With exquisite tenderness, he rubbed some of the ointment onto her hand. A tingle of pleasure crept up her arm.

'Followed by the Grand Canyon.'

'Just a big hole.' He looked up, eyes narrowed, daring her to find something lewd in the statement.

She contained all facial movement. She wasn't doing anything to jeopardise the hand rubbing. 'And then a helicopter ride over the Hoover Dam.'

The words *big dyke* were spilling out of his mouth when Gayle poked her head around the door. Jasper grimaced. Simone provided air cover by awkwardly pulling her hand away and saying *so anyway* really loudly. Yep, absolutely nothing to hear here. They exchanged a conspiratorial glance.

'What the fuck is going on?' Gayle's nostrils flared. 'You pair had better not be flirting.'

Had they been? She looked at Jasper. He was focussing hard on putting the cap on the tube.

'Don't worry,' he said. 'She's not my type.'

Clearly they hadn't been.

'Ouch!' she said with forced levity. 'Aren't you afraid you'll hurt my feelings?'

'You have feelings?'

'Touché.'

'Simone,' said Gayle, 'if I find out you have so much as *thought* about Jasper in anything other than a professional capacity, I will haunt your dreams like Freddie Kruger, and I will tear you a new one with my massive knifey hands, do you understand?'

'I'm not sure. By *a new one*, do you mean *anus*?'

She could sense Jasper's amusement, which would have been more gratifying had he not just confirmed her *he-doesn't-fancy-you* suspicions so audibly.

Gayle was staring at them both. 'Get some volunteering done, will you? Steve's gathered you a pile of sheets dirtier than the Holy Shroud of Turin.'

'I just need to put this dressing on,' said Jasper, 'and then I will release her back into her day of servitude.'

Gayle stomped off, turning the air blue as she went.

He placed some gauze over the mark. She wondered if the skin would blister. He smoothed medical tape around the edge of the fabric, his touch as soft as a sigh.

Another figure appeared at the door. It was Hozan, holding his camcorder, but not pointing it at her this time.

Jasper let go of her hand and gestured to the device. 'You need to put that away before Gayle sees you. She's on the warpath.'

Hozan nodded mutely, then sauntered off.

Jasper gathered the first aid bits together. 'So, as I think I was asking before I permanently scarred you, have you spoken to him yet?'

'No.' At least not since Hozan had said what he'd said at the funeral.

'You really should. He's a fascinating character. You won't meet anyone else like him.'

'I'm alright, thanks.'

'Seriously. You can learn a lot from him. He's a genius.'

'Like I say, I'm good.'

'Hmm. Oscar Wilde *and* easily scared. You are full of surprises.'

'Is this reverse psychology? Because it isn't working.'

He grinned, showing off his faint dimples. 'I'd better get started. Busy day.' He headed for the door.

'I'm not scared of him!' she shouted to his back.

He made the sound of a chicken.

'I'm not!'

He waved over his shoulder. 'I'll catch you later.'

Ugh, he was so aggravating when he was being all superior and knowy. She gazed out of the window at Hozan's car. Fine. When she'd done yet more laundry and helped set up for the gardening class scheduled for later, maybe she'd go and bloody well find out what all the fuss was about.

Chapter Twenty-Nine

It was the following morning, and Hozan was back to reading in the front seat of his car, when she finally plucked up the courage to speak to him. There had been a huge downpour the previous evening, cleaning the air of its grittiness after the dry spell, and the petrichor was strong in her nostrils. Somehow the car remained as dirty as it had been before.

'I wondered when you would make yourself known to me,' he said without looking up.

'I brought you a coffee.'

He reached out and took it, his gaze still fixed on the pages. Was there a third eye concealed beneath all that hair?

'So you like reading?'

She was off with the awkward first date questions again.

He placed the cup in the instrument's nook behind the steering wheel. 'I always preferred the flow of ink to the flow of blood.'

'Who doesn't, amirite?'

Eww. Thank god no one was around to see how cringy she was being. This was a mistake. There was no way she could have an actual conversation with this man.

Hozan fixed her in his piercing amber gaze. 'I have biscuits.'

She hesitated. 'What kind?'

'Many kinds.'

She hadn't had breakfast yet. Sod it. In for a penny. She ventured around to the passenger side.

The car was full of stuff. Like really full. The back seat was piled with an assortment of clear plastic boxes crammed with shoes and clothing. The rear footwells were so full of bits of electrical equipment it was like he'd dismembered a cyborg but hadn't got round to disposing of the body. The parcel shelf sagged with books, and there was a selection of bric-a-brac on the dashboard that had grown fluffy with dust. She reached for the vintage Troll doll with its shock of gravity-defying hair.

'Don't touch that!' he barked.

She pulled her hand back as if she'd been scalded again.

'Sorry,' she said.

She should probably go. The door wasn't closed, and every ounce of her lizard brain was telling her she might be in danger – her body was physiologically gearing up for some. But there was no way *sat in his passenger seat for a few seconds then ran away* was sufficient to rub Jasper's nose in. She inhaled deeply. Hozan did the same.

'No, I'm sorry. I must remind myself you're one of us. Please, go ahead.'

She hesitated.

'I insist.'

She took the figure. It left two perfect feet marks in the surface's grime. She glided her thumb across the nicks on its nose. Her heartbeat settled a little.

Hozan reached under his chair to retrieve a squat round tin. He prised the lid off and thrust it at her, unveiling a choice of animal shapes, fig rolls or pink wafers, all options she'd not seen since she was a kid. She'd been hoping for Hobnobs.

'I'm okay, thanks.'

He grunted and thrust the biscuits at her again. She was clearly having one. She took a pink wafer and, as she gingerly bit into it, a flood of memories came to her of sitting in her dad's shed, watching him fixing a radio or some other malfunctioning appliance. It drove her mum mad that they couldn't afford replacements. What would he think of all the stuff she'd amassed in the years he'd been gone?

She finished the wafer and was disappointed not to be offered another. She glanced across at Hozan. If she wanted to know what he meant, she was going to have to ask.

'What do you mean, one of us?'

'Huh?' Traces of pink crumbs remained in his beard.

'You said you keep forgetting I'm one of you. What do you mean by that?'

'A recipient.'

'A recipient?' She twirled the troll's hair round in her fingers. 'A recipient of what exactly?'

'A nanochip.' He slurped on his coffee.

'And that is…?'

'That thing you've got inside your head.'

This was what Gayle had mentioned the day of their first run-in.

'And what does this nanochip do?'

'That all depends.' He glanced over his shoulder to ensure no one else was in earshot. 'You think your exceptional memory is an accident?' he said quietly.

She wouldn't describe it as exceptional. It broke completely when she drank alcohol.

'Yes. I have a knack for remembering things. Lots of people do.'

He looked heavenward. 'No, no, no! You ever had a general anaesthetic?'

'Yes,' she said.

'That is when they inserted it.'

'This nanochip?'

'Correct.'

'But why would they do that?'

'The government wishes to control our minds. I am a Turkish Kurd. Do you know anything about our plight?'

She did not.

'There is a long history of unrest and separatist conflict. Much blood has been spilt. Brothers, sisters, children, all dead. When I was in my twenties, I was asked to become a Ranger, which means to fight for a country that didn't recognise us as humans. For the love of my people, I could not do this, and for my treachery I was tortured.'

He described the brutality with which he and others had been treated, a terrible litany of barbarism that included beatings and electric shock treatments.

'Long nights in pitch black cells, no food, no water, the screams of others becoming one with my own, praying to Allah to release me from the pain.' He gripped the sides of the biscuit tin, knuckles white. 'When I fell unconscious, they took their chance. This is when they implanted me. They wished to subdue me, to bend me to their will, but I resisted.'

He told her how, at first, he had fuelled his brain with whatever he could to stop them controlling his mind. He had studied philosophy and poetry, feasting on the works of Rumi and Saadi, then the theologians like Fakhruddin Razi. Over time he came to realise that the neuroprosthetic (as he called it) had given him special abilities – an incredible power of recall, the ability to retain information, the capacity to put together seemingly unrelated things and draw conclusions from them. He had always been a gifted pupil, but afterwards, he could understand hard-to-grasp scientific principles, and he became fluent in several languages. He also discovered the experiments weren't limited to his country or that era; they dated as far back as the fifties, perpetrated by the CIA. Trials were happening all over, on different races, ages and sexes, from old men to young women, just like her.

At first, she'd interjected. There were moments that seemed so credible, so rooted in reality, that they could almost be plausible, and she'd wanted to probe further. But after a while, she realised that Hozan didn't want to be grilled, he wanted to unburden himself, to get his thoughts out like a stream of consciousness that might not bear close scrutiny, but needed to be born witness to. And so she just let it wash over her. There was no ranting or raving as she'd originally anticipated. He spoke very softly and gently, like a kindly uncle who had decided to take her into his confidence. There was something indescribable that radiated from him, a core of innocence and wonder that had somehow stayed anchored in his soul, despite the agonies to which he had been subjected.

It was getting on to an hour later when he told her his reason for the recordings. He was building a dossier of evidence, a precaution in case anything was to happen to him, just as it had to Frank Olson, a scientist murdered after the CIA mind-control program *MKUltra* went horribly wrong.

'It's not an accident you are here,' he said. 'Unseen forces are shaping your fate.'

She was reminded of the mix-up that had landed her here. You could say that again. But that had been a freak occurrence, a silly misunderstanding she'd been too cocky to take seriously. What must it be like to have experienced genuine persecution, and to now live your life under its constant shadow to the point of delusion?

'Don't make it easier for them,' he said. 'Don't share yourself for all to see. If they know that they gave you this power, they will want it back.'

An immense sadness swept over her that this clearly intelligent man had been reduced to sleeping in a car, conjuring up conspiracies to try and make sense of how his life had turned out.

'Would you not give it back, Hozan?' she said. 'Be rid of it if you could?'

He shook his head and said something she didn't understand. The words sounded mellifluous. Something from the Qur'an perhaps?

'It is Rumi,' he said. '*The wound is the place where the light enters you.* It is a curse, but also a blessing. People who need help, I can translate for them. People seeking asylum, I offer advice. This thing is going to save us all, Simone. I won't have left my homeland in vain.'

He closed his eyes and hung his head. Simone waited a minute or so for him to continue. When he didn't, she waited a minute more. After a third, he began to softly snore. She could easily have left then, made the escape she'd been so eager for previously, but she sat for a while longer. She didn't doubt he had the capabilities he had described. But what a woeful waste of talent. The things he could do with that brain! He had been failed by the system; a once brilliant man reduced to this. Anger bubbled up like a spring. The dismay at what he'd recounted lodged like a burr in her skin. What was Gayle thinking, letting him live out his existence in a cramped car when surely, by now, he could have received housing? And what exactly was Jasper doing to help? Wasn't there some programme he could go on, some medication he could take to make him more capable of integrating with the world? Did he have a case worker looking out for him? What about his family? Where were they in all of this? She got out the car and gently closed the door. She was going to give Jasper a piece of her mind.

Chapter Thirty

She didn't get the chance to speak to Jasper straight away. This served only to increase her frustration, further amplified by an annoying email from Tony that she picked up on her afternoon break. He was asking her to do a shit-ton more work on this potential opportunity he'd been banging on about. Consequently, when their paths did cross, she had a well-rehearsed script on abandonment and dereliction of duties which she gave him with both barrels.

'Woah. Easy tiger!' He seemed more amused than abused by her outburst.

'Don't *easy tiger* me!'

'Are you okay? You appear to be experiencing a serious lack of self-interest. Do you need to lie down?'

The flush in her chest spread to her face. A guttural moan escaped her throat. 'Ugh!'

'Crikey,' he said. 'What did Hozan say to you?'

'He thinks I have a chip in my head.'

He laughed. 'You've definitely got one on your shoulder!'

Her hands clenched. If it wasn't such a cliche, she'd have beaten her fists against his chest like some 1950s starlet.

'I'm kidding!' he said.

'I'm not in the mood for jokes.' She sounded like her mother.

Jasper glanced at his watch. The guy wore an analogue watch, for fuck's sake, like it was still the nineties!

'Do you want to grab a coffee?' he said. 'It's practically home time and Gayle's out at a funding meeting. She won't know if you bunk off for a bit.'

This took the wind out of her sails a little. 'What kind of coffee?'

The murky, clumped granules in this place were for genuine stimulant emergencies only.

'I'll shout you a proper one. At that place up the road.'

There were toilets she needed to clean – Gayle was still laying it on thick – and a pile of ironing she could scale, but she could always come in early again tomorrow.

'Fine!' she said.

The coffee shop was a tiny little place, most of its footprint taken up with the counter and the Tiffany-blue coffee machine that sat on top of it. The smell of the roasted beans was an instant balm to her jangled nerves. Jasper instructed her to grab the only remaining table whilst he ordered. She watched as the barista, a pretty girl with an ugly fringe who knew him by name, flirted with him as she made the drinks. It was odd. She hadn't really considered him at large in the general population, interacting with people, or being *fancied* by them. Sure, he had the physique of an Action Man and the temperament of a puckish puppy, but she'd only ever really considered him within the confines of her own playroom.

'One very pink beetroot latte with oat milk.' He handed her the drink.

'Thanks.'

He'd gotten himself a croissant and a black coffee. He placed them on the table and eyed her curiously. 'Not going to take a photo of your drink for *the gram*?'

Apart from the occasional check-in on the girls, her self-imposed hiatus from the platform continued. Now, whenever she was at a loss as to what to do for a few minutes, she grabbed a sudoku or a crossword book. She felt much better for it.

'I see *you* have a keen real-life follower.' She motioned to the barista.

'Who, Roxy? She's lovely, but far too young for me.'

That was so typically right-on of him. The woman must have been at least mid-to-late twenties, which surely wasn't an obscene discrepancy; certainly less than what stood between her and Marcus.

He opened a sugar and slowly and deliberately added half of the packet to his drink. She'd noticed that about him: all his actions and movements were so *intentional*. Not in a self-conscious way, just that he carefully considered everything. She wondered about his background and how he'd come to be so assured.

'You asked me about Hozan and why I wasn't doing more to help him,' he said. He stared at his cup as he stirred, as if expecting an apparition to appear in it. He'd suddenly become very serious. 'It's a tough one.' He tapped the spoon on the rim of the cup and then gently placed it on the saucer. 'Hozan is a Turkish Kurd. Do you know anything about that situation?'

She hadn't expected to hear that question in a lifetime, let alone twice in a day. She filled him in on their conversation, her frustration rising as she did so.

He nodded. 'I get it. I really do. And I don't pretend to know a great deal about what's going on over there. Geopolitics, ethnopolitics, that's way above my paygrade. But did he tell you much about afterwards?'

He hadn't.

'Hozan sought asylum in the UK in the late nineties. He'd have still been in his twenties, if you can imagine that?'

She couldn't.

'He sold everything he had to come to the UK. Two and a half thousand miles, in who knows what conditions, presumably in fear of his life the whole way. And then he arrives on British soil, hoping to make a new life for himself. The process is meant to take six months, but at that point the system had really started coming under pressure, so I think it took much longer. During that time, he wasn't entitled to accommodation, and he couldn't work or earn money, so he was entirely at the mercy of the state. On top of that, his father was killed. He couldn't return to Turkey – it wouldn't have been safe – nor could he send any financial support for his mother. So he had to deal with his crushing grief and his feelings of inadequacy here in this weird no man's land. No friends. No family. No home. It must have been unimaginably difficult.'

Simone had a mental image of when she'd moaned to Jasper and Street Pete about her mortgage. She swallowed hard at the memory. First world problems.

'At that point, the story gets less clear. We assume he was granted leave to remain, but neither Gayle nor I have found any record of him, and he claims not to have any personal ID. As you know, he doesn't trust authority, so I wouldn't be surprised if Hozan isn't his real name. He was on the streets and off the grid for a long time.'

'How the hell did he survive?'

'You tell me. But he did.'

'Surely he's entitled to a bed though?'

'Our place, the accommodation at least, it's meant to be a

temporary thing. If we don't know who he is, we can't work out what he's entitled to, and therefore he gets the bare minimum.'

He tore a little off his pastry but made no attempt to eat it.

'Luckily,' he said, 'back when he first came to our attention, someone had the idea of giving him a vehicle, so he became a fixture in the car park instead. He's not doing anyone any harm, and he seems content enough to have found somewhere as stable as he's ever likely to get.'

'But couldn't you still be helping him mentally?'

'To do what?'

'You know. Join the real world.'

He laughed bitterly. 'The last time I looked, that wasn't such a great place to live.'

It was a rare display of disillusionment from him.

'So you've given up?'

'Anything but primary care is denied to non-citizens. I'm worried if I dig too deep, I'll learn something about his status that I don't want to know. Besides, the downsides of treatment are often a high price to pay. Antipsychotics can shrink the brain, cause tics and spasms, and come with a higher suicide incidence.'

'A real Sophie's choice.'

'Precisely. As you have so eloquently pointed out before, I'm no psychiatrist, but from what I can tell, whilst the drugs dull the senses and curtail the emotions, they can't remove the memories.' He shook his head sadly.

'But the life he could live if he was…' She stopped herself.

'Were you going to say *normal?*'

She nodded, abashed.

'Define *normal*,' he said.

'But he patently believes things that aren't true!'

'Who doesn't to a certain extent? Who hasn't incorrectly read something into a look, or a text message, or the way someone spoke to us? It's all a spectrum.'

'Are you suggesting we're all mentally ill?'

'I'm saying we all suffer from irrational thoughts.'

'I don't!'

'Really?' He leaned forward. 'Simone, you think buying shoes will make you happy!'

'No, I don't!'

'Really? Haven't you ever convinced yourself that if you bought those shoes, or that dress, or that fancy flat, then everything in your life would magically fall into place?'

Yes. She'd thought all those things, but didn't everyone?

'Just because your delusion is one that more people buy into,' he said, 'doesn't mean that you're not suffering from a form of madness. It's just a more sociably acceptable kind.'

He did his signature cross-between-a-smile-and-a-shrug thing. Was that where the word 'smug' came from? It was maddening, but there was something in what he said.

'Fine. You win.'

He looked up at the ceiling, as if calling on a higher power. 'This is meant to be a conversation, not a competition.' He sighed. 'And besides, making people *normal* isn't the only way. Accepting difference. Learning to live with it. Acknowledging people as they are. He's just a man. Sure, his life choices and experiences are different from ours, but that doesn't make him less worthy of our love and attention. Same goes for anyone. We're all just a little bit lost, trying to find our way as best we can.'

She examined Jasper's open face. How had he ever felt lost? His whole bearing screamed *sorted*. He was, without doubt, the most philosophically minded person she'd ever spoken to. To think she'd considered herself out of his league when, intellectually and emotionally, he was obviously superior. A myriad of questions formed on her lips. There was so much more she wanted to ask him, so much more she felt she might learn from him. But where to start?

He checked his watch. 'You'll be relieved to know it's home time.'

Nope. She'd never been less relieved for a day to end. He offered her the remains of his croissant, which she ate whilst he took their empties back up to Roxy. She hoped the barista didn't take it as a sign of interest; she wasn't so old and jaded to have forgotten the exquisite ache of an unrequited crush. But it did beg the question: exactly what age did Jasper like his girlfriends to be?

Chapter Thirty-One

Come Friday afternoon, she hadn't seen Jasper all day. She ignored the nagging disappointment at not being able to shoot the shit with him. She had, however, spent a good deal of time with Tasha, of which he would doubtless disapprove, so perhaps it was better their paths hadn't crossed.

She was increasingly surprised by what good company Tasha was. The girl was also incredibly resourceful, far more than even she had been at that age. Inspired by the gardening session they'd had that week, Tasha had persuaded Gayle to let her assist in making some raised beds out of old discarded pallets. For once, Simone had brought in suitable clothing for a day of DIY – a tatty pair of combat trousers and an old vest that had seen better days.

'You could almost pass for homeless,' the girl joked.

'Gee, thanks!' She'd sweated off the day's make-up, and her damp hair was piled on her head in a messy topknot. Still, they'd made something from nothing, and it felt good.

'I'm parched,' she told the girl. 'Do you need some water?'

'No. I'm going to start digging.'

'Okay, back in a bit.'

She'd stupidly left her water bottle in the dining room when they'd had lunch, so she traipsed back there. But when she entered the room, she found it occupied by a motley group of women sitting in a small circle.

'Oh, sorry, I...' she hesitated. Should she grab the water bottle or leave them to it? She hovered by the door, indecisive.

'Are you new here?' A middle-aged woman stepped forward. Her hair was dyed an unnatural jet-black colour, making her skin look bilious.

'Yes.' She supposed two weeks was still relatively new.

'I'm Mandy. Come in. We won't bite.'

'Cheryl might,' someone else said.

A stick-thin woman with a face like a boxer – presumably Cheryl – growled.

Mandy waved a dismissive hand. 'D'you wanna drink?'

'No, really, I'm fine, I was just going to get some water.'

'Sit yourself down.' Mandy gently pulled her towards one of the chairs. 'I'll get you one.'

Mandy clearly assumed she was here for ... whatever this was.

'You're very sweet,' she told her, 'but I shouldn't be here. I'm not homeless.'

'Me neither,' said Mandy. 'Not anymore anyways.'

Cheryl tutted. Which must have been hard, because her two front teeth were missing.

'Still good to come for the sessions,' said Mandy. 'This is a safe space.'

Simone pulled away from her. 'There's been a mistake.'

'Hey.' Mandy took her arm again. 'We've all been there. It's tough being the new person.'

'But—'

'Sit the fuck down, for fuck's sake!' Cheryl barked with such ferocity that she immediately sat the fuck down.

'Cheryl's not been coming long,' explained Mandy, 'but she'll get there.'

'I'm fucking angry, not deaf!' snarled Cheryl, spittle escaping from between the gap in her gnashers.

Mandy shrugged and fetched Simone a water. She was being very lovely for a woman who didn't understand the appropriate hair colour to complexion ratio. Her brain scrabbled for a solution. Maybe she'd have some of the drink, then make her escape by pretending to need the toilet.

'We're just waiting on Doctor Adams,' said Mandy.

Who was Doctor Adams, and what were these women here for? She didn't have to wait long for the answer, because at that moment, the door to the dining room opened.

Mandy tapped her on the arm. 'Here he is.'

There he was.

Dr *Jasper* Adams clocked Simone. Simone clocked Doctor Jasper Adams. Both of their faces clocked up a compelling WTAF look.

'Got a newcomer,' Mandy told him.

'So I see.' His mind was clearly going through similar convolutions to the ones Simone's was.

'Hello,' he said uncertainly.

'Hello,' she said back.

'I'll need to take some details, so if you can perhaps come over to the table for a second.'

Once at the far side of the room, he went through the motions of handing her a form to complete. 'What are you doing here?' he whispered.

'It's a horrible misunderstanding.' She took a pen from him. 'Cheryl shouted at me and I didn't know what to do!'

'Shit!'

It was only the second time she'd seen him remotely frazzled.

'What are they here for?'

'Anger management. It's a talking therapy session to get them to deal with their problems without resorting to maladaptive coping mechanisms.'

'Like aggressively shouting at me?'

'They have trust issues.'

'They'll have even more if they find out who I really am.'

'Double shit.'

She completed the paperwork. There were audible signs of restlessness behind her: a chair leg scraping across the floor, someone coughing, Cheryl shouting at whoever was coughing to *cover their fucking mouth, they weren't five.*

'I could just leave,' she said.

'It'll make them think they can all go.'

'So I have to stay?'

'We're making really good progress.'

Cheryl was pacing like a caged tiger, ready to rip the innards out of someone.

'Really?'

'Shh,' he said.

'Okay, Doctor, what do you suggest?'

'It's probably best if you stay.'

'Brilliant.'

'It's only an hour. Just sit, listen, and avoid saying anything.'

'That shouldn't be a problem.'

And that would have all been fine if, at precisely fifty-three minutes in (she was counting), Cheryl hadn't become overwhelmingly annoyed at her continued muteness.

'What about Little Miss Silent over there. What's your story?'

The women had been describing how they came to be homeless, a depressingly vivid catalogue of abuse, domestic violence and addiction that had been hard to hear. One of the women had been forced into prostitution by her own mother. Each story was a layer of shit in the already massive shit sandwich life had served up for them.

She turned to Jasper, panicked.

'Now, Cheryl,' he said, 'it's Simone's first time with us. If she's not ready to share her story, she doesn't have to.'

But Cheryl wasn't taking no for an answer. Even Mandy seemed keen to hear what she had to say.

'Don't be scared,' she said, patting Simone on the shoulder like she was a child. 'It's good to talk.'

Jasper cast her a look that she couldn't interpret.

'In your own time,' shouted Cheryl, which tonally she took to mean *tell us your sodding story now or you might lose your front teeth too*.

She surveyed the women's faces, uncertain how to proceed. She could very easily make something up; she'd found it easy to improvise in drama at school. And she really didn't want to be emotionally unbuttoning herself with Jasper in the room. But equally, wouldn't lying in this situation be a betrayal of these women's confidences? A further kick in the lady balls from which they already had little protection. She mentally tossed a coin. She was going to have to say *something*.

'We didn't have much money growing up,' she began. 'My dad was a trucker, and he was away quite a bit. My mum was permanently dissatisfied with her lot; she wanted a more lavish lifestyle than he could afford to give her. It didn't help that she was younger than him. I guess I was the unhappy accident that permanently called time on the life she thought she deserved.'

Mandy nodded sagely.

'At some point she decided I could be her meal ticket. Or that she could live her life vicariously through me.'

'What the fuck does vicariously mean?' demanded Cheryl.

'To do something via someone else,' said Mandy, who was clearly not as daft as her choice of hair colour suggested.

'Exactly. So she pushed me to do the things she'd liked to have done. Dance classes. Little acting jobs. Beauty contests.'

Jasper raised an eyebrow at that.

'If I'm honest, I enjoyed the attention. At first. But then it was like my life wasn't my own anymore. Because we were always off to some audition, or class, or stupid pageant, I couldn't hang around with the people I wanted to. Then on my twelfth birthday, she pinched my arm, just under here...' She grabbed one of her triceps. 'Told me I was getting fat. So then she started controlling what I ate, making me exercise twice a day.'

'What about your dad in all of this?' asked Mandy.

'She was good at hiding what was going on. And I didn't want to worry him; it was hard enough for him not being able to provide for us in the way he wanted to. Anyway, one day he came home with a puppy for me. I was thirteen and I think he sensed I needed the company. My mum was apoplectic.'

'That means really mad,' said Mandy, who was getting more intriguing by the second.

'According to her, this puppy was ruining everything: he stopped us from going to bookings at the weekend, he was distracting me, making a mess of the furniture. We argued about it loads. Then one day when I refused to leave him, she picked Bailey up and threw him at me. I wasn't quick enough to catch him and he must have fractured his skull when he fell. He died. When my dad asked what happened, she said he'd escaped through an open door and had been hit by a car, but he stopped working away not long after. I think he sensed something wasn't right. He got a job in a warehouse. It was less money, which really pissed her off, but things settled down. Then he died suddenly. I was sixteen.'

'Ah, mate,' muttered Mandy.

'Then we really did have no money, and no other family to help. Things escalated. She had me modelling clothes, then underwear, which paid a lot better. And then … well, then I tried to run away a couple of times, but by that point I didn't have many'—she laughed bitterly—'*any* close friends to call on. I got into a relationship with a photographer; he was a lot older than me, but it was a way out. I moved to his flat in Camden. He kicked me out when he got bored of me, so then it was up to me to support myself. That's pretty much it.'

Cheryl shifted in her seat, ready for the cross-examination ('cross' being the operative word), but Jasper cut across her.

'We're going to have to wrap things up. That's our hour.'

She couldn't get out of there fast enough. Screw the water bottle; she'd collect it next week. She sneaked off to the office to retrieve her phone. It was Friday afternoon; she'd escaped dental rearrangement by Cheryl, and she really, really needed a drink. Thank heavens the girls would be back tomorrow. Only when she checked her messages, Ziggy and Nancy weren't at the airport awaiting their flight back. Instead there was some rambling text saying they'd decided to stay longer; a whole week longer. Goddammit! She knew for a fact Marcus wouldn't be available. Great. Just great. She was staring down the barrel of a second weekend watching shit television and drinking wine on her own. She kicked the wastepaper basket near Gayle's desk, sending empty Pot Noodle pots flying everywhere.

'Well, that class didn't work.' Jasper was at the door.

'For fuck's sake!' She knelt down to retrieve the pots, angrily throwing them back into the bin.

'I came to say thanks for that in there,' he said.

'For what?'

'Going along with it. I take it the acting classes bit was true because that was pretty convincing.'

'What makes you think it's not all true?'

'Because…' He cleared his throat. 'It's not, is it?'

It was a mistake to have said anything. She should tell him it was all bullshit, wipe that stupid concerned look off his face. But it wasn't. It had all happened. And why should she have to make other people feel better by denying her own experience? This was why you should never talk about your feelings, because then you got feelings about talking about your feelings, and before you knew it you were sinking into a swamp of the bastard things. She removed the full bin liner and angrily tied the top of the bag.

'I had a shitty mum. Big deal. You heard what those women have been through. Mine's nothing by comparison.'

Jasper ran his palm across his mouth, like he was trying to wipe away a bad taste. 'It's not nothing, Simone. It's never nothing if it makes you feel bad.'

'It was years ago.'

He gestured to the rubbish she was wielding like a weapon. 'It's clearly raised some tough feelings.'

'This has nothing to do with what happened in there.'

He did that all-knowing look, which was especially infuriating because they both knew he was right.

'I was meant to have plans for this weekend,' she said. 'It turns out I don't.'

He leaned against the desk. He was turning something over in his head, wondering whether to say it.

'Don't you dare say that's what you get for dating a married man. I don't need your puritanical judgment, thank you very much.'

He opened his mouth, closed it, then opened it again. 'Actually, and I will almost certainly regret this, I was going to ask if you wanted to come out with me tomorrow night?'

'Please don't take pity on me, for god's sake!'

Pity was the most demeaning of all the emotions, along with its bedfellow sympathy, which was just condescension with a fancy bow on it. Yet more great reasons not to share anything, with anyone, ever.

'I'm not taking pity on you, Simone.'

She huffed.

'I'm fucking not, okay!' His eyes blazed with exasperation. It was the first time she'd ever heard him properly swear.

'Okay,' she said, suddenly contrite. She put the bag down, as if in surrender.

He rubbed his jaw, massaging the tension out of it. 'The person I was meant to be going out with is sick, so really you'd be doing me the favour. I could use the company.'

'I'm not known for my favours.' She sounded like a tetchy teenager.

'Yeah, well, you're not known for your company either,' he said, unblinking.

She laughed, a breathy chortle that bubbled unbidden out of her throat. Jasper laughed too, relieved the tension had been broken.

'Come on,' he said.

What would a night out with Jasper even entail? It might be interesting to find out.

'Please,' he wheedled.

It wasn't like there was anything else to do.

'Alright,' she said.

His face brightened. 'Okay. Cool. I'll come and collect you at eight.'

He was out the door when a thought struck her.

'How?' she shouted after him. 'You don't know where I live.'

He reappeared, reached into his back pocket, and pulled out the form she'd completed. 'Au contraire,' he said with a self-satisfied grin. 'I'll see you tomorrow night.'

Chapter Thirty-Two

He turned up at one minute to eight. She opened the door to find him casually dressed in knee-length khaki shorts and a marl grey T-shirt that, thanks to the straps of his rucksack pulling it tight across his chest, she could clearly see the contours of his pecs under.

She'd spent the day wondering what the hell she should wear. Something that said *I didn't try too hard*, but that also conveyed *seriously hot even when not trying too hard*. She had clearly hit pay dirt because Jasper looked at her cream full-length hippie dress and tan wedge sandals with some interest.

'Is that what you're wearing?'

Okay, that wasn't the reaction she was expecting.

'Why? What's wrong with it?'

'It might get dirty.'

'Why, what are we doing?' she asked.

'What do you think we're doing?'

'I don't know. Drinks?'

She'd wanted to text him to ask, unsure whether she should

218

eat first, but she didn't have his number. She'd erred on the side of caution and had a snack.

He glanced shiftily at the roses around the flat's front door, then back at her. 'You didn't think this was a date, did you?'

'No!'

Not a *date* date at least. But if not drinks, what?

'I was asking you to do some outreach with me.'

'Outreach?'

'Finding vulnerable people. Giving them advice. Handing out a few leaflets.' He gestured to the rucksack.

'Like a blue plaque tour, but of homeless people?'

He chuckled. 'Kind of like that.'

Her face was flushing.

'Are you blushing? I don't think I've seen you blush before, and I've seen Gayle break a toilet door down on you.'

The capillaries in her face redoubled their efforts. 'I didn't think it was a date.'

He chuckled again.

'I didn't!' she said.

'Okay, okay.' He held up his hands. 'You didn't think it was a date.'

His nipples were unignorable under his top. They were enjoying this as much as he was.

'It's weird to see you embarrassed. I thought your emotional spectrum lay somewhere between *couldn't care less* and *couldn't care lesser.*'

She considered slamming the door in his face.

'And are you wearing one of those outfits that says *I didn't try too hard,* but that you agonised over for ages? Like you might pick if you thought you were going out on a date.'

She pulled one of the roses off the bush and threw it in his face. 'Just because you're a psychologist doesn't mean you know everything about everyone.'

He flicked a petal off his shoulder.

'I'm not even wearing nice underwear,' she said. 'Here, I'll show you.'

'That's not necessary.'

'No, please, I insist.'

He covered his eyes as she made to reveal her pants.

'Woah! I was teasing you!'

She dropped her skirt, and he dropped his hands.

'It's okay,' he said. 'I know you wouldn't date someone like me.'

She hunted for a hint of disappointment in his voice.

'You do outreach on a Saturday night. Why would *anyone* want to date someone like you?'

'It's only once a month, and honestly, you don't have to come if you don't want to.'

'I'll get changed.'

He groaned. 'I'll make myself comfortable, shall I?'

'I won't be long.'

'Do you need me to Google *homeless outreach attire* for you?'

She smilingly closed the door in his face.

They headed east. It was one of those glorious balmy evenings you get in London, the day's mugginess having subsided into a warm hug. Delicious smells of a hundred different cuisines permeated the air. Jasper explained how it was a good time to head out because, by that time, many homeless people had settled into their pitches for the night, unlikely to be moved on by police whose attentions had turned instead to the drunk and disorderly.

The task was simple – for him at least. Brief chat, check they were okay, highlight the services available, give them a leaflet. No judgment, no hard sell. She was terrified. It was difficult enough talking to people at the shelter, but those on the street?

'Just be yourself,' he said. 'Actually, on second thoughts…'

She punched his arm.

'Ow!'

They wandered down various alleyways and back streets, none of which she'd set foot in before. Dotted along them, like human litter, were the people who'd been discarded to live amongst the flotsam and jetsam. It was like seeing the city from a completely different angle, turned inside on itself, all the viscera and sinew on the outside. Jasper told her of all the ways the authorities attempted to 'cleanse' the streets – the anti-vagrancy laws, the unnecessary shuttering of doorways, the deliberate jet-washing of pavements upon which people were sleeping. Yet still they persisted, inserting themselves into nooks and crannies in the hopes of safety or slumber, because what other choice did they have?

They met an old man whose face was still swollen from a beating he'd received from a random stranger; a middle-aged former soldier, for whom a spiral of mental health issues had taken him from the front line to the breadline; a woman, probably younger than her ravaged face suggested, who refused any idea of help, but offered herself up instead, should Jasper be interested in her services. Every time he knelt to speak to them, she stayed on the sidelines, unsure what to say. But despite him being so assured, so gently persuasive, no one had taken a leaflet; in fact, no one had seemed remotely interested in getting help. It was frustrating as hell.

'How do you keep going?' she asked him.

'It's not their fault. They've been woefully let down time and again. It's little surprise they're sceptical.'

It was starting to get dark. They'd been out for over two hours and her flip-flops were rubbing between her toes, so she was glad to stop for their next 'customer'. The guy was sat by the vent of an air conditioning unit behind a stretch of curry houses. He had keen eyes and was, seemingly, completely sober. Jasper crouched down next to him.

'How are you doing, mate?'

'How do you think I'm doing?' He had a thick north-eastern accent.

'My name's Jasper and this is Simone. We're here to check in and see if there's anything we can do to help you this evening?'

'A night at The Ritz wouldn't go amiss.'

Jasper held out a leaflet. 'Can't do that, but there are resources you can access.'

'I don't need leaflets, pal,' he said dismissively. 'I need money.'

'You can't argue with that,' said Simone.

The man eyed her curiously. 'What's a dazzler like you doing in an alleyway like this?'

'I'm asking myself the same question.'

'Where's that accent from?' asked Jasper, like it wasn't obvious.

'Newcastle.'

'Ah well,' she said. 'Better to be homeless here than housed there, eh?'

The man's peeved expression creased into a smile. 'Don't be dissing the motherland!'

'Come on, mate. I've been to Newcastle. It's as cold as Antarctica and Eldon Square is like Dante's nine circles of hell.'

The man nodded his head in agreement.

'Don't get me wrong, I really like what you've done with the place.' She gestured to his patch. 'You've feng shuied your cardboard arrangement, and the socks drying on the air-con is a lovely touch. But you deserve better, right?'

The man nodded again.

'Plus, Jasper here has a Jesus complex that is out of control, and today he has chosen you as the person he's trying to save. That's nice, isn't it?'

The man agreed.

'So will you put your completely understandable cynicism to one side, take the leaflet and call the number? Because the sooner we hit our targets for the evening, and I don't even know what those are, the sooner I get to sink into a hot bath. Sorry, I know you don't have that option.'

'Fair enough, pet.' He took the leaflet.

'But you must call. This isn't toilet paper; this is potentially life-changing information. Yes, the government are a bunch of fuck-trumpets, and yes, it isn't going to be easy to leave this beautiful sanctuary you've created, and yes, everything is stacked against you, but there are people out there who aren't total wankers waiting to do whatever they can to help. But that has to start with a phone call. Do you have a phone?'

'Aye.'

'Great. You probably won't call, but we'd really fucking love it if you did.'

'I'm going to.'

'Cool.'

The man turned his attention back to Jasper. 'That's one canny lass you've got there.'

'She's not my girlfriend,' said Jasper just as Simone pointed out he wasn't her boyfriend.

'Well, whatever you are, cheers for stopping by.'

They walked away, her heart beating a little more strongly than it had been. She'd got someone to engage! Once they'd reached the main road, Jasper stopped and put his hand on her arm.

'Simone. That was…'

He had an intensity about him. Was he going to lay into her for breaking protocol?

'…badass,' he said.

'Badass good, or badass bad?'

'Badass amazing!'

'Really?'

'Yeah. Like, you were rude to him, but in a totally caring way. And he responded really well. It was only a minute, but you made a proper connection. You could be good at this!'

'Noooo. I am not good at this.'

But he was looking at her through slitted eyes.

'Don't look at me like that,' she said.

'I think you should do another one.'

'I think I should quit whilst I'm ahead.'

'One more and then we can quit.' He was shifting from foot to foot, like he'd made some grand discovery and couldn't wait to tell people about it.

'What's up with you?'

He regarded her in that weird way again.

'Wait a minute,' she said, cottoning on. 'I see what's going on. You're like Henry Higgins in *My Fair Lady* when he gets Eliza Doolittle to speak proper.'

'To speak *properly*,' he corrected her, a smile playing on his lips.

'You think we've had some kind of breakthrough here, don't you?'

He nodded fervently.

'We haven't. It's part of my job to persuade and cajole. That's what I do to make up for my lack of empathy.'

'Lack of empathy. Sure. We'll gloss over the fact that you're clearly well-acquainted with the finer details of *My Fair Lady*, a *musical* known for its uplifting and joyous qualities.'

'Fine. So I like musicals.'

He did his best Rex Harrison, all bemused disbelief. 'What a surprising *guttersnipe* you are.'

'Ah, so you like musicals too, do you?'

'My mum is a fan. You, however...' He wiggled an accusatory finger at her. 'I think you might actually care.'

'I don't.'

'What about the suits?'

'I was proving a point.'

'Maybe that was true then. But now? Now you really do want to help. I'm witnessing my very own *Pygmalion*.'

His eyes narrowed. The amusement had been replaced by something else. Not surprise but ... pride maybe? No one had been proud of her for a long time. Least of all herself.

'On the subject of guttersnipes,' she said, keen to move things on, 'didn't you say something about one more? Come on.'

'After you, milady.' He bowed deeply.

'You are such a dick.'

'Charmed, I'm sure.'

'Can I grab a soft drink first? I'm gasping.'

'You may.'

Nighttime had finally lain its velvet cloak over the city. She ducked into a shop whose vivid strip lighting made her vision pulse. She checked her reflection in the mirrored rear of the fridge from which she pulled a water. She was no Audrey Hepburn, in so many ways, but she could view the face that looked back at her with greater compassion than she had been able to. *Okay, final push*, she mouthed.

———————————

They heard the man before they saw him, his plaintive moans audible above the thrum of the city. He was doubled over on the floor, contorting and writhing as if in considerable pain, his joggers halfway down his legs, soiled boxers on show. She'd been hoping for a happy drunk, not someone acting like they were in the grip of a zombie apocalypse.

'Jesus. What's wrong with him?' she asked.

'He'll have smoked something.' Jasper tried to get his attention without success.

'Like what?'

'Spice, most likely.'

She'd joked about spice before, but had never seen anyone on it in real life.

'Is he in pain?'

'No. But the hallucinations make you agitated.' He struggled to get the man into the recovery position. 'Can you help me?'

She didn't want to touch him, but she bent down and talked soothingly as they manoeuvred his resistant body into place. She'd barely got his legs bent when he suddenly sat bolt upright, opened his eyes, and projectile vomited all over her.

It took her a moment to register what was happening, puke pooling around her belly where she'd crouched down. She shot upright and attempted to brush it off, only that meant she now had some stranger's sick on her hands, as well as all over the jersey playsuit she'd changed into earlier. The realisation hit her brain just as the smell hit her nostrils. She'd never been good with vomit, and this situation was like vomit to the power of vomit, with an extra helping of … fuck … she was going to throw up. Her stomach heaved, the wet fabric clinging to her abdomen despite the involuntary contraction. She urgently breathed through her mouth, trying to quell her body's disgust, but her salivary glands had gone into overdrive, preparing for the inevitable onslaught. A couple of uncontrollable heaves later and there it was, a great acrid outpouring of the water she'd drunk, the scrambled eggs she'd had before coming out, the remains of her tuna salad lunch, all splattering violently and loudly onto the cobbles at her feet. If Jasper seeing her in this state wasn't bad enough, she was horrified to note his hand on her neck, his fingers acting as a makeshift band to keep the hair from her face.

'I'm sorry,' she managed between heaves, 'I really can't deal with it when people are sick.'

'Shhh,' he said, his other hand gently rubbing her back. 'Just get it all out.'

After a minute or so, she felt confident she'd emptied her stomach. She took a mouthful of water, swilled it across her soiled tongue and spat it out. God, this was so embarrassing.

'Turns out you're as good with sick as I am with blood,' he said with a small smirk.

How long had he waited to get his own back for that?

'I can't believe you're bringing that up now.'

'I'm not the one bringing stuff up.' He pointed at the pool of vomit.

Its sour smell caught in her throat again. 'Oh god, don't.'

The words had barely left her mouth before a further mix of bile and foaming saliva tagged onto their coat-tails.

'Sorry,' he said when she'd finished. 'It was a cheap shot.'

She took another drink and then rinsed off her hands and feet, emptying the bottle.

Jasper examined her face far more closely than was welcome after she'd nearly retched up a lung. 'You really are as white as a sheet,' he said.

She stared back at him, sang-froid returning. 'You're not.'

His face remained straight long enough for her to think that maybe the joke was too inappropriate, but then a succulent laugh escaped from his parted lips, a rich guffaw that seemed to reverberate off the walls. Her own wasn't far behind, her cheeks swelling momentarily as her brain wondered what possible cause for mirth might exist given the circumstances, but then it erupted from her with full force. Within seconds, their laughter had taken on a self-powering momentum of its own, increasing in pitch and magnitude as they each replayed the ridiculousness of their situation over in their heads. She hadn't laughed like that for years, not the kind of laughter that hurt the temples and weakened the knees and had you clawing for breath.

When it finally subsided, she thought to check on the homeless man, barely stifling a second bout of hilarity when she saw he was viewing them with catatonic impartiality, all signs of distress gone.

'Seriously, though,' she managed. 'I'll never get a cab like this, and I can't get on the tube.'

Jasper examined the full extent of the damage on her clothes. 'I don't live very far. You should come back to mine and get cleaned up. I feel responsible.'

'That's because you are responsible.'

'I'm so sorry.'

'What about this guy?'

Jasper dropped onto his haunches. 'You okay, mate?'

The man was in far better shape than he had been. He nodded mutely.

'How far away is your place?' she asked.

'About a fifteen-minute walk.'

She pointed to the vomit on her, revulsion returning. 'I'll pretend this is a fashion statement, shall I?'

He was thinking. He took a Swiss army knife from his pocket, cut the bottom off the water bottle, and used it as a scoop to remove the worst of it. She would have been impressed by his ingenuity had it not been for the fact he was scraping regurgitated food off her. The ribbing about the Swiss army knife could wait.

He then took off his T-shirt and handed it to her. She would have been impressed by his generosity had it not been for … oh my god, okay, she was impressed. If his body had looked delectable beneath his clothes, out of them it was, to put it mildly, TASTY AF. Every morsel of it was in exactly the place it was meant to be, each muscle sculpted into the perfect version of itself.

In the pale streetlights, the overall effect was of a walnut statue, sanded and buffed to a smooth subtle sheen.

'That should cover the worst of it if you'd prefer to head home,' he said, calm as you like.

Her treacherous hormones told her she was heading wherever that torso was going. 'Do you have alcohol?' she asked.

'I have red wine in.'

'Great. I need a drink.'

Jasper's place was in a large nondescript sandy-coloured block of ex-council flats, the only character being provided by the boxy balconies tacked on at various junctures along its façade.

'Did you orchestrate this so I had to come back?' she asked.

'Do men often pull elaborate ruses to do that?'

He'd be surprised at some of the crap she'd heard with precisely that aim.

He opened the front door. 'Boring as it may sound, if I wanted to get you back to mine, I would just ask.'

It was a modest place, with a lounge, a kitchen and a bedroom branching off from the small square hallway into which she'd stepped.

'The shower room is through the bedroom. There are towels in the cupboard. There should be an unopened toothbrush in there too.'

She passed through the bedroom. It was sparsely decorated, but surprisingly stylish, with elegant mid-century furniture and a bed with both a throw and cushions. She wasn't sure what she'd been expecting; one of those hippie wall hangings they ship in from India perhaps? The shower cubicle was small, but the water flow was powerful. As she squeezed some body wash onto her hands, the fragrance of bergamot mingling with the steam, she was grateful to finally have the smell of bile out of her nostrils.

At first, she attempted to keep her face out of the water; she hadn't brought any make-up out with her. Then again, he'd seen her covered in another man's stomach contents, so perhaps seeing her without slap was no biggie. Even so, she mussed her hair in the mirror afterwards, and made the best use of the smudges of black that remained under her eyes. When she stepped back into the bedroom, a pair of jersey drawstring shorts and three T-shirts had been laid out on the bed.

'There's a choice of tops there,' he called. 'I figured you'd have a preference. The bottoms are the most adjustable I have.'

She checked the labels. Gap. George. Next. 'I think I preferred the vomit,' she shouted back.

'You can go home in the towel if you like.'

She chose the George one, an inexpensive band T-shirt rip off. It would suit the smudgy eyes and messy hair.

In the lounge, also mid-century in style, he'd laid some snacks out on a teak coffee table, and chill tunes emanated from a small speaker. He handed her a glass of wine.

'That's a good look on you,' he said.

'Very funny.'

'I'd better make myself decent too.'

Pity. She was just getting to the point where she could look at him without staring at his pecs. She helped herself to some dips and crisps and then had a nosy at the shelves that ran the full width of the wall. There were a lot of books, a mish-mash of self-help texts, airport paperbacks and more meaty fodder about human behaviour. She pulled one, *The Social Animal*, off the shelf and read the epigraph.

Man is by nature a social animal... anyone who either cannot lead the common life or is so self-sufficient not to need to, and therefore does not partake of society, is either a beast or god.

Did not having any social engagements that weekend make her a beast?

'Cheers, Aristotle.'

There were only two photographs in the whole room. One of Jasper with an older woman with very pale skin, big red-rimmed glasses, and a smile that would light up the London Eye. The other was of him with a pretty pale blonde, possibly the one she'd seen him with at Secret Cinema.

He reappeared wearing the Gap T-shirt. She disliked it even more now she knew what it was covering.

She pointed at the photo. 'The ex-girlfriend?' It was odd to have kept the photo if so, but it would be just like him.

'Sister.'

She took another quizzical glance at the face in the frame. So they had different dads?

'I'm adopted.'

'Oh.'

That was the last thing she expected.

'I'm sorry.'

'That I was adopted? Don't be. Could have been worse – could have *not* been adopted.'

'I just mean—'

'Don't worry. I've been through the angry, rejected, woe-is-me stage. I was quite the tearaway when I was younger.'

'You, a tearaway? Did you wear your school tie a bit looser than it should have been?'

'No, we're talking police involvement-level naughtiness.' He chewed the inside of his mouth. 'But I got lucky. Mum never gave up on me.'

'No adopted dad?'

'No.'

The rug of assumption had been well and truly pulled from under her feet.

'Was it weird being...' She wasn't entirely sure how to phrase the question.

'Go on...' he said, amused.

'... *Black,*' she hazarded, 'in a white family?'

He grabbed his face in mock surprise. 'You mean I'm gonna stay this colour?'

'Eh?'

'Sorry. Steve Martin reference. Out of the film *The Jerk*. It's a comedy about a white guy raised in a Black family. I used to say it when I was a kid and people asked me the same thing. Amused me no end.'

She sat down and drew her legs up onto the sofa. 'Aren't psychologists meant to make people feel at ease?'

He sat at the other end of the sofa and pulled the coffee table closer to them. 'You're thinking of medical doctors. Psychologists are meant to challenge people's assumptions to force them to think differently about themselves.'

She sensed he was about to go into another of his long speeches, so she pointed at the other picture. 'Your mum, then?'

A broad grin spread across his face. 'Yes. That's Pat.'

It transpired that Pat, already single mum to Jessica, decided there was room in her heart for another kid. Jasper, who had been in foster care for three years since birth, was that kid. It clearly hadn't been an easy road for them. Apart from all the standard challenges that come with adoption, he described the difficulties of feeling dislocated from his cultural roots. There had been no playbook for interracial adoption back then; the feeling that any family was better than no family persisted, and the impact of not exploring great chunks of a child's heritage wasn't understood.

'I'm mixed race,' he clarified, 'and it wasn't like I was the only kid like me at school. This is London, after all. But a lot of my mates called me Bounty Boy.'

She was starting to feel tipsy; drinking on an emptied stomach would do that to you.

'As in *the taste of paradise?*'

The look on his face suggested she'd blundered again.

'No! As in brown on the outside, white on the inside. I think that's when I really started acting out.'

He poured them another drink and went on to describe a few incidences – involving truancy, weed and graffiti – that could easily have been described as high jinks by someone other than Jasper.

'So when the turnaround?' she asked.

'Pat wasn't having it. She went to work. She incorporated more of my culture into our home life; learned how to make jerk chicken and lots of other Jamaican food; went completely overboard on the Bob Marley posters and records. Then she set out to make friends in the Afro-Caribbean community. Took me to Brixton markets and community centre events there. Just imagine what they thought of us three, turning up at these rowdy socials, my mum trying to do the butterfly to Chaka Deamus & Pliers dressed in her twinset!'

His eyes glistened at the memories he continued to relate.

'I was mortified at the time, but it worked. I stopped being an idiot and I knuckled down. What can I say? I have the best mum in the world.' He glanced at her over his glass. 'Sorry,' he said. 'That's not very tactful. That business with your mum must have been tough.'

She took a large swig of her wine. 'Not really. I've always dealt with my emotions by not having any.'

'You know having emotions doesn't make you damaged or weak, right? It makes you human.'

'Just because I'm on your couch, Doctor, doesn't mean I'm *on your couch*.'

'You are so frustrating, woman! You think that not talking about your feelings is a superpower. It isn't. It's your greatest weakness.'

She needed to change the subject. 'If I did have a superpower, it would be Atmokinesis.'

'Which is…?'

'The ability to control weather. Like Thor.'

'You watch superhero movies?'

'Yep.'

'Isn't that a bit nerdy?'

'What, because I'm attractive, I can't like nerdy things?'

'Who said you were attractive?'

She gently kicked him, then left her leg breaching the middle cushion divide.

'Although this is the best I've seen you,' he said. 'Au naturel suits you.'

She had the urge to hide behind one of his cushions. Instead, she shook her glass at him like you might a waiter. 'I've finished my wine. More please!'

'Stay there, your highness.'

He fetched the wine. They must have been drinking from deceptively large glasses because there was nothing left in what had been a full bottle when he finished the refill.

He settled back down on the sofa. 'So, you don't have any brothers or sisters?'

'I did, but I consumed them.'

'You consumed them?!'

'I had a growth on my ovary; discovered it when I was twenty. I was worried I might have cancer, but it turned out to be a teratoma. Some people call them an evil twin. It was all hair and teeth and skin and body bits. Really freaky shit.'

He winced, clearly revulsed. She enjoyed that she could shock him.

'What impact does that have?'

'It messes around with your reproductive lifespan. And, well, I'm already thirty-five.'

'And yet you have the jadedness of a much older woman.'

'I try. But yeah, it means I might not be able to have kids.'

She watched for his reaction. Most people she revealed this information to, including previous boyfriends, greeted it with condolences bordering on the pathological.

'Jesus,' he said. 'That's a relief! One of you is more than enough.'

It was the perfect response.

'I think my mum would have been happy to suffer from a similar affliction,' she said.

'Well, we have that in common at least.' He raised his glass.

'Did you ever try to find your birth parents?'

'I tried. But they didn't want to know.' He shrugged. 'I'm sure they had their reasons.'

She was starting to see why a belief that certain behaviours were preordained, and therefore outside the control of the individual, might be of comfort to him. Silence settled on them. She sank further into the cushions. If she'd been out with the girls, they'd have only just been getting started. She was grateful to have her feet up on a comfy sofa, and for Jasper's easy company.

'How did you get into reputation management?' he asked.

'I don't recall telling you I was in reputation management.'

'I looked you up on LinkedIn.'

'Why?'

'Because I couldn't find you on Instagram.' He said it in a matter-of-fact way, like there was no subtext to him searching for her at all.

Simone explained that when the photographer threw her out,

she'd got a job in experiential marketing, handing out product samples and the like. She'd had to share cheap, awful digs with a bunch of other disillusioned girls, but it had been the leg up she needed. Naturally forthright, staff management followed. Then the account handling side, helping with ideas and selling them to clients. She was freelancing for Dixon & Astley when they decided to create an arm of the business dedicated to events. She headed it all up. She was just waiting to be made a partner and to be added to the board, which is where the big bucks finally happened.

'Don't you have to smile and be pleasant to be a promotional girl?' he asked.

'I can smile. I didn't get to be a Miss London finalist without being able to switch on the charm.'

'What was your platform?'

'World peace.'

'How were you going to secure that?'

'By having perky tits.'

He laughed. 'Do you like your job?'

'Does anyone?'

'I like mine.'

'You're the exception.'

'It's frustrating and heartbreaking and hard, but hugely rewarding. If I can help just one person…'

'You'd be doing a terrible job and falling way short of any reasonable targets that should be expected of you.'

'Yeah. Probably.' He smiled.

'Gayle clearly doesn't like it.'

'Not at all. She loves it.'

'But—'

'I know she comes across as being a ballbreaker. But she needs to. All too often, shelters are unsafe places to be, what with drug abuse, violent behaviour and the like. She works really hard to ensure Cedar Lodge isn't like that, precisely because she loves it.'

She'd never noticed before, but when he spoke earnestly, one of his fuzzy eyebrows kinked slightly, like there was a hidden scar holding the skin taut whilst the rest moved freely around it. He barely moved his jaw at all, the words seemingly emerging unbidden from his soft lips. Brilliant backchat aside, there was an immense authenticity to him. He was, she realised, the kindest person she knew. And quite possibly the smartest too. A fortnight ago, she'd imagined working in a shelter was a pretty low bar to have set yourself, but now she understood it to be a vocation. And, against the backdrop of the life he might have had, a startling achievement. She bet Pat and Jessica were immensely proud of him.

'Are you still there?'

He'd said something.

'Huh?'

'I said the woman is a closet softie, like someone else I know.' He put his glass down. 'You did really well tonight.'

She was squiffy enough to take the compliment. 'It's not often I go out and have someone chuck up on me.'

Despite the whole chundering episode, she was grateful the girls had decided to stay in America an extra week.

'If this *had* been a date,' he said, 'it definitely would have been a memorable one.'

He looked directly at her in a way that, had this been any other man or any other circumstance, she would have interpreted as *charged*. But he was probably messing with her. She wanted to say something witty and provocative to call his bluff, only her mind was drawing a blank. What time was it? They'd been talking for ages. What time did the tubes stop in this neck of the woods? She should probably think about going if she didn't want to stump for a cab home. He really was good company though. Very engaging, relaxed, insanely sexy company. She wondered if his bottom half was as attractive as his top half, or where the smooth hair-freeness stopped, and the springy moss of his pubic hair started. She wondered what it would be like to lean forward and kiss him, for those pillowy lips to meet hers; to feel his tongue in her mouth, his hands snaking up her legs and into the baggy leg of the shorts he'd lent her. Her pants were in a ball inside her playsuit in the bathroom; would he be surprised to feel her nakedness there? How long before he was begging her to fuck him? Or that she was begging him to fuck her? She stared hard back at him, shifted slightly in the chair, felt the vague moistness of her pussy as she did so. She hadn't had truly satisfying sex in a while. Her thing with Marcus was on a fast track to nowhere, she knew that. She'd imagined that was its charm, but Marcus wasn't a nice guy, he wasn't even that interesting. She didn't have stimulating, thought-provoking conversations with him like she did with Jasper. No, she didn't want Marcus's ungracious groping hands on her. She wanted Jasper's gentle assured fingers tiptoeing over her body like it was a globe to be explored. The idea unhitched itself from her subconscious and floated before her. Shit. She really, really wanted to sleep with Jasper. Of course, she'd always considered the prospect. He was fit, she was fit, and the idea of how their two bodies might slot together was an inevitable consequence of them being in the same orbit as one another. The problem, she understood in that moment, was that she really wanted Jasper to *want* to sleep with her. Not for sport. Not for the sake of winning some unspoken competition between them. Not because he was a man and every hole was a goal. No. She really wanted him to want to because, in some small but significant way, he might like her like she now realised she liked him.

He was still looking at her. She returned his gaze through heavy-lidded eyes. Was something going to happen?

'Excuse me one sec,' he said.

He got up and left the room. Had he gone to get more wine? To go to the toilet? To remove the pile of retro jazz mags from under his bed? Maybe he was getting a condom? She hoped she looked okay; there was no mirror in which she might check herself out. Were they really going to do this? Should they? Would Gayle be able to tell on Monday? Who cared, that was then. Right now, she just wanted to feel the full weight of his attention, and his body, on her. She'd worry about the consequences later. She arranged herself on the sofa in as effortlessly a sexy way as possible, rested her head against one of his scatter cushions, and closed her eyes to imagine what deliciousness might lie in wait.

Chapter Thirty-Three

It was a crack of light through the drawn curtains that woke her. Where was she? Her brain slowly cranked into gear. Jasper's flat. Something had happened last night. Something had changed between them. She had... No, *they* had...

Only this wasn't his bedroom, this was definitely his lounge. They weren't naked and spooning in his neat little bed. She was still on the sofa. Still fully dressed. The only change from her last memory of the evening was the addition of a light sheet over her body, and a dark pool of dribble on the cushion under her head. Bollocks! Somewhere between the meaningful looks and him coming back into the room, she'd fallen asleep. She retrieved her phone from the floor. It was 5:30am.

Why hadn't he woken her? Any normal man would have made some noise, gently nudged her back to consciousness. Hell, any normal man would have shoved a hard-on into the small of her back and hoped for the best. What was wrong with him? Or worse, what was wrong with her? Perhaps she'd misread the signals, but she was usually pretty good with signals, especially the sexual ones. She was no mathematician but, under normal conditions, lots of wine plus shared sofa plus no pants equals serious boning. But these weren't normal conditions. Jasper wasn't a normal guy. In fact, he wasn't like anyone she had ever met. He was…

She brought up the Uber app on her phone. She needed to get out of here.

Chapter Thirty-Four

A whole family of bats had taken up residence in her stomach as she approached the shelter's office on Monday morning. She'd spent the rest of the weekend replaying the circumstances of Saturday night over and over in her head. She'd half-expected Jasper to text her on Sunday to check that she was okay. When he hadn't, she'd told herself that he might not have her number; just because she'd written it on the form didn't mean he'd saved it to his phone. But having run the idea past the girls on a WhatsApp chat, they'd decided that was as unlikely as one of Hozan's theories, of which she'd also apprised them. She needed to accept that, unlike her, he hadn't spent the rest of the weekend picking over the details of their time together like a starving vulture over carrion.

She stopped at the door, took a deep breath, and went inside. Gayle was at her computer, staring intently at the screen, but when she saw Simone, she stood up and started applauding, beating out a slow and steady rhythm that made her large watch jangle. Simone glanced at Jasper in confusion, but he wasn't giving anything away.

'So, you did it,' said Gayle.

'What?'

Was she talking about her and Jasper? Was she about to get a massive bollocking?

'Steve's benefits came through.'

'What?'

'You should have received his advance this morning. A deal's a deal.'

'What deal?'

She sounded like an imbecile.

'I said if you sorted his benefits, you could leave early.'

She'd forgotten all about that agreement.

'Won't my probation officer have something to say about that?'

'I can deal with him.'

'What about that filing I was going to start on?'

'What? Did you mean your nails?'

Gayle looked to Jasper for recognition of the joke, but he was staring intently at Simone. All the other plans she'd had for the week ran through her head. After the disappointment of what didn't happen, she'd channelled her energies into something more productive on Sunday. She'd spoken to Wei about coming in and doing a little pamper session for everyone – nothing major, just manicures and pedicures – but she'd found a news story about someone doing something similar, and it had provided a real boost to everyone. She'd ordered some salad seeds, compostable pots, and a small vinyl greenhouse for Tasha to help her get her little cottage garden going. She'd even considered cleaning Hozan's car. But none of that was likely to happen now; she was going back to work.

'Unless, for any reason, you wanted to stay on?' said Gayle.

She looked at Jasper. Jasper looked at her. Gayle looked at both of them.

'What the hell is up with you pair? Simone, you look like a cat took a shit in your Gucci handbag. Jasper, you look like, well, you look like you could have been the cat.' She scrutinised their faces. 'Have I missed something?'

Jasper stayed resolutely schtum.

'No,' she said, chin lifted, face hot. 'You've not missed anything. Absolutely nothing of interest has happened. Nada. Nought. Zip. Zilch. Diddly squat. Toss all. On a scale of one to interesting, my weekend ranks as not very.'

'Can't say I'm not pleased to hear it,' said Gayle. 'Still, you'll be back with your reputation management buddies, managing reputations like a reputation managing dynamo before you know it. I'm sure they'll be thrilled to have you back.'

'I'm sure they will,' she said, still glaring at Jasper. 'And I'll be absolutely thrilled to be back.'

She spent the morning aggressively deep cleaning the bathrooms, locking the door behind her so she wouldn't be disturbed. At lunch, she intended to sneak out and get something stodgy and fattening to eat, but Tasha collared her before she got the chance.

'Gayle says you're leaving early.'

'Seems like it.'

'You pleased?'

She knew she should be, but a pang of melancholy tugged at her ribs. It was like the last day of a holiday, the anticipation of normality both a reason for contentment and disappointment. She still had this last day to enjoy, but the real world – her other one – was already encroaching, its fingertips tightening their grip.

'I guess.'

'I know this is going to sound weird,' said Tasha, 'and you can say no, but I wondered if you'd come to my next scan with me?'

'Umm.'

'I'm not asking you to be her godmother or anything. I don't want anything from you. I guess it was just nice to have someone there the last time. I asked Hozan, but he said ultrasound waves cause Havana Syndrome, and something about health attacks by Russia. You know what he's like.'

She smiled for the first time that day. Yep. She knew. 'When is it?'

'Not for a few weeks. I can give you some petrol money. Maybe.'

'I don't need you to give me petrol money.'

'Is that because you won't come with me?'

She recalled how Tasha had been treated at the maternity hospital last time. It was a very small thing to ask. 'No, it's because I'll come with you anyway. And we can take the tube.'

'Okay. Cool.'

'Cool.'

'Also,' said Tasha, 'we thought we'd have a little picnic for you this afternoon. It won't be much. Steve's made some cupcakes. They are awful, so don't eat any. Hozan is bringing his biscuit tin, and I'm making a quiche.'

'Well, if you're making a quiche, how can I say no?'

She was touched. Perhaps they did this for everyone, but even so, it demonstrated a generosity of spirit she continued to be surprised by. She wished there was something else she could offer them, something that might have a lasting impact on their lives.

'See you outside at three-ish?' asked Tasha.

She nodded. She'd have to forego her big lunch, but she could eat all her feelings back at her desk tomorrow. Why wasn't she finding the notion particularly appetising?

By the time she joined the three of them on a picnic blanket outside, she'd settled on the best possible way to spend the remaining couple of hours of her community service.

'Do not tell Gayle,' she said, 'but I'm going to teach you all how to beg. Efficiently. So you can make the money you need to move on when you're ready to.'

'But begging's illegal,' said Tasha.

'I know. But it's also criminal how difficult it is to get the help you deserve, so, you know, needs must. And if you do what I tell you, no one will really know.'

Hozan smiled. 'Are we going to play them at their own game?'

She nodded. Kind of, she guessed. She'd spent her lunch hour doing some internet research. There were a surprising number of studies conducted on how best to solicit money from people. Context was everything. People were more generous when exposed to pleasant smells, so it stood to reason that a pitch outside a bakery or launderette would boost donations. Wearing a tie increased the likelihood of people giving you money, so Steve should wear his suit.

'Have you still got it?' she asked.

'Yep.'

Being very specific about the amount of money needed gave the impression it had a non-nefarious use and thus increased consideration. Creating a sign that referenced the good fortune of the potential donor, not the bad fortune of the receiver, boosted empathy and giving. And reciprocity, particularly offering something intriguing or interesting in exchange for cash, could overcome reluctance to give.

'Steve, when were you born?'

He gave the date and then began describing the exact circumstances of his birth.

'Not now,' she said. 'Hozan, what day was that?'

They watched as Hozan quickly counted something on his fingers.

'Tuesday.'

She checked the answer on her phone. He was right. Steve whistled.

'And what was at number one in the charts that week?'

Hozan rattled off an answer. Again, he was correct.

'I think with Tasha acting as a sidekick, you have a regular old sideshow there. Invite people to bet a few pounds on whether you'll get it right or not.'

'But Hozan won't want to draw attention to himself,' said Tasha.

Hozan noted the hand Tasha was resting on her belly. 'If it helps Tasha, I'll try it.'

'You don't need to.'

He looked sternly at her. 'I'll try it.'

'I think you could also be doing an excellent sideline in pub quizzes. But let's start small.'

She helped herself to a large slice of quiche – Tasha really was an amazing cook – and watched as the idea took on life. Tasha suggested they could run a mini workshop with some of the other day visitors on the quiet, since they too could benefit from this information. Steve was getting misty-eyed about seeing his son again. She wondered if she should stay to the end of the week and see what other proactive ideas she might come up with, but then the chattering stopped. Jasper was standing over them, eyebrows raised.

'Good afternoon, Jasper,' said Hozan.

'When were you going to tell me there was quiche?' He was wearing the third T-shirt from the selection he'd offered her.

'And cakes,' said Steve.

'I heard about the cakes.'

Steve nodded. 'Yeah, the kitchen never was my strong suit. There was this one time—'

Jasper cleared his throat. 'I wondered if I might borrow Simone for a few minutes.'

'Actually,' she said, 'we were just—'

'Yep,' Tasha butted in. 'You can take her.'

'All yours,' said Steve.

Her eyes widened in remonstration. They gazed innocently back. She stood up and let Jasper lead her away until they were out of earshot.

'A little picnic, eh?' he said. 'You've really made an impression. Nice one.'

'Are you patronising me?'

'Why do you always assume I'm patronising you?'

'Because you're a very patronising person.'

'Or perhaps it's because you think it's too far beyond the realm of possibility that you could have done something praiseworthy?'

'Just wanted to squeeze in a bit of last-minute psychoanalysis?'

'No. I came to say goodbye.'

'Oh.'

The word escaped her mouth involuntarily, like a gasp. She'd expected to see him later, hoped that they might still discuss Saturday's turn of events. Perhaps she'd harboured the teeniest fantasy that he'd ask her to go for a drink later, she would accept, and maybe they would…

'I've got an appointment,' he said, 'but I thought it would be courteous to come and say thanks for all your help. You should be proud of yourself.'

'You really are upping the condescension stakes. Maybe you should give me a pat on the head whilst you're at it?'

She was being a bitch.

'I imagined you'd be happier you were going.'

'Sure, I'm happy. I'm ecstatic. I'm over the fucking moon.'

'You don't appear very happy.'

She glared at him through sullen eyes.

'What's wrong?'

Great. Now he'd asked her outright. Why did he have to be

such a grown-up, ffs. Psychologists, man. They were all so … probing. And up front. And insightful. And sexy. Really bloody sexy.

'Uggghhhhh!'

It was a guttural cry, something from the recesses of her soul. And what was she meant to say? That she was deeply disappointed that he hadn't taken advantage of her. That it was as though some inalienable law of the universe had been violated – a rupture in the sex-time continuum. That somehow, in the last two and a half weeks, her opinion of herself had become inextricably intertwined with his opinion of her. And his failure to want to fornicate with her had come as both a refreshing revelation and an undermining of everything she valued about herself. Not only would she come across like a petulant idiot, but worse, she would give away the fact that his physical ambivalence towards her mattered. Like really mattered. There was absolutely no way she would ever give him the satisfaction by asking him. No bloody way.

'Why didn't you try and sleep with me?' she said.

He seemed genuinely taken aback. 'When? On Saturday?'

'Yes, of course on Saturday. Why didn't you try it on?'

'I'm just not that kind of guy.'

She threw up her hands. 'Come on! Every guy is that kind of guy.'

'I like you. I really do. But … I…' His face took on a pained expression. 'Not like that.'

Wow. There it was. Verbal proof, like she needed it. They hadn't been playing some will-they-won't-they game to ramp up the tension. He really didn't fancy her. And why would he? Why would someone like Jasper like someone like her? Sure, he said he liked her, but find someone on the planet Jasper didn't like. If a shark bit his leg off, he'd find a way to warm to it. Something about nature versus nurture, delivered in his easy, agreeable, nonjudgmental way. But he didn't fancy her. Didn't think of her *like that*. Which would be fine had it not been for the fact that she'd made it quite clear that it was precisely *like that* that she liked him.

'Gee, thanks.' Any notion of staying for the rest of the week quickly evaporated.

'No, what I mean is—'

She cut across him. 'It's fine. You don't need to explain. You're some morally superior specimen that isn't led by his dick. It's fine. Really, it's fine.'

'I don't think you think it's fine.'

He had that stupid concerned look on his face again.

'Don't tell me what I think, Jasper. That would make you like all the others. And you're...' She trailed off. She didn't need to blow any more smoke up his arse.

'I just meant—'

'I need to go to the toilet.' She walked towards the building.

'Hey!' he called after her.

She didn't stop.

'Simone!'

She upped the pace, but he caught up with her. She was reminded of the very first day that she'd met him.

'Would it be so terrible to just be friends?' he said.

'Oh my god. You're giving me the friend chat?! I don't need any more friends.'

They both knew this to be a lie.

'I really do have to go to the toilet.'

'I'm not stopping you.'

Only he was. There was some unseen pull about him. A gravitational field that with each orbit, each bants-filled interaction, had drawn her closer and closer into its rarefied atmosphere. He stepped aside, moving the celestial body that would remain unexplored out of her way.

He reached out as she passed him, his fingers lightly brushing against her arm. 'I'm here whenever you need me.'

Why did she feel like she was going to cry? She definitely didn't want to cry.

'Don't forget about us, okay,' he said.

Fuck. Her upper nostrils were tingling and everything. Time to rally.

'How could I? I've got the scar tissue to remind me. See?' She held up her fist to show him the still-angry patch of scalded skin, and then slowly and deliberately mimed cranking up her middle finger.

He smiled. Christ, that bloody smile.

'I hope to see you around.'

'Not if I see you first,' she said, which made no sense whatsoever.

On the toilet she texted Tony to let him know she'd be back early. He was thrilled, even if she wasn't. The client on whom she'd done the cursory research during Toiletgate – the Wolfe bloke – had invited them to pitch for a full corporate PR and events job promoting a series of new developments he had in the offing. He was creating apartments with hybrid office spaces beneath them. Apparently, it was going to be big. As in, *clear the decks, this is all you're going to be thinking about for weeks* big. Which was just what she needed to put the last couple of confusing weeks behind her.

On the way back past the seemingly empty office, a voice rang out.

'Oi, Duchess, come in here a second!'

Gayle was on the floor doing press-ups. She jumped to her feet. 'You weren't going to leave without saying goodbye, were you?'

'Yes.'

Gayle laughed. 'You're not such a bad sort, you know.'

'That means so much coming from charity's answer to Charles Bronson.'

'I hope you're taking something away with you.'

'Yeah. Scabies.'

Gayle chuckled. 'You made a difference. It all makes a difference, you know.'

She appreciated this moment of relative softness from Gayle, but she wasn't convinced.

'Being alive,' said Gayle, 'none of it's easy.'

Had she been talking to Jasper? But no, surely doctor–patient confidentiality was a thing, even when you weren't officially a patient.

'Go easy on yourself,' said Gayle.

'Never. I've still not forgiven myself for a lacklustre dream I had back in the noughties.'

'Well then, at least go easy on others.'

Hmm. Even her childhood imaginary friends had complexes, given how she'd held them to account.

Gayle held her arms out. 'Bring it in.'

'I'm fine.'

'Come on.'

'Honestly—'

'You know you want to.'

'Really, I'm—'

Gayle ignored her entreaties and enveloped her in a massive all-encompassing bear hug. When she finally let go, she flexed her bicep. 'Sure you don't want a last little feel?'

'Okay, fine.'

She tentatively reached out a hand towards the bulging flesh. As soon as her fingers made contact, Gayle shouted *boo* really loudly into her face.

Back outside, Hozan, Steve and Tasha got up to greet her.

'Time for me to get off.' Her voice wobbled.

Hozan shook her by the hand. 'Remember what I said. Don't make it easy for them.'

'I'll be careful.'

Next was Steve, with his comedy haircut and daft tracksuit.

'Thanks for sorting my money out, mate.'

'If I hear you've spent a penny of it on betting, I'm going to get Gayle to remove your thigh bone and then I'm going to beat you to a bloody pulp with it.'

'I won't let you down.'

'Kids need their dad, Steve.'

'I know.'

She turned to Tasha. 'And as for you, young lady. I'll be seeing you soon anyway, right?'

'That's the plan.'

She had the urge to reach out and touch her belly. That poor kid, inside that poor kid, like shitty-life Russian dolls. Should she give her a hug? Tasha didn't strike her as the hugging kind. Better not to invade her personal space.

'Are you going to be okay?' said Tasha.

Surely she should have been asking the girl that, but Tasha was observing her in that characteristic way of hers.

'I'll be fine,' she said, waving a dismissive hand.

She would be. She'd be fine. She just didn't feel it right now.

Chapter Thirty-Five

'Hi, Simone. How was your holiday?'

Nora had sashayed into the office kitchen where Simone was having a bowl of cereal, her usual posh coffee and croissant ritual now seeming too excessive.

'Great, thanks.'

'I bet you're sad to be back, aren't you?'

She was, but not in the way Nora meant. She'd woken up early with a weird mix of nerves, anticipation and melancholy lodged in her throat, like a hairball that she'd not yet managed to cough up.

'You're looking very casual today,' said Nora. 'Still in the San Fran vibes, eh?'

Simone had attempted to squeeze herself into one of her standard work outfits this morning, but having worn flat shoes and relatively non-constrictive waistbands for a fortnight, it was like mild torture. She'd opted instead for some wide-legged pants and a short-sleeved shirt. Work was challenging enough without having to navigate it in corporate bondage gear.

'No clients in today, so...'

Nora, by contrast, was almost dressed in a tiny high-waisted skirt, tight polo shirt and towering platform sandals. Remembering all the times she'd seen Ollie ogling her, she had the sudden urge to guide Nora to a better, less-sexualised version of herself.

'Did you know Winston Churchill once said skirts were like speeches?' she began. 'They should be long enough to cover the subject and short enough to maintain interest.'

It was a quote her dad often used when she was heading to school with her skirt waistband rolled over.

Nora was gazing at her phone and only half listening. 'Who's Winston Churchill?'

'Prime Minister of Britain.'

'When did he get in?'

Okay, change of tack required.

'What I mean is, if you don't feel comfortable, you don't have to wear such short skirts.'

'I want to wear this.'

'Do you? Or do you feel like you have to wear it, you know, for people to find you attractive?'

Nora glanced up from the screen. 'Do people find me attractive?' Her eyes lit up. 'Which ones in particular?'

'Probably all of them, if we're honest.'

'Well, that's a nice thing, isn't it?'

'That depends,' said Simone. 'What if it means they don't see you for your other virtues?'

'You think I should show off my boobs too?'

This wasn't going well.

'I'm just saying I've been where you've been and—'

'You've had everyone in the office fancy you?' Nora seemed doubtful, which, given what they were discussing, was far more annoying than it should have been.

'What I mean is, I don't want you to feel any pressure to look a certain way or wear certain clothes. I want this to be your choice.'

Was she mansplaining? Was it possible to mansplain if you were a woman? She found the whole thing very confusing.

Nora cocked her head to one side and smiled sympathetically. 'Thanks. I really appreciate it. I'll think about what you've said.' She went back to scrolling.

That was a start at least.

'Great.'

She really needed to get her head into gear. Tony would be in shortly, and she still had some reading about this potential new client to do.

'Nora.'

'Hmm?'

'Can you make sure there's enough Post-its, pens and pads in the boardroom for the meeting on the Wolfe pitch this morning?'

Nora's thumb paused in its perpetual flicking. 'I don't know if I should. Is that not exploitative?'

'Well, you are still an employee, so it's okay for me to ask you to do things.'

'Is that in the sisterhood rule book?'

Was she messing with her?

'No, it's in your contract of employment.'

'Still, perhaps I should check the details.'

'I tell you what,' said Simone. 'I'll get the Post-its, shall I?'

'If you're sure.'

Nora went back to scrolling and she went back to her desk. Some people just couldn't be helped.

Ollie swivelled round in his chair as she entered the boardroom. He had Steri-Strip stitches across his nose, and bruises like viola petals under his eyes.

'You're back then,' he grunted.

'You *nose* it.'

'Come on, you pair,' said Tony. 'I need you to put your differences to one side.'

'You're right,' she said. 'Time to repair that *broken bridge* between us.'

'Go fuck yourself,' said Ollie.

'You're *no-stril* upset, are you? I have no idea who that man was.'

'If I find out you do, I will take you down to Chinatown.'

'Hah!' she said. 'You're about as gangster as Vanilla Ice.'

'That's enough,' said Tony. 'Can we crack on? Simone, you're going to head this up.'

'What the fuck, Tony!' shrieked Ollie.

'I can't put you in front of one of London's most powerful landlords looking like some posh cage fighter. When your face is sorted, then you can face the client.'

Ollie went into an immediate sulk.

'Besides, Simone has certain advantages that we'll need to exploit.'

'That's right, Ollie,' she said. 'This is predominantly an event brief, requiring the full gamut of my extensive experience.'

The response was going to be a total ball-ache. They had less than three weeks to come up with a full programme of events, one that would not only creatively beat anything Wolfe's incumbent agency might come up with, but also exceed the company's previous column inches and sales, all on a reduced budget. It was going to mean early mornings, late nights, and calling in a lot of favours from suppliers to get it all costed in time.

'I was talking about your tits,' said Tony.

Ollie sniggered.

'He's a notorious ladies' man.'

'But—' she said.

'We need to play to our strengths.'

'But—'

'What are you wearing anyway? You look like a 1950s sailor. You just need a doughboy hat. I need more legs and cleavage tomorrow.'

'But—'

'Exactly. More butt too. Whatever it takes, yeah?'

Miraculously, she'd somehow forgotten how much of a bellend Tony was. It was okay, though, because she was in charge and Ollie would have to play second fiddle to her. She just needed to get it done and then, maybe, she'd finally get her promotion.

Back at her desk afterwards, she received a message from Marcus.

How's Mother Theresa? Fancy a little 'missionary' work later on this eve? Bryony is going to Max's school play.

Shouldn't you be going too?

He sent back a ROFL emoji. She didn't respond. He was typing again.

I'd much rather be behind the bike sheds with you.

She shook her head. How had she ever found this shit endearing? Or more appallingly, arousing? Why was she wasting her time on him? She sometimes wondered if he represented some kind of father figure for her, a mature influence in her life. But Marcus was nothing like her father. Her dad had been a lovely man who worshipped her, whilst Marcus was an immature selfish prick who wanted everything on his own terms. It was incredible she hadn't seen it before. Well, there was no taking back what she'd done, but she could exert what little power she had now.

She tapped out a message.

Grow up, Marcus. It's over. Go be a father to your sons.

He sent a line of question marks back.

She didn't respond. There was too much other stuff going on.

Chapter Thirty-Six

The following fortnight passed by in a blur. The opportunity with Wolfe was by far the biggest thing she'd worked on, a potential annual revenue of over two million pounds if it came off. Tony was acting like a sweaty limpet, shadowing every meeting, questioning every decision, insisting on being more closely involved than he'd ever bothered to be before. Proof, if it was needed, that this was *BIG*. She was glad for the distraction. Left to her own devices, she risked running out of energy; she wasn't sleeping particularly well, and she was unable to shake a vague feeling of ambivalence towards the task at hand. Sure, she really wanted to win it and put Ollie back in his box. Plus, Tony had all but promised that if she pulled this off, the directorship was hers. But her usual hunger had been tempered with a gnawing feeling of the inanity of the whole endeavour.

She'd built up a dossier on Wolfe Holdings, and it made for interesting reading. It was a behemoth, a multi-headed beast of a corporation, spawning more subsidiaries and satellite businesses than a spider might eggs. It enjoyed a presence on notable boards across the capital, pulling levers in the public sector in a way she hadn't realised private companies could. She'd spoken to Tony about it, wondered out loud if the whole organisation didn't seem suspicious. He'd regarded her like she'd grown a second head and told her she was getting soft. *We're in reputation management,* he'd said. *People with good reputations don't need them managed.*

As for Wolfe, she was on her way now to meet him for the third time. The first two occasions, he had been far less 'avuncular' and far more 'creepy uncle' than his online pictures suggested. He was in his late fifties, with oddly dyed hair, the ghost of his greyness hovering just below the surface of a peculiar auburn brown that made his skin seem jaundiced. His face bore the expression of a man who could get whatever he wanted, although a better barber had clearly never made the list. At their last meeting he'd invited her to a charity gala Wolfe Holdings was hosting. It was the very last thing she needed, given how much was left to do for the response, but Tony had insisted she go: she needed to see what other people in their employ did to put on a show, and to butter Wolfe up, obviously.

In the cab on the way there, she allowed herself a moment to think about how everyone was getting on back at the shelter. Who had replaced her? Was there some other thirty-something woman enjoying banter with Jasper? She'd been meaning to text Tasha, and perhaps get his number – she still had his T-shirt and shorts to return, and he still had her playsuit – but her mind was frazzled. The brain space required to create a casually worded and not-at-all leading message was beyond her capabilities. It was hard to explain to anyone who hadn't been involved in a pitch just how all-encompassing and draining they could be. Still, she would be seeing Tasha soon enough, and when everything had settled down at work, well, maybe then she'd find the time to pop in.

Chapter Thirty-Seven

The gala was being held in a five-star hotel in Covent Garden in one of the city's largest traditional ballrooms. Simone had used it a couple of times before and knew the astronomical prices it commanded. This whole thing was a chance for Wolfe to lean on his contacts to raise money for his company's chosen charities, a common practice in large businesses. It was crazy really, given how Wolfe could easily have supported them out of his own bursting coffers, which would also save the expense of all this pomp and ceremony.

She did a quick tour of the venue and checked out the menu, the floral arrangements, the AV set-up, and the list of things up for auction. It was all nondescript. If this was the kind of thing they were up against, the ideas her and her team were developing would blow this standard fare out of the water.

She was going to be at a table with Wolfe himself, a pleasure she was happy to put off until the very last minute, so she headed to the bar to help kill some time before she'd need to take her seat. As she approached it, though, she saw a familiar silhouette. She took in the twisted afro hair with the low fade, the light brown neck, the broad shoulders, the peachy bottom, the handkerchief being taken out of the trouser pocket. It couldn't possibly be, could it?

'Jasper?'

He spun around. Holy shit: it was.

'Simone?'

He was wearing a slim-fit tuxedo in which he looked immeasurably hot and surprisingly at home. She couldn't wrap her head around what was happening. The universe kept on conspiring to put them together.

'Why are you here?' she asked.

He seemed equally bewildered to see her.

'I'm here as a plus one.'

Her heart sank. 'Oh cool. Who's your date?' She tried to keep her voice even.

He nodded in the direction of a woman talking animatedly to two jocular older ladies. She was a petite blonde with a shattered bob, wearing a white trouser suit, bright red stilettos and matching lipstick. She'd spotted her earlier and thought she was envy-inducingly stylish.

'Do you recognise her?' he asked.

She was similar in appearance to an actress whose name she'd forgotten.

'It's my sister,' he clarified.

'Huh?'

'You saw her picture in my flat.'

She wasn't sure she wanted to be reminded of his flat, or the conversation that had followed on her last day at the shelter, but he had moved on. He explained how Jessica led the partnerships team for a charitable trust, one that Wolfe Holdings supported through their Corporate & Social Responsibility arm.

'They're beneficiaries of some of the obscene amounts of money she tells me will get bandied around this evening.'

Simone went to sneak another glance at Jessica, but she was heading towards them anyway.

'Pass me my drink, bro. God, my feet are already killing.'

'Mine too,' said Simone.

'Oh hello.' The woman looked her up and down. 'Who are you?'

'Simone, this is my very forthright sister, Jessica. Jessica, this is my friend Simone.'

Jasper passed Jessica a glass of what looked like straight whisky. She eyed Simone curiously.

'Simone? As in the babe from work you were banging on about?'

His eyes widened. 'No. A different Simone.'

'Really? Only you said she was really pretty with dark hair, so I just assumed…'

Jessica smirked. She knew exactly what she was doing. Jasper put his hand over her mouth. It was gratifying to see him properly uncomfortable for once.

'She's not my real sister,' he said.

Jessica slapped his hand away. 'And you said she had a smoking hot body.'

'I would never say that.'

It was true, he wouldn't, even if he thought it.

'Okay, just to be clear,' said Jessica, 'you're not the Simone who has some weird arrangement with a married man.'

'Jesus,' said Jasper. 'It would've been better to be brought up in a children's home.'

'No, that's not me,' said Simone, very much enjoying the display of sibling teasing. 'No married boyfriend. At least, not anymore.'

Jasper raised a questioning eyebrow.

'We broke up.'

'I'm sorry.'

'Are you?'

'Not really.'

They were staring at one another.

'Yeah,' said Jessica. 'I'm going to leave you two *friends* to it.'

Simone turned, apologetic. 'No please. I'm interrupting your night.' She really wanted to make a good first impression.

'Don't stress. I have to do the rounds, work the crowd. I just needed to get this.' She raised the glass, downed the drink in one, grimaced, and then collected herself. 'It was nice to meet you, not-that-Simone. Hopefully I'll meet you again.' She marched off.

'She seems pretty cool.'

'Really? I can't stand her.'

Simone laughed.

'Can I get you a drink?' he said.

'Gin and tonic please.'

She had no plans to drink too much, but she'd need something to get through it: Wolfe had a reputation for liking a tipple, and being sober around drunk people you *liked* was torture enough. Unsurprisingly, Jasper got served immediately.

'So, you've been talking about me, huh?' She played with her straw, moving the ice around the glass.

'I may have mentioned you.'

An endorphin rush of joy engulfed her. 'May you have?' Her half-smile expanded into a smirk.

'Let's change the subject,' he said.

'Okay.' She took a step back, like he was a work of art that she needed to view in its entirety. 'Did you borrow that tuxedo for the night?'

'Why?'

'It's a little tight on you,' she teased.

'No, it's all mine.'

'Perhaps you've been comfort eating since I left?'

'No, I haven't.' He undid his jacket and held it open so she could get a better view.

'Yep, you've definitely been piling on the pounds. Look at that belly.'

With measured fingers, he untucked the shirt from the waistband of his trousers and lifted the fabric, revealing the four perfect glazed buns of his lower abs. 'What, *this* belly?' He studied her face, waiting for a reaction.

It took all her willpower not to reach out and run her hand along their ridges. She frowned up at him. 'My mistake. Must have been a trick of the light.'

He winked and tucked the shirt back in. 'Speaking of tight clothing, how are you breathing?'

She was wearing a simple emerald satin gown with a cinched-in boned waist.

'Less breathing and more shallow panting.'

'Like a dog.'

'Exactly. Look.' She stuck her tongue out.

'Charming.'

They both laughed.

'You look very nice,' he said.

Her hair was up in a chignon bun, and she was conscious she was wearing quite a lot of make-up.

'Really? Didn't you say you liked the natural look?'

'I do. But I also like this look.'

Her insides liquified.

'How is everyone?' she asked quickly.

'All fine. Gayle is a bit stressed because another one of our funding sources has gone, but she's working hard to get a replacement.'

'And the others?'

'Interesting you should ask. They've been going offsite a lot more. You wouldn't have any idea what they're up to, would you?'

'No.'

'Hmm. I didn't think so. I'm sure they'd like to hear from you; you'd be welcome to come back any time.'

'I know.'

She told him all about Wolfe and the response. 'But I'm hoping when that's done, I can pop back in. I've not forgotten I owe you a coffee.'

'And I owe you a fun evening.'

'Do you mean go out?' she hazarded.

'I don't mean more outreach.'

'So, like drinks, or dinner.'

'If you like.'

She took a sip of her drink. 'That sounds a lot like a date.'

'Does it?'

'Is it?'

'Would you like it to be?'

'Would you?'

He smiled. 'Yes. I would obviously like to go out on a date with you.'

'But you said you didn't think of me *like that*.'

'When?'

'The day I left the shelter.'

He cocked his head to one side, trying to recall their conversation. Then his face cleared. 'No, you idiot! I meant I wouldn't take advantage of you like that. I know you have a wonky notion of what chivalry is, Simone, but really! I'm not some opportunist. I won't so much as kiss a woman unless I really like her.'

'Oh.'

'And may I remind you, you had a boyfriend.'

'Oh.'

'And you really were very annoying.'

'Why, thank you.'

'But it turns out that you *not* being around is appreciably more infuriating than you being around.'

A cacophony of optimistic thoughts ricocheted around her head.

'You say the sweetest things.'

A voice came over the AV system telling everyone to take their seats as dinner was about to be served.

'I should go,' she said reluctantly.

'Me too.'

'You'll call me though?'

'I will, if you're happy to give me your number.'

'But you had it on—'

He gave her another of his *what do you take me for* faces. Of course he wouldn't have made a note of her number unless she'd given him express permission to do so. She tapped it into his phone. It took a restraint she didn't know she possessed to not ask him to leave right there and then. Or to suggest perhaps their first date could be in her bed, directly after this event. But no, she didn't need to rush into anything; it was enough that they were going on a date together!

As she walked away, she put an extra little sashay into her step. She glanced over her shoulder as she did so, and with a feeling suspiciously akin to happiness, saw he was smiling and shaking his head.

The dinner and the auction were intensely boring compared to the preamble. Food-wise, they had done what so many 'posh' places did, piling the food up in a little tower on the plate, as if by elevating the constituent parts, they could elevate the quality. It didn't work. She then watched as people with more money than sense bid stupid amounts on things that they almost certainly didn't need. It was obscene. Still, at least Jessica was benefiting. Did good outcomes, even if they were aided and abetted by subjectively bad people, still create a net good effect? What would Jasper think? She wanted to find him and ask him, but instead she had to content herself with responding to the progressively more inane crap dribbling from Wolfe's increasingly slurring mouth. By the time the coffee was served, and she excused herself to go to the toilet, the man could barely focus. There was a queue for the bathroom directly outside the ballroom, so she went further around the corridor and found one that was quieter. When she emerged, she was startled to see Wolfe loitering outside.

'Are you lost?' she asked.

He leered at her, lips peeling back to show red wine-stained teeth. 'Where d'you get to?'

She pointed to the very obvious sign on the toilet door behind her.

'Visiting the little girl's room, hey?'

A million termites crawled beneath her skin. He wasn't lost. He had followed her.

'We should probably be getting back,' she said.

He stepped in front of her, momentarily swaying like a tower in the wind, before placing a hand on the wall behind her to steady himself. 'There's no rush.' The other hand snaked to her side, and he ran it up and down her hip bone as if she was a cow whose readiness for market he was checking. 'I didn't think I could see any panties.'

The guy couldn't have seen a fucking elephant if she'd had one in the seamless knickers she was most definitely wearing. He was sozzled, but that didn't make him any less of a lecherous arsehole. She pressed herself as far into the wall as possible and weighed up her options. She should tell him to go fuck himself; he had no right to follow her, no right to touch her. But she also knew what the backlash to that would entail. Tony would have an aneurism.

Then again, Tony wasn't the one who had some dickweasel's hand snaking up towards her tits.

'Simone?'

Shit. It was Jasper.

'What's going on?'

He was clearly trying to calculate exactly what he'd stumbled across.

'Nothing. It's fine.'

She cast him a look that attempted to convey this was just some rich dickhead getting handsy, and he didn't need to get involved.

'Yeah, she's fine, pal,' said Wolfe.

'It doesn't look fine.'

'Me and Siobhan here were discussing some business, weren't we, Siobhan?'

'It's Simone,' said Jasper.

Wolfe closed his eyes and shook his head, as if Jasper was a figment of his own imagination that he could blink away. He scowled when the apparition didn't comply.

'You know you don't have to put up with that, don't you?' said Jasper.

'He's just drunk.'

'That's no excuse.'

'Is this your boyfriend?' asked Wolfe.

She really hoped the answer to that might soon be yes.

'No.'

'Then tell him to get lost.'

'Jasper, please, can you leave it?'

'Not unless you're happy with him groping you?'

'I'm not groping her, mate. She's into it.'

'Are you?' Jasper asked.

As much as she loved the idea of him stepping in to protect her, this needed to be handled carefully.

'I don't need you to look after me.'

'I never said you did. I'm just asking if you're okay.'

'Can you tell this twat to fuck off?' said Wolfe.

Jasper squared up.

'He's just leaving,' she said quickly.

'Am I?'

'I need a piss,' said Wolfe. 'Make sure he's gone by the time I get back.' He stumbled into the ladies' toilets.

'I just need to keep him sweet for tonight,' she explained. 'He's too drunk to do anything anyway.'

Jasper's face was etched with confusion. 'This isn't right.'

'If I can just get this promotion—'

'You shouldn't have to be manhandled for your job!'

'It is what it is. I don't mind.'

'You don't mind?! That's somehow worse!'

Of course she minded. Her soul ached with the effort of trying to withstand the entitlement people like Wolfe had internalised as acceptable. The times they made you feel like you were in sexual debt to them because they'd bought you a drink, or given you a job, or paid you a compliment. It was all part of a continuum of aggression arising from their basic failure to see women as equals. But she wouldn't topple the Patriarchy by telling Wolfe to sod off. The only thing she would topple were her chances of a promotion, and why should she suffer double the injustice? And besides, who the hell was Jasper to judge how she dealt with these situations?

'It's my body,' she said defensively. 'I can do what I like with it.'

'I'm not disputing that.'

'You don't understand what it's like.'

Sure, he understood prejudice. She couldn't imagine the bigotry and discrimination to which he'd been subjected. But he had never, would never, could never know what it was like to be a woman living with the omnipresent dread of upsetting certain male egos for fear of what repercussions might ensue.

'You're right,' he said. 'I don't understand. I'm just saying if you continue to give pieces of yourself away so easily, how can you ever know your true value?'

'So you're saying I brought this on myself?'

'No!' He ran his hand over his face, rubbed his chin in frustration. 'Fuck! I'm sorry, I just saw you with him and … I didn't mean it like that.'

They waited in painful silence as someone else loped past them to the bathroom door. As the door opened, she saw Wolfe emerge from a cubicle. She panicked.

'I need you to go.'

'Simone—'

'For god's sake, Jasper! What part of *fuck off* don't you understand?'

The words were out before she even registered them. His face fell. She knew she'd hurt his feelings, but he'd hurt hers too.

He held up his hands in surrender. 'You're right. I don't want to be *that guy*. I'm going.'

The moment he decided to comply with her wishes was the moment she really didn't want him to.

'Jasper, please—'

'I need to go.' He turned and strode away.

She wanted to run after him. Ten minutes ago, she'd been harbouring the idea of not returning to Wolfe's table, but seeking his out instead. She wanted to go back to his flat, kick off her wretched shoes, and liberate herself from this stupid dress. She wanted to pull on one of his labelless T-shirts and talk about life, the universe and everything. Instead, they'd had their first argument and she now had to work out how Wolfe could be satisfied she'd been a gracious enough guest without having to let him screw her.

Chapter Thirty-Eight

She awoke to the sound of drilling in her brain. Or was it a one-man band trying to run the hundred metres? Whatever it was, it was swiftly followed by pain, the dull thud of sledgehammer against concrete. Full-on body nausea completed the holy trinity of stinking hangover. She'd clearly decided to have more than a couple of drinks after all. She prised her eyes open. This wasn't her bedroom; it was a hotel room. This also hadn't been in the plan for the evening. Dread and paranoia intermingled with all the other sensations she was feeling. She shifted in the bed and felt a warm body beside her. The body was naked. As was she.

Nooo. Please tell her she hadn't actually slept with Wolfe. She tried to piece together what had happened, but her head wasn't yet playing ball. She knew he'd tried it on, so far so predictable, but he'd been wasted. And even if she'd been drunk, she'd have found a way to not sleep with him. She always found a way. But maybe this time she didn't. Maybe this time she'd actually done the thing she promised herself she would never do. She refused to turn around. What was that weird thought experiment with the cat in the box? The one where it was dead and alive at the same time. This was like that. For as long as she didn't look, it would be like whatever happened, hadn't. She pulled the covers more tightly around her, but in doing so disturbed the other occupant of the bed. An arm folded over her and a familiar voice added to her mental chatter.

'I knew you'd be back.'

It was Marcus. Her body relaxed and relief flooded through it. It was only Marcus. But why the hell would she be with him? He wasn't even at the gala. No, the surprise guest of the evening had been…

Fuck.

She got a sudden mental image of Jasper in his tuxedo. Of their flirting. Of him asking her out on a date. And of him walking away from her after their row. She must have gotten drunk after that, and then called up the one person who wouldn't judge her.

'Time for a quickie?'

She didn't move when Marcus pressed his hard-on against her bum cheek. Didn't say anything as he shuffled into position behind her. It was too late for all of that. The damage was already done.

Chapter Thirty-Nine

I t was two days before the big Wolfe meeting, and she was watching the sun slowly set across the Thames through the shattered top of The Shard, eating takeout straight from a carton. It was yet another late night in the office, desperately trying to pull everything together in time. Her phone pinged. It was probably Tony, stressing about something or other, but not so much that he'd considered staying late to help. Ollie was also long gone. She knew better than to hope it might be Jasper. She'd heard nothing from him since the gala a week ago, and despite the crippling workload that threatened to exclude all else, their argument still glowed white hot in her mind. She'd wanted to text him, apologise for letting the stress of the situation get to her, and talk it through, but the contusions of shame left by Marcus's touch prevented her from doing so.

She flipped the phone over. It was a diary reminder. Tasha's scan. Damn it. In the general madness, she'd completely forgotten she was meant to be going with her tomorrow. There was no way she'd be able to; there was still so much to do. Tony had already given her a couple of talking-tos about her head not fully being in the zone. He had a point. She was listless and distracted. It was as if she was inside a goldfish bowl with everything slightly removed and distorted. The girls had been back for a while, and she still hadn't seen them. She'd meant to do so a few nights ago, but she'd flaked out, the idea of overcoming her own social inertia too torturous. It was like she was dragging a kettlebell around with her.

The scan's diary entry morphed into an accusatory finger pointing out of the screen. Her hopes of making time for the shelter were dead, and the ghost of them haunted her. The truth was, her enthusiastic 'future self' was now her apathetic present one, and she hated herself for her predictability. She messaged Tasha, a perfunctory text, no more than she needed to say. She was sorry, but she wasn't able to go. She hoped she was okay. She'd come and see her when work had quietened down. There was still that possibility, wasn't there? But then that would mean bumping into Jasper. Perhaps it was better to put the whole episode behind her. When she pressed send, she persuaded herself it was in Tasha's best interests – she had work to do, people to impress, a promotion to get. And if she had more money, she could help more, couldn't she?

She switched off her notifications and tucked her phone back into her bag; she didn't need any further distractions this evening, least of all a confrontation with Tasha. She needn't have bothered, though, because by the time she got home several hours later, the message had been read, but absolutely no reply had been forthcoming. Tasha clearly didn't care either way.

Chapter Forty

Forty-eight hours later, she was in Dixon & Astley's main boardroom, watching herself go through the motions as Wolfe and two of his cronies, plus Ollie and Tony looked on. The whole thing had thus far been an exercise in self-restraint. The meeting had begun with her trying very hard not to throw a jug at Tony's face when, even with five grown men in the room, he deemed it her responsibility to *play mum* and pour everyone a glass of water. She'd then been forced to mentally shave time off her painstakingly rehearsed script. Tony had used ten of the allotted ninety minutes to ask Nora to come into the room, sweeping his arm like a circus master on her arrival, and announcing that *this, gentlemen, is why I got into PR!* And of course, there had been the general disparaging chit-chat about 'her indoors' and the 'ankle-biters', all delivered with a level of snide eyerolling that made her want to scream. There was so much macho bullshit being bandied around, the air reeked of it. It was a good job she was wrapping up the final idea, because, with Wolfe looking at his phone more than the PowerPoint document she'd agonised over, her performative enthusiasm was becoming harder and harder to fake. She had no idea why he was even part of the pitch process – surely the guy had far more important things to do than worry about a tiny fraction of the marketing plan? Still, despite the storm raging within, her audience's reaction indicated her presentation had been well-received.

'So,' she concluded, 'as I hope we've demonstrated, if you award us the account, we'd be ready to hit the ground running with any one of these ideas. We'd anticipate getting the space filled before you've so much as started excavating.'

'Very impressive,' said Wolfe. 'I can see you've all put a lot of effort in.'

Ollie nodded. 'It's not every day we get the opportunity to work with someone of your immense stature.'

Trust him to prove it was possible to both suck up and dribble at the same time. He had, of course, done practically nothing to help, but clearly he was hedging his bets in case she landed it. The question was, *was* she landing it?

Wolfe cast around to his cronies. 'If everyone's in agreement, I'd say we've got ourselves a new partner.'

Everyone nodded. Ollie looked like his head was going to spin 360 degrees and he might projectile vomit on Wolfe's fancy suit, but he managed a plastic smile.

Wolfe's gaze fell on her. 'And as for you, young lady…'

His mouth stretched into a self-satisfied grin that gave her the instant ick. This was how the three little pigs must have felt.

'It seems you and I are going to be seeing a lot more of one another.'

'I'm sure you'll be far too busy for all the detail.'

She desperately hoped there was someone other than this cartoon villain with whom she'd liaise day-to-day. But she could worry about that later, because right now, she was quietly celebrating the fact that she would finally get that promotion.

'This calls for champagne,' said Tony, clapping his hands. 'Simone, ask Nora to do the honours.'

Given the circumstances, she was happy to fetch a couple of bottles and the flutes herself. She did a little victory dance in the kitchen and then returned to the room composed. Once everyone had a drink, Tony rose to his feet.

'So, can you tell us where this next site is going to be? You've been keeping it all very quiet.'

Wolfe hadn't disclosed the details for the response; they'd had sight of the general plans, but not the location in which they would reach fruition.

'We're under NDA,' Tony added. 'Your secret's safe with us.'

'It's in Whitechapel,' said Wolfe. 'On Stepford Street.'

Simone flinched. That was the street the shelter was on. Hearing it out of Wolfe's mouth, in this incongruous setting, brought back the hollowing rot of self-loathing about what had unfolded since she left. Still no word from Jasper or Tasha. But surely it was mere coincidence that this was where Wolfe's next operation would be happening? Odd synchronicities lending perceived significance to unrelated events – there had been a few recently. But where exactly was the site? She'd been up and down that road, and there hadn't been an obvious place where a development could easily be slotted.

'It's some old hospital,' said Wolfe. 'Not been operational for years. Being used as a soup kitchen or something.'

This must be a joke. Tony must have disclosed her community service whilst she was out of the room, and they'd agreed to play a trick on her.

'Very funny,' she said. 'I know full well that's a council property.'

'Which can be sold off for affordable housing,' said Wolfe.

'But this isn't affordable housing. This is, strictly speaking, fucking obscenely priced housing.'

Wolfe smiled, appreciating the reference to just how much money the development stood to make, but she hadn't meant it as flattery.

'There's a legal loophole. Isn't there, Graham?'

One of the cronies went into some lengthy explanation about not having to fulfil policy obligations due to calculations of residual land value versus a developer's financial viability assessment. It was impossible to keep up. She didn't need to. The gist was that he was very definitely not joking, and was very much planning on the shelter being his next plot.

'But it's currently being used, no?'

She was trying to play it cool, like she had no emotional investment in the answer to the question. Tony fired a warning look across the boardroom table.

'Not for very much longer,' said Graham. 'Their council funding has just been cut. If it's not a going concern, then it's closing.'

'And then I get to sweep in and scoop it up.' Wolfe grinned like a killer whale.

'Couldn't they get a grant? Or raise the funds?' She kept her voice even.

Wolfe let out a horrible low rumble of amusement. Ollie, the simpering cockwipe, joined in.

'A leaking boat is a sinking boat,' said Wolfe. 'Other funding will take too long, and no one in the neighbourhood will rally to save a shelter. It's a blight. This will increase the value of their own properties. Mark my words, it'll take a miracle to stop this.'

'But what happens to the people who live there?'

'Who cares?' said Wolfe. 'The bottom line is more important than a bunch of bums.' He drained his glass and gestured that he wanted another.

She tried to unball her fists, then took some levelling breaths and considered making her excuses and taking some time out in the toilets. She was like the unopened champagne bottle in front of her; the pressure of repressed energy fizzed inside, a million bubbles of resentment and frustration ready to erupt. The idea that Tasha, Hozan, Steve and the rest could be displaced once more had loosened the cork.

'You can't do that,' she said quietly. Her heart quickened.

'Simone...' Tony's tone was reproachful.

'I think you'll find I can,' said Wolfe.

'Just because you can doesn't mean you should.'

Wolfe looked at her through slitted eyes. 'Maybe it's time you left us big boys to talk things through.'

'Do you think?' She levelled him her steeliest stare.

'You've done a great job with your pretty pictures, but now we need to get down to business.'

Condescending prick.

She turned to Tony. 'Are you going to let him talk to me like that?'

'If you're about to make a scene about a few down-and-outs, then yes.'

Ollie sniggered.

'Don't you dare,' she said, rounding on him. 'You've done fuck all on this, so don't think you get to sit there and take any of the credit.'

'Is it the wrong time of the month?' said Ollie, knowing exactly which buttons to push. 'You have been a bit on edge these last few weeks.'

'I'm not on edge because of a period, you misogynistic shitstain. It's because it's the wrong thing to do. There must be loads more sites you could pick?'

'There aren't,' said Wolfe.

'But I know them.' Desperation tinged her voice. 'They're decent people who just need a break.'

Wolfe's face registered some curiosity at how she might know them, but not enough to actually ask. 'Then you can help them pack their bags, can't you?'

'Why would you do this?' Her mercury was rising. 'It's not like you need the money!'

'You're being hysterical,' said Tony.

'Brilliant!' she hissed. 'The old hysteria accusation. Men strongly object to something, that's *passion*; women do the same, they're mentally ill.'

Tony looked like she'd pointed out a material fact, rather than highlighted the irony.

'I'm not bothered because I have a uterus, you moron. I'm bothered because I have a conscience.'

What was she doing? She needed to let it go. People were fucked by Big Corp every single day. This was a battle far bigger than her.

'Go home,' said Tony. 'Get yourself a hot water bottle and a bar of chocolate. We can talk tomorrow.'

'I'm not on my fucking period!'

'Perhaps I need to take my business elsewhere?' said Wolfe.

'That won't be necessary,' said Tony.

Simone felt like her skin was on fire. This wasn't just about the shelter. This was also about her sense of agency, or lack thereof.

'Do you know he felt me up at that event you made me go to?'

'That was kind of the point of sending you,' said Tony.

'Would you be happy with your daughter getting groped at work?'

'She's a minger. It wouldn't happen.'

'You need to grow a pair.'

He cocked his head, canine-like, weighing something up. She imagined she could see an understanding between them, an appreciation of all the effort she'd made for him and his business.

'You're right,' he said eventually.

'Thank fuck for th—'

'You're fired.'

'What?'

Ollie's eyes sparkled with unadulterated joy. If he could have grabbed popcorn, he would have done.

'You heard me,' said Tony.

She shook her head in disbelief. 'You can't do that.'

'I just have.'

She swallowed hard. 'I've worked my ass off for you.'

Nausea flooded through her. It was inconceivable that he'd actually sack her. This was posturing, surely, playing up to the audience in the room. Yes, she'd overstepped the mark, but there were procedures. Processes. The ten years of blood and tears she'd poured into the place. And who the hell was going to manage the account?

'Ollie, I assume you can pick this up,' said Tony as if he'd read her thoughts.

Ollie now had a look of such intense rapture on his face, he might have been getting sucked off by invisible angels.

'Of … of course,' he spluttered.

This wasn't what she'd intended to happen. Sure, she was tired of being devalued. Tired of being objectified. Tired of the silent judgment of people when she didn't act like she was expected to. Tired of the groupthink. Tired of being at the wrong end of the gendered power spectrum. Tired of repeatedly being put on and knocked off a pedestal of someone else's making. But she was also just tired, right? It had been a rough few months. No matter how unjust Wolfe's actions were, the fact was she had everything riding on this. No matter how much she hated the job, she still couldn't afford to *not* have it.

'Tony…'

She asked him to reconsider; tried joking that it had been her wayward womb to blame after all. She despised herself for her neediness.

'You're losing it,' he said. 'You've gone weak. I'm going to have to ask you to leave.' He opened the boardroom door. 'Ollie, if you can help Simone get her stuff together.'

'The shit I've done for you,' she said.

Ollie took her by the arm, but she wrenched it away.

'Don't touch me. You lay a single finger on me, and I will tear your bollocks off and turn them into earmuffs.'

Ollie shrank from her.

She made for the door on shaky legs but stopped at its threshold. If this was happening, if she really was being cast aside like a toy they'd grown bored of, she had to say something to let them know it wasn't okay.

'I will get you all back for this.' The words sounded hollow to her own ears.

Ollie, Tony and Wolfe all chuckled.

'I very much doubt it,' said Tony.

Back at her desk, she found a couple of plastic bags and stuffed things into them. Nora asked her if she was okay, but she wasn't paying any attention. Her fight or flight response had kicked in and it had chosen flight. She just wanted to be out of there as soon as possible. Her drawers were full of shit: pointless corporate excreta that included USB dongles, adapters and chargers from obsolete tech, three rulers, two staplers, enough Post-its to cover the building, and a box of business cards. Well, she wouldn't be needing those. The personal gear was more telling of a life squandered at work: deodorant, toothpaste and toothbrush, make-up bag, cystitis treatments, cold & flu tablets, a packet of probably unneeded contraceptive pills, unused gym kit, a jumper with the label still attached that she'd forgotten she'd bought, and two pairs of heels. She considered nabbing the laptop, but she already had backups of her work files on a personal cloud, and she wouldn't give Tony the satisfaction of accusing her of stealing from him. There was also her desk plant, an unwieldy peace lily that was almost a metre tall, but she'd be blowed if she was leaving it here with these bastards. She picked it up, half hiding her face in its foliage, and made for the lift.

Once she reached the building's reception, she put everything down. There was no way she was getting on the tube with this lot. She'd need to order a cab. She took a deep breath and steadied her trembling hands. She'd be okay, even if her body was telling her otherwise. She unlocked her phone to find she'd missed a call – from Jasper of all people. Her stomach did a 360. There was no message. No text or WhatsApp. Who even makes calls nowadays? Was he getting in touch to apologise for the other night? She wouldn't let herself hope that, and besides, she needed to warn him about Wolfe's plans.

He answered in two rings. 'Simone, thank goodness. Have you seen Tasha?'

There were no pleasantries. No *how are yous* or *I've missed yous*. Still, after what had just happened, it felt good to hear his voice.

'Tasha? No, why?'

'She didn't come back to the shelter last night. She's never missed curfew before. Do you know where she went after the scan?'

Her stomach went into freefall. 'I didn't go to the scan.'

There was a condemning silence at the other end of the line.

'I had to prepare for a meeting.'

Still nothing.

'I told her I couldn't go.'

She sounded even more pathetic than when she'd originally made the excuse. And what had she missed it for in the end?

'Do you have any idea where she might be?' he said.

'No, none.'

'Fuck.'

He was obviously concerned, which meant now she was. She didn't want to add to his woes, but she also needed to warn him about Wolfe's plans.

'There's something else.'

She heard raised voices in the background.

'Hang on,' he said. 'Gayle needs me.'

'Jasper, this is important. Wolfe, you know, that guy at the gala.' He'd know full well who she was talking about. 'He's planning on buying the shelter.'

'What? It's not for sale.'

'Not yet. But he's got wind of the funding problems. He thinks it's just a matter of time before the council offload it.'

'How do you know this?'

'I had a meeting with him today.'

She explained what little she knew as quickly as possible, the words rushing out so that he knew her intel was a result of a professional encounter, not a personal one. She distinctly heard Gayle shout *shit a brick* at someone or something in the background.

'Gayle's going to do her nut. I need to go. If you hear from Tasha, message me, okay?'

'But Jasper—'

The line went quiet. Goddammit! She desperately wanted to call him back, tell him what else had happened in the meeting; perhaps to have him offer her some words of comfort. But there was no time for that because she needed to find Tasha. London only had nine million people living in it – ten thousand of them homeless and a hundred thousand on the brink of homelessness. How on Earth was she supposed to find one single solitary girl?

Chapter Forty-One

She parked up as close to the junction as possible, which wasn't very close because the whole area was double-red-line central. She had finally found a permit-free street about five minutes' walk away from the underpass to which she was now headed. She'd initially tried calling Tasha, which unsurprisingly hadn't worked. She'd then spent a fruitless hour searching how to locate someone's phone without needing an app or spyware. Not possible. She'd then reluctantly messaged Marcus who had called in a favour from a guy he knew in surveillance. He'd given her a couple of square miles to try on the outskirts of town.

She'd driven around for almost two hours, preferring to be in the car deluding herself that she'd find the girl, rather than sat at home deriding herself for losing her only source of income. But then she'd recognised the road that led towards Dagenham, the one they'd taken to the slum flat, and recalled the encampment to which Tasha had paid special attention. She grabbed her bag and jogged towards it, ignoring the angry grumbles of her stomach. She'd not eaten anything since breakfast, and it was getting on towards six o'clock; she'd have to grab something soon.

How they'd imagined this was a good place to make camp was anyone's guess. As well as the ear-splitting traffic that ran overhead, it was at the heart of one of those immense multiple intersections you find in London, the kind where no one is entirely sure which lane of traffic they need to be in, and therefore subject to the additional cacophony of frustrated drivers honking and howling around it. Still, desperate times called for piss-poor decision-making. She crossed as soon as there was a gap in the traffic, only half-noting the bike festooned in fake flowers which stood in memory of some poor cyclist who'd fallen foul of the carnage.

Now what? Half of the tents had been abandoned, their frames fractured and crumpled. The rest were zipped up with no immediate signs of life. It wasn't like she could go around knocking on the doors.

'Tasha!' she shouted. 'Tasha!'

Nothing.

'Tasha! If you're here, please come out.'

Still nothing. What if she wasn't here?

'I have money. I will pay anyone for information pertaining to the whereabouts of Tasha…' she paused. She couldn't remember her second name. And what was with the officious lingo?

'How much money?' A man's voice. It came from a tent about ten yards away.

'You're such a twat,' came the rejoinder.

The zip unfastened and Tasha appeared, clutching a can of fruit cider. She stumbled over the fabric of the tent's opening.

'How did you find me?' she asked. Her eyes were glassy.

'Lucky guess.'

'Not for me.'

'Everyone was worried.'

'Ask her for the money,' came the voice from inside the tent.

Its limp flap obscured whoever was inside. Tasha's jaw tensed.

'And pass me the cider,' he said.

Tasha sighed, closed her eyes, and emptied the can's contents into her mouth before throwing it into the tent.

'Oi, you dickhead.'

Tasha turned to her. 'You can take that look off your face. I'm not harming the baby. It's already dead.'

'Oh Tasha. What happened?'

'No heartbeat.'

The girl hiccupped. It would have been comedic were it not for the tragic news she'd relayed.

'At least you can have a drink now,' came the voice.

Tasha made a grand sweep of her hand towards the tent. 'The father, ladies and gentlemen.'

'Are you okay?'

Tasha shrugged. 'It's not like I meant to get pregnant, is it?'

'It's my super sperm.' The tent's occupant chuckled.

'I know you didn't, but that doesn't make this any easier to deal with.'

She imagined what it must have been like for her to get that news alone. If only life had an undo button, she would press it and go back and be there for her.

'What do you care anyway?' said Tasha.

A police siren wailed overhead. The smell of the fumes was making her feel light-headed.

'Can we go for a walk?'

'Why?'

'Because I think maybe you want to?'

Tasha's slack face suggested otherwise, but she didn't say no.

'Come on.'

'Get some cider if you're going out,' came the voice.

Tasha didn't reply.

They were close to the Thames, so it was in that direction that they headed. When they were in sight of the river, its surface dappled with the sun's fragmented amber reflection, she hazarded another question.

'Has the baby already...?' She wondered if she would need to be induced.

Tasha shook her head. 'I've got an appointment to discuss my options.'

'I could come with you.'

Straight away, the girl's back was up. 'Hah!' she barked. 'Like you did last time?'

'Tasha, I'm so sorry, I had a job to do.' *Had a job* being the operative words.

She sat at a concrete bench near the river's edge and put her bag next to her, wondering if the physical boundary might encourage the girl to sit too. She didn't. The Thames Barrier stretched before them, its peculiar construction looking like silver hooded monks standing sentinel across its expanse with only their heads visible above the waterline.

'Why are you even pretending to care?' said Tasha.

'I'm not pretending.'

'Come off it,' she scoffed. 'You obviously prefer things to people.'

She stepped towards the bench, grabbed Simone's bag, and disconcertingly cradled it like a baby. She instinctively tried to take it from her, but Tasha backed away towards the steel balustrades separating them from the water.

'See,' she said. 'How much is this worth anyway? It could probably pay my rent for a month.'

And the rest.

'You can have it. Take it. Sell it. Whatever you want.'

'No. Why should I make you feel better? You can't buy people off. I only wanted a bit of your time.'

'I know. I made a mistake.'

Tasha blinked back tears.

'If I can just have the bag for a second…'

She needed to call Jasper and let him know Tasha was okay. Ish. But the girl was staring into the middle distance, like a plan was taking shape in her head.

'Maybe I'd be doing you a favour if I threw it in there.'

'Please don't do that.'

Tasha shrugged. 'Do you know what? Fuck it.'

She took a backswing of the bag. Simone was off the bench as quickly as possible, but not quickly enough. It was already arcing upwards, following the path of an invisible rainbow over the railings. It seemed to slow slightly as it reached its zenith above a paddling swan, then continued its downwards trajectory. It landed in the water with a surprisingly small splash given the magnitude of problems its loss would cause. It quickly sank beneath the surface.

'Fuck's sake, Tasha, that had my whole life in it!'

Her phone, her purse, her house and car keys. She stared wide-eyed at the place it had gone in, then at Tasha, then at the river again. Her brain refused to accept its disappearance, as if perhaps the girl had pulled off some sleight of hand trick. Tasha's face was also a mask of disbelief that she'd actually done it, her eyes wide, her mouth agog. Then she rallied.

'Well, what a sad and lonely life you must have,' she shouted. She turned tail and ran off in the direction from which they'd come.

Simone attempted to steady herself. Her heart was pounding. With shaking hands, she checked her jeans pockets in case, by some miracle, she'd put her keys in there. She hadn't. She sat back down and tried to think. She'd have to find a phone box and call someone, assuming it was still possible to get through to an operator and reverse the charges. But who? On what number? All her contacts were in her phone. She knew the landline to Dixon & Astley's, but the chances of anyone being there at this time was slim; almost as slim as the chances Tony would be prepared to help her if he *was* there. She wished she'd eaten. Her empty stomach murmured its agreement. Her head felt like it was full of cotton wool. She could try and get through to Marcus via the paper, but without a direct line, there was every chance she'd be cut off before she got close. Ziggy and Nancy would be god-knows-where on a Friday night, and without any money, she couldn't risk cabbing to their places on the off-chance they were in. Maybe she should call the shelter? At the very least try to get a message to Jasper to let him know what had happened. Perhaps he'd come and rescue her, but even as she entertained the idea, she knew she wouldn't throw herself on his mercy. And there was no way Tasha would help. She must be ten miles away from Brixton, at least a forty-minute taxi ride. She'd just have to go home and hope that a) she could break in and b) she had enough cash knocking around to pay whatever astronomical fare a black cab would charge for the journey. She stood up, relieved to have a plan of sorts, only no sooner had she done so than her skin became clammy, an icy sweat spread across her face and her footsteps faltered, their momentum petering out to a stumble.

Then everything went white.

Chapter Forty-Two

'Can you hear me?'

She was in a vehicle. Moving. The cab. She must have fallen asleep.

'If you can hear me, squeeze my hand.'

Why would the cab driver be holding her hand? Perhaps it was some new service. Like getting your name on a cup at Starbucks. How nice. She squeezed the hand.

'Okay, that's good.'

She really was very tired though. Perhaps just another five minu— but hang on, if the cab driver was holding her hand, how were they driving? She tried to open her eyes, but it was like her eyelashes had weights on them.

'You're going to be okay,' came the voice. A woman's. There really weren't enough female cab drivers in London.

'We're getting you to the hospital.'

The hospital? She hoped it wasn't too far out of the way. She really wasn't sure how much cash she had in the flat. Wait, why the hell would they be going to the hospital? And then she felt it: the searing pain at the top of her skull, like someone was trying to scoop her brains out with a rusty spoon. She tried her eyelids again. This time they half opened, revealing a green overall-clad woman bending over her.

'You had a fall. Got a nasty cut to your head.'

She struggled to sit up, gripped by a sudden panic.

'Woah, easy. Let me help you.'

She got upright. Her top was covered in blood. She felt for the cut, but the woman stayed her hand.

'Probably best not to. But don't worry, we're not far away now; they'll get you sorted.'

The events leading up to her fall came back in a rush. She wished she'd stayed unconscious.

'I lost my phone,' she said.

'Is there anyone you'd like me to contact?' the paramedic asked. 'Your next of kin?'

She fixed her gaze on the woman's kind eyes. She was older, but not by much.

'No.' She suddenly felt very small. 'There's no one.'

Chapter Forty-Three

She'd been in the hospital for one night, but when she got home, everything had changed. The whole edifice of her life had come tumbling down, and it wasn't going to be as easy to stitch back together as the wound on her head had been. She'd ended up with eighteen staples. She'd fallen back against the concrete bench, splitting her scalp open and being very fortunate not to have suffered a concussion – at least not one that had yet shown itself. Apparently, given the lack of personal identifying belongings, the passer-by who found her assumed she'd been mugged. Nope. Just fainting from woefully low blood sugar.

After showering, she stood in front of her bathroom mirror and angled another behind her to assess the damage. She'd made a right mess of it, alright, the sutures like giant ants crawling in her blood-matted hair. She ran her fingers along them like braille. What did they say? *You're a fuck up.*

There would be no washing her hair for a couple of days, but what did that matter? She wouldn't be going anywhere, at least not until her new bank cards came through. And then where? Then what? Sure, she would see the girls at some point, but the last thing she wanted to do was sit in some bar listening to all the amazing times they'd had. But what *did* she want to do? What did she even *like* doing? It was almost too cliched to admit, but after the last couple of months, she had no idea who the heck she was anymore.

She had received an email from work this morning. *Employment terminated effective immediately.* She would receive four months' severance pay, provided she *didn't make a fuss*. She should start a complaints procedure and take Tony to court for unfair dismissal, but the email had outlined the catalogue of wrongdoing that had left them no choice but to let her go. Of course, it was Ollie's trumped-up charges of workplace bullying of which she was apparently 'guilty' – the hatchet job was complete.

She went and laid down on her bed. She longed for sleep, yet the whirring blades of her restless mind refused to stop. She'd had plenty of time to think about what Tasha had said. Maybe her dig about preferring things to people had been true. She was out of practice with people. Things, they were easy. Things didn't let you down. They didn't betray you, or leave you, or die on you. Things could be replaced. But she was surrounded by stuff now and what did it serve her? A hole in her soul had opened up, and it would not be filled with stupid trinkets. These *laughable proxies for happiness*, as Jasper would probably call them. Where was he right now? Had he found Tasha? What would Gayle have said about the Wolfe news? Trying to make sense of everything that had happened was like trying to make sense of a dream. She gazed around her room and considered the sheer volume of things she owned. Books she'd never read, clothes she'd never worn, handbags she'd never used. Shame nibbled at her. Those people at Cedar Lodge who had barely anything, and here she was saddled with all this shit. She was a prisoner of her possessions, crushed by their collective weight. The whole thing was a *clutterfuck*. She was *stuffocating*.

She had the sudden overwhelming urge to build a bonfire and watch it all go up in flames. To be rid of the evidence of her material gluttony. She would happily pile each and every item onto a pyre and let it blacken and char, watch as great acrid columns of poisonous vapour curled up into the atmosphere, a prolonged puff of smoke and then, as if by magic, gone, just like her bag.

She lifted a small marble jewellery tray from her bedside table, tested its heft in her hands, and then launched it with all her might towards a picture frame on the opposite wall. The shards of glass fell as noisily as her sobs.

Chapter Forty-Four

She swung the front door open, expecting the figure behind the remaining pane of glass to be a courier with her new phone. It wasn't. It was Jasper. Her skin came alive, each nerve ending thrumming at the sight of him. And then she remembered how totally arsed-up everything was.

He gestured to the plank she'd crudely hammered over the door panel she'd smashed to gain entry. 'What the hell happened?'

'I lost my keys. Had to break in.'

She spun around and showed him her injury.

'Jesus. Did you axe your own head instead of the door first?' He was joking, but his face belied genuine concern. 'I've been calling you.'

'I also lost my phone. And my purse. And my job.'

'What's that *The Importance of Being Earnest* quote? The one about losing one of those could be considered a misfortune, but all of them looks like carelessness.'

'I think that's it.'

She must look a complete mess. She still hadn't washed her

hair and, although she'd had some sleep last night, her eyes were somehow both swollen and sunken at the same time. She was also mortified to be wearing the T-shirt and shorts she'd borrowed from him.

He tilted his head and scrutinised her. 'May I come in?'

She turned and led him up the stairs, her emotions intensifying with every step. She'd spent the last twenty-four hours trying to get a handle on everything, but now the world's hottest psychologist was on her landing. Her former stunted emotional spectrum was far preferable to this new flywheel of feelings that never seemed to run out of energy. She ushered him into the lounge.

'Oh nice. Did you get that idea out of House Beautiful?'

He was referring to the boxes and black bin bags that she'd stuffed with all the crap she wanted rid of, piled up by the fireplace.

'Can I get you a cup of tea?'

She sounded like some prim spinster. She was about to articulate as much when Jasper tapped her on the shoulder.

'Hey.' He opened his arms and invited her into them. 'Come here.'

It was the last thing she'd been expecting, but the exact thing that she needed. She stepped forward and let him curl his arms around her, his muscle and sinew a shield against the raging shitstorm in her head.

'What the hell happened?' he said.

His body felt as solid as she'd expected it to. Of course it did. He was, literally, a solid bloke. He smelt just as he had that night on the sofa, all woody and musky and delicious. If she could just stay here, she wouldn't have to think about the trash fire that was her life.

'You don't have to tell me if you don't want to,' he said.

Where to start? Ollie. Tony. Wolfe. Tasha. The fall. Her job. Her bloody life. She was determined not to cry, so instead a salad of words tumbled out, and all the while he gently rubbed her back like he was trying to rub the sadness out of her. It had been a long time since she'd been held in that way – without judgment or expectation. After she'd finished, he gently lifted her chin so he could meet her gaze.

'You know none of this is your fault, right?'

'I mean, it kind of is.' She felt like a teddy with all its stuffing on the outside.

'It isn't. You need to cut yourself some slack.'

A single tear ran down her face. Traitorous eyes. He pulled out his handkerchief and wiped it away with a featherlight sweep of his thumb.

'Okay, that's out of my system.'

'Simone…' he said with gentle reproof.

Another tear escaped from her other eye. He wiped that one away with his other thumb.

'Okay, it definitely is now.'

'It's okay to be upset.'

'I don't want to be upset.' Another tear ran down her face. Stupid feelings. 'And that's before I've even gone into what's happening with the shelter.' She groaned. 'I'm so sorry you ever had to cross paths with me.'

'Hey, that's not your fault either,' he said. 'And I'm not sorry for what's happened. It meant I got to meet you.'

Her eyes brimmed again. She tried to compose herself, clenching her jaw until it ached, but the rising tide of emotion wouldn't be quelled. But what started as a quivering breath, a tentative release of tension, transformed into something else entirely: a full-on gurgling laugh that bounced off the walls, carrying with it the frustrations of the last forty-eight hours. This clearly wasn't the reaction he had been expecting.

'Perfect.' He pushed her away in mock offense. 'I'm trying to be all sincere and this is how you treat me.'

She couldn't help it. 'I think that's the cheesiest thing anyone's ever said to me.'

'You are intolerable.'

'*I got to meet you,*' she mimicked, still chuckling.

'Why don't you put your Doc Martens on and properly trample all over my feelings?'

'I'm sorry.' She snorted. She was relieved to know everything was still functioning in the piss-taking department.

'It's fine. It's called displacement. You can't deal with the enormity of your feelings, so you have to take the mickey. Classic example.'

'Which feelings?'

'The feelings you have for me,' he said.

'Ha! I have feelings for you, do I?'

'Without question.'

'Actually, you're right.'

'I know I am.' He took a step towards her, his confidence returning.

Simone took a step back. 'Antipathy. That's a feeling.'

'Hmm.' He took another step nearer.

'Ambivalence.' She stepped back again. 'That's also a feeling.'

He smiled and took another step.

'Revulsion.' She bumped into the wall behind her.

'You say the sweetest things.' He came so close that the celestial patterns of his irises were visible. 'Just so you know, I'm going to kiss you now.'

'Oh are y—'

And then his lips were on hers. Not urgently or forcefully; just the merest whisper of a kiss; one that sought permission to go further. She granted it by pressing back against him. Still looking directly into her eyes, he tilted his head and gently licked across the opening of her mouth, but she felt it in a hundred places beyond her lips.

'Hmm. You taste good.'

She lightly sucked his lower lip into her mouth. 'You too.'

He put his hand behind her neck. She wound her arms around his back. And then he kissed her again. It was hard to describe the sensation of having his mouth on hers. It certainly wasn't how she'd been kissed before. The intensity of having him watch her the whole time was a definite turn on, but it was the selflessness with which he did it that made her insides coil with desire. It was like she was a vessel he wanted to pour his affection into, with no expectation of getting anything back. Jesus, if this was the starter, she wanted all in on the main course. She reached for his junk, testing to see if he was experiencing this in the same places she was.

His eyes widened momentarily. 'What if I told you I only want a kiss?'

'I'd tell you that's very disappointing to hear.'

'I don't want to take advantage of you.'

'I am all for being taken advantage of.'

'You're emotionally vulnerable.'

'I am also very turned on.'

'We haven't even been on a date.'

'That doesn't usually stop me.'

'Lovely!' said Jasper.

'Just shut up and kiss me again.'

This time the kiss went deeper, more urgent. It was a kiss that was going places. The sexual gods had awoken and there was only one way they were going to be appeased. Jasper pressed himself against her. She ground herself against him, the seam of the shorts settling in just the right place to magnify each rhythmic movement. It was like sinking into quicksand; she couldn't have pulled herself away if she wanted to. She needed to consume and be consumed by him.

'I think we should close that.' He nodded in the direction of the blind.

She pulled him towards the window, unwound the cord, and let it fall.

'I think we should open these.' She unbuttoned his trousers.

He littered kisses along her collarbone, making her scalp prickle. He tugged on her shorts. 'These are going to have to go.' He loosened the bow and they dropped to the floor.

'These too, I'm afraid.' She tugged his cargo pants down over his bottom.

He kicked off his trainers and deftly wriggled out of the trousers. She leant in to taste his lips once more, delaying the inevitable removal of the final layer. She was unable to recall the last time she'd slept with someone for the first time and been sober. But impatience got the better of her. She wrestled his T-shirt off him, relishing seeing in close-up the same body parts she'd lusted after from afar. The faint ridges that ran across the edge of his pecs where they met his breastbone; his hair-free, taut, unyielding skin; his perfect dark nipples that lined up with the outer edge of his six-pack. She wanted to take one into her mouth, see what it tasted like, but would he think that was weird?

He was under her T-shirt, undoing her bra.

'What kind of sex are you into?' she breathlessly whispered into his ear.

'Is there a menu?' He cupped her breast.

'I'm serious.'

She'd never felt the need to please someone more.

His hand stayed and he looked directly into her eyes. 'Simone. You don't have to perform for me. You just need to enjoy yourself. That's the kind of sex I'm into.'

She could just melt into him. She'd never felt more turned on, but perhaps there was no need to rush. She could take her time and savour the moment. She put an arm's distance between them and unhurriedly removed her top, then slowly and deliberately took off her bra. She'd always been confident about her body, but as his eyes slowly traced the curves of her boobs, she felt painfully self-conscious.

'They'll do, I guess.' He winked.

'Will they now? And what have you got for me?'

He pointed to his own chest. 'These?'

'Nuh-uh. The rest of it.'

The outline of his erection was clearly visible in his tight-fitting boxer shorts. She became apprehensive all of a sudden. It was always nerve-wracking making the acquaintance of a penis, especially when you had grown so fond of the owner to which it was attached. She imagined it was like being introduced to someone's kid for the first time. Would you like them? Would you want to spend more time with them? It was probably shallow, but this shit was important if you were going to be in a relationship. Uh-oh. Relationship. She tucked the idea away to revisit later. Best to tackle these things one shag at a time.

'Okay, fine.' He tucked his thumbs into the waistband of his boxers and very slowly unpeeled them, past the pronounced ridges of his lower abdomen, past the blackness of his tight pubic hair, past the point of no return. His dick sprang out like a jack-in-the-box. It had a slight curve, like it was cocking its head and inviting her to come play, but it was as irresistible as the rest of him.

'I think I can work with that,' she said.

The boxers fell to his ankles and he stepped out of them. 'I've shown you mine, now you show me yours.'

She removed her knickers.

'Eww, is it meant to look like that?!'

He was joking, of course.

'You asshole!'

'I really like you too. Come here.' He pulled her towards him, grabbed her by the bum, and lifted her up so she was straddling him. 'Crikey, you're heavier than you look.'

She joy-snorted. 'And you are far weaker.'

'Do you have a bed? I'm pretty certain that sofa won't be able to handle what we're about to do.'

'It's that way.' She pointed back out onto the landing.

'Hnngg.' He pretended to stagger.

She laughed again.

'We're also going to need a condom,' he said. 'I don't tend to carry them around with me.'

'Tut-tut. Were you not a boy scout?'

'No, but I'm pretty certain that wasn't one of the badges.'

They'd reached the bedroom, and even though the flat was otherwise unoccupied, she kicked the door closed behind them.

'Alexa, play some music. Volume five.'

She didn't need the dude downstairs hearing anything of what was about to transpire; this was going to be just for her.

Two hours and more than one condom later, they lay in bed. Jasper was stroking her hair and she didn't even care how greasy it was. He tentatively parted it, taking a closer look at her wound.

'Did it hurt when you fell from heaven?'

They both burst out laughing.

'I once had someone say that to me for real.'

'That's because you are very, very hot.' He kissed her head.

She shivered with pleasure. 'So what made you come?'

She couldn't believe that he was really here, in her bedroom.

'I think it was that thing you did with your finger, mainly.'

She cackled. 'I meant back here. Today.'

He comically hit his head, pretending he really had imagined she'd meant it sexually. 'Well, first off, I was worried. I called you. A few times. Then I sent a couple of messages, but none got read. I figured that was odd, given how ordinarily you're surgically attached to your phone.'

She playfully hit him, her hand making contact with unyielding muscle.

'And I owed you an apology. I'm sorry for being a dick at the gala. The truth is I saw you with that guy and I … I don't know, I was worried about getting hurt.'

'I don't think he'd have taken you in a fight.'

'Not physically, you dope! I thought about texting you every day since then but … I guess I still harbour some abandonment issues that I wanted to work through.'

She had a sudden, horrible flashback of waking up in bed with Marcus. With the tsunami of shit she'd been dealing with, her mind had offered her some small respite by keeping that in the sidebar of her consciousness. But there it was. Should she tell him what had happened? She didn't want to say or do anything that could spoil this moment. Equally, she wanted to be completely transparent with him. She tossed the thought this way and that. They hadn't been seeing one another, so did she need to mention it at all? But if it came out later, would he feel aggrieved that she'd kept it from him?

'Anyway,' he said, 'you might have convinced yourself you can switch your emotions on and off, but it turns out I can't.'

He bent over and kissed her deeply. She decided now wasn't the time.

'Is that why you work at the shelter,' she said when they came up for air, 'rather than literally anywhere else?'

He considered this. 'I don't know how anyone can see what these people have been through and then walk away.'

She was reminded of some reels Nancy and Ziggy had posted

of an organised tour of San Francisco's tent cities, tickets for which had set them back thirty dollars. She'd been shocked by the cynical profiteering at work, and she told Jasper about it now. How weird to think that, had fate taken a different turn, she would have been there with them, probably not thinking twice about snapping away with her camera.

'I'm not surprised.' He had far more shocking stories of poverty and disaster tourism that he shared.

'And dare I ask what's happening at the shelter?'

He told her that, as feared, the council had confirmed the shelter's funding was being cut.

'I don't know when they were planning on telling us if we hadn't asked. Gayle's investigating alternative accommodation for everyone, but until the shutters come down completely, there's nothing official we can do. She's doing her nut about Tasha. I should probably call her and let her know.'

He grabbed a towel, wrapped it around himself, and went to retrieve his phone from the shorts on the lounge floor. She missed him the second he left.

'What will happen to Hozan?' she asked when he returned.

It wasn't like he could just pitch up in another shelter's car park.

'I don't know.' Jasper's mouth set in a grim line. 'I really don't know.'

She had temporarily allowed herself to forget everything, but the real world was crowding in once more.

He sat down heavily on the edge of the bed. 'What kind of a world is it where rich idiots can consider other people's suffering to be good business, or worse, entertainment?'

Her brain's synapses glittered with the germ of something. She rolled onto her side. 'What did you say?'

'How can it ever be reasonable to use people's suffering for profit or entertainment?'

The thought burst through its fleshy membranes and into her consciousness.

'That's brilliant,' she said.

'What is?'

'That idea.'

'What idea?'

'What if we ran an event? At the shelter. An authentic homeless experience. *Twenty-four hours in the life* kind of thing. As a fundraiser.'

'Are you kidding?'

'No. I'm deadly serious.'

The idea was like a magnet, drawing others to it.

'We could invite a bunch of influencers along. They love that kind of shit.'

'Why would anyone want to stay in a homeless shelter unless they had to?'

'Because influencers are insecure attention seekers who think the validation they get from other people, whilst doing things those other people won't get the chance to do, will in some way make their vacuous, pointless lives more meaningful.'

More ideas careered around her head. Why hadn't she considered it before? This was how she'd get her own back. Scupper Wolfe's chances of getting the shelter. It was perfect.

'We could do a fundraiser at the same time. Double up.'

'How would you even organise it?'

'Please! You are looking at a three-time Eventex Award winner.'

Finally, it was time to put her skills to good use, and if she could get her revenge in the process, well, that was extra delicious.

'But what would we do with the residents?' asked Jasper.

'Temporarily put them up in a hotel?'

'How? There's no money, remember?'

She got up off the bed and opened her wardrobe doors. In neat fabric hangers were the things she hadn't packed up for the charity shop: the designer handbags she'd amassed over the last fifteen years or so.

Jasper shook his head. It was a rather excessive collection.

She nodded her tacit agreement. 'I think it's time I finally sold some of these…'

Chapter Forty-Five

Going to a designer exchange place in Camden hadn't been an ideal first date venue, but they'd come away with more than enough money for a couple of nights in a B&B for everyone. At one point she wondered whether she should hand the cash straight over to Gayle, rather than risk its investment in her idea, but Jasper had told her it was better to try something that might have a long-term impact. She still wasn't over the fact that he had come back for her, that they had finally ended up in bed together. She had a million unanswered questions for him, but she'd had to drag herself away to find Tasha. With Jasper holed up at her place, she'd returned to the intersection where, thankfully, Tasha was still ensconced.

'You're back, are you?' said the girl.

She was sat on a camping mat outside the tent, reading a book. At least she wasn't smashed this time.

'Yep. I've come to fetch you.' She'd already decided that she wasn't taking no for an answer.

'I'm not some kid playing out who you get to call back in for dinner.'

'True. But if you were my kid, I would actually do that. I would make sure that every single night you came back home, and you had a decent meal inside you.'

'Yeah, right.'

'Yeah, right. Tasha, I don't know a great deal about your background, and I don't know the shit you've been through, but I'm guessing your parents are either dead or assholes. Because only complete douchebags would let someone as warm and caring and smart and lovely as you end up somewhere as shitty as this.'

The girl seemed completely unmoved.

'This isn't where you belong and this isn't what you deserve,' said Simone.

Tasha continued to glare at her impassively.

'Just come with me now.'

'Where to? The shelter's closing.'

'How do you know that?'

Tasha shrugged. Perhaps Gayle had got hold of her.

'I've got an idea to keep it open, but I'm going to need your help.'

The tent's zip opened and a head emerged. 'What the fuck's going on?'

She'd expected any boyfriend of Tasha's to be some ripped-sweater long-haired goth type, but this guy was just your typical hoodie. He wasn't much older than Tasha.

'Go back to sleep,' Tasha told him.

'I can't with this shit happening in me earhole.' He nodded at Simone. 'Who's this?'

'Just someone I know from the shelter.'

'Tell her to fuck off,' the lad said.

'Don't tell me what to do.'

'What the fuck is up with you?'

'You tell her to fuck off if you want her to fuck off,' said Tasha.

'Oi, fuck off!'

'Fuck you!' said Simone.

'Is she some kind of lesbian?' he asked Tasha.

Simone was wearing a bandana to cover her greasy hair and a pair of dungarees. Stereotyping moron.

'Yeah, the straight kind,' said Tasha.

'Are you screwing her?' he asked.

'Don't be stupid.'

'Don't call me stupid.'

'You are stupid.'

'Was that baby even mine?' he said, apropos of nothing.

'Well, it wasn't hers, was it, you idiot?!'

'Don't call me an idiot.'

'You are an idiot.'

The guy turned from Tasha in a huff. They really were still just a pair of kids.

'I'm sorry about the baby,' said Simone.

He groaned. 'Don't get her going about the baby. She's done nothing but blub about it. I told her, it's a blessing.'

'It's not a blessing, you inconsiderate dickhole,' Simone said. 'It's a horrible tragedy.'

Tasha turned to her with questioning eyes.

'It is. It's a tragedy and I am so sorry that I wasn't there for you. You would have been an amazing mum; and one day you will be an amazing mum. But not if you stay here. If you stay here, you're going to lose whatever fight you have left in you, and that will be an even greater tragedy. You're smart, you're talented and you're special. It doesn't have to be this way.'

'Doesn't it? So what exactly am I meant to do?'

'You can come and stay with me for a while.'

'I knew you were a fucking lesbian!' said the boyfriend.

'Shut up, you little turd.'

She felt bad for him. That was Jasper's influence exerting itself. He probably had his own issues to contend with, but dragging Tasha down with him wasn't going to help either of them. A truck rumbled overhead.

'It's not much quieter, if I'm honest, but it's warm and safe. Just until you get on your feet.'

'Don't listen to her, babe. It's you and me, innit?' The boy slung his arm around Tasha's shoulder.

'Tasha, I am a horrible cynical fuck. I don't do feelings, or at least I didn't think I did, but I can't let you throw your life away. It means too much.'

'But what am I going to do?'

Okay, she hadn't dismissed the idea out of hand.

'I'm not sure. But right now, I need your help. This idea to try and save the shelter, I can't do it without you. *We* can't do it without you.'

'And then when I've served my purpose, or you're busy with work again—'

'Then you can tell me I'm being a twat, and I'll course correct.'

Tasha slowly shook her head. 'Maybe you believe that now, but...'

She trailed off. Perhaps she wouldn't be persuaded? After all, what reason did she have to trust her? What reason did she have to trust anybody? But she refused to leave her here; she wouldn't do it. She got down on her hands and knees.

'Okay, I'm begging you.' She interlaced her fingers and looked deep into the girl's eyes. 'I am literally begging you. Please come with me now. Please.'

Tasha took a deep breath.

'You're not seriously considering it, are you?' said the boyfriend. 'Let's just have a drink and forget this dick.'

Tasha didn't answer him.

'Seriously, babe,' he said. 'If you go, that's it, we're over.'

Tasha pressed her lips together and pulled at a stray piece of cotton at the hem of her T-shirt. She then stood up and went inside the tent.

The boyfriend gave Simone the finger. 'I win. Unlucky lezza!'

His smile disappeared the moment Tasha reappeared with her rucksack.

'I'm not fucking about here, Tash,' he said. 'If you leave, there is no coming back.'

'What are you gonna do? Change the zips?' She flicked her hair over her shoulder. 'As for you. Get up. You're embarrassing yourself.'

Simone got up.

'Come on,' said Tasha. 'Let's get out of here.'

When they got back to the flat, Jasper opened the door.

'So are you two together now?' the girl said.

'Ugh. Him?!'

'Her?! Are you serious?'

Tasha smiled and handed him her rucksack. 'Great. I'm gonna start calling you mum and dad.'

Jasper flinched and looked like he was about to launch into a big speech, probably about boundaries or something.

'Jokes.' Tasha continued up the stairs.

'She okay?' he whispered.

'I'm fine!' she shouted.

They had talked about the miscarriage on the way back. She was being incredibly pragmatic about it all. She described her sadness for the baby, but also a mixture of guilt and relief that it hadn't proved a viable pregnancy. The foetus had stopped developing not long after her first scan. Simone had reassured her that there was no right or wrong way to experience loss, and whatever worked for her was what worked for her.

'So is anyone going to tell me what's going on?' Tasha called down the stairs.

'Yes,' Simone said. 'But let's order something to eat first.'

Chapter Forty-Six

This was the first time she'd seen Ziggy and Nancy since they'd returned from America. They'd chatted lots on their WhatsApp group, so they already knew about the job thing. Still, she was genuinely touched when Ziggy insisted on buying the wine when she met up with them at her local pub.

'Before we talk about anything else,' said Simone, 'I need to bounce an idea off you. I'm thinking of running an event at Cedar Lodge. A spooky sleepover type thing, like a Haunted Homeless Shelter.'

'*Is* it haunted?' asked Nancy, eyes wide.

'Artistic license. It's a former psychiatric hospital, so it's not such a leap to imagine some bad shit went down there. I'm thinking a bit of atmosphere. People carrying candles. A bit immersive. Perhaps a few escape-room-style touches dotted around. Nothing too complicated, but you get the idea.'

'Can we come?' they both said in unison.

'So I'm on to something?'

'Are you kidding?' squeaked Nancy. 'It sounds amazing!'

Ziggy's eyes narrowed. 'But why?'

'Why what?'

'Are you being forced to do kind-hearted things against your will? Do you need to use our safe word?'

'It's being threatened with closure.'

She told them all about Wolfe. The information had started to sink in, but her pulse still quickened and the red mist descended at the injustice of it.

'You must really care about the place,' said Nancy.

'I'm just doing what anyone would do.'

'Would you do that, Ziggy? Give up your spare time to raise money for a homeless shelter you only learned existed a month ago?'

'Nope,' said Ziggy.

'Neither would I,' said Nancy.

'And Nancy is Insta's answer to Lady Di,' said Zig. 'I've never seen you so passionate about anything.'

'Shut up!' Simone's cheeks were reddening.

'Serious, Sim,' said Nancy. 'We're the ones who went away, but you're the one who's acting like they've had a life-changing experience.'

'You're going to get a life-changing injury in a minute if you don't stop saying nice things about me.'

'That's more like it,' said Ziggy.

'And will this psychologist be there?' asked Nancy.

A big stupid grin spread across her face. She might have mentioned Jasper a few times. And yes, he would be.

'He sounds far too good to be true,' said Ziggy. 'Are you sure he's not reverse gaslighting you?'

'What would that entail?'

'Making you believe you're a much better person than you actually are. Telling you that you teach sign language or cure cancer when you're drunk.'

'No. No gaslighting. It's literally the very last thing he's capable of.' She was still grinning like an idiot.

'Sim's in love!' said Nancy.

'No, I'm not.'

'Are you sure?'

'I'm too busy for all that.'

She and Jasper hadn't yet managed to spend a great deal of time together, as much as she yearned to do so. She wanted to ensure that Tasha didn't get spooked and run off again. She was currently convalescing at home after a procedure to remove the remains of her pregnancy. Jasper's sister, Jessica, was between places, so she was staying in his bedroom and he had the couch, meaning going back to his wasn't an option. When she'd asked if this amounted to sexist gallantry – since women were perfectly capable of sleeping on sofas – he had kissed her on her nose, told her that the pupil had become the master, and suggested as soon as Jessica moved out that they watch Star Wars together. She'd wanted to ask if he meant all nine films, which would be suggestive of the fact he saw some long-term future for them, but asking someone a straightforward question about their intentions towards you was a lousy way to start things off. Far better to ease yourself in with some good old-fashioned second-guessing.

'I'll also need to tap into your networks, if that's okay? We need to make a big splash, get as many people talking about the shelter as possible.'

'Cool,' said Ziggy.

'Really?'

'Yeah. Why so doubtful?'

'I don't know. I wasn't sure if it was *on brand*.'

'You're a mate, you dickhead. We're here for whatever you need us for.'

'Yeah, Sim, you dope,' said Nancy. 'Group hug!'

The tell-tale tickle of emotion welled up in her again. Jesus. She was becoming emotionally incontinent. She enveloped them both in a hug. They weren't perfect friends, but they were hers, and they were going to come through when it counted.

Chapter Forty-Seven

Gayle was in the office shouting at someone on the phone. She attempted to emphatically hang up, which was far harder on a mobile than it would have been on a landline.

'What's with the get-up?' she asked. 'Have you gone over to the dyke side?'

She looked at Jasper. Was he going to pick Gayle up on her derogatory language?

He waved a hand in front of her face. 'This isn't the conversation you're looking for.'

He was probably right. They had other priorities.

'It doesn't matter how many Star Wars references I hear, you know, I'm not watching it.'

Gayle observed their exchange with the air of a woman being forced to wear a tripe facemask. 'Oh I get it. You two finally porked then?'

'You make it sound so romantic,' said Jasper.

'Seriously, though, what's with the head scarf?'

Simone told Gayle what had happened and showed her the wound.

'Shit a brick! Was it her hairy gash that swung the deal, J?'

Tasha, who had been loitering by the door, made a puking sound.

'As for you, young lady, I was worried sick.'

'I'm sorry,' said Tasha.

'It's alright. You can make it up to me. Gary's not come in again. Lazy git. There's Love Island couples more committed than him.'

Tasha tutted. 'Has the food drop been?'

'About ten minutes ago.'

'Fine. I'll see what I can rustle up.' She sloped off.

'And how are you, other than the head?' asked Gayle.

'I'm good.'

'You look like shit.'

'I've missed you too.'

Gayle scoffed.

'You can say it,' said Simone.

'Say what?'

'You've missed me.'

'I've missed you in the same way I'd miss my piles if I ever got rid of them. So what's so important that it couldn't wait for me to come up with a good enough excuse not to be here?'

'We're going to get the money to tide you over.'

'And the shopping list I made this morning is going to win the Booker Prize.'

Gayle explained how she'd contacted everyone she knew to see if there were any emergency funds she could tap into until they sourced a more permanent solution. No one had been able to offer any help.

'So unless you're about to magic a golden goose out of your arse, we're screwed.'

'How long before you reckon you might secure something?' asked Simone.

'At least a couple of months. But I've got six weeks tops before the shutters come down.'

'I've got an idea.'

'Shake a bucket outside?'

'Even better.'

She told Gayle her plan. She'd fleshed it out properly since she'd spoken to Nancy and Ziggy, running her ideas by them to gauge interest. It was going to be called *Asylum*. She liked that it nodded to the idea of refuge and protection, so they could talk about the place being a homeless shelter now, but also hark back to its days as a psychiatric facility. A mashup between the two. She'd got a contact in theatrical prop hire who owed her a favour and could get them gurneys, old wheelchairs, straightjackets and treatment beds with restraining straps to set the tone.

There'd be a ton of activities on offer. Things like a padded isolation room where people would be invited to sit stimulus-free for an hour; freezing cold hydrotherapy baths, originally thought to calm the nerves in disturbed patients; hypnotherapy masquerading as *mesmerism*, named after the German physician who had induced trance-like states to deal with energy blockages. Wei was going to perform cupping to purge excess bodily humours and restore balance in the body. And there would be personality diagnosis through Rorschach inkblot tests. Essentially a whole load of things that had their genesis in some of the more horrifying treatments from the so-called Age of Reason, but that had the capacity to leave participants energised, more self-aware and more in touch with themselves than when they first came through the door.

For it to feel truly immersive, they'd also need to conjure a creepy atmosphere. There'd be a Ouija board for anyone wishing to commune with Cedar Lodge's 'previous occupants' who, they would claim, stalked the corridors at night. They'd keep the electrics off and equip people with torches. What with a few ceiling tiles removed here, a banging door there, it would be easy to let people's imaginations and lack of sleep do the rest. She was conscious that much of it wasn't strictly related to old-school psychiatric care, but it was okay to play fast and loose with some conventions to ensure people had a memorable time. It was a bit distasteful if you examined it too closely, but there were event companies out there making top money from dropping people into a simulated apocalypse, or actually kidnapping them and subjecting them to low-level torture – all in the name of entertainment. At least this was for a genuinely good cause.

The whole time she described her idea, Gayle peered at her through mistrusting eyes.

'Why would anyone put themselves through that voluntarily?'

'Because they are bored, rich millennials who just want to feel something.'

'And how much do you think this will make?'

'I think we should do it as a *pay what you think it's worth* event.'

A mushroom cloud of expletives erupted from Gayle's mouth. 'So we might not make anything?!'

'This way we get plenty of exposure and the chance of donations from a wider group of people. And if the guest list has a good time, there's a potential cash boost from them too.'

She'd consulted the girls about it. They'd talked about the phenomenon whereby, when they were paid for a post, they'd do the bare minimum to justify the fee, but give them something for free and suddenly they were canaries in a mine, telling everyone who would listen about it. Buying a ticket to a charity gig? Nothing special in that. But raising awareness for a good cause, and publicly making a grand gesture of donating to the cause themselves? That was like meth to the social media mavens. *No one*, Ziggy had said with staggering self-awareness, *cares about anything more than they care about looking like they care about something*.

'How many people and how many nights?' asked Gayle.

'One night. Around thirty people. Exclusivity makes these things more desirable. Scarcity is the currency in which these people trade.' She also told her about the hotel idea for the current residents.

Gayle tilted her head from side to side, weighing up the options. 'Okay,' she said eventually.

'Really?'

'It beats selling a kidney.'

'You sure?'

'Yep. I'm all out of ideas. Let's give yours a go.'

Jasper seemed as surprised as she was that Gayle had acquiesced so quickly. He was very, very beautiful when he was surprised, so much so that what she really wanted to do was take him to the nearest accessible toilet and remove all his clothes. But that would have to wait. It looked like they had work to do.

Chapter Forty-Eight

F or the next two weeks, she was in her element. She'd forgotten how much she loved organising events, and without Tony and Ollie to get in her way, she was crushing it, the different strands from her almighty Gantt chart all coming together.

The team were all playing their part. Tasha was in charge of catering, putting together a supper just like patients might have eaten back in the day. She'd borrowed metal trays from a local Thali restaurant into which she planned to unceremoniously slop the food. Steve was housekeeping, starching sheets and collecting moth-eaten grey scratchy blankets that were destined for landfill from an army surplus outlet. Hozan was mostly on observation duty, wandering around and regarding the work underway with abject suspicion, but he understood what was at stake, and was happy that they were trying their best against *The Man*.

The volunteer-led craft sessions had been given over to the creation of props, things like old patient case notes and signs to help people navigate their way around. What they lacked in finesse would be made up for by blocking up the windows and keeping the lights off, so the details wouldn't really be seen.

Jasper continued to hold his usual sessions with guests and visitors. It was agony not being able to pick up where they'd left off in bed that day; she was bobbing on a fast-flowing river of affection, gaining momentum with every snatched minute she spent with him. It wasn't a sensation she was entirely comfortable with. She'd spent her adult life thinking of men like perms: they may seem like a good idea at the time, but they never are. She expected some huge fall to happen at any moment, a Niagara-grade drop that would leave her dashed on the rocks. But every time the doubts became unwieldy, and she imagined perhaps he didn't feel the same way, he would suggest a walk around the block, or a brief tea break, during which his hand would seek hers out, letting her know in the sweetest of ways that it really had occurred, and he really hadn't regretted it.

Ziggy and Nancy kept their word to drum up interest. They'd been at the opening of yet another swanky bar where they'd bumped into one of London's biggest club promoters. They casually asked if he'd heard about this event that everyone was talking about. The guy had pretended to know exactly what they meant, and then, later on, had his PA circle back to ask for details about how he might get on the guest list. Having secured that person's interest, it was then a case of rinse-and-repeat for other leading influencers. Before long, they'd been proactively contacted by some of the biggest names on the social media circuit, all asking to be included. It was like a Ponzi scheme, but with social currency at stake versus cold hard cash. The potential guest list kept on getting bigger – in both length and ego – until they had their pick of the bunch. With a day to go, Simone had been contacted by two journos for *What's On* style digital magazines, asking to come and cover everyone's arrival. It was bonkers. All of which meant that, by the time the evening swung round, she was absolutely crapping herself that the whole thing might be a terrible, disappointing let-down.

The fact that, two hours in, it didn't seem to be bombing, made her even more nervous.

'What's the vibe with everyone?' she asked. 'Are people enjoying it do you think?'

She'd taken Ziggy and Nancy to one side to garner opinion. The atmosphere was decidedly buoyant, but it was impossible to be in all places at once, so she was having to trust that everyone was doing what they needed to.

'Babe,' said Ziggy, who, ever keen to show off her arse, had decided on a backless hospital gown as her outfit of choice. 'Apparently the Mindfulness Maven just posted she'd had an out-of-body experience in the isolation room, Mr E has been livestreaming himself crying over the plight of poor people, and Jason Reynolds – only the UK's biggest lifestyle vlogger – wants to talk to you about his upcoming birthday party. So, yeah, I think things are working out.'

Her shoulders relaxed a little. 'Okay. But what I really need is for this to make money.'

Nancy gave Simone's arm a cuddle. 'It's going to make money,' she said.

Was it? The JustGiving page that Gayle had set up was off to a slow start; just over six hundred pounds in donations had come in. Sure, she was hoping attendees would bolster the coffers by the end of the event, but they were also relying on this capturing the public's imagination. Thus far, her influencers hadn't proved particularly influential, even if the event was trending on socials.

'Stop relentlessly refreshing pages, and go and enjoy yourself,' said Nancy.

That might be a step too far, but she should try to not spend every second in a state of perpetual panic. What would be would be.

'In other news,' said Ziggy, 'we need to talk about Jasper.' She gave a chef's kiss. 'I can see why you might want to do the whole *look into my eyes, look deep into my eyes* thing with *that*.'

That was exactly what she was hoping to do after this was over.

Nancy murmured her agreement. 'And I absolutely adore Wei!' she said. 'Where have you been hiding him all this time?'

It was odd that the girls had now met both Wei and Jasper. It was like she was a maypole, and the different ribbons of her life were intertwining around her. The truth was she'd always been a bit embarrassed about going to Wei's: he was markedly no-frills compared to the upmarket places the girls frequented, but she'd been an idiot to care; they clearly didn't. She was beginning to understand that friendships were like most things in life – you got out what you put in – and with these pair she'd skirted along, providing the bare minimum. After all this was over, she was going to try and be a better friend to them.

'Thanks for everything, guys.'

'Aww. You're welcome!' said Nancy.

'Are we free to go now?' asked Ziggy. 'That guy who does cocktails on TikTok has said I can strap him to a gurney and take him for the ride of his life. So, you know, priorities.'

'Yes. Go. Have fun. But don't forget to tell everyone to include the link to the JustGiving page if they're posting.'

By the time the pale light of dawn bled in through the gaps in the newspapered windows, and the guests were filtering out to be greeted by a throng of fanboys and girls wanting to catch a glimpse of their mobile-screen idols, they had reached just under fifty percent of their target.

'OMG,' said Ziggy. 'We've been invited to an afterparty at the Hot House!'

The Hot House was a huge loft on Brick Lane where a bunch of hugely successful twenty- and thirty-something influencers lived together, collaborating creatively, and churning out content around the clock.

'This is next-level shit!' said Nancy, her entrepreneurial moxie briefly usurping her butter-wouldn't-melt persona.

'Are you coming, Sim?' said Zig. 'They said you'd totally be welcome.'

No, she bloody well wasn't going. Her plan not to charge everyone had backfired. Those privileged tight-arsed cockwombles. Coverage was all well and good, but cold hard cash was what they really needed, and barely anyone who had been there that night had donated.

'Hey,' said Nancy, 'it's going to be okay. It's still early in the morning. Most people will only just be waking up to the posts and stuff. There's every chance more donations will come in. You're worrying over nothing.'

But it would have been easier to swallow a brick than it would her disappointment. 'You guys go on. I'm going to finish up here then check in with the others.'

Once all the guests and helpers had left, they reconvened in the lounge. Jasper gave her a hug.

'Long night, huh?'

'Yeah.' She wanted to collapse into him.

'I'm absolutely knackered,' said Tasha.

Gayle was sat at a table with Steve, the eyes wide stare of the sleep-deprived lending her face a gormless air. 'I can't believe it.'

'I know,' said Simone. 'After all that.'

'I didn't think they had it in 'em.'

She agreed. 'Unutterable, selfish pricks.'

'To think I considered twatting one for filming me without asking.'

'Don't hold back the next time you get the opportunity.'

'And all along they were planning this?' said Gayle.

'To totally do a number on us.'

'Eh?' Gayle blinked.

'You were right all along. You said it was risky doing *pay what you think it was worth*. I'm sorry I didn't listen.'

'What the fuck are you talking about?' said Gayle.

'We're only at half the total. I blew it.'

Gayle's eyes were getting more manic by the second. 'Do you know who Demetri D is?'

'Yeah, he's that dickhead who asks poor people for money and then gives them crisp packets stuffed with cash if they lend him some.'

He'd been one of the guests, but she hadn't spoken to him. There was something about his performative morality that irked the shit out of her.

'Well, that dickhead just gave us ten thousand pounds.'

'Eh?'

She looked more closely at Steve. His mouth was working like an oxygen-starved fish. He picked something up off his lap: an envelope bulging with cash.

'Is that real?' asked Jasper.

Steve nodded. 'I think so.'

'Oh my god.' Simone ran over, took the envelope, and pulled out a wad of fifties as thick as a paperback book.

'What happened?' she said.

'I dunno,' said Steve. 'He asked me if he could film me chatting to him, and I said I was fine with it. I was telling him about everything that had happened, the whole Twelve Steps and that. Then he asks me if I have twenty quid for a cab home later. I thought it was a bit weird, because, you know, he could just use

Uber and pay on account. But I appreciated him listening so I said *of course, pal*, and I gave him twenty quid. He gave me this back.'

Simone pulled out her mobile and frantically searched for the guy online. Sure enough, his latest Tik Tok was of him giving Steve a bundle of cash.

'How can he afford to do that?' asked Jasper.

'Said he'd set up a Crowdfunder campaign, got the others involved, so he could spring it on us,' said Steve. 'I think he's just a really good guy.'

She really did have to stop pre-judging people.

'Weren't you tempted to do a runner with it?' She riffled through the notes again. The possibility that all that money would represent to someone like Steve.

'Of course. I'm only human. But I could never face our kid again if I did that. And step twelve is to help others. I'd say this gets me off to a decent start.'

The man never ceased to surprise her. 'You are a wonder.'

Steve whistled. 'You're not doing too badly yourself, mate.'

'Let's not start sucking each other's saucy bits just yet,' said Gayle, even though she was clearly gearing up to do just that. 'We're not there yet.'

Tasha looked up from her phone. 'The other total has just gone up too,' she said.

Simone refreshed their JustGiving page. Sure enough, the thermometer had shot up by another couple of thousand pounds. Her hands trembled. She refreshed the page. Another hundred dropped into the pot.

'Holy shit.' She caught Jasper's gaze. 'It's actually happening!' she shrieked.

He nodded, still pretending to be as calm as you like, but his eyes were gleaming as he pulled his handkerchief out of his pocket. 'It looks that way.'

Gayle sang 'We're in the Money'. Steve joined in. Tasha bayed like a wolf. Hozan, who had watched all this unfold, simply bowed his head in silent prayer.

She refreshed the page again. More money had come in. The girls had been right, it was simply a matter of time before they exceeded their total. It was like someone had let off a party cannon in her chest as happiness and disbelief fluttered like confetti through her body. She'd never experienced anything like it. Ten minutes ago, she could have slept where she stood; now every nerve was ignited with the surfeit of energy coursing through her. There was, she was certain, absolutely nothing that could topple her from this feeling.

Then the door burst open.

Chapter Forty-Nine

'Ollie?'

'Who?' said Jasper.

'He's that work colleague I told you about.'

But what was he doing here?

'There she is.' Ollie sauntered over to her, slow clapping. His chinos and shirt looked like he'd slept in them, and his eyes were bloodshot.

'Are you drunk?' she said.

'I should be. I had a shot for every time I thought about what a skank you are.'

'Hey!' Jasper was up out of his seat.

She held up a hand.

'Did you really think it would be this simple?' said Ollie.

His pupils were dilated and he was having difficulty controlling his jaw. She recognised the signs; he was coked up to the eyeballs.

'What would be?'

'Saving your shithole of a shelter.'

So he'd got wind of what was going on. But she wouldn't be intimidated.

'We've raised enough money to cover the gap for three months.' She lifted her chin. 'I think we're going to raise more.'

'Whoop-de-do. Your naivety is almost charming. Did you not for a second wonder how Wolfe knew this place was struggling for funds?'

In all the furore and everything that had happened since, it hadn't really crossed her mind.

'Because he created the funding issues in the first place, you idiot.' Ollie spun around to see the reaction his words might have. Nobody said anything, but both Jasper and Gayle looked like bulls, ready to charge. She stayed them with a glance. If this was true, and she feared it was, it would be better to let him talk.

'You're bullshitting,' she said.

'Nuh-uh,' said Ollie. 'Wolfe's the one who's been leaning on the shelter's funding sources. A posh lunch here. A scratched back there. It's all been very carefully orchestrated.'

'How do you know this?'

'Because he likes to talk. He's like any narcissist. It's not enough to pull off the trick, he has to explain how it was done. It's all been quite irritating if I'm honest – talking down to me like I'm some lackey. I'm pretending to lap it all up until I work out how I can use the fat cunt to my advantage.'

Her brain whirred. 'But what he's doing is corruption.'

Ollie sneered. 'The thing you never grasped, Simone, is that sure, money is useful, but influence is what gets you the boardroom backslaps and the keys to the fancy bathroom. And by *influence* I don't mean those idiots on Insta. I'm talking genuine power. The kind that comes from status and breeding. Influence is the real currency in life, and your problem is that you don't have any.'

It was like a hole had opened up in her chest and fetid water had rushed in. It was grotesque that Wolfe could care so much for profits and so little for people.

'You know it's funny,' said Ollie. 'I wasn't sure whether I should put the police on to you that night at Secret Cinema, but then I figured it might be fun to spook you a bit.'

Her head whipped back. 'You did what?'

'Have you not worked that out yet either?' A leer emerged from his grinding teeth. 'Simone, Simone, Simone. All it took was a little tip-off. I was disappointed you didn't have any drugs on you; I always assumed you were a coke whore.'

'That's rich, coming from you.'

'But then you let your fiery little temper get the better of you, didn't you? Got yourself arrested anyway!'

It felt like the air had been sucked out of her lungs. He had to be lying.

'The conviction was pure poetry. They must have really disliked you.'

'There's no way you could engineer that.'

'Couldn't I? The simple fact is, I know people. Who do you know?' He gestured around the room.

He didn't recognise Steve, although Steve knew exactly who he was. Again, Simone wordlessly warned him off doing anything crazy.

'That doesn't stack up,' she said. 'Why work at D&A if you have that kind of leverage?'

'Because knowledge is power. And where better to uncover the kind of knowledge that can be incredibly powerful than at the very place where people come to cover up their dirty secrets?'

The notion he would be so calculating gave her goosebumps. As did the knowledge that he would and could have gone to such lengths just to spite her. One thing was clear: it didn't matter how much money they raised. If this was what they were up against, Gayle wouldn't be securing additional funding. She sat down before her legs buckled and dropped her head into her hands. When Hozan had said it was no accident she was there, she had taken it as the ramblings of a disordered mind. It turned out he'd been inadvertently right all along. Ollie had managed to royally screw her over. She only glanced up when she heard the crack of a fist puncturing plasterboard.

'For fuck's sake!' shouted Gayle. 'Where's Hozan's bleedin' camcorder when you need it?'

Hozan eyed Gayle in a curious way. 'You told me my camcorder wasn't allowed.'

'I know!' She laughed sourly.

Hozan seemed in two minds about something, but then he pointed to his lapel. 'But no one told me I couldn't have this one.'

Gayle stopped rubbing her knuckles. 'Eh?'

'No one told me I wasn't allowed this one,' he repeated. Again, he pointed to the buttonhole on the lapel of his suit. There was the tiniest little glint where fabric should be.

'Are you joking right now?' said Simone, barely daring to believe he might have a tiny camera hidden there. But Hozan was to joking what ballerinas were to plus-size clothes.

He pulled a phone out of his jacket pocket. On the screen was a grainy version of them all.

'Are you telling us you recorded that?' asked Gayle.

Hozan's great eyebrows furrowed.

'It's okay, Hozan,' said Tasha. 'Did you?'

He nodded. He passed Simone the phone, then removed the pin and placed that in her palm. It was no bigger than her fingernail in length and width. She gently nudged it around her hand.

'Where did you get the money for this?'

'Begging. Like you taught me.'

Sweet Jesus. It was pure poetry.

'You beautiful, brilliant man!'

Ollie's addled brain had caught up with events. 'The cretin has a secret camera?!'

'Don't you dare call him that!' Jasper was over like a whippet after a rabbit. Steve and Gayle jumped to their feet.

'Don't touch him!' she said, despite wanting Ollie to sustain a second broken nose for his hatefulness. 'We physically hurt him, we're in proper trouble. He's going to be screwed enough when Wolfe has to back down.'

'Ha!' said Ollie. 'How's that happening? Are you going to call the police?'

'No. I'm going to call an organisation that's far more powerful. The *press*.'

He seemed wholly unconcerned. She couldn't wait to knock that look off his stupid, snivelling face. She took out her mobile, brought Marcus's number up, and prayed he'd answer. He did.

'I was wondering when you'd be in touch,' he said.

'I have a story for you.'

'Is it a saucy one? You've not been returning any of my messages.'

'I'm about to make it up to you.' She gave him a précis of what had happened, her excitement building as she went. This was potentially significant, wasn't it? They had proof of Wolfe's misdeeds.

'Not as much pussy as I was hoping for, to be honest,' he said when she finished.

'Get your head out of the gusset for one second!'

But his tone hadn't been playful.

'I'm not interested in the story.'

'But you heard, we have proof.'

'You've got nothing. Wolfe's dodgy dealings are well known. He's got holding companies within holding companies, hiding things even *he* probably doesn't know about. One story isn't going to do anything.'

'I'm not trying to topple an empire,' she said, 'I'm trying to save the shelter!'

Ollie sniggered. It was obvious to everyone this wasn't going how she'd hoped.

'I know Wolfe,' said Marcus. 'He's a friend.'

Of course he was. Of course they were all part of some extended boys club, with their power and their entitlement and their constant and unerring ability to shaft her every which way. She couldn't bear everyone looking at her, disappointment etched on their faces.

'Jesus, Marcus,' she said quietly. 'These are people's lives.'

'I know. And I publish stories about them being destroyed every day. If you think a few down-and-outs are going to move the needle, you're wrong.'

She rubbed her temples. Her head throbbed.

'Babe,' he continued, 'trust me. The shit that passes my desk, the things people do, it would make your hair turn white. It's cute you got yourself a conscience, but the world is fucked, and there's nothing you or I can do about it. Hang on, I've got another call coming in. I'll call you back.'

She stared at the screen. That wasn't it, was it? The whole thing was slipping away like dander on the wind. It had all been for nothing.

Ollie pulled an exaggerated sad face. 'Ahh, was Mr Marcus Millner not interested? There, there.'

The mention of his name caught her off guard. She'd not said it out loud, had she?

Ollie frowned at her. 'I've been given full access to your emails, you dimwit. They make for very interesting reading. What was the last one? Something about a blowjob you owed him. All very colourful.'

Jasper looked up sharply.

'Here I am,' said Ollie, 'a bona fide member of the in-crowd. Whereas you've resorted to boning the in-crowd.'

'Simone?' said Jasper. 'Is this true?'

'Not in the way he's making it sound.'

Jasper's face was a maelstrom of confusion and dismay.

Ollie pointed between them. 'Are you two...? Oh, I do apologise.'

'Go suck a bag of dicks, Ollie!' she barked. 'Jasper, let's go outside. I can explain.'

He was shaking his head; processing; judging.

'Please,' she said.

When he stepped into the corridor after her, his face was as expressive as wet cement. She could already feel the change in him.

'There's nothing going on between Marcus and I,' she said. 'I promise you.'

'So what was he talking about?'

She explained how she'd asked for Marcus's help in tracking Tasha down. 'It was a stupid joke.'

He relaxed a little. 'So when you told me you'd finished with him, that was true. Nothing else has happened between you?'

She swallowed hard. Fuck. She'd kept meaning to tell him about the night of the charity event, but with every passing day it had become more difficult, more awkward, until eventually she'd changed tactics and convinced herself it was irrelevant. But all this time it was incubating like a parasite, waiting for the perfect conditions in which to crawl out and wreak maximum damage.

'Something did happen.'

He closed his eyes and exhaled through his nose. 'Go on.'

'That night at the gala. I ended up in bed with him. But I was drunk...'

Any hope that he might take the news in his usual sanguine way quickly dissipated.

'Oh, you were drunk, were you?' His voice was thick with sarcasm. 'Well, that's okay then.'

'I know it's not great. I felt terrible the next day, and I thought about telling you. But equally, we weren't officially dating, so—'

'No, no, you're right.' He pointed a finger at her. 'We forgot to shake on it, didn't we? I forgot to bring out my standard twenty-page document with the wax seal that says we wouldn't go off and screw other people that very night.'

'Hang on a minute. You walked away from me.'

He threw up his arms. 'You told me to fuck off, remember? I was hurt. Did you ever consider that? In fact, did you ever stop to think about me at all?'

'But you never called me afterwards!'

'Why the hell was it my responsibility to do so? Most relationships are two people for a reason. It's give and take. And I came to see you.'

'Eventually.'

'Some of us have proper jobs to do.'

It was a low blow, and her first instinct was to retaliate, but she needed to pull the joystick back a little and stop the whole thing from plummeting.

'I'm sorry,' she said. 'I was pissed off.'

But he was wound up, his usual measure gone.

'That's as may be, but most normal people talk about these things. They find a way through this shit. How did you think it was going to work? That you'd go and sleep with Marcus every time we argued? That's not how adults go about things.'

'Oh, so you're calling me a child?'

His jaw worked like he was chewing something over. It was clearly leaving a bitter aftertaste.

'No, I don't think you're a child,' he said eventually. 'Do you want to know what I do think though? I think you use sex as a proxy for power. You conflate being fuckable with being loveable, and you use your body as leverage in situations where you think who you are isn't enough.'

'Oh god, thanks for the pseudo-scientific psychobabble.'

'Say I'm not right.' He was looking imploringly at her.

'You're not my psychologist, Jasper. You don't know what's going on in my head.'

'You're damned right I don't. You act like you like me, like there's some connection between us, but then the moment things get a bit spicy… What about this Marcus? Have you ever stopped to think that maybe you really like this guy? You've been seeing him a while.'

'Don't be stupid. He's never going to leave his wife for me.'

'And that's the only thing holding you back?'

'No. I mean…'

She was fucking it up.

'Why do you even want to be with me?' he said. 'Am I some kind of novelty act? A bit of rough. A mixed-race guy to add to the collection. Or perhaps it was all just a bit of fun to help your time here pass more quickly?'

Her face betrayed her.

'Oh, so it was?'

'At first, maybe. But not now.'

'Think about it, Simone. I don't have money. I don't have influence. I don't have a team of intelligence people I can lean on in emergencies. This is all I have to offer. And deep down, I'm not sure you think it's enough.'

She couldn't think straight. Everything was too emotionally raw.

Her phone rang. She instinctively looked at the screen. It was Marcus. Jasper had seen it too. She rejected the call.

'I need some space,' she said.

He nodded, resigned. 'Here you go. I'll give you all the space in the world.' He walked off down the corridor without a backward glance.

Marcus rang again. This time she picked up. Perhaps there was still hope for the story.

'Hey,' he said. 'Sorry about that. Where are you now?'

'I'm at the shelter. I lost my job.'

'I know, I heard.'

'Who from?'

'Tony.'

'You know Tony?'

'I know everyone,' he said, like this shouldn't be news to her. 'But it's okay. I can help.'

'How?'

'I can get it all put back the way it was. I'll send you a car. Come and meet me. I'm at the hotel. I miss you.'

'I can't just—'

'Abandon them? Of course you can. They're not your responsibility. If you're worried what they'll say, pretend you have a meeting with me. To discuss the story. Come on. Come back to me. Let's give it another go.'

'But—'

'Drop me a pin. The car's on its way.'

He hung up.

The darkness of the corridor crowded in on her. Marcus made it all sound so easy. Forget all about the shelter and put the pieces back the way they were. Everything she'd worked for, everything she'd sacrificed for her job, the thing with her mum, it would finally have been worth something. It wasn't like she had anything else to offer these people. There were no moves left to play. She'd tried her hardest to help, and it hadn't been enough.

And what about Jasper? Early doors, Wei had questioned whether her experience at the shelter was like a holiday romance. Incredibly intense and meaningful at the time, but the emotional impact would soon fade. Did he have a point? Annexed from her real life, had Jasper's appeal been magnified? Had she been swept along, without really considering the broader context within which anything between them would need to function? Was whatever they had going on destined to go wrong? They'd already had two major arguments and they hadn't so much as been on a proper date yet. Of course she liked him. But she'd liked someone before, and he'd made another woman pregnant. Even if she could persuade him to give her another chance, with that knowledge tucked away in her back pocket, how soon before the Hindenburg of further doubt floated overhead, casting its huge shadow as she waited for the whole thing to come crashing down?

What was it he'd once said about determinism? You can never be truly independent of the influence of other people, no matter how much you tell yourself you are, or how much you might like to be. And you can never be free of yourself. You can never entirely escape the person you are or the conditioning you've had. She was who she was. Simone Stephens: Cynical. Rational. Fuckable.

She closed her eyes and pressed her head to the cool wall, turning over the tangle of thoughts, grasping for the loose thread to pull on to help straighten it all out. Marcus was right when he said the world was screwed. Perhaps it was time to stop fighting against that and surrender herself to the inevitability of it, even if it meant she was letting everyone down.

She headed back to the lounge.

'I'm going to have to head out,' she told them.

'What's wrong?' asked Gayle.

'Nothing!'

But of course, her face gave it away.

'I'm going to go and speak to him in person. Find the angle. Make it work.'

Tasha looked searchingly at her. She wasn't buying it either. 'You're lying.'

'There are details we need to go over. He needs to understand what evidence we've got.'

Tasha shook her head. 'No, something's not right. I know what lying looks like, and I know what leaving looks like.'

'Tasha, listen—'

'No. I won't!' she shouted. 'I'll never listen to you again, you lying cow. You've not changed at all. You're still a selfish, materialistic bitch!'

Ollie followed her out of the shelter, relishing in watching her moral failure play out in real time. The world outside was turning in exactly the same way as it had been. Life carried on. It always did.

'Why are you even here?' she said to him. 'Wolfe was always going to get what he wanted. Did you really need to come and rub everyone's face in it?'

His mouth had finally stopped wobbling like a ventriloquist dummy's. The cocaine crash would come soon. The exhaustion, the headaches, the depression, and the feeling that there isn't a single pleasurable thing left to enjoy in the world. Welcome to the club.

'You're the kind of scrote who watches a parade passing from your balcony, then takes their trousers down and shits all over it. Does that make you happy? Does that bring you contentment? Are you not privileged enough? You're already in a lofty position; crushing people underfoot doesn't get you that much higher, you know.'

He leered. 'This has nothing to do with them. And I couldn't care less about Wolfe's plans. I just like to win.'

She wasn't sure she'd ever hated anyone more than she hated him.

The car pulled up, a sleek dark Jaguar, with smoky glass windows. She opened the door.

'It doesn't matter how many times you win, Ollie; to me you'll always be a tiny scrap of smegma clinging to the skin creases of someone else's bellend. Have a great comedown.'

She got in, slammed the door and told the driver to take a detour via her flat. Her phone pinged. It was Marcus.

Hurry up. I've only got a few hours before I need to be somewhere.

She tapped out a reply.

Just going to get changed into something less comfortable. Promise it'll be worth the wait.

If she was going to do this, she may as well do it properly.

Chapter Fifty

S he walked through the door wearing a pleated checked mini-skirt, white shirt, red ribbon tied at her neck, blue blazer and white knee-length socks. It was a costume she'd purchased for a Halloween party once – she'd gone as Gogo Yubari, the Japanese assassin from *Kill Bill*. She shrugged off a large rucksack.

'Woah, a schoolgirl vibe,' said Marcus. 'I like it.'

'I've escaped from my boarding school and I'm after some fun.'

'You look like a very fuckable doll.'

Marcus looked the same as he always did with his white bathrobe loosely tied over flesh that was tending towards doughiness.

'You should get a photo,' she suggested.

'I should,' he leered.

She watched as he unlocked his phone, held it up, and heard the fake shutter-click.

'I knew you'd be back. Again.'

'You know me better than I know myself,' she demurred.

'All that caring shit. It's a nice little distraction, but there's no future in it. Oestrogen getting the better of you.'

She put a finger to her mouth and bit the end of it. 'I don't know what I was thinking.'

'Come here.'

She skipped to his side of the bed. He put his phone on the bedside table and lifted her skirt.

'You're wearing knickers. I'm disappointed.'

'I figured you'd want something to remove with your teeth.'

He smiled a heavy-lidded smile. He was already turned on.

'What did you say you were studying?'

'Advanced fucking,' she purred. 'It's a new subject. The curriculum has changed a bit since you were a boy.'

'Clearly. And how do you think you're going to do?'

'I don't know. I've been a bit distracted recently. I've not been doing as much studying as I should have been.'

'I could help you cram tonight.'

'That's a nice offer.'

'I'm a nice guy.'

Even in role play, that was a little hard to swallow. But he was a *powerful* guy, and that was what counted.

He pulled open his dressing gown. The end of his cock glistened, taut and expectant. 'So what's the first lesson?'

She reached into her small cross-body bag. 'These?' The cuffs he'd bought tinkled as she pulled them out. 'A little bit of revision before we move onto something new?'

'Anything to help.'

Marcus had booked his usual room, which featured a gauche metal four poster bed complete with vertical bar headboard. She cuffed his hands directly above his head, then put her bag on the bedside table. The contents spilled from it as it did so.

'Whoopsie!' she said.

'Why don't you take my dick in that pretty mouth of yours, and lick it like a lollipop?'

'What if my parents find out I've been taking sweets from strangers?'

'I won't tell.'

She smiled coquettishly. 'Okay. I just need to get a picture. For my coursework.' She grabbed her mobile from the bedside table, then stepped back from the bed.

'Oh wait! This isn't my phone. It's yours. Silly me.' She didn't make any moves to swap them back. 'I must have got mixed up. All that oestrogen. Ovaries, man. Total twats.' The cutesy voice had gone.

'Eh?' said Marcus.

'I'm saying, women's bits, huh. Amirite?'

'I'm not sure what this is, but it's not working for me.'

His cock was wilting like a carrot left too long in the salad drawer. Simone turned her attention to his phone.

'And what about all those silly little opinions we have? And those crazy notions of equality.'

'What are you doing with my phone?'

She'd been tapping away the whole time. It had been almost too easy to get him to unlock it for her. 'I'm just getting a few numbers.'

'What for?' His tone had finally shifted from annoyance to concern.

'I'm thinking of sending them something.'

'What something?'

'The video.'

'Christ.' He gazed heavenward. 'Not that Wolfe shit again. When are you going to get it into your thick skull that nobody cares?'

Where was the nice guy now?

'Not *that* video.' She pointed to her throat. '*This* video.'

'What the fuck are you going on about?'

'You've seen a hidden camera before, right? You guys use them all the time, don't you?' She pointed to the tiny pin at the centre of her bow. 'Come on, Marcus. Wave.'

He twisted in the cuffs.

'Oh that's right, you can't. Now. Let's see who might be interested.' She scrolled through his contacts. 'Your wife?'

'Hah!' he barked. 'Breaking news. Man has bit on the side. So what? You know what our arrangement is.'

'That's a fair point. Thanks for the heads-up. I'll send her number to myself anyway, just in case.'

She emphatically tapped on the screen.

'Your father-in-law, however? He doesn't know about your little understanding. Be a hell of a way for it to come out!'

'Come on, Simone. A joke's a joke. Let me out of these cuffs.'

An attempt at conciliation. She was clearly on to something.

'What were your kids' names again? Max and Elliot? Imagine a video of their dad popping up in their TikToks. The shit they'd get at school would die down eventually. And with a doting father like you on hand, I'm sure they're resilient, well-rounded kids who can handle some gentle trolling.'

'Don't fuck with my kids.'

'And I wonder if the editor of *The Metro* might think it was a laugh to run the story. He'd probably go with some gently massaged version of the truth to spice it up a bit. *Rival newspaper editor meets schoolgirl for S&M sessions.*'

'You're not a schoolgirl.'

'I know. But they never see my face. And from what you were saying, it all sounded a lot like I was, didn't it?'

'You scheming bitch!'

He twisted some more, trying to get free, but she'd been very careful to tighten the cuffs just the right amount.

'That's the biggest compliment you've ever paid me.'

The idea had come to her at the flat. She'd been rooting around in a box, looking for the cuffs, when she happened across a picture of her mum. The sight of it made her catch her breath. She'd tried her best to erase all traces of her, removing all photos, possessions and the rare gifts she'd given; forensically clearing the flat like a serial killer might a crime scene. She didn't want anything remaining that might pin her to the woman.

But she'd missed this one picture. The image was only small, but her mum's face filled it, her soft bouncing curls almost bursting beyond the boundaries of the frame, her neck disappearing into the pussybow of a striped seersucker blouse. She was beautiful, physically at least, her high cheekbones not needing the accentuation of her unnaturally pink blusher, and her feline pale blue eyes glittering from beneath garish green lids.

The thing that stood out most, though, was the smile on her face. A genuine, heartfelt smile. She couldn't recall her mum ever being happy, had never considered that there'd been a time when anything other than resentment and hostility coursed through her blackened heart. But here was a sliver of evidence to the contrary. When did it all start going so wrong for her? When did she decide to be the vindictive cow that she became?

And then she was struck by a thought so profound, and yet so obvious, her head reeled. If everything we become is an inevitable consequence of everything that has gone before, perhaps her mum couldn't help becoming the heartless hollowed-out harridan she'd morphed into. Perhaps something, potentially innocuous but completely beyond her control, had set in motion a series of tiny missteps, which, taken consistently over time, had led her further away from this seemingly happy person someone had once captured on camera.

But the implications were almost too great to bear. Because if she could empathise with Tasha, with Steve, and with Hozan, as she had learned to, if she could see that not everything was as black and white as she had believed, that meant that she had to extend her mum the same courtesy.

The picture became fuzzy and indistinct in her hand.

And what did that mean for her own story? Was she destined to continue to play the part in which she'd typecast herself or did the plot twist of the shelter mean she had no choice but to accept her script had been rewritten without her realising?

She'd reached into her handbag to get a tissue, which is when she'd spotted Hozan's camera. She'd lifted it to the window, a tiny onyx stone that glinted as the light played off its lens. She'd taken a steadying breath, letting the air fill her lungs, feeling the pressure in her chest build. Then her diaphragm retracted, the spent air rushing out through her nostrils, and with it any doubt she might have had. The answer was obvious. Not really a decision at all, but in fact the natural outcome of everything that had happened to her up to that moment. She would try and do the right thing, which meant trying one last thing.

A litany of expletives poured from Marcus's flushed, angry face. She went to the mini bar, popped open one of the single-serve bottles of fizz, and slowly and deliberately poured herself a glass. She sat down on the end of the bed, out of kicking range, and nonchalantly took a sip.

'Get it all out of your system.'

Marcus started calling for help.

'I slipped the reception staff a little sweetener on the way up, told them it might get a little racy and it was best not to disturb us. And there's no one either side of us. I checked.'

'I am not fucking about, Simone,' he roared. 'I'll fucking bury you. You'll never work in media again.'

'Ah, thank you. It's a shitty industry. I'm probably better off out of it.'

'What do you want?' Desperation clung to his words now. 'Do you want me to run the fucking Wolfe story?'

'I'm not a sadist.' She pouted. 'I know you can't do that. And you were right, I can't save the world, but I can save the shelter. I want you to advise him to back off.'

'Why would he do that?'

'Because it's an excellent PR story for him. I know all the plans he's got in the pipeline; I've seen the rumblings happening on the web about his dodgy practices. He's sailing a little close to the wind and, like it or not, the event has raised the shelter's profile. There's a lot of attention trained on it. If suddenly he's involved in its redevelopment … well, why risk putting everything else in the spotlight? Far easier to make it a poster child for all the wonderful support he's offering local communities. He comes out the good guy.'

It was like a turbo-charged version of the stuff D&A were selling him as part of the pitch, but with a far bigger profile than his current CSR programme.

'Do that,' she said, 'and he'll find it far easier to slip under the radar on future ventures.'

'You want him to publicly support the shelter?'

'That's about the size of it.'

Her breezy tone belied her nerves. Even as she spoke the words, she called their credibility into question. It had seemed like a good idea when she hashed it out at home, but now…

'So are you ready to have a little word, or shall I get to work on your contacts list?'

'There's no saying he'll even go for it.'

'You're going to have to be very persuasive then, aren't you?'

He regarded her with pure malevolence. She almost felt sorry for him. It was an invidious position to put him in, but in the long run it was barely a moment's discomfort; for the people at Cedar Lodge, it was a potential lifetime.

'Pass me the phone,' he said eventually.

'Nuh-uh. Probably best we go speakerphone. No mention of my being here, obvs.'

Wolfe answered after the third ring. These old people and their habit of using mobiles for making and taking calls; it was adorable! Once the pleasantries were dispensed with – the pleasantries being Wolfe calling her a meddlesome slag when he heard about the event and the fact that a few press outlets had been sniffing around the story – Marcus set to work. She had to give it to him, he was one smooth-talking bastard. By the end of the conversation, he'd convinced Wolfe that it was the property mogul's idea all along. She hung up the phone. How had it been so easy? Was this how business was done in the upper echelons?

'Satisfied?' said Marcus.

'More satisfied than I've ever been in bed with you before.'

'You bitch.'

'Why, thank you.'

'Now are you going to let me go?'

No. She had no intention of releasing him whilst she was still in the vicinity.

'I'll send someone up with the keys,' she told him.

'At least cover my cock up, for fuck's sake!'

She examined it for the very last time. It aroused as much desire in her as a bloated albino slug might.

'No.'

'You can't leave me with my dick out. I'm totally defenceless here!'

'Aww. Are you feeling vulnerable? Exposed? Frustrated someone else is in control? Are you feeling undermined? Exploited? Used? Fearful? That must be awful for you.'

He looked like he wanted to kill her. It was infinitely preferable to him wanting to fuck her. She buttoned up her blazer, gathered her bits up into her small bag, picked up the rucksack, and opened the door.

'Told you I'd give you a night to remember, though, didn't I?'

And with that, she winked and left.

Chapter Fifty-One

She was more nervous than she'd ever felt as she ran up to the shelter doors. After a quick change in a hotel toilet, she'd grabbed a cab. All the way back she attempted to type and retype the right message to let Jasper know what she'd done. In the end, she decided the element of surprise might work in her favour; she didn't want him running off before she got the chance to tell him what she needed to. She found him in the first place she looked, in the office, sat at a desk, blankly staring at a wall.

'Hey,' she said.

His head pivoted towards her, incomprehension writ large on his face. He stood up. 'You're back?'

'Yes.'

'Why? Did he have to go and see his wife?'

It was a cheap shot, but an understandable one.

'I need to show you something.' She retrieved the photo of her mum from her handbag and approached him as she might an unexploded grenade.

'That's my mum.'

He tentatively took the picture from her outstretched hand. 'She looks like you.'

'Looked. She's dead. She killed herself.'

'Oh. I'm—'

'Don't say anything. Not yet. I've never told anyone this before, and if you interrupt, I might not get it out.'

He looked like he had a lot to say, but he tempered himself. He sat back against the desk. There was barely a foot between them.

'Okay. I'm listening.'

She looked down at her hands. 'I think I'm a really bad person,' she began. 'I could have saved her, and I didn't.'

Her fingers blurred and a salty droplet splashed onto her hand. She brushed the tears away.

'She'd threatened to do it loads of times before. Ever since Dad died. Every time she split up with one of her many boyfriends, every time she didn't get her own way with something. She said it to doctors, to friends, everyone. She was a drama queen.'

She picked at a nail, tore it down to the quick.

'She only ever took an interest in my life when something was going wrong in hers. She was less like a mum, and more like the crap friend who ditched you when they got a boyfriend, only to come crawling back after a breakup.'

A saffron strand of blood appeared across the angry pink skin.

'This particular time, she called and said she was finally going to do it. Told me she had some pills and a bottle of brandy, and that unless I went to see her that night, I would never see her again. I was busy at work – I was always busy at work – and it was easier to assume she was lying. I didn't go and see her. I didn't call back later to check on her. I don't even recall thinking about her again that day. I just had my head down, working on a presentation. I got the call the day after. For once, she was telling the truth. It was her final power play.'

He shifted his weight.

'Hang on, I've not finished. I didn't even cry when I found out. If anything, I was relieved. At least that's what I told myself. I threw myself into my work, more so than before, and became fixated on this idea of being promoted. You were right, if I could just get more money, more security, more things, then I'd be whole. And getting a promotion would make sense of her death, wouldn't it? Make sense of the fact I'd chosen work over her. Like it had to have been worth something, right? I don't know, you're the psychologist.'

'I think…'

'Wait. I'm not done. I'm not saying this for your sympathy. I'm saying it so you can understand who I really am. I worry that my indifference to her death means I'm incapable of loving anything. I worry I won't ever be able to let my guard down when it comes to relationships. I worry that I'm going to end up like her: some sad, embittered, lonely old woman. That I won't ever be able to trust someone enough to truly be vulnerable with them. I worry that I don't know what real love even feels like. And I worry that a bit of me is broken. Horribly, irreparably, profoundly broken. But if we're destined to never speak to one another again, I want you to know that I've never wanted to believe I might be capable of properly loving someone, that I might just be able to overcome all this stupid fucking prior conditioning, more than I've wanted to since meeting you.'

She sobbed, a full stop to her unburdening.

He pulled her towards him, gripping her tightly in his enfolded arms. It felt too good. Tearing herself away from this was going to be harder than telling him had been.

'I don't think you're a bad person,' he whispered into her hair.

'Hmm.'

'You're here, aren't you? You came to do something good.'

'But—'

'Shhh,' he murmured. 'We all have bits that are broken. But one man's trash…'

It was too much to hope that he thought of her as treasure.

He gently took her chin and raised her face to his. 'I don't believe you're damaged goods, Simone. I think you're a box marked *fragile* that deserves to have been handled with far more care.'

She clenched her jaw and let a long breath out of her nose. He was just trying to make her feel better. He still wouldn't want her in any material sense. She'd shown her hand, and he now knew she was holding nothing but dysfunction and neuroses. This was the moment where he let her go, back to her flat, back to her empty, pointless existence. Only he didn't. What he actually did was lean down and ever so tenderly put his lips to hers.

'I'm sorry,' he whispered into her mouth.

'What for?'

'For being jealous. For being insecure. For saying and doing stupid things because I was feeling jealous and insecure.'

She allowed a tiny chink of optimism to penetrate her emotional armour.

'But I'm glad you felt that way,' she whispered back.

She hazarded a kiss, but he pulled away from her. He put his hands on her shoulders and gazed at her intently. Had she blown it?

'No, Simone. Jealousy. Possessiveness. They're not necessarily signs someone cares about you. They can be signs someone cares about themselves at your expense.'

'I know.'

She leaned in, but he continued to hold her away from him.

'I'm serious. You're worth more than that. Far more.'

She took in every morsel of his sexy, earnest face. How could she imagine she was incapable of feelings when a torrent of them was raging within her? 'I know,' she repeated. She really was starting to know.

He kissed her properly then, an urgent if-I-don't-do-it-now-I-never-will kiss, one that she repaid with interest. It probably would have gone further, right there in the office, had it not been for Tasha walking in on them.

'I'm sorry, what?!' She looked thunderous. 'Didn't you fuck off and leave us about two hours ago?'

Of course, she hadn't even told them what had happened.

'Shit! Yes! I have some news for you all.' Her heart quickened with excitement. 'Tasha, get everyone together in the lounge.'

The girl arched her neck. She was giving off some serious *fuck you* energy. 'What did your last slave die of?'

'It'll be worth it, I promise.'

Tasha cast Jasper her best Judas vibes. He shrugged.

'Fine.' She swung around, braids whipping against her back.

The lounge was like a hospital waiting room, everyone sat exhausted yet expectant on uncomfortable plastic chairs.

Gayle was out of hers the moment she entered. 'You're like an unflushable turd.'

'I know, I know, but give me a second.'

She quickly gave them the very edited highlights. Wolfe was their new sponsor.

Gayle peered at her, doubtful. 'How the fuck did you manage that?'

'I'd rather not say.' She looked quickly at Jasper. 'It didn't involve bodily fluids though, I promise.'

'It's okay.'

Steve whistled. 'This reminds me of the time…' He stopped himself. 'Actually, this is a pretty unique situation, isn't it?'

Even Tasha allowed herself a grin at that.

'So we get to stay?' asked Hozan.

'Hozan. You were right when you said your gift was going to

save us all. I'm sorry I ever doubted you. I believe this is yours.' She took the tiny camera out of her bag and handed it to him. 'Thank you for the loan.'

'And I was right when I said you were special.' He placed his hand on her shoulder and said something in a language that she didn't understand.

'Is that some wisdom of Rumi?'

'No, I was saying *this calls for a biscuit.*'

Gayle appeared at their side. 'I can't believe it.'

'I know.' She expected to be showered with expletive-riddled praise at any moment.

Gayle looked at her earnestly. 'He's normally such a tight-arsed bastard with his biscuits.'

Simone laughed.

'Seriously, though,' said Gayle, 'how do we know he'll follow through?'

'With the biscuits?' quipped Tasha. 'I know where he keeps them if he doesn't.' She offered Simone a small smile that hinted very strongly at reconciliation between them.

'Wolfe's an asshole,' Simone said, 'but he knows a good PR opportunity when he sees one. And if he doesn't, well, then there's always the option of blackmailing the council. But we've got a while to think about it.'

'We?' questioned Gayle.

'I've got nothing else to do at the moment.'

Jasper pulled her to him once more. 'You're a very resourceful woman. I'm sure you'll think of something.'

'Alright everyone,' Gayle called out, clearly uncomfortable with their public display of affection. 'Don't stand around gawping. This isn't Gogglebox, and we've still got a job list longer than a Gwyneth Paltrow acceptance speech to get through. Hop to it.'

Everyone filtered out, but Jasper wouldn't let go of her.

'So, do you want to be my girlfriend?' he asked. 'Officially.'

'What are we, seven?'

She really, really, really wanted to be his girlfriend, but just thinking about seven-year-olds gave her this weird compulsion to remind him that she probably couldn't have kids. She'd been thinking about it a lot recently. Her feelings for him reminded her of an old neighbour who refused to get her dog neutered, despite it causing unwanted pregnancies in the neighbourhood. The woman's defence had been that she loved the dog too much, she couldn't bring herself to – literally – cut off its chance to procreate. At the time, Simone had thought there were billions of dogs in the world, how could that one be so special that you knew it deserved to genetically continue its lineage? But she was starting to understand what the woman meant.

'Are you sure? What about the whole...' she gestured to her pelvic area.

'I want to be with you, you chumnut, not your reproductive capabilities.'

'But—'

'How about we cross that bridge when we come to it?'

He made everything sound so reasonable, so drama free. To him, life was a blanket, something to relax under the weight of. To her, it was a starchy duvet cover, something to be wrestled into submission. But he'd said *when*, not *if*. Like there was no question that he was in it for the long haul. The idea made her unspeakably happy.

'Okay,' she said.

'Nothing else to add?'

'No.'

'Really?' He placed his palm on her brow. 'You must be coming down with something. Perhaps you should come back to mine for a little R&R. My sister's away.'

She was starting to flag. It had been a long, long night.

'Can we watch Midsomer Murders?'

'Hah! Very funny.'

'What? I really like cosy detective series. If some fading TV star is getting bludgeoned to death with a Victoria sponge, I'm all in.'

She really did. It was a guilty pleasure she'd never admitted to anyone. It would be like Wolverine admitting he liked knitting.

'You've got to be kidding me.'

'Don't say anything bad about Midsomer Murders.'

'I don't need to. It's all been said.'

'I'm serious. That's what you've let yourself in for. Every Sunday afternoon.'

'This relationship is over.'

'We're going to have to make polite conversation when I turn up here on Monday.'

'Okay, I might give you another chance.'

She tugged him towards the door, but he stood his ground.

'How about we compromise with Inspector Morse?' he said.

'How about you do Poirot, I'll do the Phantom Menace?'

'Alright, you surprising little creature. It's a deal.'

'But first we need to clear up,' she said.

He groaned. 'There is such a thing as being too good, you know.'

'You only have yourself to blame.' She reached for a sticky-out eyebrow and smoothed it against his face. 'Kiss me.'

'You didn't say please.'

'Please.'

He pressed his lips to hers and all bodily exhaustion temporarily melted away. Then he kissed her nose.

'Come on,' he said. 'The sooner we get it done, the sooner I can get *you* done.' His eyes flashed and his mouth set in a wolfish twist.

Damn. She'd been mad to suggest they stay and help. They should be calling a cab and hurtling headlong to his place and all the deliciousness that lay ahead. Instead, she would have to let the flavour of that tender kiss sustain her, for the next few hours at least. She took his hand in hers, felt its thereness, said a silent thanks to the universe that this was how things were unfolding, and headed out to find the others.

Chapter Fifty-Two

'Guess what?' said Wei.

'You're pregnant?' asked Simone.

'What makes you say that?'

'That belly. You look about five months gone.'

She had come to see Wei to return some bits he'd left at Cedar Lodge.

'It's like Dolly says. *My weaknesses have always been food and men, in that order.* I've let myself go.'

'Go where? On a fast train to type two diabetes?'

'Who are you to speak? Those bags under your eyes are so black I thought the bin men had forgotten their collections this week.'

'That's a bit laboured. Three out of ten for effort though,' she said.

'I'll never reach your standards, great high priestess of put-downs.'

'Just as well. We'd only fight like cat and overweight dog.'

'Miaow!'

'Oi, that's my line,' she said. 'Seriously though. What?'

He sat down on his stool. 'My auntie called.'

'Did she want her hairstyle back?'

'Put your claws away for a second and lie down. I'll give you a nice head massage.'

'I'd love to, but I'm short on cash. I only came to drop this round.' She put the bag on the side.

'I've not got anyone in for half an hour. Come on.'

She'd gladly take a freebie.

'So why did your aunt call?'

Wei's fingers went to work on her temples. 'My mum wants to speak to me.'

This was big news.

'Why didn't your mum just call?'

'She didn't know how I'd feel about it.'

'How do you feel about it?' She peeked at him. She didn't have to ask; his eyes were wide like a child's. He was clearly delighted. 'What happened?'

'She went to a conference in Shanghai. Led by the first woman to come out publicly as the mother of a gay son. My auntie went with her. She attended a free counselling session and another woman described how she'd already lost her son once when she found out he was gay, but that didn't mean she needed to lose him forever.'

Tears pooled in his eyes and spilt over onto her face.

'Apparently, my mum cried for three hours,' he choked. 'And then told my auntie she felt the same.' He wiped his nose. 'Sorry. How unprofessional.'

'And how does David feel about all this?'

'He did want to kill her. But then I told him she makes the best spring rolls, so now he's looking at sofa beds for when she comes to stay.' His face creased into more joyous tears.

'Oh Wei. I'm so happy for you. Everyone deserves to have a shitty mum in their life.' She got off the bed and gave him a hug.

'And what about everything she did? Are you ready to forgive her?'

'Of course. She couldn't help it. There's so much stigma around being gay in my culture. I'm sure if I was my mum, with her background and upbringing, I'd have behaved in the same way.'

'You sound like Jasper.'

'And how is Gandhi?'

Her belly still did funny things at the mention of his name. She was insanely happy. It was like her brain, or maybe her heart, had a 'reserved' section in it this whole time and it was just waiting for its VIP guest's arrival for the party to begin.

'We're now officially boyfriend and girlfriend!'

Wei fluttered his fingers near his eyes. He was going to cry again. 'How does that feel?'

'Like finding the perfect pair of jeans.' Her phone pinged. 'Hang on, that might be him.'

Whenever they weren't together, they were messaging. A lot. But it wasn't Jasper, it was Tony. She was wondering when he'd be in touch.

Well played.

What was?

A message popped back almost immediately.

Don't act the innocent with me.

She sent back the wide-eyed emoji face.

Ollie's gone.

Oh no. What happened?

Like you don't already know.

Okay, so maybe she'd taken the footage they'd recorded of Ollie calling Wolfe the c-word, edited it down, put it on a loop, and then sent it to Wolfe anonymously using a prepaid SIM card.

It was him or the account.

Good call.

Want a job?

Of course she wanted a job. She was nursing a credit card balance the size of a small country's national debt.

Hmm.

With the promotion.

She tapped out a message.

I wouldn't come back to work for you if you were the last man on Earth. I would rather eat the contents of my food bin than spend a second longer in that hell hole. I can only hope that your ample years of self-neglect means that, as I text, an embolism is forming in your clotted arteries, ready to unleash a stroke of epic proportions in your disgusting, diseased, haemorrhoid of a body.

And then she deleted it. She was better than that. Instead, she just texted *no*. It was incredibly empowering.

Name your price.

She was done negotiating with emotional terrorists. She didn't even bother to respond.

'I need to get a job,' she said to Wei.

'You should do your own events. That last thing you did was amazing.'

'I'll just set up my own agency, shall I?'

'Why not?'

'Because there are hundreds of event agencies out there. To be successful you need an angle. Something different. Something no one else is offering.'

'So come up with one.'

'Yeah, like it's that eas—'

A thought scuttled across her brain like a mouse.

'—y. Hang on a minute. I have an idea.'

'What is it?'

'Shh! I need to get it down.' She picked up her phone and began to make copious notes.

The front doorbell rang.

'Alright, Rockefeller. You're going to have to plan your world domination elsewhere. That's my next client.'

She jumped off the bed and made for the door, but then turned back. 'Wei. Crazy question, but you and David wouldn't like to have dinner at mine at some point, would you? With Jasper?'

'Aww. At this rate you'll be asking me to be a bridesmaid at your wedding!'

'You'd need to lose a few pounds first,' she said.

He launched a packet of cotton wool at her. 'Isn't love meant to make you softer?'

'You're thinking of body lotion.'

'Get out,' he said. 'Send me some dates. We'd love to come.'

Chapter Fifty-Three

It had been a while since she'd last stood on a doorstep with a man with his dick out, but here she was again.

'Sorry love. Just having a wazz.' The man zipped his trousers up.

'Don't worry, I've seen far worse.'

Jasper gave her hand a squeeze. He looked deliciously edible in his bright yellow puffer jacket and fleece-lined snow boots. She wasn't quite sure how it had happened, but these evenings spent walking the streets with him, helping with his outreach, had become her favourite way to spend time. The city unveiled its secrets after dark; an unseen side that she hadn't known was there. Messy. Beautiful. Enveloping. Brutal.

Tonight was particularly cold, and the man's sleeping bag looked like it could no more keep him warm than a bun could a hot dog. Jasper offered him a leaflet and went into his spiel, patiently explaining the services available even as the man shrugged, disbelieving.

Incredibly, Wolfe had done as he'd said he would. Marcus had made a big splash about his philanthropic deeds in the paper, the kind of whitewashing not even Johnny Depp playing the Lone Ranger could top. But this wasn't a fairy tale, and sadly not all baddies get their comeuppance. At least later on she would curl up on the sofa with Jasper with a mug of hot chocolate in hand and a movie or box set on the TV. Or they might listen to music and chat. Their conversations hadn't become any less sparky than when they'd first met, but at least now they got to take out their frustrations with one another in the bedroom.

She would also use these evenings as a recruitment drive. It was early days, but she had set up her own event agency, staffed in-part by homeless people. She had pitched her services at not-for-profit and purpose-driven companies, nothing that would risk her contravening her D&A non-compete clause, but the reception had been strong enough to suggest she was on to something. Sometimes Tasha would join them on their jaunts – far more approachable for the youngsters – and persuade them to apply for a position. It had been Tasha who had come up with the idea of the six-week system: bed, board, and intensive training in various skills required to help Simone run the events, such as DJing, silver service waitressing, and flower arranging. Gayle had offered up two rooms at the shelter for these rookie recruits, and so far eighty percent of them had stuck it out and now worked for her full-time, getting themselves back on track because of the income they were bringing in. Perhaps one day she'd start discussions with other shelters about replicating the training model, enabling her to properly scale up.

In the meantime, the occasional private party for some spoiled rich kid that Ziggy and Nancy fired her way was enough to top up the coffers and keep the mortgage paid.

Wei had also caught the altruistic bug, and with David's help was planning on opening a little nail and coffee bar. It would be somewhere to which the increasing number of people escaping unrest in Hong Kong could come, work, hang out, and learn the idiosyncrasies of the city to help them feel less disoriented and socially isolated.

Steve had stayed gamble-free and had got himself a job with Walthamstow council, doing repairs and maintenance on housing association places. He still turned up for his Twelve Step sessions at the shelter, and the last time Jasper had seen him, he'd brought his wife and son along. The signs were positive.

As for Hozan? Well, Hozan was still Hozan, and no worse for that.

She wasn't naïve enough to think she could save everyone. There was no delete key that could remove the endless cycle of shit that a lot of people on the streets had been subjected to, but occasionally they would stumble across a kid or a recently arrived migrant, devoid of options but not yet devoid of hope, to whom she would pass a card and extend the offer of gainful employment. The whole thing was an imperfect solution; they were the tiniest little drop in an ocean of people drowning. If she could rescue just one person from the ignominy of homelessness … well, if she did only manage to rescue one person, she'd be doing a bloody terrible job. But she'd never been bad at any job she'd put her mind to, and she wasn't about to start now.

Acknowledgments

First up, many thanks to the team at One More Chapter, including: Charlotte Ledger for doing more than any mortal should be capable of; Bonnie Macleod for picking up the mantle with such patience and enthusiasm; Laura Burge for her excellent copyediting; Federica Leonardis for her keen proofreading; Lucy Bennett for her striking front cover and Emma Petfield and Chloe Cummings for their marketing smarts.

Also, to my agent Kate Barker, who supplied a hearty dose of just get the hell on with it whenever I needed it (and boy, did I need it).

Thanks to the Amazon Algorithm. I'm not sure you're sentient yet, but just in case, loving your work. Feel free to bring the magic for this book.

Much gratitude to all the friends and family who <u>are</u> going to evangelise to their networks about how great this book is, even though at least 30 percent of them secretly thought it was a bit too sweary / a bit too different to my first one / a bit too cringe in the sex scene department.

Finally, to the two people who get me up in the morning, Jimbob and Edgar. Perhaps if you got me up in the afternoon instead, I wouldn't be quite so grumpy.

ONE MORE CHAPTER

YOUR NUMBER ONE STOP

FOR PAGETURNING BOOKS

The author and One More Chapter would like to thank everyone who contributed to the publication of this story...

Analytics
Abigail Fryer
Maria Osa

Audio
Fionnuala Barrett
Ciara Briggs

Contracts
Sasha Duszynska Lewis

Design
Lucy Bennett
Fiona Greenway
Liane Payne
Dean Russell

Digital Sales
Hannah Lismore
Emily Scorer

Editorial
Laure Burge
Kate Elton
Arsalan Isa
Charlotte Ledger
Federica Leonardis
Bonnie Macleod
Jennie Rothwell

Harper360
Emily Gerbner
Jean Marie Kelly
emma sullivan
Sophia Walker

International Sales
Bethan Moore

Marketing & Publicity
Chloe Cummings
Emma Petfield

Operations
Melissa Okusanya
Hannah Stamp

Production
Emily Chan
Denis Manson
Simon Moore
Francesca Tuzzeo

Rights
Rachel McCarron
Hany Sheikh
Mohamed
Zoe Shine

The HarperCollins Distribution Team

The HarperCollins Finance & Royalties Team

The HarperCollins Legal Team

The HarperCollins Technology Team

Trade Marketing
Ben Hurd

UK Sales
Laura Carpenter
Isabel Coburn
Jay Cochrane
Sabina Lewis
Holly Martin
Erin White
Harriet Williams
Leah Woods

And every other essential link in the chain from delivery drivers to booksellers to librarians and beyond!

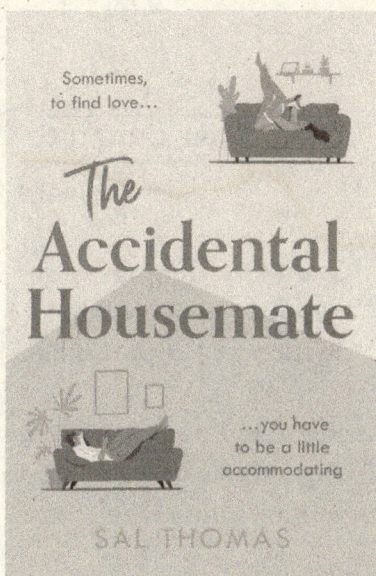

Sometimes, to find love, you have to be a little accommodating…

Cath Beckinsale is in a jam. She's a single mum of three, with her 40th birthday in sight and a precarious hold on employment. And she can't quite let go of her late husband Gaz, whose ashes are still in an urn on the kitchen table.

To make ends meet a student lodger seems like the perfect solution – after all, what's one more child in the house? But when Dan flies in from the US with guitar and chest hair on display, it's immediately clear that he's no teenager, but someone who quickly sends life in an unexpected direction.

Available in paperback and eBook now!